A.L.O.

A.M.S.

R.H.S.

Contents

The Mansion on the Hill   3

On the Carousel   53

The Double Zero   66

Forecast from the Retail Desk   82

Hawaiian Night   106

Drawer   115

Pan's Fair Throng   118

The Carnival Tradition   133

Wilkie Fahnstock: *The Boxed Set*   227

Boys   239

Ineluctable Modality of the Vaginal   247

Surplus Value Books: Catalogue Number 13   264

Demonology   291

Demonology

The Mansion on the Hill

The Chicken Mask was sorrowful, Sis. The Chicken Mask was supposed to hustle business. It was supposed to invite the customer to gorge him or herself within our establishment. It was supposed to be endearing and funny. It was supposed to be an accurate representation of the featured item on our menu. But, Sis, in a practical setting, in test markets — like right out in front of the restaurant — the Chicken Mask had a plaintive aspect, a blue quality (it was stifling, too, even in cold weather), so that I'd be walking down Main, by the waterfront, after you were gone, back and forth in front of Hot Bird (Bucket of Drumsticks, $2.99), wearing out my imitation basketball sneakers from Wal-Mart, pudgy in my black jogging suit, lurching along in the sandwich board, and the kids would hustle up to me, tugging on the wrists of their harried, underfinanced moms. The kids would get bored with me almost immediately. They knew the routine. Their eyes would narrow, and all at once there were no secrets here in our town of service-economy franchising: *I was the guy working nine to five in a Chicken Mask*, even though I'd had a pretty good education in business administration, even though I was more or less presentable and well-spoken, even though I came from a good family. I made light of it, Sis, I extemporized about Hot Bird, in remarks designed by virtue of my studies in business tactics to drive whole families in for the new *low-fat roasters*, a meal option that was steeper, in terms of price, but tasty nonetheless. (And I ought to have known, because I ate from the menu every day. Even the coleslaw.)

Here's what I'd say, in my Chicken Mask. Here was my pitch: *Feeling a little peckish? Try Hot Bird!* Or *Don't be chicken, try Hot Bird!* The mothers would laugh their nervous adding-machine laughs (those laughs that are next door over from a sob), and they would lead the kids off. Twenty yards away, though, the boys and girls would still be staring disdainfully at me, gaping backward while I rubbed my hands raw in the cold, while I breathed the synthetic rubber interior of the Chicken Mask — that fragrance of rubber balls from gym classes past, that bouquet of the gloves Mom used for the dishes — while I looked for my next shill. I lost almost ninety days to the demoralization of the Chicken Mask, to its grim, existential emptiness, until I couldn't take it anymore. Which happened to be the day when Alexandra McKinnon (remember her? from Sunday school?) turned the corner with her boy Zack — he has to be seven or eight now — oblivious while upon her daily rounds, oblivious and fresh from a Hallmark store. It was nearly Valentine's Day. They didn't know it was me in there, of course, inside the Chicken Mask. They didn't know I was *the chicken from the basement, the chicken of darkest night-mares,* or, more truthfully, they didn't know I was a guy with some pretty conflicted attitudes about things. That's how I managed to apprehend Zack, leaping out from the in-door of Cohen's Pharmacy, laying ahold of him a little too roughly, by the hem of his pillowy, orange ski jacket. Little Zack was laughing, at first, until, in a voice wracked by loss, I worked my hard sell on him, declaiming stentoriously that *Death Comes to All.* That's exactly what I said, just as persuasively as I had once hawked *White meat breasts, eight pieces, just $4.59!* Loud enough that he'd be sure to know what I meant. His look was interrogative, quizzical. So I repeated myself. *Death Comes to Everybody, Zachary.* My voice was urgent now. My eyes bulged from the eyeholes of my standard-issue Chicken Mask. I was even crying a little bit. Saline rivulets tracked down my neck. Zack was terrified.

What I got next certainly wasn't the kind of flirtatious attention I had always hoped for from his mom. Alex began drumming on me with balled fists. I guess she'd been stand-ing off to the side of the action previously, believing that I was a reliable paid employee of Hot Bird. But now she was all over me, bruising me with wild swings, cursing, until she'd pulled the Chicken Mask from my head — half expect-ing, I'm sure, to find me scarred or hydrocephalic or other-wise disabled. Her denunciations let up a little once she was in possession of the facts. It was me, her old Sunday school pal, Andrew Wakefield. Not at the top of my game.

I don't really want to include here the kind of scene I made, once unmasked. Alex was exasperated with me, but gentle anyhow. I think she probably knew I was in the middle of a rough patch. People knew. The people leaning out of the storefronts probably knew. But, if things weren't already bad enough, I remembered right then — God, this is horrible — that Alex's mom had driven into Lake Sacandaga about five years before. Jumped the guardrail and plunged right off that bridge there. In December. In heavy snow. In a Ford Explorer. That was the end of her. *Listen, Alex*, I said, *I'm confused, I have problems and I don't know what's come over me and I hope you can understand, and I hope you'll let me make it up to you. I can't lose this job. Honest to God.* Fortunately, just then, Zack became interested in the Chicken Mask. He swiped the mask from his mom — she'd been holding it at arm's length, like a soiled rag — and he pulled it down over his head and started making simulated automatic-weapons noises in the directions of local passersby. This took the heat off. We had a laugh, Alex and I, and soon the three of us had repaired to Hot Bird itself (it closed four months later, like most of the businesses on that block) for coffee and biscuits and the chef's special spicy wings, which, because of my position, were on the house.

Alex was actually waving a spicy wing when she offered her life-altering opinion that I was too smart to be working for Hot Bird, especially if I was going to brutalize little kids with the creepy facts of the hereafter. What I should do, Alex said, was get into something positive instead. She happened to know a girl — it was her cousin, Glenda — who managed a business over in Albany, the Mansion on the Hill, a big area employer, and why didn't I call Glenda and use Alex's name, and maybe they would have something in accounting or valet parking or flower delivery, you know, some job that had as little public contact as possible, something that paid better than minimum wage, because minimum wage, Alex said, wasn't enough for a guy of twenty-nine. After these remonstrances she actually hauled me over to the pay phone at Hot Bird (people are so generous sometimes), while my barely alert boss Antonio slumbered at the register with no idea what was going on, without a clue that he was about to lose his most conscientious chicken impersonator. All because I couldn't stop myself from talking about death.

Alex dialed up the Mansion on the Hill (while Zack, at the table, donned my mask all over again), penetrating deep into the switchboard by virtue of her relation to a Mansion on the Hill management-level employee, and was soon actually talking to her cousin: *Glenda, I got a friend here who's going through some rough stuff in his family, if you know what I mean, yeah, down on his luck in the job department too, but he's a nice bright guy anyhow. I pretty much wanted to smooch him throughout confirmation classes, and he went to . . . Hey, where did you go to school again? Went to SUNY and has a degree in business administration, knows a lot about product positioning or whatever, I don't know, new housing starts, yada yada yada, and I think you really ought to . . .* Glenda's sigh was audible from several feet away, I swear, through the perfect medium of digital telecommunications, but you can't blame Glenda for that. People protect themselves from bad luck, right? Still, Alex wouldn't let her cousin refuse, wouldn't hear of it, *You absolutely gotta meet him, Glenda, he's a doll, he's a dream boat,* and Glenda gave in, and that's the end of this part of the story, about how I happened to end up working out on Wolf Road at the capital region's finest wedding- and party-planning business. Except that before the Hot Bird recedes into the mists of time, I should report to you that I swiped the Chicken Mask, Sis. They had three or four of them. You'd be surprised how easy it is to come by a Chicken Mask.

Politically, here's what was happening in the front office of my new employer: Denise Gulch, the Mansion on the Hill staff writer, had left her husband and her kids and her steady job, because of a wedding, because of the language of the vows — that soufflé of exaggerated language — vows which, for quality-control purposes, were being broadcast over a discreet speaker in the executive suite. Denise was so moved by a recitation of Paul Stookey's "Wedding Song" taking place during the course of the Neuhaus ceremony ("Whenever two or more of you / Are gathered in His name, / There is love, / There is love . . .") that she slipped into the Rip Van Winkle Room disguised as a latecomer. Immediately, in the electrifying atmosphere of matrimony, she began trying to seduce one of the ushers (Nicky Weir, a part-time Mansion employee who was acquainted with the groom). I figure this flirtation had been taking place for some time, but that's not what everyone told me. What I heard was that seconds after meeting one another — the bride hadn't even recessed yet — Denise and Nicky were secreted in a nearby broom closet, while the office phones bounced to voice mail, and were peeling back the layers of our Mansion dress code, until, at day's end, scantily clad and intoxicated by rhetoric and desire, they stole a limousine and left town without collecting severance. Denise was even fully vested in the pension plan.

All this could only happen at a place called the Mansion on the Hill, a place of fluffy endings: the right candidate for the job walks through the door at the eleventh hour, the check clears that didn't exist minutes before, government agencies agree to waive mountains of red tape, the sky clears, the snow ends, and stony women like Denise Gulch succumb to torrents of generosity, throwing half-dollars to children as they embark on new lives.

The real reason I got the job is that they were short-handed, and because Alex's cousin, my new boss, was a little difficult. But things were starting to look up anyway. If Glenda's personal demeanor at the interview wasn't exactly warm (she took a personal call in the middle that lasted twenty-eight minutes, and later she asked me, while reapplying lip liner, if I wore cologne) at least she was willing to hire me — as long as I agreed to renounce any personal grooming habits that inclined in the direction of Old Spice, Hai Karate or CK1. I would have spit-polished her pumps just to have my own desk (on which I put a yellowed picture of you when you were a kid, holding up the bass that you caught fly-fishing and also a picture of the four of us: Mom and Dad and you and me) and a Rolodex and unlimited access to stamps, mailing bags and paper clips.

Let me take a moment to describe our core business at the Mansion on the Hill. We were in the business of helping people celebrate the best days of their lives. We were in the business of spreading joy, by any means necessary. We were in the business of paring away the calluses of woe and grief to reveal the bright light of commitment. We were in the business of producing flawless memories. We had seven auditoriums, or *marriage suites*, as we liked to call them, each with a slightly different flavor and decorating vocabulary. For example, there was the *Chestnut Suite*, the least expensive of our rental suites, which had lightweight aluminum folding chairs (with polyurethane padding) and a very basic altar table, which had the unfortunate pink and lavender floral wallpaper and which seated about 125 comfortably; then there was the *Hudson Suite*, which had some teak in it and a lot of paneling and a classic iron altar table and some rather large standing tables at the rear, and the dining stations in Hudson were clothed all in vinyl, instead of the paper coverings that they used in Chestnut (the basic decorating scheme there in the Hudson Suite was meant to suggest the sea vessels that once sailed through our municipal port); then there was the *Rip Van Winkle Room*, with its abundance of draperies, its silk curtains, its matching maroon settings of inexpensive linen, and the *Adirondack Suite*, the *Ticonderoga Room*, the *Valentine Room* (a sort of giant powder puff), and of course the *Niagara Hall*, which was grand and reserved, with its separate kitchen and its enormous fireplace and white-gloved staff, for the sons and daughters of those Victorians of Saratoga County who came upstate for the summer during the racing season, the children of contemporary robber barons, the children whose noses were always straight and whose luck was always good.

We had our own on-site boutique for wedding gowns and tuxedo rentals and fittings — hell, we'd even clean and store your garments for you while you were away on your honeymoon — and we had a travel agency who subcontracted for us, as we also had wedding consultants, jewelers, videogra-

phers, still photographers (both the arty ones who specialized in photos of your toenail polish on the day of the wedding and the conventional photographers who barked
directions at the assembled family far into the night), nan-
nies, priests, ministers, shamans, polarity therapists, a
really maniacal florist called Bruce, a wide array of
deejays — guys and gals equipped to spin Christian-only
selections, Tex-Mex, music from Hindi films and the occasional death-metal wedding medley — and we could get
actual musicians, if you preferred. We'd even had Dick
Roseman's combo, The Sons of Liberty, do a medley of "My
Funny Valentine," "In-a-Gadda-Da-Vida," "I Will Always
Love You" and "Smells Like Teen Spirit," without a rest
between selections. (It was gratifying for me to watch the
old folks shake it up to contemporary numbers.) We had a
three-story, fifteen-hundred-slip parking facility on site,
convenient access to I-87, I-90 and the Taconic, and a staff
of 175 full- and part-time employees on twenty-four-hour
call. We had everything from publicists to dicers of crudités
to public orators (need a brush-up for that toast?) — all for
the purpose of making your wedding the high watermark of
your American life. We had done up to fifteen weddings in a
single day (it was a Saturday in February, 1991, during the
Gulf War) and, since the Mansion on the Hill first threw
open its door for a gala double wedding (the Gifford twins,
from Balston Spa, who married Shaun and Maurice Wick-
ett) in June of 1987, we had performed, up to the time of my
first day there, 1,963 weddings, many of them memorable,
life-affirming, even spectacular ceremonies. We had never
had an incidence of serious violence.

■　　■　　■

This was the raw data that Glenda gave me, anyway, Sis. The arrangement of the facts is my own, and in truth, the arrangement of facts constitutes the job I was engaged to perform at the Mansion on the Hill. Because Glenda Manzini (in 1990 she married Dave Manzini, a developer from Schenectady) couldn't really have hated her job any more than she did. Glenda Manzini, whose marriage (her second) was apparently not the most loving ever in upstate history (although she's not alone; I estimate an even thousand divorces resulting from the conjugal rites consummated so far at my place of business), was a cynic, a skeptic, a woman of little faith when it came to the institution through which she made her living. She occasionally referred to the wedding party as *the cattle;* she occasionally referred to the brides as *the hookers* and to herself, manager of the Mansion on the Hill, as *the Madame,* as in, *The Madame, Andrew, would like it if you would get the hell out of her office so that she can tabulate these receipts,* or, *Please tell the Hatfields and the McCoys that the Madame cannot untangle their differences for them, although the Madame does know the names of some first-rate couples counselors.* In the absence of an enthusiasm for our product line or for business writing in general, Glenda Manzini hired me to tackle some of her responsibilities for her. I gave the facts the best possible spin. Glenda, as you probably have guessed, was good with numbers. With the profits and losses. Glenda was good at additional charges. Glenda was good at doubling the price on a floral arrangement, for example, because the Vietnamese poppies absolutely had to be on the tables, because they were so . . . *je ne sais quoi.* Glenda was good at double-booking a particular suite and then auctioning the space to the higher bidder. Glenda was good at quoting a figure for a band and then adding instruments so that the price increased astronomically. One time she padded a quartet with two vocalists, an eight-piece horn section, an African drumming ensemble, a dijeridoo and a harmonium.

The other thing I should probably be up-front about is that Glenda Manzini was a total knockout. A bombshell. A vision of celestial loveliness. I hate to go on about it, but there was that single strand of Glenda's amber hair always falling over her eyes; there was her near constant attention to her makeup; there was her total command of business issues and her complete unsentimentality. Or maybe it was her stockings, always in black, with a really provocative seam following the aerodynamically sleek lines of her calves. Or maybe it was her barely concealed sadness. I'd never met anyone quite as uncomfortable as Glenda, but this didn't bother me at first. My life had changed since the Chicken Mask.

Meanwhile, it goes without saying that the Mansion on the Hill wasn't a mansion at all. It was a homely cinderblock edifice formerly occupied by the Colonie Athletic Club. A trucking operation used the space before that. And the Mansion wasn't on any hill, either, because geologically speaking we're in a valley here. We're part of some recent glacial scouring.

On my first day, Glenda made every effort to insure that my work environment would be as unpleasant as possible. I'd barely set down my extra-large coffee with two half-and-halfs and five sugars and my assortment of cream-filled donuts (I was hoping these would please my new teammates) when Glenda bodychecked me, tipped me over into my reclining desk chair, with several huge stacks of file material.

— Andy, listen up. In April we have an Orthodox Jewish ceremony taking place at 3 P.M. in Niagara while at the same time there are going to be some very faithful Islamic-Americans next door in Ticonderoga. I don't want these two groups to come in contact with one another at any time, understand? I don't want any kind of diplomatic incident. It's your job to figure out how to persuade one of these groups to be first out of the gate, at noon, and it's your job to make them think that they're really lucky to have the opportunity. And Andy? The el-Mohammed wedding, the Muslim wedding, needs prayer mats. See if you can get some from the discount stores. Don't waste a lot of money on this.

This is a good indication of Glenda's management style. Some other procedural tidbits: she frequently assigned a dozen rewrites on her correspondence. She had a violent dislike for semicolons. I was to double-space twice underneath the date on her letters, before typing the salutation, on pain of death. I was never, ever to use one of those cursive word-processing fonts. I was to bring her coffee first thing in the morning, without speaking to her until she had entirely finished a second cup and also a pair of ibuprofen tablets, preferably the elongated, easy-to-swallow variety. I was never to ask her about her weekend or her evening or anything else, including her holidays, unless she asked me first. If her door was closed, I was not to open it. And if I ever reversed the digits in a phone number when taking a message for her, I could count on a pink slip that very afternoon.

Right away, that first A.M., after this litany of scares, after Glenda retreated into her chronically underheated lair, there was a swell of sympathetic mumbles from my coworkers, who numbered, in the front office, about a dozen. They were offering condolences. They had seen the likes of me come and go. Glenda, however, who keenly appreciated the element of surprise as a way of insuring discipline, was not quite done. She reappeared suddenly by my desk — as if by secret entrance — with a half-dozen additional commands. I was to find a new sign for her private parking space, I was to find a new floral wholesaler for the next fiscal quarter, I was to *refill her prescription for birth-control pills*. This last request was spooky enough, but it wasn't the end of the discussion. From there Glenda started getting personal:

— Oh, by the way, Andy? (She liked diminutives.) What's all the family trouble, anyway? The stuff Alex was talking about when she called?

She picked up the photo of you, Sis, the one I had brought with me. The bass at the end of your fishing rod was so outsized that it seemed impossible that you could hold it up. You looked really happy. Glenda picked up the photo as though she hadn't already done her research, as if she had left something to chance. Which just didn't happen during her regime at the Mansion on the Hill.

— Dead sister, said I. And then, completing my betrayal of you, I filled out the narrative, so that anyone who wished could hear about it, and then we could move onto other subjects, like Worcester's really great semipro hockey team.

— Crashed her car. Actually, it was my car. Mercury Sable. Don't know why I said it was her car. It was mine. She was on her way to her rehearsal dinner. She had an accident.

Sis, have I mentioned that I have a lot of questions I've been meaning to ask? Have I asked, for example, why you were taking the winding country road along our side of the great river, when the four-lanes along the west side were faster, more direct and, in heavy rain, less dangerous? Have I asked why you were driving at all? Why I was not driving you to the rehearsal dinner instead? Have I asked why your car was in the shop for muffler repair on such an important day? Have I asked why you were late? Have I asked why you were lubricating your nerves *before* the dinner? Have I asked if four G&T's, as you called them, before your own rehearsal dinner, were not maybe in excess of what was needed? Have I asked if there was a reason for you to be so tense on the eve of your wedding? Did you feel you had to go through with it? That there was no alternative? If so, why? If he was the wrong guy, why were you marrying him? Were there planning issues that were not properly addressed? Were there things between you two, as between all the betrothed, that we didn't know? Were there specific questions you wanted to ask, of which you were afraid? Have I given the text of my toast, Sis, as I had imagined it, beginning with a plangent evocation of the years before your birth, when I ruled our house like a tyrant, and how with earsplitting cries I resisted your infancy, until I learned to love the way your baby hair, your flaxen mop, fell into curls? Have I mentioned that it was especially satisfying to wind your hair around my stubby fingers as you lay sleeping?

Have I made clear that I wrote out this toast and that it took me several weeks to get it how I wanted it and that I was in fact going over these words again when the call from Dad came announcing your death? Have I mentioned — and I'm sorry to be hurtful on this point — that Dad's drinking has gotten worse since you left this world? Have I mentioned that his allusions to the costly unfinished business of his life have become more frequent? Have I mentioned that Mom, already overtaxed with her own body count, with her dead parents and dead siblings, has gotten more and more frail? Have I mentioned that I have some news about Brice, your intended? That his tune has changed slightly since your memorial service? Have I mentioned that I was out at the crime scene the next day? The day after you died? Have I mentioned that in my dreams I am often at the crime scene now? Have I wondered aloud to you about that swerve of blacktop right there, knowing that others may lose their lives as you did? Can't we straighten out that road some-how? Isn't there one road crew that the governor, in his quest for jobs, jobs, jobs, can send down there to make this sort of thing unlikely? Have I perhaps clued you in about how I go there often now, to look for signs of further tragedy? Have I mentioned to you that in some countries DWI is punishable by death, and that when Antonio at Hot Bird first explained this dark irony to me, I imagined taking his throat in my hands and squeezing the air out of him once and for all? Sis, have I told you of driving aimlessly in the mountains, listening to talk radio, searching for the one bit of cheap, commercially interrupted persuasion that will let me put these memories of you back in the canister where you now at least partially reside so that I can live out my dim, narrow life? Have I mentioned that I expect death around every turn, that every blue sky has a safe sailing out of it, that every bus runs me over, that every low, mean syllable uttered in my direction seems to intimate the violence of murder, that every family seems like an opportunity for ruin and every marriage a ceremony into which calamity will fall and hearts will be broken and lives destroyed and people branded by the mortifications of love? Is it all right if I ask you all of this?

Still, in spite of these personal issues, I was probably a model employee for Glenda Manzini. For example, I managed to sort out the politics concerning the Jewish wedding and the Islamic wedding (both slated for the first weekend of April), and I did so by appealing to certain aspects of light in our valley at the base of the Adirondacks. Certain kinds of light make for very appealing weddings here in our valley, I told one of these families. In late winter, in the early morning, you begin to feel an excitement at the appearance of the sun. Yes, I managed to solve that problem, and the next (the prayer mats) — because K-Mart, *where America shops,* had a special on bathmats that week, and I sent Dorcas Gilbey over to buy six dozen to use for the Muslim families. I solved these problems and then I solved others just as vexing. I had a special interest in the snags that arose on Fridays after 5 P.M. — the groom who on the day of the ceremony was trapped in a cabin east of Lake George and who had to snowshoe three miles out to the nearest telephone, or the father of the bride (it was the Lapsley wedding) who wanted to arrive at the ceremony by hydrofoil. Brinksmanship, in the world of nuptial planning, gave me a sense of well-being, and I tried to bury you in the rear of my life, in the back of that closet where I'd hidden my secondhand golf clubs and my ski boots and my Chicken Mask — never again to be seen by mortal man.

One of my front-office associates was a fine young woman by the name of Linda Pietrzsyk, who tried to comfort me during the early weeks of my job, after Glenda's periodic assaults. Don't ask how to pronounce Linda's surname. In order to pronounce it properly, you have to clear your throat aggressively. Linda Pietrzsyk didn't like her surname anymore than you or I, and she was apparently looking for a groom from whom she could borrow a better one. That's what I found out after awhile. Many of the employees at the Mansion on the Hill had ulterior motives. This marital ferment, this loamy soil of romance, called to them somehow. When I'd been there a few months, I started to see other applicants go through the masticating action of an interview with Glenda Manzini. Glenda would be sure to ask, *Why do you want to work here?* and many of these qualified applicants had the same reply, *Because I think marriage is the most beautiful thing and I want to help make it possible for others.* Most of these applicants, if they were attractive and single and younger than Glenda, were shown the door. But occasionally a marital aspirant like Linda Pietrzsyk snuck through, in this case because Linda managed to conceal her throbbing, sentimental heart beneath a veneer of contemporary discontent.

We had Mondays and Tuesdays off, and one weekend a month. Most of our problem-solving fell on Saturdays, of course, but on that one Saturday off, Linda Pietrzsyk liked to bring friends to the Mansion on the Hill, to various celebrations. She liked to attend the weddings of strangers. This kind of entertainment wasn't discouraged by Glenda or by the owners of the Mansion, because everybody likes a party to be crowded. Any wedding that was too sparsely attended at the Mansion had a fine complement of *warm bodies*, as Glenda liked to call them, provided gratis. Sometimes we had to go to libraries or retirement centers to fill a quota, but we managed. These gate crashers were welcome to eat finger food at the reception and to drink champagne and other intoxicants (food and drink were billed to the client), but they had to make themselves scarce once the dining began in earnest. There was a window of opportunity here that was large enough for Linda and her friends.

She was tight with a spirited bunch of younger people. She was friends with kids who had outlandish wardrobes and styles of grooming, kids with pants that fit like bedsheets, kids with haircuts that were, at best, accidental. But Linda would dress them all up and make them presentable, and they would arrive in an ancient station wagon in order to crowd in at the back of a wedding. Where they stifled gasps of hilarity.

I don't know what Linda saw in me. I can't really imagine. I wore the same sweaters and flannel slacks week in and week out. I liked classical music, Sis. I liked historical simulation festivals. And as you probably haven't forgotten (having tried a couple of times to fix me up — with Jess Carney and Sally Moffitt), the more tense I am, the worse is the impression I make on the fairer sex. Nevertheless, Linda Pietrzsyk decided that I had to be a part of her elite crew of wedding crashers, and so for a while I learned by immersion of the great rainbow of expressions of fealty.

Remember that footage, so often shown on contemporary reality-based programming during the dead first half-hour of prime time, of the guy who vomited at his own wedding? I was at that wedding. You know when he says, *Aw, Honey, I'm really sorry,* and leans over and flash floods this amber stuff on her train? You know, the shock of disgust as it crosses her face? The look of horror in the eyes of the minister? I saw it all. No one who was there thought it was funny, though, except Linda's friends. That's the truth. I thought it was really sad. But I was sitting next to a fellow *actually named Cheese* (when I asked which kind of cheese, he seemed perplexed), and Cheese looked as though he had a hernia or something, he thought this was so funny. Elsewhere in the Chestnut Suite there was a grievous silence.

Linda Pietrzsyk also liked to catalogue moments of spontaneous erotic delight on the premises, and these were legendary at the Mansion on the Hill. Even Glenda, who took a dim view of gossiping about business most of the time, liked to hear who was doing it with whom where. There was an implicit hierarchy in such stories. *Tales of the couple to be married caught in the act on Mansion premises were considered obvious and therefore uninspiring.* Tales of the best man and matron of honor going at it (as in the Clarke, Rosenberg, Irving, Ng, Fujitsu, Walters, Shapiro or Spangler ceremonies) were better, but not great. Stories in which parents of the couple to be married were caught — in, say, the laundry room, with the dad still wearing his dress shoes — were good (Smith, Elsworth, Waskiewicz), but not as good as tales of the parents of the couple to be married trading spouses, of which we had one unconfirmed report (Hinkley) and of which no one could stop talking for a week. Likewise, any story in which the bride or the groom were caught *in flagrante* with someone other than the person they were marrying was considered astounding (if unfortunate). But we were after some even more unlikely tall tales: any three-some or larger grouping involving the couple to be married and someone from one of the other weddings scheduled that day, in which the third party was unknown until arriving at the Mansion on the Hill, and at which *a house pet was present.* Glenda said that if you spotted one of these tableaux you could have a month's worth of free groceries from the catering department. Linda Pietrzsyk also spoke longingly of the day when someone would arrive breath-lessly in the office with a narrative of a full-fledged orgiastic reception in the Mansion on the Hill, the spontaneous, over-whelming erotic celebration of love and marriage by an entire suite full of Americans, tall and short, fat and thin, young and old.

In pursuit of these tales, with her friends Cheese, Chip, Mick, Stig, Mark and Blair, Linda Pietrzyk would quietly appear at my side at a reception and give me the news — *Behind the bandstand, behind that scrim, groom reaching under his cousin's skirts.* We would sneak in for a look. But we never interrupted anyone. And we never made them feel ashamed.

You know how when you're getting to know a fellow employee, a fellow team member, you go through phases, through cycles of intimacy and insight and respect and doubt and disillusionment, where one impression gives way to another? (Do you know about this, Sis, and is this what happened between you and Brice, so that you felt like you personally had to have the four G&Ts on the way to the rehearsal dinner? Am I right in thinking you couldn't go on with the wedding and that this caused you to get all sloppy and to believe erroneously that you could operate a motor vehicle?) Linda Pietrzsyk was a stylish, Skidmore-educated girl with ivory skin and an adorable bump on her nose; she was from an upper-middle-class family out on Long Island somewhere; her father's periodic drunkenness had not affected his ability to work; her mother stayed married to him according to some mesmerism of devotion; her brothers had good posture and excelled in contact sports; in short, there were no big problems in Linda's case. Still, she pretended to be a desperate, marriage-obsessed kid, without a clear idea about what she wanted to do with her life or what the hell was going to happen next week. She was smarter than me — she could do the crossword puzzle in three minutes flat and she knew all about current events — but she was always talking about *catching a rich financier with a wild streak and extorting a retainer from him,* until I wanted to shake her. There's usually another layer underneath these things. In Linda's case it started to become clear at Patti Wackerman's wedding.

The reception area in the Ticonderoga Room — where walls slid back from the altar to reveal the tables and the dance floor — was decorated in branches of forsythia and wisteria and other flowering vines and shrubs. It was spring. Linda was standing against a piece of white wicker latticework that I had borrowed from the florist in town (in return for promotional considerations), and sprigs of flowering trees garlanded it, garlanded the spot where Linda was standing. Pale colors haloed her.

— Right behind this screen, she said, when I swept up beside her and tapped her playfully on the shoulder, — check it out. There's a couple falling in love once and for all. You can see it in their eyes.

I was sipping a Canadian spring water in a piece of company stemware. I reacted to Linda's news nonchalantly. I didn't think much of it. Yet I happened to notice that Linda's expression was conspiratorial, impish, as well as a little beatific. Linda often covered her mouth with her hand when she'd said something riotous, as if to conceal unsightly dental work (on the contrary, her teeth were perfect), as if she'd been treated badly one too many times, as if the immensity of joy were embarrassing to her somehow. As she spoke of the couple in question her hand fluttered up to her mouth. Her slender fingertips probed delicately at her upper lip. My thoughts came in torrents: *Where are Stig and Cheese and Blair? Why am I suddenly alone with this fellow employee? Is the couple Linda is speaking about part of the wedding party today? How many points will she get for the first sighting of their extramarital grappling?*

Since it was my policy to investigate any and all such phenomena, I glanced desultorily around the screen and, seeing nothing out of the ordinary, slipped further into the shadows where the margins of Ticonderoga led toward the central catering staging area. There was, of course, no such couple behind the screen, or rather Linda (who was soon beside me) and myself *were the couple* and we were mottled by insufficient light, dappled by it, by lavender-tinted spots hung that morning by the lighting designers, and by reflections of a mirrored *disco ball* that speckled the dance floor.

— I don't see anything, I said.

— Kiss me, Linda Pietrzsyk said. Her fingers closed lightly around the bulky part of my arm. There was an unfamiliar warmth in me. The band struck up some fast number. I think it was "It's Raining Men" or maybe it was that song entitled "We Are Family," which played so often at the Mansion on the Hill in the course of a weekend. Whichever, it was really loud. The horn players were getting into it. A trombonist yanked his slide back and forth.

— Excuse me? I said.

— Kiss me, Andrew, she said. — I want to kiss you.

Locating in myself a long-dormant impulsiveness, I reached down for Linda's bangs, and with my clumsy hands I tried to push back her blond and strawberry-blond curlicues, and then, with a hitch in my motion, in a stop-time sequence of jerks, I embraced her. Her eyes, like neon, were illumined.

— Why don't you tell me how you feel about me? Linda Pietrzsyk said. I was speechless, Sis. I didn't know what to say. And she went on. There was something about me, something warm and friendly about me, I wasn't fortified, she said; I wasn't cold, I was just a good guy who actually cared about other people *and you know how few of those there are.* (I think these were her words.) She wanted to spend more time with me, she wanted to get to know me better, she wanted to give the roulette wheel a decisive spin: she repeated all this twice in slightly different ways with different modifiers. It made me sweat. The only way I could think to get her to quit talking was to kiss her in earnest, my lips brushing by hers the way the sun passes around and through the interstices of falling leaves on an October afternoon. I hadn't kissed anyone in a long time. Her mouth tasted like cherry soda, like barbeque, like fresh hay, and because of these startling tastes, I retreated. To arm's length.

Sis, I was scared. What was this rank taste of wet campfire and bone fragments that I'd had in my mouth since we scattered you over the Hudson? Did I come through this set of coincidences, these quotidian interventions by God, to work in a place where everything seemed to be about *love*, only to find that I couldn't ever be a part of that grand word? How could I kiss anyone when I felt so awkward? What happened to me, what happened to all of us, to the texture of our lives, when you left us here?

I tried to ask Linda why she was doing what she was doing — behind the screen of wisteria and forsythia. I fumbled badly for these words. I believed she was trying to have a laugh on me. So she could go back and tell Cheese and Mick about it. So she could go gossip about me in the office, about what a jerk that Wakefield was. *Man, Andrew Wakefield thinks there's something worth hoping for in this world.* I thought she was joking, and I was through being the joke, being the Chicken Mask, being the harlequin.

— I'm not doing anything to you, Andrew, Linda said.
— I'm expressing myself. It's supposed to be a good thing.

Reaching, she laid a palm flush against my face.

— I know you aren't . . .
— So what's the problem?

I was ambitious to reassure. If I could have stayed the hand that fluttered up to cover her mouth, so that she could laugh unreservedly, so that her laughter peeled out in the Ticonderoga Room . . . But I just wasn't up to it yet. I got out of there. I danced across the floor at the Wackerman wedding — I was a party of one — and the Wackermans and the Delgados and their kin probably thought I was singing along with "Desperado" by the Eagles (it was the anthem of the new Mr. and Mrs. Fritz Wackerman), but really I was talking to myself, *about work,* about how Mike Tombello's best man wanted to give his toast while doing flips on a trampoline, about how Jenny Parmenter wanted live goats bleating in the Mansion parking lot, as a fertility symbol, as she sped away, in her Rolls Cornische, to the Thousand Islands. Boy, I always hated the Eagles.

Okay, to get back to Glenda Manzini. Linda Pietrzsyk didn't write me off after our failed embraces, but she sure gave me more room. She was out the door at 5:01 for several weeks, without asking after me, without a kind word for anyone, and I didn't blame her. But in the end who else was there to talk to? To Marie O'Neill, the accountant? To Paul Avakian, the human resources and insurance guy and petty-cash manager? To Rachel Levy, the head chef? Maybe it was more than this. Maybe the bond that forms between people doesn't get unmade so easily. Maybe it leaves its mark for a long time. Soon Linda and I ate our bagged lunches together again, trading varieties of puddings, often in total silence; at least this was the habit until we found a new area of common interest in our reservations about Glenda Manzini's management techniques. This happened to be when Glenda took a week off. What a miracle. I'd been employed at the Mansion six months. The staff was in a fine

mood about Glenda's hiatus. There was a carnival atmosphere. Dorcas Gilbey had been stockpiling leftover ales for
an office shindig featuring dancing and the recitation of
really bad marital vows we'd heard. Linda and I went along
with the festivities, but we were also formulating a strategy.

What we wanted to know was how Glenda became so
unreservedly cruel. We wanted the inside story on her personal life. We wanted the skinny. How do you produce an
individual like Glenda? What is the mass-production technique? We waited until Wednesday, after the afternoon
beer-tasting party. We were staying late, we claimed, in
order to separate out the green M&Ms for the marriage of
U.V.M. tight end Brad Doelp who had requested bowls of
M&Ms at his reception, *excluding any and all green candies.*
When our fellow employees were gone, right at five, we
broke into Glenda's office.

Sis, we really broke in. Glenda kept her office locked
when she wasn't in it. It was a matter of principle. I had to
use my Discover card on the lock. I punished that credit
card. But we got the tumblers to tumble, and once we were
inside, we started poking around. First of all, Glenda
Manzini was a tidy person, which I can admire from an
organizational point of view, but it was almost like her
office was empty. The pens and pencils were lined up. The in
and out boxes were swept clean of any stray dust particle,
any scrap of trash. There wasn't a rogue paper clip behind
the desk or in the bottom of her spotless wastebasket. She
kept her rubber bands banded together with rubber bands.
The files in her filing cabinets were orderly, subdivided to
avoid bowing, the old faxes were photocopied so that they
wouldn't disintegrate. The photos on the walls (Mansion

weddings past) were nondescript and pedestrian. There was nothing intimate about the decoration at all. I knew about most of this stuff from the moments when she ordered me into that cubicle to dress me down, but this was different. Now we were getting a sustained look at Glenda's personal effects.

Linda took particular delight in Glenda's cassette player (it was atop one of the black filing cabinets) — a cassette player that none of us had ever heard play, not even once. Linda admired the selection of recordings there. A complete set of cut-out budget series: *Greatest Hits of Baroque, Greatest Hits of Swing, Greatest Hits of Broadway, Greatest Hits of Disco* and so forth. Just as she was about to pronounce Glenda a rank philistine where music was concerned, Linda located there, in a shattered case, a copy of *Greatest Hits of the Blues.*

We devoured the green M&Ms while we were busy with our reconnaissance. And I kept reminding Linda not to get any of the green dye on anything. I repeatedly checked surfaces for fingerprints. I even overturned Linda's hands (it made me happy while doing it), to make sure they were free of emerald smudges. Because if Glenda found out we were in her office, we'd both be submitting applications at the Hot Bird of Troy. Nonetheless, Linda carelessly put down her handful of M&Ms, on top of a filing cabinet, to look over the track listings for *Greatest Hits of the Blues.* This budget anthology was released the year Linda was born, in 1974. Coincidentally, the year you too were born, Sis. I remember driving with you to the tunes of Lightnin' Hopkins or Howlin' Wolf. I remember your preference for the most bereaved of acoustic blues, the most ramshackle of musics.

What better soundtrack for the Adirondacks? For our meandering drives in the mountains, into Corinth or around Lake Luzerne? What more lonesome sound for a state park the size of Rhode Island where wolves and bears still come to hunt? Linda cranked the greatest hits of heartbreak and we sat down on the carpeted floor to listen. I missed you.

I pulled open that bottom file drawer by chance. I wanted to rest my arm on something. There was a powerful allure in the moment. I wasn't going to kiss Linda, and probably her desperate effort to find somebody to liberate her from her foreshortened economic prospects and her unpronounceable surname wouldn't come to much, but she was a good friend. Maybe a better friend than I was admitting to myself. It was in this expansive mood that I opened the file drawer at the bottom of one stack (the *J* through *P* stack), otherwise empty, to find that it was full of a half-dozen, maybe even more, of those circular packages *of birth-control pills*, the color-coated pills, you know, those multihued pills and placebos that are a journey through the amorous calendars of women. All unused. Not a one of them even opened. Not a one of the white, yellow, brown or green pills liberated from its package.

— Must be chilly in Schenectady, Linda mumbled.

Was there another way to read the strange bottom drawer? Was there a way to look at it beyond or outside of my exhausting tendency to discover only facts that would prop up darker prognostications? The file drawer contained the pills, it contained a bottle of vodka, it contained a cache of family pictures and missives the likes of which were never displayed or mentioned or even alluded to by Glenda. Even I, for all my resentments, wasn't up to reading the letters. But what of these carefully arranged packages of photo snapshots of the Manzini family? (Glenda's son from her first marriage, in his early teens, in a torn and grass-stained football uniform, and mother and second husband and son in front of some bleachers, et cetera.) Was the drawer really what it seemed to be, a repository for mementos of love that Glenda had now hidden away, secreted, shunted off into mini-storage? What was the lesson of those secrets? Merely that concealed behind rage (and behind grief) *is the ambition to love?*

— Somebody's having an affair, Linda said. — The hubby is coming home late. He's fabricating late evenings at the office. He's taking some desktop meetings with his secretary. He's leaving Glenda alone with the kids. Why else be so cold?

— Or Glenda's carrying on, said I.

— Or she's polygamous, Linda said, — and this is a completely separate family she's keeping across town somewhere without telling anyone.

— Or this is the boy she gave up for adoption and this is the record of her meeting with his folks. And she never told Dave about it.

— Whichever it is, Linda said, — it's *bad.*

We turned our attention to the vodka. Sis, I know I've said that I don't touch the stuff anymore — because of your example — but Linda egged me on. We were listening to music of the delta, to its simple unadorned grief, and I felt that Muddy Waters's loss was my kind of loss, the kind you don't shake easily, the kind that comes back like a seasonal flu, and soon we were passing the bottle of vodka back and forth. Beautiful, sad Glenda Manzini understood the blues and I understood the blues and you understood them and Linda understood them and maybe everybody understood them — in spite of what ethno-musicologists sometimes tell us about the cultural singularity of that music. Linda started to dance a little, there in Glenda Manzini's office, swiveling absently, her arms like asps, snaking to and fro, her wrists adorned in black bangles. Linda had a spell on her, in Glenda's anaerobic and cryogenically frigid office. Linda plucked off her beige pumps and circled around Glenda's desk, as if casting out its manifold demons. I couldn't take my eyes off of her. She forgot who I was and drifted with the lamentations of Robert Johnson (hellhound on his trail), and I could have followed her there, where she cast off Long Island and Skidmore and became a naiad, a true resident of the Mansion on the Hill, that paradise, but when the song was over the eeriness of our communion was suddenly alarming. I was sneaking around my boss's office. I was drinking her vodka. All at once it was time to go home.

We began straightening everything we had moved — we were really responsible about it — and Linda had gathered up the dozen or so green M&Ms she'd left on the filing cabinet — excepting the one she inadvertently fired out the back end of her fist, which skittered from a three-drawer file down a whole step to the surface of a two-drawer stack, before hopping and skipping over a cassette box, before free-falling behind the cabinets, where it came to rest, at last, six inches from the northeast corner of the office, beside a small coffee-stained patch of wall-to-wall. I returned the vodka to its drawer of shame, I tidied up the stacks of *Brides* magazines, I locked Glenda's office door and I went back to being the employee of the month. (My framed picture hung over the water fountain between the rest rooms. I wore a bow tie. I smiled broadly and my teeth looked straight and my hair was combed. I couldn't be stopped.)

My ambition has always been to own my own small business. I like the flexibility of small-capitalization companies; I like small businesses at the moment at which they prepare to franchise. That's why I took the job at Hot Bird — I saw Hot Birds in every town in America, I saw Hot Birds as numerous as post offices or ATMs. I like small businesses at the moment at which they really define a market with respect to a certain need, when they begin to sell their products to the world. And my success as a team player at the Mansion on the Hill was the result of these ambitions. This is why I came to feel, after a time, that I could do Glenda Manzini's job myself. Since I'm a little young, it's obvious that I couldn't *replace* Glenda — I think her instincts were really great with respect to the service we were providing to the Capital Region — but I saw the Mansion on the Hill stretching its influence into population centers throughout the northeast. I mean, why wasn't there a Mansion on the Hill in Westchester? Down in Mamaroneck? Why wasn't there a Mansion on the Hill in the golden corridor of Boston suburbs? Why no mainline Philly Mansion? Suffice to say, I saw myself, at some point in the future, having the same opportunity Glenda had. I saw myself cutting deals and whittling out discounts at other fine Mansion locations. I imagined making myself indispensable to a coalition of Mansion venture-capitalists and then I imagined using these associations to make a move into, say the high-tech or bio-tech sectors of American industry.

The way I pursued this particular goal was that I started looking ahead at things like upcoming volume. I started using the graph features on my office software to make pie charts of ceremony densities, cost ratios and so forth, and I started wondering how we could pitch our service better, whether on the radio or in the press or through alternative marketing strategies (I came up with the strategy, for example, of getting various nonaffiliated religions — small emergent spiritual movements — to consider us as a site for all their group wedding ceremonies). And as I started looking ahead, I started noticing who was coming through the doors in the next months. I became well versed in the social forces of our valley. I watched for when certain affluent families of the region might be needing our product. I would, if required, attempt cold-calling the attorney general of our state to persuade him of the splendor of the Niagara Hall when Diana, his daughter, finally gave the okey-dokey to her suitor, Ben.

I may well have succeeded in my plan for domination of the Mansion on the Hill brand, if it were not for the fact that as I was examining the volume projections for November (one Wednesday night), the ceremonies taking place in a mere three months, I noticed that Sarah Wilton of Corinth was marrying one Brice McCann in the Rip Van Winkle Room. Just before Thanksgiving. There were no particular notes or annotations to the name on the calendar, and thus Glenda wasn't focusing much on the ceremony. But something bothered me. That name.

Your Brice McCann, Sis. Your intended. Getting married almost a year to the day after your rehearsal-dinner-that-never-was. Getting married before even having completed his requisite year of grief, before we'd even made it through the anniversary with its floodwaters. Who knew how long he'd waited before beginning his seduction of Sarah Wilton? Was it even certain that he had waited until you were gone? Maybe he was faithless; maybe he was a two-timer. I had started reading Glenda's calendar to get ahead in business, Sis, but as soon as I learned of Brice, I became cavalier about work. My work suffered. My relations with other members of the staff suffered. I kept to myself. I went back to riding the bus to work instead of accepting rides. I stopped visiting fellow workers. I found myself whispering of plots and machinations; I found myself making connections between things that probably weren't connected and planning involved scenarios of revenge. I knew the day would come when he would be on the premises, when Brice would be settling various accounts, going over various numbers, signing off on the pâté selection and the set list of the R&B band, and I waited for him — to be certain of the truth.

Sis, you became engaged too quickly. There had been that other guy, Mark, and you had been engaged to him, too, and that arrangement fell apart kind of fast — I think you were engaged at Labor Day and broken up by M.L.K.'s birthday — and then, within weeks, there was this Brice. There's a point I want to make here. I'm trying to be gentle, but I have to get this across. Brice wore a beret. *The guy wore a beret.* He was supposedly a great cook, he would bandy about names of exotic mushrooms, but I never saw him boil an egg when I was visiting you. It was always you who did the cooking. It's true that certain males of the species, the kind who linger at the table after dinner waiting for their helpmeet to do the washing up, the kind who preside over carving of viands and otherwise disdain food-related chores, the kind who claim to be effective only at the preparation of breakfast, these guys are Pleistocene brutes who don't belong in the Information Age with its emerging markets and global economies. But, Sis, I think the other extreme is just as bad. The sensitive, New Age, beret-wearing guys who buy premium mustards and free-range chickens and grow their own basil and then let you cook while they're in the other room perusing magazines devoted to the artistic posings of Asian teenagers. Our family comes from upstate New York and we don't eat enough vegetables and our marriages are full of hardships and sorrows, Sis, and when I saw Brice coming down the corridor of the Mansion on the Hill, with his prematurely gray hair slicked back with the aid of some all-natural mousse, wearing a gray, suede bomber jacket and cowboy boots into which were tucked the cuffs of his black designer jeans, carrying his personal digital assistant and his cell phone and the other accoutrements of his dwindling massage-therapy business, he was the enemy of my state. In his wake, I was happy to note, there was a sort of honeyed cologne. Patchouli, I'm guessing. It would definitely drive Glenda Manzini nuts.

We had a small conference room at the Mansion, just around the corner from Glenda's office. I had selected some of the furnishings there myself, from a discount furniture outlet at the mall. Brice and his fiancée, Sarah Wilton, would of course be repairing to this conference room with Glenda to do some pricing. I had the foresight, therefore, to jog into that space and turn on the speaker phone over by the coffee machine, and to place a planter of silk flowers in front of it and dial my own extension so that I could teleconference this conversation. I had a remote headset I liked to wear around, Sis, during inventorying and bill tabulation — it helped with the neck strain and tension headaches that I'm always suffering with — so I affixed this headset and went back to filing, down the hall, while the remote edition of Brice and Sarah's conference with Glenda was broadcast into my skull.

I figure my expression was ashen. I suppose that Dorcas Gilbey, when she flagged me down with some receipts that she had forgotten to file, was unused to my mechanistic expression and to my curt, unfriendly replies to her questions. I waved her off, clamping the headset tighter against my ear. Unfortunately, the signal broke up. It was muffled. I hurriedly returned to my desk and tried to get the forwarded call to transmit properly to my handset. I even tried to amplify it through the speaker-phone feature, to no avail. Brice had always affected a soft-spoken demeanor while he was busy extorting things from people like you, Sis. He was too quiet — the better to conceal his tactics. And thus, in order to hear him, I had to sneak around the corner from the conference room and eavesdrop in the old-fashioned way.

— We wanted to dialogue with you (Brice was explaining to Glenda), because we wanted to make sure that you were thinking creatively along the same lines we are. We want to make sure you're comfortable with our plans. As married people, as committed people, we want this ceremony to make others feel good about themselves, as we're feeling good about ourselves. We want to have an ecstatic celebration here, a healing celebration that will bind up the hurt any marriages in the room might be suffering. I know you know how the ecstasy of marriage occasions a grieving process for many persons, Mrs. Manzini. Sarah and I both feel this in our hearts, that celebrations often have grief as a part of their wonder, and we want to enact all these things, all these feelings, to bring them out where we can look at them, and then we want to purge them triumphantly. We want people to come out of this wedding feeling good about themselves, as we'll be feeling good about ourselves. We want to give our families a big collective hug, because we're all human and we all have feelings and we all have to grieve and yearn and we need rituals for this.

There was a long silence from Glenda Manzini.

Then she said:

— Can we cut to the chase?

One thing I always loved about the Mansion on the Hill was its emptiness, its vacancy. Sure, the Niagara Room, when filled with five-thousand-dollar gowns and heirloom tuxedos, when serenaded by Toots Wilcox's big band, was a great place, a sort of gold standard of reception halls, but as much as I always loved both the celebrations and the network of relationships and associations that went with our business at the Mansion, I always felt best in the *empty* halls of the Mansion on the Hill, cleansed of their accumulation of sentiment, utterly silent, patiently awaiting the possibility of matrimony. It was onto this clean slate that I had routinely projected my foolish hopes. But after Brice strutted through my place of employment, after his marriage began to overshadow every other, I found instead a different message inscribed on these walls: *Every death implies a guilty party.*

Or to put it another way, there was a network of sub-basements in the Mansion on the Hill through which each suite was connected to another. These tunnels were well-traveled by certain alcoholic janitorial guys whom I knew well enough. I'd had my reasons to adventure there before, but now I used every opportunity to pace these corridors. I still performed the parts of my job that would assure that I got paid and that I invested regularly in my 401K plan, but I felt more comfortable in the emptiness of the Mansion's suites and basements, thinking about how I was going to extract my recompense, while Brice and Sarah dithered over the cost of their justice of the peace and their photographer and their *Champlain Pentecostal Singers*.

I had told Linda Pietrzsyk about Brice's reappearance. I had told her about you, Sis. I had remarked about your fractures and your loss of blood and your hypothermia and the results of your postmortem blood-alcohol test; I suppose that I'd begun to tell her all kinds of things, in outbursts of candor that were followed by equal and opposite remoteness. Linda saw me, over the course of those weeks, lurking, going from Ticonderoga to Rip Van Winkle to Chestnut, slipping in and out of infernal sub-basements of conjecture that other people find grimy and uncomfortable, when I should have been overseeing the unloading of floral arrangements at the loading dock or arranging for Glenda's chiropractic appointments. Linda saw me lurking around, *asked what was wrong and told me that it would be better after the anniversary, after that day had come and gone,* and I felt the discourses of apology and subsequent gratitude forming epiglottally in me, but instead I told her to get lost, to leave the dead to bury the dead.

After a long excruciating interval, the day of Sarah Danforth Wilton's marriage to Brice Paul McCann arrived. It was a day of chill mists, Sis, and you had now been gone just over one year. I had passed through the anniversary trembling, in front of the television, watching the Home Shopping Network, impulsively pricing cubic zirconium rings, as though one of these would have been the ring you might have worn at your ceremony. You were a fine sister, but you changed your mind all the time, and I had no idea if these things I'd attributed to you in the last year were features of the *you* I once knew, or whether, in death, you had become the property of your mourners, so that we made of you a puppet.

On the anniversary, I watched a videotape of your bridal shower, and Mom was there, and she looked really proud, and Dad drifted into the center of the frame at one point, and mumbled a strange *harrumph* that had to do with interloping at an assembly of such beautiful women (I was allowed on the scene only to do the videotaping), and you were very pleased as you opened your gifts. At one point you leaned over to Mom, and stage-whispered — so that even I could hear — *that your car was a real lemon and that you had to take it to the shop and you didn't have time and it was a total hassle and did she think that I would lend you the Sable without giving you a hard time?* My Sable, my car. Sure. If I had to do it again, I would never have given you a hard time even once.

The vows at the Mansion on the Hill seemed to be the part of the ceremony where most of the tinkering took place. I think if Glenda had been able to find a way to charge a premium on vow alteration, we could have found a really excellent revenue stream at the Mansion on the Hill. If the sweet instant of commitment is so universal, why does it seem to have so many different articulations? People used all sorts of things in their vows. Conchita Bosworth used the songs of Dan Fogelberg when it came to the exchange of rings; a futon-store owner from Queensbury, Reggie West, managed to work in material from a number of sitcoms. After a while, you'd heard it all, the rhetoric of desire, the incantation of commitment rendered as awkwardly as possible; you heard the purple metaphors, the hackneyed lines, until it was all like legal language, as in any business transaction.

It was the language of Brice McCann's vows that brought this story to its conclusion. I arrived at the wedding late. I took a cab across the Hudson, from the hill in Troy where I lived in my convenience apartment. What trees there were in the system of pavement cloverleafs where Route Seven met the interstate were bare, disconsolate. The road was full of potholes. The lanes choked with old, shuddering sedans. The parking valets at the Mansion, a group of pot-smoking teens who seemed to enjoy creating a facsimile of politeness that involved both effrontery and subservience, opened the door of the cab for me and greeted me according to their standard line, *Where's the party?* The parking lot was full. We had seven weddings going on at once. Everyone was working. Glenda was working, Linda was working, Dorcas was working. All my teammates were working, sprinting from suite to suite, micromanaging. The whole of the Capital Region must have been at the Mansion that Saturday to witness the blossoming of families, Sis, or, in the case of Brice's wedding, to witness the way in which a vow of faithfulness less than a year old, a promise of the future, can be traded in so quickly; how marriage is just a shrink-wrapped sale item, mass-produced in bulk. You can pick one up anywhere these days, at a mall, on layaway. If it doesn't fit, exchange it.

I walked the main hallway slowly, peeking in and out of the various suites. In the Chestnut Suite it was the Polanskis, poor but generous — their daughter Denise intended to have and to hold an Italian fellow, A. L. DiPietro, also completely penniless, and the Polanskis were paying for the entire ceremony and rehearsal dinner and inviting the DiPietros to stay with them for the week. They had brought their own floral displays, personally assembled by the arthritic Mrs. Polanski. The room had a dignified simplicity. Next, in the Hudson Suite, in keeping with its naval flavor, cadet Bobby Moore and his high-school sweetheart Mandy Sutherland were tying the knot, at the pleasure of Bobby's dad, who had been a tugboat captain in New York Harbor; in the Adirondack Suite, two of the venerable old families of the Lake George region — the Millers (owner of the Lake George Cabins) and the Wentworths (they had the Quality Inn franchise) commingled their tourist-dependent fates; in the Valentine Room, Sis, two women (named Sal and Martine, but that's all I should say about them, for reasons of privacy) were to be married by a renegade Episcopal minister called Jack Valance — they had sewn their own gowns to match the cadmium red decor of that interior; Ticonderoga had the wedding of Glen Dunbar and Louise Glazer, a marriage not memorable in any way at all; and in the Niagara Hall two of Saratoga's great eighteenth-century racing dynasties, the Vanderbilt and Pierrepont families, were about to settle long-standing differences. Love was everywhere in the air.

I walked through all these ceremonies, Sis, before I could bring myself to go over to the Rip Van Winkle Room. My steps were reluctant. My observations: the proportions of sniffling at each ceremony were about equal and the audiences were about equal and levels of whimsy and seriousness were about the same wherever you went. The emotions careened, high and low, across the whole spectrum of possible feelings. The music might be different from case to case — stately baroque anthems or klezmer rave-ups — but the intent was the same. By 3:00 P.M., I no longer knew what marriage meant, really, except that the celebration of it seemed built into every life I knew but my own.

The doors of the Rip Van Winkle Room were open, as distinct from the other suites, and I tiptoed through them and closed these great carved doors behind myself. I slipped into the bride's side. The light was dim, Sis. The light was deep in the ultraviolet spectrum, as when we used to go, as kids, to the exhibitions at the Hall of Science and Industry. There seemed to be some kind of mummery, some kind of expressive dance, taking place at the altar. The Champlain Pentecostal Singers were wailing eerily. As I searched the room for familiar faces, I noticed them everywhere. Just a couple of rows away Alex McKinnon and her boy Zack were squished into a row and were fidgeting desperately. Had they known Brice? Had they known you? Maybe they counted themselves close friends of Sarah Wilton. Zack actually turned and waved and seemed to mouth something to me, but I couldn't make it out. On the groom's side, I saw

Linda Pietrzsyk, though she ought to have been working in the office, fielding calls, and she was surrounded by Cheese, Chip, Mick, Mark, Stig, Blair and a half-dozen other delinquents from her peer group. Like some collective organism of mirth and irony, they convulsed over the proceedings, over the scarlet tights and boas and dance belts of the modern dancers capering at the altar. A row beyond these Skidmore halfwits — though she never sat in at the ceremony — was Glenda Manzini herself, and she seemed to be sobbing uncontrollably, a handkerchief like a veil across her face. Where was her husband? And her boy? Then, to my amazement, Sis, when I looked back at the S.R.O. audience beyond the last aisle over on the groom's side, *I saw Mom and Dad.* What were they doing there? And how had they known? I had done everything to keep the wedding from them. I had hoarded these bad feelings. Dad's face was gray with remorse, as though he could have done something to stop the proceedings, and Mom held tight to his side, wearing dark glasses of a perfect opacity. At once, I got up from the row where I'd parked myself and climbed over the exasperated families seated next to me, jostling their knees. As I went, I became aware of Brice McCann's soft, insinuating voice ricocheting, in Dolby Surround Sound, from one wall of the Rip Van Winkle Room to the next. The room was appropriately named, it seemed to me then. We were all sleepers who dreamed a reverie of marriage, not one of us had waked to see the bondage, the violence, the excess of its cabalistic prayers and rituals. Marriage was oneiric. Not one of us was willing to pronounce the truth of its dream language of slavery and submission and transmission of property, and Brice's vow, *to have and to hold Sarah Wilton, till death did them part, forsaking all others,* seemed to me like the pitch of a used-car dealer or insurance salesman, and these words rang out in the room, likewise Sarah's uncertain and breathy reply, and I rushed at the center aisle, pushing away cretinous guests and cherubic newborns toward my parents, to embrace them as these words fell, these words with their intimations of mortality, *to tell my parents I should never have let you drive that night, Sis. How could I have let you drive? How could I have been so stupid? My tires were bald — I couldn't afford better. My car was a death trap; and I was its proper driver, bent on my long, complicated program of failure, my program of futures abandoned, of half-baked ideas, of big plans that came to nought, of cheap talk and lies, of drinking binges, petty theft; my car was made for my own death, Sis, the inevitable and welcome end to the kind of shame and regret I had brought upon everyone close to me, you especially, who must have wept inwardly, in your bosom, when you felt compelled to ask me to read a poem on your special day, before you totaled my car, on that curve, running up over the berm, shrieking, flipping the vehicle, skidding thirty feet on the roof, hitting the granite outcropping there, plunging out of the seat (why no seat belt?), snapping your neck, ejecting through the windshield, catching part of yourself there, tumbling over the hood, breaking both legs, puncturing your lung, losing an eye, shattering your wrist, bleeding, coming to rest at last in a pile of moldering leaves, where rain fell upon you, until, unconscious, you died.*

Yet, as I called out to Mom and Dad, the McCann-Wilton wedding party suddenly scattered, the vows were through, the music was overwhelming, the bride and groom were married; there were Celtic pipes, and voices all in harmony — it

was a dirge, it was a jig, it was a chant of religious ecstasy —
and I couldn't tell what was wedding and what was funeral,
whether there was an end to one and a beginning to the
other, and there were shouts of joy and confetti in the air,
and beating of breasts and the procession of pink-cheeked
teenagers, two by two, all living the dream of American
marriages with cars and children and small businesses and
pension plans and social-security checks and grandchil-
dren, and I couldn't get close to my parents in the throng; in
fact, I couldn't be sure if it had been them standing there at
all, in that fantastic crowd, that crowd of dreams, and I realized I was alone at Brice McCann's wedding, alone among
people who would have been just as happy not to have me
there, as I had often been alone, even in fondest company,
even among those who cared for me. I should have stayed
home and watched television.

This didn't stop me, though. I made my way to the reception. I shoveled down the chicken satay and shrimp with
green curry, along with the proud families of Sarah Wilton
and Brice McCann. Linda Pietrzsyk appeared by my side, as
when we had kissed in the Ticonderoga Suite. She asked if I
was feeling all right.

— Sure, I said.

— Don't you think I should drive you home?

— There's someone I want to talk to, I said. — Then I'd
be happy to go.

And Linda asked:

— What's in the bag?

She was referring to my Wal-Mart shopping bag, Sis. I
think the Wal-Mart policy which asserts that *employees are
not to let a customer pass without asking if this customer*

needs help is incredibly enlightened. I think the way to a devoted customer is through his or her dignity. In the shopping bag, I was carrying the wedding gift I had brought for Brice McCann and Sarah Wilton. I didn't know if I should reveal this gift to Linda, because I didn't know if she would understand, but I told her anyhow. *Is this what it's like to discover, all at once, that you are sharing your life?*

— Oh, that's some of my sister.

— Andrew, Linda said, and then she apparently didn't know how to continue. Her voice, in a pair of false starts, oscillated with worry. Her smile was grim. — Maybe this would be a good time to leave.

But I didn't leave, Sis. I brought out the most dangerous weapon in my arsenal, the pinnacle of my nefarious plans for this event, also stored in my Wal-Mart bag. The Chicken Mask. That's right, Sis. I had been saving it ever since my days at Hot Bird, and as Brice had yet to understand that I had crashed his wedding for a specific reason, I slipped this mask over my neatly parted hair, and over the collar of the wash-and-wear suit that I had bought that week for this occasion. I must say, in the mirrored reception area in the Rip Van Winkle Room, I was one elegant chicken. I immediately began to search the premises for the groom, and it was difficult to find him at first, since there were any number of like-minded beret-wearing motivational speakers slouching against pillars and counters. At last, though, I espied him preening in the middle of a small group of maidens, over by the electric fountain we had installed for the ceremony. He was laughing good-naturedly. When he first saw me, in the Chicken Mask, working my way toward him, I'm sure he saw me as an omen for his new union. *Terrific! We've got a chicken at the ceremony! Poultry is always reassuring at wedding time!* Linda was trailing me across the room. Trying to distract me. I had to be short with her. I told her to go find herself a husband.

I worked my way into McCann's limber and witty reception chatter and mimed a certain Chicken-style affability. Then, when one of those disagreeable conversational silences overtook the group, I ventured a question of your intended:

— So, Brice, how do you think your last fiancée, Eileen, would be reacting to your first-class nuptial ceremony today? Would she have liked it?

There was a confused hush, as the three or four of the secretarial beauties of his circle considered the best way to respond to this thorny question.

— Well, since she's passed away, I think she would probably be smiling down on us from above. I've felt her presence throughout the decision to marry Sarah, and I think Eileen knows that I'll never forget her. That I'll always love her.

— Oh, is that right? I said, — because the funny thing is I happen to have her *with me here,* and . . .

Then I opened up the small box of you (you were in a Tiffany jewelry box that I had spirited out of Mom's jewelry cache because I liked its pale teal shade: the color of rigor mortis as I imagined it), held it up toward Brice and then tossed some of it. I'm sure you know, Sis, that chips of bone tend to be heavier and therefore to fall more quickly to the ground, while the rest of the ashes make a sort of cloud when you throw them, when you cast them aloft. Under the circumstances, this cloud seemed to have a character, a personality. *Thus, you darted and feinted around Brice's head,*

Sis, so that he began coughing and wiping the corners of his eyes, dusty with your remains. His consorts were hacking as well, among them Sarah Wilton, his betrothed. How had I missed her before? She was radiant like a woman whose prayers have been answered, who sees the promise of things to come, who sees uncertainties and contingencies diminished, and yet she was rushing away from me, astonished, as were the others. I realized I had caused a commotion. Still, I gave chase, Sis, and I overcame your Brice McCann, where he blockaded himself on the far side of a table full of spring rolls. Though I have never been a fighting guy, I gave him an elbow in the nose, as if I were a Chicken and this elbow my wing. I'm sure I mashed some cartilage. He got a little nosebleed. I think I may have broken the Mansion's unbroken streak of peaceful weddings.

At this point, of course, a pair of beefy Mansion employees (the McCarthy brothers, Tom and Eric) arrived on the scene and pulled me off of Brice McCann. They also tore the Chicken Mask from me. And they never returned this piece of my property afterwards. At the moment of unmasking, Brice reacted with mock astonishment. But how could he have failed to guess? That I would wait for my chance, however many years it took?

— Andy?

I said nothing, Sis. Your ghost had been in the cloud that wreathed him; your ghost had swooped out of the little box that I'd held, and now, at last, you were released from your disconsolate march on the surface of the earth, your march of unfinished business, your march of fixed ideas and obsessions unslaked by death. I would be happy if you were at peace now, Sis, and I would be happy if I were at peace; I would be happy if the thunderclouds and lightning of Brice and Sarah's wedding would yield to some warm autumn day in which you had good weather for your flight up through the heavens.

Out in the foyer, where the guests from the Valentine Room were promenading in some of the finest threads I had ever seen, Tom McCarthy told me that Glenda Manzini wanted to see me in her office — before I was removed from the Mansion on the Hill permanently. We walked against the flow of the crowd beginning to empty from each of the suites. Our trudge was long. When I arrived at Glenda's refrigerated chamber, she did an unprecedented thing, Sis, she closed the door. I had never before inhabited that space alone with her. She didn't invite me to sit. Her voice was raised from the outset. Pinched between thumb and forefinger (the shade of her nail polish, a dark maroon, is known in beauty circles, I believe, as *vamp*), as though it were an ounce of gold or a pellet of plutonium, she held a single green M&M.

— Can you explain this? She asked. — Can you tell me what this is?

— I think that's a green M&M, I said. — I think that's the traditional green color, as opposed to one of the new brighter shades they added in a recent campaign for market share.

— Andy, don't try to amuse me. What was this green M&M doing behind my filing cabinet?

— Well, I —

— I'm certain that I didn't leave a green M&M back there. I would never leave an M&M behind a filing cabinet. In fact, I would never allow a green M&M into this office in the first place.

— That was months ago.

— I've been holding onto it for months, Glenda said.

— Do you think I'm stupid?

— On the contrary, I said.

— Do you think you can come in here and violate the privacy of my office?

— I think you're brilliant, I said. — And I think you're very sad. And I think you should surrender your job to someone who cares for the institution you're celebrating here.

Now that I had let go of you, Sis, now that I had begun to compose this narrative in which I relinquished the hem of your spectral bedsheet, I saw through the language of business, the rhetoric of hypocrisy. Why had she sent me out for those birth-control pills? Why did she make me schedule her chiropractic appointments? Because she could. *But what couldn't be controlled, what could never be controlled, was the outcome of devotion.* Glenda's expression, for the first time on record, was stunned. She launched into impassioned colloquy about how the Mansion on the Hill was supposed to be a *refuge,* and how, with my *antics,* as she called them, I had sullied the reputation of the Mansion and endangered its business plan, and how it was clear *that assaulting strangers while wearing a rubber mask is the kind of activity that proves you are an unstable person, and I just think, well, I don't see the point in discussing it with you anymore and I think you have some serious choices to make, Andy, if you want to be part of regular human society,* and so forth, which is just plain bunk, as far as I'm concerned. It's not as if Brice McCann were a *stranger* to me.

I'm always the object of tirades by my supervisors, for overstepping my position, for lying, for wanting too much —

this is one of the deep receivables on the balance sheet of my life — and yet at the last second Glenda Manzini didn't fire me. According to shrewd managerial strategy, she simply waved toward the door. With the Mansion crowded to capacity now, with volume creeping upward in the coming months, they would need someone with my skills. To look after the cars in the parking lot, for example. Mark my words, Sis, valet parking will soon be as big in the Northeast as it is in the West.

When the McCarthys flung me through the main doors, Linda Pietrzsyk was waiting. What unfathomable kindness. At the main entrance, on the way out, I passed through a gauntlet of rice-flingers. Bouquets drifted through the skies to the mademoiselles of the capital. Garters fell into the hands of local bachelors. Then I was beyond all good news and seated in the passenger seat of Linda's battered Volkswagen. She was crying. We progressed slowly along back roads. I had been given chances and had squandered them. I had done my best to love, Sis. I had loved you, and you were gone. In Linda's car, at dusk, we sped along the very road where you took your final drive. Could Linda have known? Your true resting place is forested by white birches, they dot the length of that winding lane, the fingers of the dead reaching up through burdens of snow to impart much-needed instruction to the living. In intermittent afternoon light, in seizure-inducing light, unperturbed by the advances of merchandising, I composed my proposal.

On the Carousel

Is the celluloid of Los Angeles — in editing-room strips, unassembled by freelancers — influenced by the lives of this city? Or are the lives of Los Angeles influenced by this high-profile movie business? Or is the relationship between the two fluid, circular, and continuous, and therefore not to be separated into two discrete quantities — Los Angeles and the movie business? Who has *time* for questions? Lily is late. If Thea wants to have juice for godsakes, she's not so late that she can't stop for juice, since she has borrowed her friend Ellen's Mercedes — her own is in the shop. Thea can have juice even though Evan is after school being I.Q.-tested and she's supposed to pick him up and then she's supposed to pitch a woman at the Fox lot and the script needs another writer, another in a series of writers, some entire sewing circle of writers. *Here's how the back end works,* according to the letter of agreement that came from the lawyer this morning — 2½% net, which is frankly embarrassing, her lawyer told her, and the term of license is all wrong, way too short, the term is ridiculous even if it is a small movie, the story of a strong, sympathetic woman from the South and her conflicts with the political and social institutions of small-town America in the early decades of this century — just right for a self-starting independent director who's not bound by the constraints of the studios. Lily's not sure if she's attracted to the script because she herself is a strong, sympathetic woman from the South (relocated to the Brentwood area) or rather if the action of pitching the script reconfigures her in a way, so that suddenly she feels stronger and more powerful. She's not exactly sure if all this legal language is really coherent, the language at the center of the deal (as her lawyer describes it), or whether language itself clutters up what otherwise might be simple. Language hangs in potential, as with preedited strips of footage at the editing facilities, like confetti or Christmas tinsel or strips of fly paper in dingy coffee shops of the unvisited downtown section of Los Angeles. The language of her town, the cinematic lexicon, is seductive and dangerous, but it enables her, when transmuted into her occasionally generous paychecks, to afford better than the McDonald's on Pico. So why are they here? According to what rationale? *Do they even have juice at McDonald's?* she asks Thea in the rearview. *Honey, do you want to stop here at McDonald's?* And what's Thea doing in the backseat, anyhow? *Don't you want to come sit up here with me? I hate that feeling that I'm just driving you around and that's all I'm good for,* but Thea says she likes it in back, and she's playing with a doll that looks exactly like, or not exactly like but extremely close to the woman who was in the luggage commercial with Lily four years ago, when she was sitting in the baggage claim area at DFW — they had rented it overnight for an astronomical sum — and she was dressed in a conservative, pinstripe suit with a hemline about so, sitting with one of those fancy new rolling suitcases, a suitcase with rolling *and* pivoting mechanisms (the corporate people told her), and as the cameras turned she pulled this sleek gray suitcase from the baggage carousel, and, according to instructions from her Austrian director, said, as though a future of unlimited possibility were hers, *It makes every other piece of luggage obsolete.* Meanwhile, as she was getting comfortable between takes, there was this blonde, this beautiful, radiant but finally vacuous blonde sitting on the edge of the carousel beside her and this blonde made Lily uncomfortable, as though she were creeping toward Lily, riding around and around on the carousel driven centrifugally toward Lily to pounce on her like a succubus or a particularly rapacious condor, embodying a message of obsolescence, the inevitable obsolescence of older women actors (thirty-four years old), this blonde actually trying to render her obsolete, a young waitress from some Rodeo Drive luncheonette getting the big break, while Lily was coming to the end of her streak of well-paying but shallow roles in commercials. Once you have met this particular blonde you don't forget her. Lily wonders if she became a producer *because of her work in commercials* — because commercials taught her how to exaggerate wildly with the appearance of total conviction. The point being that Thea's doll looks like the blonde who had climbed from the baggage carousel to steal Lily's career, whom Lily never really saw except in the undertow of some sleep-deprived vision in DFW, likewise she can't really be sure that the doll looks *exactly* like the blonde anyhow, since she's trying to drive *and* keep an eye on the clock and she's also dangerously interested in a copy of a magazine on the passenger seat which is open to an article about a big new production of some musical by Rogers and Hammerstein — with rich Technicolor photos — and she should be back at school to pick up Evan, who's being I.Q.-tested because they suspect there's something wrong with him, because, in fact, Evan is preoccupied with musicals to the exclusion of all other cultural productions and that's how the magazine came to be in the front seat in the first place, because Evan was looking at it. There's a circular aspect to this, to the way she grew up with a brother with a certain neurological difficulty and now has a son who might well have a similar neurological difficulty, among his eccentricities refusing eye contact, refusing to be touched, excessive interest in musical comedy. Is she able to care for Evan because of her brother, or will Evan in turn make some lasting contribution to her relationship with her brother (who continues to live robustly and to make primitivist paintings)? She would assuredly weep about all this, curse God or the heavenly planning commissions responsible for such things, had she more time. Traffic is heavy and that's the one good reason to stop at the McDonald's on Pico, which is a *drive-thru*, that oasis outside of the traffic, into which you go inching forward and then around and out. She's reminded temporarily of her husband. He's a really, really great guy, puts up with her twists and turns, and he's terrific looking, with a lot of forehead, and a thatch of hair upon his chest and he's hardworking, and there are really no problems at all, really, *you know how these things are,* but they are taking the hard right at the drive-thru entrance to the McDonald's on Pico, and there's a car in front of her, completing its fast-food order, which seems to be, when handed through the window, something for a child, because there is the bright packaging that comes with the *Happy Meal*, which also contains, undoubtedly, its fully poseable action figure. *Collectors go mad for this stuff.* She imagines that the action figure is the blonde on the baggage carousel turning endlessly, stuck in some nexus of recurrences. Then the Saturn (before her) pulls up six feet and stops suddenly, and the car behind her (in the rearview), a banged-up Dodge Omni, stops suddenly, and she looks at the man in the tinted drive-thru window of McDonald's, at his amiable, open features. He's laughing. However, his expression scrambles as she gazes upon it, disappears in the window, such that the tinted window has suddenly an uncanny fullness, and then she looks at Thea, who is in the backseat, muttering directorial instructions to her blond doll. On the menu wall next to her, next to Lily and Thea, a voice rumbles from a two-inch woofer, *Order, please?* And Lily thinks, *yes, order, please,* but says instead, *Happy Meal and a large orange juice,* uncertain if orange juice is really possible here in this zone of fast-food particulars. She glances out the passenger window, and it will be the casualness of this glance that will frighten her later on. What if she had not looked? What if she had not, as if in reverie, found, before her, the origin of all disorder — like a villain of westerns upon his dark steed — in baggy jeans and mesh T-shirt and backwards baseball cap, removing *his weapon* from the cinched waist of baggy jeans. His underwear is definitely Calvin Klein, she notices. And it's an automatic weapon, though she knows nothing of these, of revolvers or semi-automatic or automatic weapons, except what the films of her city have shown her. Has each scriptwriter in the metropolis thus been witness to such an incident? Or is it only Lily, who wants only to make films about powerful women opposing rigid, small-town social institutions, who is now, unfortunately, going to experience weaponry firsthand? Have all the kids who discharge these firearms been to see the movies in which weapons technologies so often appear? Do the films generate the weapons or vice versa, or are the guns somehow spontaneously generated? The kid with the weapon has no idea that she's in a rush to go see the I.Q.-testers about Evan's disability and therefore to discuss Evan's tendency to sing entire musicals from memory — *South Pacific* and *Oklahoma!* — and this boy obviously doesn't know that *Thea just wants juice* or that Lily is still living off the paycheck from a commercial in which she pronounced the words, *It makes every piece of luggage obsolete,* and if this boy did know these things, he might shoot her anyway. This is not the best block, but it is not the worst block either, and the argument that she just shouldn't have driven here will not be adequate, but there is no time for the argument, in any case, because now *the boy starts shooting.* He's a teenager, and the gun is turned, thank God, away from Lily, and this boy's ass, amid a billowing of shorts over the margin of baggy trousers, is pressed against the passenger window of Ellen's Mercedes. He appears to be firing into a crowd, into the parking lot adjacent to the drive-thru slip, into a crowd of other teenagers, teenagers schooled in secret handshakes and semaphoric gesticulations and certain uniforms, teenagers now scattering, and Lily reaches back and grabs Thea by the hair and says, *You*

are going to have to unbuckle yourself and get yourself down,
and Thea says, *But I don't want to,* and she says, *I don't care
what you want, just get down,* and she has to be a little rough
with her daughter, as soon as Thea has sprung the belt,
shoving the girl's strawberry blond head down after the rest
of her down into the footwell between backseat and front,
after which she launches herself between the seats, over an
armrest, to cover her giggling daughter with her arms, *Will
one body stop a hailstorm of bullets from entering a second
body? Will this water and blood and bile stop a bullet or is
that just the stuff of movies?* She imagines that she should
be composing desperate pleas, *I love my daughter and I love
my son even though he has certain difficulties and I love my
husband and I only stopped here for juice, though I am not
sure that McDonald's even serves juice, and I think you
should just let me drive on out of here and we can forget about
the history of trouble between our two peoples,* but she doesn't
think any of these things, really, and Thea says, *Mom, you're
squishing me,* but the truth is that Lily is actually, at this
moment, thinking about luggage. *Rolling suitcases are really
an improvement, if you should find that you are going in and
out of a number of airports in a short period of time — on a
promotional junket, for example.* She happened to notice in
DFW, where they filmed the luggage commercial, that the
airport was so enormous that you had to take a train to get
from one end to the other. DFW was as big as Manhattan
someone told her. Or maybe that was Denver. *In airports
this enormous, the rolling and pivoting mechanisms of contemporary luggage design will certainly be an improvement
over portage-style suitcases.* Lily's conviction is that the rolling
design is so profound that it will cause further alteration in

the way Americans travel. They will change planes more often. They will go to more motels. She releases Thea for a moment, to peek over the margin of the rear window, in a reloading silence, just before the kids from across the parking lot begin to *fire back* — directly at Ellen's Mercedes — and the sound of these bullets is like the kernels of Cineplex Odeon or Sony Theatres popcorn inflating in a patented *steam-popping apparatus,* or it is like a rambunctious Independence Day celebration; her similes are optimistically nonlethal, though the bullets nonetheless perforate the side of Ellen's Mercedes. Lily hopes there is no actual tendency for *gas tanks to explode under these circumstances,* that the bluster of cinema is responsible for this cliché. *Mom, what's happening?* Thea asks, and Lily says, *Please, keep your head down, okay?* And the kid, the boy, reclining against the side of the Mercedes begins to lope off toward the rear of her car, but before he does so he stops and looks into the backseat, through the lightly tinted glass, he eclipses all the light in the car, filling the window with the butt of the gun and his face and his mesh t-shirt, and his hairless chest underneath, and he looks in at Lily, and their eyes meet, and then bullets rain down again from across the parking lot. The sewing circle of writers will come back to this again and again trying to understand how we could live so close to this boy and never understand the meaning of his smile, how he smiles nervously *and* hopelessly *and* menacingly, all these meanings in one smile — he's just a kid, not old enough to vote, not old enough to avoid voting — and then another car screeches to a halt beside the Mercedes, a black Jeep, late model, yes, Lily is sitting up, though this is the wrong posture to take, and the Jeep draws the fire, though so far not a single *arterial fountaining* has she seen, and there are likewise no cries of pain, no spontaneous oaths of revenge. Everyone is concentrating. Would she know if she were hit? The boy leaps into the backseat of the Jeep, and the back door flaps, unclosed, as the Jeep goes over an edge of curb and sidewalk and out onto Pico, completing its drive-thru circuit, and then a car from the parking lot, with boys and girls cursing, loads up at once and gives chase, and then all is silent.

It could be optioned — the story of the attractive professional woman caught in the crossfire at a local McDonald's, taken hostage by renegade gangsters bent on seizing control of the local government, bent on revolution, bent on assassinating local government officials, and her husband, a mild-mannered actor and screenwriter who infiltrates the cadre of separatist revolutionaries at their fearsome ghetto redoubt using only the tools of the trade he has learned from action films. The prejudicial vigilante justice on which he thus embarks brings him and his wife closer together. This vigilante justice could be optioned for much better terms than the 2½% promised her for the tale of small-town America and the strong woman character.

— Are you all right? she asks Thea. She takes diminutive hands into her own. They are sitting up, in the backseat.
— Any broken bones?
— What happened, Mom?
— That man was firing a gun. I don't have any idea why. Are you all right?

Thea says nothing, and resumes the contemplation of her doll. *It makes every other piece of luggage obsolete.* Lily starts the Mercedes and they ease out onto Pico, which fills with traffic, as if nothing out of the ordinary has taken place, which indeed nothing has. They go as slowly as the Sunday drivers of Laurel Canyon. Lily's breaths are shallow.

— Mom? Thea says.

— Yes, darling?

— We forgot our food.

— I think you're right. Do you want to go back?

— No.

Lily wouldn't go back anyway, and there isn't time since she is late, really late, to pick Evan up from his I.Q. test. But she pulls the car over nonetheless, double parks, though it is still as if recent events were a projection upon some screen somewhere — at the Chinese theater, or in Century City; she double parks by a public telephone, gets out, dials 911. Eleven minutes later, the operator takes her call. Lily pronounces her words emphatically, as though delivering lines, *I was witness to gunfire on Pico at the McDonald's, there was this really young boy and he was firing an automatic weapon into a crowd nearby, a crowd of teenagers, and my daughter and I . . .*

— How did you know it was an automatic weapon? replies the operator.

— Well, I've seen them in the . . . I mean, when he fires off so many rounds in a minute . . . It must be a . . . It was almost a hundred bullets, I'd say, maybe a hundred and fifty, you should see the side of my car. I mean, it's not my car . . .

— Thank you very much —

— Don't you want to take my name?

No, the operator wants no such thing and the line is disconnected, and Lily looks back into the car, where Thea is playing with her doll, where Thea is whistling quietly, gently.

The traffic is heavy. She dials 911 a second time, and goes through the whole thing again, the conversation identical; again the operator asks, *How did you know it was an automatic weapon?* and asks in addition how Lily is able to identify *the perp* if she was crouching in the backseat using her body as a shield and asks furthermore why Lily was at McDonald's in search of juice, since everybody knows it's only Coke, Diet Coke, and Sprite. *As if Lily's story were a test screening* and the emergency operator one of those disgruntled teens in search of narrative credibility problems who's more interested in flirting with pals in the back row. Once the interview has become antagonistic, Lily hangs up, and there is no choice but to proceed to Evan's school, though the way Lily's foot trembles on the gas pedal suggests that this is not a good time to be driving.

— Thea, I would really like it if you would come sit in the front seat.

Her anxious tone finally works the magic, and Thea, pliable and sweet, levers herself between the seats and tumbles into the front. She leans against Lily as they are heading down Melrose. Lily thinks briefly, once more, of luggage. Where is her husband now? Could she call him? Has she done everything she might do to make her husband happy and to put him at ease? She once had collagen injected into her lips. She once fucked him in a doorway. Should she get a breast job? Should she abandon acting for good? Should she raise her children in another town and lead a quiet life? Should she leave off speaking the Latinate vocabulary of attorneys? Should she whisper the last of her movie pitches? Should she climb off the baggage carousel, where she has spent years locked in a metaphysical and purely imaginary struggle with a blonde, a fully poseable action figurine, a doll with the multiple polymer outfits? Should she walk here among the streets? Should she get out of the car, out of the city where the car-pooling lanes are always empty, where every vehicle has its radio up loud and solitary drivers are singing lamentations and arias to the lifeless melodies of classic rock stations, arias that treat of a city *where lives are influenced by demographically calculating mass-market fictions?* Are all these questions equally ridiculous?

Last night Evan asked her to read to him in bed. The time of night when streetlights and sunset vie for eminence, when the layer of haze dims each until it is like the incomplete luminosity of faded paintings of the great masters, smudged on a ceiling of some monastery in the mad latitudes of southern Europe. She knelt at the edge of Evan's bed, and tried to get him to make eye contact for ten seconds, as she does each night — it's good practice, making eye contact. When Evan was done looking into her eyes, he announced that he wanted to tell her about *Carousel* by Rodgers and Hammerstein, and he gave her again the exact date of composition (1945) and reminded her about how it was based on a play by a Hungarian (Ferenc Molnár) and told her of the women of the northeast with their thankless small-town jobs, and how, in the ashen landscapes of industrial New England, the only thing to look forward to was the fair, when carousels and ferris wheels would come to town, and the women waited for the fair, and they courted the unhappy men at the fair, and sang, each of them, upon the rotating platform of the carousel, threading their way between the gilded horses, their hair pinned up and their lips painted, wearing their fine dresses, and then Evan began to sing to her, her boy with perfect pitch, and she whispers now to the sleeping Thea, beginning to sing herself, her hands clammy and tight upon the wheel, Evan's reedy little voice inherited from her, there in his bedroom, here in the car, *Words wouldn't come in an easy way, round in circles I would go . . . I'd let my golden chances pass me by.*

The Double Zero

My dad was for midwestern values; he was for families; he was for a firm handshake; he was for a little awkward sweet-talking with the waitress at the HoJo's. Until he grew to the age of thirty-four he worked at one of those farms owned by a big international corporation that's created from family farms gone defunct. Looked like a chessboard, if you saw it from the air. This was near Bidwell, Ohio. Don't know if it was Archer Daniels Midland, Monsanto, some company like that. The particular spread I'm talking about got sold to developers later. I guess it was more lucrative to sell the plot and buy some other place. The housing development that grew up on that land, it was called Golden Meadow Estates even though it didn't have any meadows. That's where we lived after Dad got laid off. He'd been at the bar down by the railroad when the news came through.

So he took the job at Sears, in the power tools dept. About the same time he met my mom. She'd once placed in a beauty contest, Miss Scandinavian Bidwell. They got married after dating a long while. My mom, probably on account of her beauty crown experience, was eager for my dad (and me too, because I showed up pretty soon) to get some of that American fortune all around her. She was hopeful. She was going to get her some. The single-story tract house over in Golden Meadow Estates, well, it was a pretty tight fit, not to mention falling down, and we were stuck next door to a used-car salesman nobody liked. I heard a rumor that this guy Stubb, this neighbor, had dead teenagers in the basement. The Buckeye State had a national lead in serial killers, though, so maybe that wasn't any big surprise. My mother convinced my dad that he had to get into some other line of work, where there was a better possibility of advancing. *Was he going to spend his whole life selling power tools?* Her idea was raising Angora rabbits. He went along with it. They really multiplied, these rabbits, like I bet you've heard. They were my chore, matter of fact. You'd get dozens of these cages with rabbits that urinated and shat all over everything if you even whispered at them, and then you had to *spin* their fur, you know, on an *actual loom*. If you wanted to make any kind of money at all. I didn't have to spin anything though. I was too little. But you get the idea. Turned out my mother didn't have the patience for all that.

Next was yew trees. Some chemical in the yew tree was supposed to be an ingredient in the toxins for fighting cancers. Maybe my mother was thinking about that cluster in town. I mean, just about everybody in Golden Meadows Estates sported a wig, and so it wasn't newsworthy later when they found that the development had been laid out on an old chromium dump. Meantime, we actually had a half acre of yew trees already planted on some land rented from the nylon manufacturer downtown, and there were heavy metals there too, which must have been fatal to the yew trees. The main thing is they cooked up this chemical, the yew chemical, in the laboratory by the end of the year.

Mom made a play for llamas. She went down to the Bidwell public library. To the business section. Read up about llamas. But what can you do with a llama anyway? Make a sweater? *Well, that's how we settled on ostriches.* The ostrich is a poetic thing, let me tell you. Its life is full of dramas. The largest of birds on planet Earth. The ostrich is almost eight feet tall and weighs three hundred pounds and it has a brain not too much bigger than a pigeon's brain. It has two toes. It can reach speeds of fifty miles an hour, and believe me, I've seen them do it. Like if you were standing at the far end of the ostrich farm we had, the Rancho Double Zero, and you were holding a Cleveland Indians beer cup full of corn, that ostrich would come at you about the speed an eighteen-wheeler comes at you on the interstate. Just like having a pigeon swoop at you, except that this pigeon is the size of a minivan. The incredible stupidity on the ostrich's face is worth mentioning too, in case you haven't seen one lately. They're mouth-breathers, or anyhow their beaks always hang open a little bit. That pretty much tells you all you need to know. Lights on, property vacant. They reminded me of a retarded kid I knew in grammar school, Zechariah Dunbar. He's dead now. Anyway, the point is that ostriches are always trying to hold down other ostriches, by sitting on them, in order to fuck these other ostriches, without any regard to whether it's a boy or girl animal they're trying to get next to. And speaking of sex and ostriches, I'm almost sure that the men who worked on my father's farm tried to have their way with the Rancho Double Zero product. With a brain so small, it was obvious that the ostrich would never feel loving congress with some heartbroken Midwestern hombre as any kind of bodily insult. Actually, it's amazing that the pea-sized brain in these ostrich skulls could operate the other end of them. Amazing that electrical transmissions could make it that far, what with that huge bulky midsection that was *all red meat*, hundreds of pounds of it, as every brochure will tell you, *but with a startlingly low fat content*. In fact, *tastes like chicken*, as my grandma said before the choking incident. Okay, it was almost like the ostrich was some kind of bird. But it didn't look like a bird, and when there were three or four hundred of them, running around in a herd at fifty miles an hour, flattening rodents, trying to have sex with each other, three or four hundred of them purchased with a precarious loan from Buckeye Savings and Trust, well, they looked more like conventioneers from some Holiday Inn assembly of extinct species. You expected a mating pair of wooly mammoths or a bunch of saber-toothed tigers to show up any moment.

I'm getting away from the story, though. I really meant to talk about ostrich eggs. After ten years of trying to get the Rancho Double Zero to perform fiscally, my parents had to sell the whole thing and declare bankruptcy. That's the sad truth. But it was no shame. Everybody they knew was bankrupt. Everybody in Bidwell, practically, had a lien on their bank account. When we were done with the Double Zero, we had nothing left but a bunch of ostrich eggs, the kind that my parents used to sell out in front of the farm, under a canopy, for people who came out driving. There were three signs, a quarter mile apart, *See the Ostriches! Two Miles!* And then another half-mile. *Ostrich eggs! Five dollars each!* Then another. *Feed the ostriches! If you dare!*

I remember giving the feeding lecture myself to a couple from back East. They were the only people who'd volunteered to feed the ostriches in weeks. I handed them the Cleveland Indians cups. They were dressed up fine. *You can either put some of this corn in your hand and hold it out for the ostriches, but I sure wouldn't do that myself, because I've seen them pick up a little kid and whirl him around like he was a handkerchief and throw him over a fence, bust his neck clean through. Or you can hold out the cup and the ostriches will try to trample each other to death to get right in front of you, and then one of those pinheads will descend with incredible force, steal the entire cup away. Or else you can just scatter some corn at the base of the electrified fence there and get the heck out of the way, which is certainly what I'd do if I were you.* Who would come to Bidwell from anywhere, I was asking myself, unless they were trying to avoid a massive interstate manhunt? Probably this couple, right here, laughing at the poor dumb birds, probably they were the kind of people who would sodomize an entire preschool of kids, rob a rich lady on Park Avenue, hide her body, grind up some teenagers, and then disappear to manage their investments.

Anyhow, that ranch came and went and soon we were in a used El Dorado with 120,000 miles on it. I was in the backseat, with five dozen unrefrigerated ostrich eggs. Dad was forty-eight, or thereabouts, and he was bald, and he was paunchy, and, because of the failure of all the gold-rush schemes, he was discouraged and mean. If he spoke at all it was just to gripe at politicians. He was an independent, in terms of gripes. Just so you know. Non-partisan. And the only hair left on his ugly head, after all the worrying, was around those two patches just above his ears, just like if he were an ostrich chick himself. Because you know when they came out of the shell, these ostrich chicks looked like human fetuses. In fact, I've heard it said that a human being and an ostrich actually share forty-eight percent of their DNA, which is pretty much when you think about it. So Dad looked like an ostrich. Or maybe he looked like one of those cancer survivors from Golden Meadow Estates who were always saying they felt like a million bucks even though it was obvious that they felt like about a buck fifty. Mom, on the other hand, despite her bad business decisions, only seemed to get prettier and prettier. She still spent a couple of hours each morning making up her face with pencils and brushes in a color called *deadly nightshade*.

In terms of volume, one ostrich egg is the equivalent of two dozen of your regular eggs. It's got two liters of liquefied muck in it. That means, if you're a short order cook, that one of these ostrich eggs can last you a long time. A whole day, maybe. The ostrich shell is about the size of a regulation football, but it's shaped just like the traditional chicken eggshell. Which is something I was told to say to tourists, *Note your traditional eggshell styling.* The ostrich egg is so perfect that it looks fake. The ostrich egg looks like it's made out of plastic. In fact, maybe the guys who came up with plastics got the idea from looking at the perfection of the ostrich egg. Myself, I could barely eat one of those ostrich eggs without worrying about seeing a little ostrich fledgling in it, because it looked so much like a human fetus, or what

I imagined a human fetus looked like based on some pictures I'd seen in the *Golden Books Encyclopedia*. What if you accidentally ate one of the fledglings! Look out! They make pretty good French toast, though.

Over the years, my dad had assembled an ostrich freak exhibition. There were lots of genetic things that could go wrong with an ostrich flock, like say an ostrich had four legs, or an ostrich had two heads, or the ostrich didn't have any head at all, just a gigantic midsection. Maybe the number of genetic abnormalities in our stock had to do with how close the farm was to a dioxin-exuding paper plant, or maybe it was the chromium or the PCBs, whatever else. It was always something. The important part here is that the abnormalities made Dad sort of happy and enabled him to have a *collection* to take away from the Rancho Double Zero, and what's the harm in that. Not a lot of room for me in the backseat, though, what with the eggs and the freaks.

The restaurant we started wasn't in Bidwell, because we had bad memories of Bidwell, after the foreclosure and all. There wasn't much choice but to move farther out where things were cheaper. We landed in Pickleville, where it was real cheap, all right, and where there wasn't anything to do. People used to kill feral cats in Pickleville. There was a bounty on them. Kids learned to obliterate any and all wildlife. Pickleville also had a train station where the out-of-state train stopped once a day. Mom figured what with the train station nearby there was a good chance that people would want to stop at a family-style restaurant. So it was a diner, Dizzy's, which was the nickname we had given our ostrich chick *with two heads*. The design of our restaurant was like the traditional style of older diners, you know, shaped like a suppository, aluminum and chrome, juke-boxes at every booth. We lived out back. I was lucky. I got to go to a better school district and fraternize with a better class of kids who called me *hayseed* and accused me of inti-mate relations with brutes.

My parents bought a neon sign, and they made a shelf where Dad put his ostrich experiments, and then they got busy cooking up *open-faced turkey sandwiches* and *breaded fish cutlets* and *turkey hash* and lots of things with *chipped beef* in them. As far as I could tell, just about everything in the restaurant had chipped beef in it. Mom decided that the restaurant should stay open nights (she never had to see my dad that way, since he worked a different shift), for the freight trains that emptied out their passengers in Pickle-ville occasionally. Freight hoboes would come in wearing that hunted expression you get from never having owned a thing and having no fixed address. Sometimes these guys would order an egg over easy, and Dad would attempt to convince them that they should have an ostrich egg. He would haul one of the eggs out of the fridge, and the hoboes would get a load of the ostrich egg and there would be a ter-rified flourishing of *change money*, and then these hoboes would be gone.

My guess is that Dad had concluded that most midwest-ern people were friendly, outgoing folks, and that, in spite of his failure in any enterprise that ever had his name on it, in spite of his galloping melancholy, he should make a real attempt to put on a warm, entertaining manner with the people who came into the diner. It was a *jolly innkeeper* strategy. It was a last-chance thing. He tried smiling at cus-tomers, and even at me, and he tried smiling at my mother, and it caught on. I tried smiling at the alley cat who lived in the trailer with us. I even tried smiling at the kids at school who called me *hayseed*. Then an ostrich egg ruined everything.

One rainy night I was up late avoiding homework when I heard a really scary shriek come from the restaurant. An emergency wail that couldn't be mistaken for anything but a real emergency. Made goosebumps break out on me. My pop burst into the trailer, weeping horribly, smashing plates. What I remember best was the fact that my mother, who never touched the old man at all, caressed the bald part of the top of his head, as if she could smooth out the canals of his worry lines.

It was like this. Joe Kane, a strip-club merchant in Bidwell, was waiting for his own dad, Republican district attorney of Bidwell, to come through on the train that night. There'd been a big case up at the state capital. The train was late and Joe was loafing in the restaurant, drinking coffees, playing through all the Merle Haggard songs on the jukebox. After an hour or two of ignoring my dad, Joe felt like he ought to try to say something. He went ahead and blurted out a pleasantry,

— Waiting for the old man. On the train. Train's running late.

Probably, Dad had thought so much about this body that was right there in front of him, this body who happened to be the son of the district attorney, that he started getting really nervous. A white foam began to accumulate at the corners of his mouth. Like in your chess games that kind of pile outward from the opening, maybe dad was attempting to figure out *every possible future conversation* with Joe

Kane, ahead of time, so he would have something witty to say, becoming, in the process, a complete retard.

He said, for example, the immortal words, — How-de-do.

— How-de-do? said Joe Kane. Did anyone still say stuff like this? Did kiddy television greetings still exist in the modern world of schoolyard massacres and religious cults? Next thing you know my father'd be saying *poopy diapers, weenie roast, tra la la, making nookie.* Just so he could conduct his business. He'd locate in his imaginary playbook the conversational gambit entitled *withering contempt dawns in the face of your auditor,* and, according to this playbook, wasn't anything else for him to do but go on being friendly, and he would.

— Uh, well, have you heard the one about how Christopher Columbus, discoverer of this land of ours, was a cheat? Sure was. Said he could make an egg stand on its end, which obviously you can only do when the calendar's on the equinoxes. And when he couldn't make the egg stand, why he had to crush the end of the egg. Maybe it was a hardboiled egg, I don't know. Obviously, he can't have been that great a man if he had to crush the end of the egg in order to make it stand. I wonder, you know, whether we ought to be having all these annual celebrations in honor of him, since he was a liar about the egg incident. Probably about other things too. He claimed he hadn't crushed the end of the egg when he had. That's not dealing fair.

To make his point, my father took an ostrich egg from a shelf where two or three were all piled up for use that night at the diner. The counter was grimy with a shellac of old bacon and corn syrup and butterfat and honey and molasses and salmonella. He set the egg down here.

— Helluva egg, Joe Kane remarked. — What is that, some kind of nuclear egg? You make that in a reactor?

— I know more about eggs than any man living, my father said.

— Don't doubt that for a second, Joe Kane said.

— This egg will bend to my will. It will succumb to my powers of magic.

— If you say so.

My dad attempted to balance the ostrich egg on its end without success. He tried a number of times. Personally, I don't get where people thought up this idea about balancing eggs. You don't see people trying to balance gourds or footballs. But people seem like they have been trying to balance eggs since there were eggs to balance. Maybe it's because we all come from some kind of *ovum*, even if it doesn't look exactly like the kind that my father kept tipping up onto its end in front of Joe Kane, but since we come from some kind of *ovum* and since that is the closest we can get to any kind of real point of origin, maybe we're all kind of dumb on the subject of *ova*, although on the other hand, I guess these *ova* probably had to come from some chicken, or vice versa. Don't get me confused. Joe had to relocate his cup of coffee out of the wobbly trajectory of the shell. A couple of times. My father couldn't get anything going in terms of balancing the ostrich egg and so why did he keep trying?

Next, Dad got down the formaldehyde jars from up on the shelf, and started displaying for Joe Kane some deformed ostriches. In his recitation about the abnormalities he had names for a lot of the birds. He showed Joe the fetus with two heads, Dizzy; *she was the sweetest little chick,* and then showed Joe one with four legs. He showed Joe two or three sets of Siamese twin ostriches, including the set called Jack 'n Jill. *This pair could run like a bat out of hell.* My dad's voice swelled. He was proud. He gazed deeply into yellowed formaldehyde.

Joe Kane tried to figure an escape. He looked like an ostrich himself, right then, a mouth-breather, a shill waiting for the sideshow, where the real freaks, the circus owners themselves, would go to any lengths, glue a piece of bone on the forehead of a Shetland pony and call it a unicorn, for the thrill of separating crowds from wallets. Wasn't there any other place for Joe to take shelter from the buckets of rain falling from the sky? Must have been a lean-to or something. On the good side of the tracks.

— This bird here has two *male appendages,* and I know a number of fellows would really like it if they had two of those. Imagine all the trouble you could get into with the ladies.

Ever notice how in the Midwest no one ever kisses anyone? That little peck on the cheek people are always giving one another back East? *Nice to see you!* Much less in evidence here in the Midwest. Probably it accounts for the ostrich farmhands and their romantic pursuits, turned down by wives, just looking for some glancing physical contact someplace, with a mouth-breather, if necessary. They came home, these working men, to wives reciting lists of incomplete chores, because of which they'd just get right back into their pickups and head for the drive-thru. They'd sing their lamenting songs into drive-thru microphones. My father had seen a man once slap another man good-naturedly on the shoulder after a friendly exchange about a baseball. This was at a fast-food joint. He was sick with envy right then. And that's why, since he'd just shown Joe Kane an ostrich fetus with two penises, he decided *to chuck Joe under the chin*, as a sign of neighborly good wishes. My father came out from around the counter — he was a big man, I think I already said, 250 pounds, and over six feet — and as Joe Kane attempted to get up from his stool, my father *chucked him under the chin*.

— Take a weight off for a second, friend; I'm going to show you how to get an ostrich egg into a Coke bottle. And when my magic's done you can carry this Coke bottle around with you as a souvenir. I'll give it to you as a special gift. Here's how I do it. I heat this egg in regular old vinegar, kind you get anyplace, and that loosens up the surface of the egg, and then I just slip it into this liter bottle of Coke, which I bought at the mini-mart up the road, and then when it's inside the Coke bottle, it goes back to its normal hardness. When people ask you how you did it, you just don't let on. Okay? It's our secret. Is that a deal?

What could Joe say? Dad already had the vinegar going on one of the burners. When the egg had been heated in this solution, my dad began attempting to cram the thing into the Coke bottle, with disappointing results. Of course, the Coke bottle kept toppling end over end. Falling behind the counter. Dad would have to go pick it up again. Meantime, the train was about to come in. Hours had passed. The train was wailing through a crossing. My father jammed the ostrich egg, which didn't look like it had loosened up at all, against the tiny Coke bottle opening, without success. Maybe if he had a wide-mouth bottle instead.

— Last time it worked fine.

— Look, I gotta go. Train's pulling in. My dad's —

— *Sit down on that stool.* Damned if you're going to sit in here for two hours on a bunch of coffees, eighty-five cent cups of coffee, and that's going to be all the business I'm gonna have all week, you son of a bitch. I know one place I can get this egg to fit. Goddamn you.

And this is where the ostrich egg broke, of course, like a geyser, like an explosion at the refinery of my pop's self-respect. Its unfertilized gunk, pints of it, splattered all over the place, on the counter, the stools, the toaster, the display case of stale donuts. Then Joe Kane, who was already at the door, having managed to get himself safely out of the way, *laughed bitterly.* My father, his face pendulous with tusks of egg white, reached himself down an additional ostrich egg and attempted to hurl it at Joe Kane. But, come on, that was like trying to be a shot-put champion. He managed to get it about as far as the first booth, where it shattered on the top of a jukebox, obscuring in yolk an entire run of titles by the Judds.

Next thing that happened, of course, was the blood-curdling shriek I already told you about. Sorry for it turning up in the story twice, but that's just how it is this time. My father, alone in the restaurant, like the bear in the trap, screamed his emergency scream, frightened residents of Pickleville for miles around, especially little kids. People who are happy when they're speculating about other people's business, they might want to make a few guesses about that scream, like that my dad was ashamed of himself because the trick with the ostrich egg didn't work, or my dad was experiencing a crisis of remorse because he couldn't ever *catch a break.* And these people would be right, but they'd be missing a crucial piece of information that I have and which I'm going to pass along. My father screamed, also, because he was experiencing a shameful gastrointestinal problem. That's right. It's not really, you know, a major part of the story, but there was this certain large food company marketing some cheese snacks with a non-nutritive fat substitute in them, and that large company was test-marketing its cheese snacks guess where? Buckeye State, of course. Where these companies test-marketed lots of products for people they figured were uninformed. These snack foods were cheap, all right, a real bargain compared to leading brands, and they had cheddar flavoring. Only problem was, since your intestine couldn't absorb the non-nutritive simulated fatty acid, it was deposited right out of you, in amounts up to two or three tablespoons. The food company was trying to find out how much of this we'd tolerate in Ohio, this oily residue that didn't come out in the wash. If you ate a whole bag, it could be *bad*. So, truth is, on top of having *egg on his face*, my dad, right then, was having a rough day, and he wasn't tolerating it too well.

You'll be wanting to know how I know all this stuff, all these things that happened to my father in the restaurant, especially since I wasn't there and since Dad would never talk about any of it. Especially not *anal leakage*. Wouldn't talk about much at all, after that, unless he was complaining about Ohio State during football season. You'll want to now how I know so much about the soul of Ohio, since I was a teenager when all this happened and was supposed to be sullen and hard to reach. Hey, what's left in this breadbasket nation, but the mystery of imagination? My mother lay in bed, hatched a plan, how to get herself out of this place, how to give me a library of books. One night she dreamed of escaping from the Rust Belt, from a sequence of shotgun shacks and railroad apartments. A dream of a boy in the shape of a bird in the shape of a story, a boy who has a boy who has a boy: each generation's dream cheaper than the last, like for example all these dreams now feature Chuck E. Cheese (*A special birthday show performed by Chuck E. Cheese and his musical friends!*) or Cracker Barrel or Wendy's or Arby's or Red Lobster or the Outback Steakhouse or Boston Market or Taco Bell or Burger King or TCBY or Pizza Hut or Baskin Robbins or Friendly's or Hard Rock Cafe or KFC or IHOP or Frisch's Big Boy. Take a right down by Sam's Discount Warehouse, Midas Muffler, Target, Barnes and Noble, Home Depot, Wal-Mart, Super Kmart, Ninety-Nine Cent Store. My stand's at the end of the line. Fresh poultry and eggs. Eggs in this county they're the biggest darned eggs you've ever seen in your whole life.

Forecast from the Retail Desk

Nobody likes a guy who can foretell the future. Let me tell you. A guy with foreknowledge of events. It's like having really bad acne. I had that, too. You'll need clinical trials probably. *The bull market will come to an end,* for example. Any idiot will tell you that, and yet a persuasive demonstration of my skills requires that I start small and build to a spectacular conclusion. The Dow, in spite of its reliance on blue chip issues, will chase NASDAQ's tail down. My own employers will come face to face with some nasty accounting practices that lead straight to a cadre of cocaine-snorting, Lexus-driving tech-fund specialists. Then some really bad international loans will surface. *Jesus, make a loan to Canada, or something.* My position, here at the retail desk, where I am not well liked, will be one of the first declared obsolete in the merger. They'll let me know first thing on a Monday, after I've been up for three consecutive nights, worrying about my brother's kid, who has leukemia.

I tell my wife this stuff, she doesn't believe me.

Here's a historical account of the first ever public demonstration of my skills: I told Bobby Erlich that he was going to get paralyzed in a motorcycle crash. This was in 1977. Erlich didn't like motorcycles or mechanical stuff of any kind. He had a tentative approach to the sciences, too, though we were sequestered there, in chemistry, at the pleasure of the New York State Board of Regents. The laboratory tables were always marbleized, always black, swept clean of hazardous accumulations. Songbirds in our town, New Rochelle, sang parochial songs, jingles, light fare. The windows were open. It was late autumn. The chemistry teacher, Miss Rydell, said, *Bobby, you work with Everett here.* No one else would work with me. Not even the two Hispanic kids. A pairing off had transpired, boys of incredible beauty with girls as perfect as in the Old Masters. What was my crime? Bobby Erlich, that blond, said nothing, accepted a glass beaker from Miss Rydell, shoved past me toward the lab station. At the beginning of the experiment, sodium and water in equal parts, I smiled genially at Bobby, thanked him for working with me, but this was simulated, because, when he still wouldn't talk, wouldn't collaborate, kept taking beakers away from me, I had no choice but to deliver his fate, which came to me with a sort of uncanny trembling that you associate with early stages of fever, as if foresight and shingles, or chicken pox, were identical: *You're going to get maimed in a horrible motorcycle accident. It's really going to hurt, too. The part you can feel, anyway. Just remember we had this chat.*

Know what, Bennett? said Erlich, *I always thought you were a jerk. And I was right.*

The exchange in its entirety. Two lines. Had I known what was going to happen I would have feigned illness and taken a city bus home, lugging my ring binder, my unused baseball glove, and the remains of my bag lunch. Why worry about the opinion of Bobby Erlich? I could just as easily have said something polite. Nevertheless, class proceeded without incident, almost like it was supposed to, despite discord between lab partners. Miss Rydell hummed as she circulated from lab station to lab station. We performed the experiment, I balanced the equation in my lab notebook — Erlich didn't know how to do it — I passed our results to the front of the class. We got an A on the homework, and afterward Bobby avoided me wherever possible, especially in chemistry class. I would see the rear view of him in the cinder-block corridors, a faded red backpack retreating.

Eventually, Erlich turned out to be, well, *gay*, the preferred colloquialisms in those days being *fag*, *mo*, *felcher*, *queer*, and so forth. Foreknowledge of his blossoming condition would have been possible among my prognostications, though in truth I had a basis for my surmises, namely that Erlich had repeatedly been beaten and tortured by the *lobotomized physical-education students* of my school, most of whom are now plumbers with collections of child pornography taped inside their vans, or this seemed to be the implication at our recent twentieth reunion. Anyhow, I didn't tell Erlich he was *gay*, I just told him he would be maimed in a motorcycle accident, and the year passed, and I was grateful every time I saw Bobby's retreating backpack on the way to band practice, where he was first flute, or easing into the Green Room backstage at one of his beloved high-school dramas. (I was property master for several of the shows that year.) I was grateful because Bobby was intact.

Then we were seventeen (along with everyone else in our class except the aforementioned *lobotomized physical-education students*). An age of promise, an age of adventures, of intoxications, of epiphanies. Bobby Erlich the seventeen-year-old meanwhile seemed to be having an *intergenerational romance*, that was the rumor, and one night he was riding in an Olds Cutlass Supreme beside this off-duty policeman from our town, Officer Meineke, a policeman with a wife and kids who nonetheless had found himself all dizzy over a flute-playing, theater-obsessed boy from the junior class of the local high school. I'm conflating characters and scenes, you understand, in order to spare certain parties bad publicity. It was rainy. It was June. That intersection at Four Corners was, and is still, noted for scofflaws trying to make it to the station before the local train pulled out. Bobby and his policeman were locked in a kiss at a stoplight, a devouring kiss, and I would like to think that in spite of my robust heterosexuality I could render that kiss for you. The instant eclipsed all the years of Bobby's woeful adolescence. It was *interstellar*. It was *pantheistic*. He wanted to see Meineke's locker, at the police station. He wanted his own dog-eared photo of Meineke as a little boy.

However, as they were sundering themselves from this embrace and preparing for its duplicate, Joey Kaye's father, who was coming home impaired from a nearby tavern, was trying to catch the tail end of a yellow traffic signal. Joey's dad: *thirty-eight miles per hour on a street zoned for thirty.* In a Honda Civic. He struck the passenger side of Meineke's

Olds, and was uninjured, since drunk. Meineke, except for a few hematomas and his reputation, was also intact. Not so Bobby. Lots of witnesses could corroborate this account. Melissa Abdow, for example, was on the corner, eating mint chocolate chip in a sugar cone (it was dripping badly). She told me the next day. In math class. She had a sequence of images lodged in her brain, she said, like evidentiary photos: *Bobby in the front seat of the car, smiling, then Bobby curled around the mashed engine of the Olds, which was right up in the front seat of the other car. Then the Jaws of Life.*

I didn't visit him in the hospital, since, like I say, he couldn't stand me. But I should have visited him, because instead I was spending weeks in my room, gorging on remorse. I lay awake nights, debating with the dead white people of philosophy about *my prophecy.* Could it be true? Did language, when you petitioned with it, cause such devastations as Bobby's crash? Did the stuff you mumbled on a bad day in chemistry class despoil a family of a policeman *who happened to like boys,* but who hadn't yet told his wife, and was then undeservedly pulled mostly uninjured from the detritus of his car alongside the paralyzed body of an underage flute-player? Did I cause all that? It was supposed to be a *joke!* And, besides, I said *motorcycle crash!* If only I had played football, if only I had worn shoulder pads, worn that war paint of football players, if only some hulking alcoholic wife-batterer in the Pop Warner League had cared enough about me to make me feel like I was more than a barnacle at New Rochelle High, then I wouldn't have had to do what I did; if only I had played football, and had heard, at the line of the scrimmage, the crunch *in which my own neck buckled,* in which the ether above me gave way and the songbirds blew the play dead for now and always, if only I had heard the hoarse commands of stretcher-bearers.

Once I told my mother she was going to inherit a lot of money from an aunt in Lithuania. What did my mother know of Lithuania? She was raised in New Jersey, and she had an Irish surname. Maybe I was trying to get *attention,* as guidance counselors had it then. Maybe I had an *active imagination.* Maybe I was trying to best my charming, handsome brother in the competition for her affections. Maybe it was because my dad had absconded at the first opportunity, back when I was in single digits. Of course, by virtue of my forecasting gift, I realized that my old man had another wife and family elsewhere, in Moline, Illinois, if you're interested. I could see their shrubs and annuals, Siamese cats, sugary breakfast cereals, *it just dawned on me.* I had known this just as I knew that the 1974 Mets would win no more than eighty games. Some days in my room, when I had exhausted a stack of pulps and *The 4:30 Movie* was a romantic comedy not to my tastes, well, I felt I could contact my father, through extrasensory perceptions. *Dad,* I would say, *this is your son Everett calling, would you be willing to accept charges? You have, by my estimation, now missed seven of my birthdays, and I feel, if you're worrying about it, that you could just go ahead and roll some of those birthday moneys into an, umm, interest-bearing account toward my education at CCNY, which will probably start in about sixteen months. I'd be happy to acknowledge receipt of a cashier's check or a money order. If you want to know my personal feelings about the fact that you have missed seven of my birthdays, I guess I would say that it's a little irresponsible, and I wonder if this had to happen to you, if your dad had to blow your childhood environment to smithereens in order to make you the kind of person who could take a seven-year business trip and forget to write. That's about all I've got today, feel free to contact me at your earliest convenience.*

My mom never had an aunt from Lithuania or any relatives anywhere besides old Hibernia, and they were mostly dead, and truth is if I lied to her about the inheritance she was going to receive it's probably because I worried about my mother. When she got home each night from the long-term convalescent home where she was an accountant, she was about as lively as a vinyl footstool. And she had to officiate in the fisticuffs between myself and my brother. *I wanted her to have something to look forward to.* She played the lottery, when the lottery became state supported, and I used to see her at the variety store. She'd be counting out the grimy singles that she kept in a drawer in the kitchen. She scrawled out numbers based on sentimental remembrances. Occasionally she took home small purses. The point here is that my prophecy is kind of inexact, and you have to use a sort of *metaphoric-analytic schema* (it's in the retail-sales training manual here on my desk) in order to understand exactly how it works its wonders.

A few contemporary forecasts. Cher will contract a grave immune disorder of unknown origins, until she reveals the nature of the voodoo that has so preserved her semblance. I was just making this point to Mrs. Rona Peregrina of Bensonhurst, in fact, while issuing a strong sell recommendation in the e-merchandizing sector. The color *yellow* will become the one color that everyone *has to be seen in.* In the Big Apple, Gotham City, below Fourteenth Street, everyone will start to wear it: canary, lemon, mustard, maize, curry, goldenrod, marigold, sunflower, ochre. Entire discothèques, places I'd never go, yellow, inside and out, the yellow of the power tie, the caution signal, the yellow of foul-weather gear, the yellow of hepatitis. What else? Books, apparently useless objects of my childhood, paperweights, shelf decorators, books will get rare. You know that volume of women's sexual fantasies that you're embarrassed about, or that science-fiction opus about *computer telepathy among Venusians?* You'll throw these out, or give them to the library, and you will never replace these books. Your kids will read screens; their contact lenses will fuse onto their eyes. And the wild language that you used to find in books *or upon stones*, language of prophecy, like when a guy from Schroon Lake, New York, or Cowan, Tennessee, calls out from his wilderness about how to interpret obscure texts rescued from caves of Egypt, texts that refer to *our last end*, this language will instead be used to write irate letters to owners of television stations who sell zirconium rings to minimum-wage earners across the land. These letters will never be read on air, if indeed, they are ever read at all. More? Every relationship you ever have, in your entire life, will end in disease. Sound far-fetched? It's not. Today you eat grilled cheese on seven-grain bread, tomorrow you clutch your gut, locate the tumor. A dog will be crossed with a sheep, because it will make wool less expensive. Most people will accept this rationale. Melvin Cushman, chief executive of that very hot venture capital firm, Vortex Solutions, will, utilizing techniques perfected by American-educated doctors in Lagos, Nigeria, have himself *cloned* as a gift for his wife, Wilhelmina, thirty years his junior. *I just love the little lady here, and I'm not about to let her go just because my pancreas is giving out.*

My brother's kid, the one with leukemia, will get sicker still.

Here's another story. I met my wife on the subway. I was on my way to a basketball game when Bobby Erlich, the paraplegic, *came wheeling into the subway car, displaying his amputated limbs.* OK, not really. I would often hear the door at the end of the car open, however, and I would think, *Here comes Erlich.* Any desperate life form that entered the space, *Evening, ladies and gentlemen, sorry to interrupt and I don't mean no one no harm but I am homeless and trying to get money for my three kids. I'm currently living here on the trains with my family.* Any unfortunate was the harbinger of a celestial accounting for yours truly, *Let there now be penitence.* Know what I mean? That night even worse things came to pass. I had changed for the Seventh Avenue line at Times Square, and by habit I waited near the rear of the train, *the empty car;* if you're ever going to know that this visible earth is only a splinter of the mystical action spinning out around you, figure on the last car. I was sitting down on the empty bench at the front end of the last car, with a book, probably something required for a class at Queens College, let's say Plato's Apologia, *And now, O men who have condemned me, I would fain prophesy to you; for I am about to die, and in the hour of death men are gifted with prophetic power.* Besides, nobody on earth messes with you if you're reading the classics. Just as I had arranged myself on this bench, and opened my book, I heard this guy coming down the stairs, making a real commotion, *Hold the train! Hold the train!* Ladies swept aside by his assault. You know those stairs at the end of the platform there? How many femurs have become bone meal on that staircase? How many hips replaced?

Hold the train. I could make out his latecomer's face, as the doors tintinnabulated and converged. He was smiling. This was the train he needed to catch. This was his quarry. Never mind hindrances that developed, the door being closed, the conductor shuttering his window, the train beginning to move, *Hold the train.* I wish he'd said something more compelling, such as *Behold, the Lord maketh the earth empty, and maketh it waste, turneth it upside down, scattereth abroad the inhabitants thereof.*

I looked up from the Apologia, saw him smiling. I knew right away. I didn't want to know. But, like I've been trying to tell you, my heart was crenelated *with scars of foreknowledge.* He was making for that spot where the plates of the two cars abutted. A bisection of chains to keep away the foolhardy. The train lurched forward, I saw *the smiler* disappear out of the region of my peripheral vision, like a bird of air lifting off. He wore a smile, he grabbed for the chain, got one leg up, his shopping bag went under, there was a silence, there was exertion, he fumbled for the bag slipping down between the cars, there was a span of blackness, there was the third rail, and then he was tumbling after his possessions, *down there.* Between platform and train. Holy God. The Apologia fell out of my hands. *When my sons are grown up, I would ask you, O my friends, to punish them.* Just as I saw him lifting off, as in falconry, out of the margin of my weak eyes, I was up off the bench, the train jumped, and there was that awful hydraulic exhalation that means *this conveyance is not going to move for a while,* this train has met *impediment upon the tracks*. The entire system of trains, all the hundreds of miles of it, all Gotham knew at once what it had done; its daily imaginings again included gristle, sinew, marrow, plasma. There had been an *incident*.

Since I was a strapping young man of well over two hundred pounds, closer to two-fifty, to be honest, I was a kind of missile being propelled forward, when the train stopped, ready to squash just about anything or anyone. I fell across the two-seater there, *into the lap of a woman*. She was irritated at first, she didn't know where we were, in the circle of creation reserved for dismemberment and sorrow, the realm of severed limbs, of triage, and she pushed back against my commodious bulk, *Move, goddamit*. I said, *Hey, excuse me, I'm really sorry, hell*. Then the woman in whose lap I had parked my large, soft posterior called weakly across the car to an MTA employee who powerlessly inhabited our car, standing nearby, *Is someone on the tracks?* The older woman stared across the car at the gathering of official presences outside, at the crowd beginning to gather around our train. *I knew he was gonna do it*. A small Hispanic boy said, clutching at his mother's hand, *What happened? What happened? What happened?* His mother shook her head.

A long two or three minutes we were locked inside, in our stationary subway car. There were faces pressed up against the outside, a wall of faces, and these faces would look down into that space under the train, never satisfied until they had apprehended *why*, and then their faces would knot uncomfortably at what information they now possessed. I resolved that I wouldn't be one of these people, one of those who *had to see*. When the door at the end of the car was at last opened from the platform by a man with a high-visibility vestment, people filed off, and the announcement began to cycle on the P.A., *lasshnnrnd genmhhnhnssbrs . . .* What a processional, all of us filing out, *Before him went the pestilence, burning coals went forth at his feet,* by arrangement of Excellent Destiny, the woman I had nearly crushed touched me on the arm, beside me now, in the queue, *Do you think he's all right?*

I thought, since I experienced trauma as a convulsion of the imagination, *Who's the guy's mother and what did he have for lunch and did he ever drive a hydrofoil and did he ever feed a dolphin and how old was he when he lost his virginity and did he know the difference between a coniferous tree and a deciduous one and who was his favorite Yankee and did he know the table of the elements and how many women did he love and who were they all and are they all happy and did they do the things they wanted to do and did he have a kid brother and did he ever play a musical instrument and what is the woman he was meeting thinking right now and what is his mother thinking and is his head separated from his neck or his leg separated from hip, his inner organs like stew upon the undercarriage of the express?* Of course, I *knew* the answers to these questions and knew the answers to others, too, through my sophisticated foreknowledge, even if my step was unsteady, even if I felt like I might pass out. I made reply to the woman; I said poetical words that had only recently occurred to me, *I have a couple of tickets to the Knicks, they're about to lose to Philadelphia, but I won't tell you the score. I was going to sell one of the tickets anyhow.*

Let's make something good out of something bad. I had never ever asked a woman out before.

The emergency guy at the door remarked, *Let's get a move on, pal, we got a situation.*

My wife, because that's who she was, my solace, my destiny, my respite, because that's the substance of what I am telling you, *detrained,* but she froze on the platform, shoulders trembling suddenly as she held a pulped tissue to her nose, and crowds surrounded us, a gathering of disgruntled New Yorkers, getting home late from the office, or trying to get home late, while down the stairs came the paramedics, with their stretchers. In every part of this story, the stretcher-bearers eventually come. To my wife, I said, *No big deal, if it's too sudden. I'd understand. I just don't feel right tonight. I don't feel like being alone.*

What kind of woman was she? What kind of woman was it who called to me from that calamity on the Seventh Avenue line? What kind of woman do I love now, with a fealty that will not cease, not till my occluded arteries send their clots up to the spongy interiors in my skull and I go mute and slack? I love the kind of woman whose hair has gone gray in a not terribly flattering way, the kind who doesn't even notice how she keeps having to buy *larger jeans,* the kind who likes big cars because she doesn't like *to be uncomfortable.* I love this woman because she is gifted with astounding premonitory skills: no matter how uncertain, how despondent, how lost her mate feels, no matter how dire the circumstances, she nonetheless predicts that *Everything will be roses.*

She gave me her number. On the fortieth day of our acquaintance, I proposed.

Soon I was living near the water in the Bronx. Not far from City Island. What I loved about that part of the world was how the swamps persisted long after the city planners had tried to do away with them. Co-Op City rising out of the swamps, the cattails and the trash, the Bruckner Express-way, kids actually attempting to fish in the rivers — unworried about hepatitis, unworried about PCB's. Old unsteady docks, skiffs that leaked, a clustering of powerboats, all in the shadow of low-cost housing. My wife and I were newly-weds in our little place with the screened-in porch in back and the quarter acre, and I had just got this job on the retail desk, where I attempt to persuade regular folks to gamble away their meager savings. Every day since I was trained I had known I was going to lose my job, and sometimes for weeks at a time I wouldn't allow my wife to touch because I was so disgusted with who I was, with the bands of useless pork on me, with my fulsome breasts, with my joyless prognostications.

You might be wondering why my brother hasn't turned up in these prophecies until now. Any idea what it is like to grow up the homely older brother of the most gifted, the most talented, the most revered kid on your block? Any idea what it is like to look at the basketball hoop in the drive-way and to see your brother sailing past it, in slow motion, grinning an unspeakable grin, dunking the ball with his off-hand, finishing a soda, lighting a firecracker, all at the same time, while the Cosa Nostra kids from up the block curse under their breaths for having again lost the two-on-one? Any idea what it's like having your own brother *beat you in a drug deal* in which he sells you a mixture of oregano and fresh basil and then, to give credence to his salesmanship, smokes some of it with you and comments on its potency?

My brother Jack refused to speak to me in the cinder-block halls of New Rochelle High, unless these halls were empty, unless we were alone, and even then he would answer only *yes* or *no* to questions having to do with what time we were to be picked up, or the hour of a certain dentist appointment. My brother carried a *golf club* everywhere he went, a seven iron, and swung at me with it. My brother swiped twenty dollars from my mother's purse, to wager on the ponies, brought back forty dollars from O.T.B., put the twenty back in her purse, left a ten in the offertory plates at Mass on Sunday. My brother never liked me, as he never liked American cars, black jeans, health foods, girls without makeup. My brother Jack never liked to talk about what didn't go his way, or about our father, or about my *second sight*. He was handsome. He liked tailored suits. He liked his socks to match his shirt.

I am well pleased with my two sons, my mom said wearily, when the two of us fought, like the time I chased him around the entire house with an ax, threatening, cursing him, swinging the ax, *I'm going to bury this thing in your skull, and then I'm going to watch your brains run out and I'm going to eat your brains.* He locked himself in the bathroom, and I was banging on the door with the dull side of the ax, until I had managed to put the ax *through* the door, and he was yelling, *Christ, he's insane, Mom, can't you get him to back off;* my mother waited patiently, until the hitch in my swing, the dormancy in me, when I turned to her, *Why has everything been so easy for him?*

My brother and I fought the whole next ten years, my brother Jack and me, as I correctly predicted, threats shouted at holidays, even after I met my wife, even after my marriage ceremony (my best man was Joey Kaye, the guy whose dad paralyzed Bobby Erlich for life). My brother missed my wedding because he'd been at a club in the Village called Silver Screen, where he said whatever he had to say in order that he might persuade one Elise, an alcoholic, to go to a motel in Yonkers with him, where he was doing lines with her on a pocketbook mirror and watching motel pornography, the swooping arc of enhanced breasts, a nipple coming in and out of focus, simulated yelps of longing. He had never seen a girl with such large tattoos, and in such unusual spots. Was it her or was it the actress on the screen who was so vocal? Elise wanted to be an actress, and her uncle had *incested* her, but she made him phenomenally happy for two hours, and he her, at least until they ran out of their talc, and then when she woke in the morning my brother was back at the car dealership, moving the *Beemers*, as he said, wearing an Armani double-breasted suit, totally forgetting that he was supposed to be at my wedding. I know all these things.

One day some years later, who should come knocking at the back door but my brother Jack, wearing clothes that eerily resembled the garb of detectives from a popular television show of the period: a designer suit in pale blue and a polyester T-shirt of dusty rose. He was at the back door, see, while my wife and I were eating deviled eggs and sprigs of parsley; here he was wearing pastel colors, smiling in a way that signaled *bad news ahead.*

What's he doing here? my wife said, loud enough that he would not mistake the words. She'd never forgiven him for missing the wedding and for sending us a set of plastic nesting bowls as a gift, and she rose up from the table on the porch, her green paper napkin still tucked in her neckline, and hastened indoors, where she turned on some opera, loud.

He rapped on the aluminum siding, though I was two feet away. We were in plain sight of one another.

Who do you think it is?

Oh, hey. A long-lost relative. A good-looking guy with a flimsy pretext.

Thought I'd drop by.

So you did.

What the hell's going on? he attempted. *I wanted to say that I feel bad about things, you know? I feel bad about things and I want to straighten it out. I thought I'd come on over and we'd have a talk. We could set things right again and we could hoist a few beers together. Talk about it all.*

He was still out on the step, and he was shading his eyes, though wearing sunglasses. He had a scrape on his cheek. There was an earnestness to his simulations.

That'd be great, I said, *but Tanya and I have an engagement, if you want to know the truth, so I only have a couple of minutes.*

What kind of engagement?

Precious Jewels and Stones show. At the Coliseum. Going to be a big rush on the first day.

It went on like that, each of us maneuvering for a purchase. One guy makes a slip, the other guy grabs for the handhold, crowds in. Soon my brother Jack began to warm to his ulterior motive. He was always a guy who couldn't sit still for long.

Why don't you come out front here, Jack said. *I got something I want to show you.*

The screen door slapped at its frame. I figured I'd get it over with. We went around the alley, between Frattelli's place and ours. Fratelli's garden hose coiled by the edge of his lawn. Frattelli's excessively healthy floribunda, a spigot on the side of our house still dripping, though I had put a washer in there only a week before. I wanted a life with a minimum of fuss. *Woe to them that are wise in their eyes.*

It was a gold Porsche.

Mergers in the automobile business will continue apace, and soon General Motors will be making Bentleys, and the same barely functioning engines that are under the hoods of American cars will soon be under the hoods of fancy foreign models, and it will be good for stock prices, and even good for the Gross National Product, but not good for cars themselves. That's the limit of my interest on the subject. What's a car, my fellow-Americans, but a system for conveyance, as I was recently telling Sasha Levin of Forest Hills, before she had time to complain about her under-performing account; I'll buy any car, a Reliant K, a Breeze, a Cavalier, I don't care too much, and Tanya doesn't either, and we tend to leave bottles rattling around in the footwells in the back seat, to take up the space where the kids should have gone. A Porsche to me was just another car, and mainly I saw behind it some Organized Crime Figure or Junk Bond Trader who rode your bumper and talked on a cellular phone while flipping you the bird. I didn't want to have anything to do with Porsches, or Jaguars, or Corvettes. I looked back at my house. I saw my wife, Tanya, in a window upstairs. A curtain fell across her face.

Isn't she a beauty? My brother said hurriedly. He meant the car.

What the hell are you doing showing me this Porsche? Let's get this over with, okay?

What's the rush?

It was dented up. In a way that, for me, exactly recalled an earlier car crash and an earlier victim, which is to say that the passenger side was mashed, one headlight completely eliminated, and I'm pretty sure the axle was bent and the front fender mangled up in there, rubbing against the oil pan. There was flourescent gunk running in my driveway.

I just hosed this driveway.

Hey, I'm sorry, Jack said. *Listen, I just want to know if I can park this in your garage for a couple of days.*

I looked at my Timex with imitation Cordovan strap and wondered *why eighteen minutes* for this request. He had his own car dealership where he worked, and his own auto mechanics who would bang out a few dents, no questions asked, and he had always boasted that he could get an inspection sticker for me *easy*. It was not a good sign, his request, and I asked why I had to have this car in my garage, and he said that he'd busted it up right nearby, out on the river road, and he had things to do, and some points on his license, and just wanted to leave it for a couple of days, wouldn't be any trouble, and he'd buy me a case of beer or something to make it worth my while.

And that was when I noticed the blood inside. The interior of the Porsche was leather, a ruddy leather interior, and there was blood on the dash, on the molded foam, where the air bag would later have gone, there was a dried splotch of blood from where some forehead had collided with the windshield, and I squinted at it discerningly, at the inevitability of another life coming to an end, the failure of it, of life leaking out on the leather.

Is this blood in this car?

What the hell are you talking about? My brother replied.

I asked if this was blood.

There's no blood in the car. I don't know what you're talking about.

Why was a spillage of blood always an emblem of my troubled march in this world, why these pieces of bodies, these cascading morsels of corporeal material, why this length of tibia broken jaggedly off at the knee, with tufts of muscle still clinging to it, why, in my dreams, the stretcher bearers, why the dead boys, why the high-impact collisions, again and again, why the spectacle of young men running into stationary objects, why the lamppost with the D.U.I. wrapped around it, a hand separated from a wrist, by some fifty feet, vertebrae like popcorn scattered across the bucket seats?

I said, *Get your goddamn car out of here now, what do you mean by bringing this thing around here? Did you kill someone, in this car? Am I accessory to all your blunders? Like I don't have enough blunders of my own? What are you doing here? I'm not related to you, I don't have even one characteristic that you have.* I started loud, admittedly, but I got quieter, because I *knew,* in the middle of my tirade I knew, this fragmentary bunch of people, this collection of lost souls, my family, they were rushing further off now, like some distant hurtling margin of the negatively spherical universe, they were further off during this conversation, and when this conversation was over, they would be *impossibly far away* — cousins, aunts, uncles, of old bipolar Eire, my father, there would be only my mother's death left to survive, my mother alone in her little house in New Rochelle one block over from a shuttered Main Street, and when my brother climbed into his Porsche — which had a left front flat, I now saw — the last of my uncertain futures would be certain.

With a fluttering of his pinky-ringed hand, my brother tried to get me to play cool. *I'm gone before you know it. Man, if I came here singing songs of love, even then you'd bounce me out on my ass.*

Now the backing away of my brother Jack, blond dealer of exotic high-performance cars, future dealership owner. I waited for the threatening language, but the silence of his departure was instantaneous. *I will not punish your sons when they commit whoredom.* I knew, I knew. I knew where the police would find the body of poor Elise from the club called Silver Screen, out by the woods at the edge of the golf course in Pelham. There's always trouble at the edge of this golf course, you know, because it's the edge of New York City, it's the beginning of the suburbs, and every threshold must have its darkness, and so Elise, who was *incested* when young, got driven to the edge of this wood, where she drank wine with my brother, and they kissed, and they cavorted, and they lived such lives as I have never lived, and then they took a dirt road there, by the edge of the canal, where there were only torched hulks of cars, stripped of all but the smoking exterior chassis, the steering column, muffler, disc brakes, upholstery all gone, my brother, at thirty-four miles per hour in an avenue zoned for twenty-five, drove into a tree, knocked her unconscious, ditched her body, flung away its wedding band, and then after the visit to me abandoned the stolen car, the car he brought into the city to impress her, or to impress someone like her, and he waded down into the lifeless river just beyond the woods, and he dove in, in his Armani suit, drifted downstream, in a narcissistic reverie. Leaving no trail.

Remember Melissa Abdow? The girl who saw Bobby Erlich's crash? Amazing thing. She called last week, at work. (The surfaces of my cubicle are appallingly clean. My rolodex is blank. Here's a photograph of Tanya wearing a yellow dress.) Melissa wanted a little advice on the inverted yield curve, *What's going to be the effect on treasuries, as a conservative type of investment?* She and her husband were trying to salt away some funds for their kid's college education. And she got my number from somebody who got it from somebody. Research, that morning, had brought in some disappointing news from the markets. It was also scrolling across my computer screen. *Full kingdom blessing* on traders of bonds, they *shall run like mighty men. The horseman lifteth up the bright sword.* That I.P.O. for the new web portal is going to sell out fast. Melissa asked about my brother. *How's Jack anyway?* Something in my tone made her ask, I knew, and yet I couldn't stop myself. If it's possible for a voice to have worry lines, Melissa's voice had them, when she was speaking to me. *My brother? My brother, Melissa?* I started and I couldn't stop. I admitted that I hadn't seen my brother in years, seven years, that he had married a lovely girl, Elise, and I didn't go to his wedding, you know, *I smote you with blasting and with mildew,* because I was ashamed; he had smashed up Elise's brother's Porsche not long before the ceremony, cut himself kind of badly, and he came to me for aid and counsel, and I drove him out of the house, *and you know how it is with brothers, Melissa, you know how it is.*

My wife keeps calling down the basement staircase to where I'm sitting here enveloped in darkness, tightening wood screws on a small racing car that I have made for my nephew, Danny. I have made him many toys. *A day of darkness, a day of clouds and of thick darkness, as morning spreads upon the mountains,* the bugs are kind of bad down here, *Take me and cast me into the sea.* This basement with its cinder blocks and its exposed bulb, this suits me. Seven years now, a biblical interval, and it was just a little thing. I was a jumpy, anxious person, hard to get along with, I suppose; amazing that I have kept my job this long, when I cannot be comforted. It was just some car that I refused to have in my garage, you would think that would be enough, that it could be forgotten. And I haven't even set eyes upon my brother's boy, except in that Christmas card that came this last year (his hair like a crown of *goldenrod*), and there's Elise, with the strawberry-highlights, I don't get too many cards, it's almost a week now here that I have been worrying about the boy, waiting for my brother to call, our Chevy is gassed and ready. There was a time when everybody knew the future, but a few wise types elected *to forget what was to come,* as we all elect, eventually, to forget the past. Forgetters raised up many children and made songs of praising, *I will lift mine eyes unto the hills, from whence cometh my help.* Please let me be wrong again. About that sick boy. Let me be wrong.

Hawaiian Night

A limbo bar festooned with streamers, by the bathhouse entrance. Tuna on shish kebab and pineapple slices in large stainless-steel serving cisterns arranged on a buffet table. At the edge of the snack bar, the undergrad who gave golf lessons, in chef's hat and lei, carving a roast pig. The carcass had menaced the staff from the walk-in kitchen fridge for *upwards of five days*. The Olson kid, chaperoned on either side by his parents, in the moment of asking if they had *cooked, you know, the pig on a spit*. Logical inquiry under the circumstances, on Hawaiian Night. No evidence, however, of a spit. Polynesian slide guitar drifted across the patio, from a concealed speaker. Don Ho.

Lena Beechwood, at Table No. 1 (my table, though she was no relation of mine), worried aloud about her crew for the Round Island Race, peppering her sentences with fine acerbities: *Pete Evans got his jib twisted in the middle of the Memorial Day course, just let the sheet right out of his hands.*

They'd placed second, when they could very well have won, and so *He won't do, won't do at all, you just can't trust him.* They could take Evans's wife, Hunter, but she was sluggish from having the twins and might not have the energy or the reflexes. Second place goes to the weary, to the inert.

Northeastern sun, that pink hatbox, drifted into a margin of haze as the kids of Hawaiian Night threw off their regulation jackets and ties or their cardigan sweaters and flats and began to caper on the lawn. The Costellos, Dan and Pete and Gretchen; the appallingly smart Sam Harvey, who intimidated everybody else's towheads; little René Hennessy, with the platinum-blond crewcut and the French accent — his parents had been transferred to the Paris office, but they made it back across the pond for August; Marilyn Wendell, who would almost certainly get as stout as her mom, and, like her mom, be the consort of all local boys *until that day.* Two dozen kids, maybe, interchangeable, by virtue of their long-standing acquaintance; interchangeable, by virtue of the physical resemblances each to each; interchangeable, by virtue of the hidden entanglements of their parents over the years, or by virtue of these times. Perhaps it was simply that all children were one phylum, one kingdom, one species, one throbbing, pulsating corpus of velocity, language, and enthusiasm.

Andrew Grimm's boy and girl were thick in the stew, though Andrew's wife had died the summer before. The Grimms had taken the cigarette boat out, at dusk, with Ellen Moss and a shaker of cocktails, to pick up house guests who'd missed the last ferry. In the course of demonstrating for Ellen just how fast the *Pretty Young Thing* could go — she on the wheel, he the throttle, Andy's wife, Debby, gazing pacifically upon the action — they had jumped a large wake. One engine failed, the craft lifted up into the air, and they began to spiral to port, to be thrown into the magnificent bay. Outboards exposed in the shadows above the three of them. Here comes tragedy. As Andy and Debby and Ellen bobbed and ducked and breaststroked, laughed nervously at first, their unmanned boat embarked on its repetitive circular course, leftward, sinisterly, coming around and bearing down again on the three swimmers, who couldn't match its forty-nine miles per hour (fifty if you tilted the engines just so), who couldn't get out of its way. The boat struck Andy's wife decisively and crushed a plurality of vertebrae. Andy Grimm served as distraught witness, with the craft circling ominously between himself and the afflicted woman. Ellen Moss called out to Debby across the water, having just sidestroked inside the perimeter of the concentric rings that the *Pretty Young Thing* made in chop and spray. *Don't move!* Then Ellen Moss, of Foyle, Decker, Greenwood and Peacock, Management Consultants, Ellen Moss of the size-four tennis skirts, of the collection of antique porcelain miniatures, Ellen Moss risked heavily insured life and limb to swim back to Debby Grimm, to remove Debby from harm's way, to hold her as she lost consciousness, Ellen Moss whispering endearments as best she could, *Just a minute or two, huh?*, while Andy watched, immobilized by the menace of events. At last, a passing speedboat threw out its coils, hauled them from the sea, and the trouble really began. Debby's pulse fibrillated and then quit. The Coast Guard spent a couple of hours trying to figure out how to put a stop to the circular imperatives, the eternal return at forty-nine miles per hour of the *Pretty Young Thing*. Then they tangled its prop in a drift net.

Yet here were Debby's kids on the lawn with the others, and it was proof that you could vanish from this sweet, colorful existence one summer, and the next summer Hawaiian Night would go off without a hitch, as with the Thursdaynight dances, so with the annual complaints about club dues, and so forth. The tennis instructor, Marla, chased Robby Pigeon out of the ice-cream line, from which he had swiped a stainless-steel scoop and was now tongue-bathing it, consuming its strawberry delights, defiling the club's make-your-own-sundae apparatus with his infantile contagions, the Grimm children right behind him, giggling. Marla, it appeared, wore plastic green palm fronds, a South Pacific plumage, over U.S.T.A.-approved whites, as she chased them past the beverage table.

Collectively the children of Hawaiian Night next divined that the leis, which had been bunched, folded, and gathered on an assembly line in Edison, New Jersey, could be untwisted, stretched, and retooled to resemble antique ticker tape, expanding to a length of nearly sixteen feet, something like the footage of Lena Beechwood's small, sleek round-the-island sailing vessel. Andy Grimm's son, last seen wearing khakis, blue-and-white-striped button-down Oxford shirt, beige corduroy jacket, and white bucks, now clad only in his trousers, emerged from a swelling population of kids carrying the orange streamer that had been his lei, like a banner proclaiming this club, this lawn, this evening, this way of life his own, where minutes before only the present had been his concern, as he raced from the end of *Court No. 3* over to the Adirondack chairs by the swimming pool, staking his claim at the site marked *Shallow water, no diving*. I confess that I held my breath as I tried, through the incantation of worry, to stave off further Grimm calamity, in which little Drew toppled over the Adirondack chairs, hovered briefly in the air, gathered gravitational freight, broke the surface of the wading end of the pool, struck bottom, cracked his skull, and then bobbed in the shallows, deceased, as Andrew Grimm, insurance executive, recited his next canto of loss. But nothing horrible would happen on this voluptuous Hawaiian Night as five, ten, twelve, fifteen kids chased each other with tropical decorations in the stiff, humid preliminaries of a late-summer storm.

The automatic sprinklers that watered the Har-Tru courts were engaged by the coming of twilight.

The children began to wet themselves down.

Ghostly, a grandfather, from a neglected constituency of grandfathers, appeared at the top of the step where I sat with a camera that I would never remove from its case. Whose grandfather I don't know, though it would not have been hard to discern convictions, familial traits, resemblances, in the salt-and-pepper fringe around back and sides, upright posture, absence of socks, cable-knit sweater in *Franconia green* ordered from one of the larger catalogues. I recognized him, of course, as it hadn't been more than a week since I had espied him in the midst of a practice swing on the first fairway, just as he dislodged, in a manner so vulnerable it provoked a yelp in me, his entire top bridge, so that golf ball and false teeth, in different directions, tumbled into that large, humiliating sand trap just over the lip of the hill.

Look at them, the grandfather said with oratorical authority. As the kids sported in tennis-court fountains. *Look at them. Thankful for nothing, not for the sprinklers, not for the moon, not for the salty wind that blows around the mist, not for the way these events get arranged. When I was their age, I had a teacher in school whose car had lost its old rusty fender. Used to see her driving back and forth from school. She always waved, was always cheerful, but it was obvious that she couldn't afford to get a new fender for her car, who the hell knows why. I think it was a Pontiac. What I did was as follows: I took up a collection among my fellow-classmates. It wasn't Christmas or Be Nice to Your Teacher Day or anything else, nor was I trying to avert punishment or suck up to my teacher or any such thing. Everyone chipped in a dollar, or maybe their parents chipped in a dollar, whatever it took. My father knew a good mechanic who in turn knew a good spare-parts man, and one thing led to another, and next day at school we presented Mrs. Pendleton with a new fender for her Pontiac. I was the same age as those kids out there, not a day older. I went through plenty of difficult times myself, times when the red ink was more plentiful around our house than the black ink, that's about how old I am, but I could still afford to help Mrs. Pendleton when I was their age.*

Hurricane coming up the coast. Almost certain now. In the coming hours, we would board up our large windows and secure our powerboats. Eternally, in this late-summer moment, Debby Grimm seemed to fall delicately out of the western sky, somewhere between here and the mainland, the *Pretty Young Thing* plunging after her, and we felt what we could bear to feel and sought refuge in our gardens or on our patios, firing up propane barbecues, lacquering ribs, shucking genetically engineered corn hybrids. *Pretty Young Thing* appeared out of the fog, and I chronicled its progress — rising up to port, skidding up on beach debris, tumbling end over end, and bursting into flames.

I felt a strong need to corner the chef, before repairing to any *limbo entertainment*. What was the recipe for that calamari? As I stole toward the club ballroom, Andy Grimm himself passed silently by, in his wake the faint but unmistakable pungencies of *remorse and survival*. Immediately, I noticed the following, catalogued on the bulletin board by the water fountain: *Eric Pigeon, fourteen-and-under tennis, gold ribbon. Handmaid's Shoppe, designer items 50% off now until Columbus Day. Lost: Male Wedding Band, call Nick Fox.*

Who would come closest to the floor, as Afro-Cuban jazz began to summon, through its familiars, all my summers past as well as the last days of the Batista regime, gambling, prostitution, Catholic heresies. Families gathered, mothers laid their arms on the shoulders of their sons, and damp infants played underneath an old grand piano that had been rolled into a corner behind draperies. Sterling McGeeney, matriculating at Yale in ten days, as had her old man and his old man, elbows flush against hips, rocked like a religious convert and slipped under the limbo bar. Married men averted their gazes. Sterling's sister, Eveline, tripped the bar, catching it on a billowing sleeve, and was disqualified. Alice Pigeon, her party dress so wet it was practically translucent, snuck under. There was a braying of wind instruments. The club manager removed pegs, lowered the bar. It was close enough to the dusty ballroom floor as to permit no passage to *the other side*, to the warehouse of infinite childhoods. Claire Barnaby, sunflower of a girl, in understated flannel skirt and pullover sweater, intent on getting under, was denied. Sterling McGeeney, despite early successes, was now also turned back. The limbo bar reverberated and the needle was lifted from the old record player and Dave, the golf manager, feigned a good-natured frustration. The next contestant was the Grimms' melancholy daughter, Celine.

Need I point out that I had no children myself, that in the tidal flux of the generations I no longer voted *with the kids*, on that side of the ballroom. Twenty-odd years of lessons in deportment and racket sports, twenty-odd years of suing for the affections of Cary Evans and Nina Oxford, twenty-odd years of stolen drinks and brain fevers and fender benders, all behind me, though I still attempted to shuffle to the Latin rhythms that accompanied this particular soirée. Neither was I among the fathers and mothers, whose free time was given over to the private-school applications of their kids, adjustable-rate mortgages, loopholes in the capital-gains tax, or the privations of long-standing marriages.

My role was to watch. I was not bad at it.

Celine Grimm, laughing, at the threshold. If she passed under, made her body narrower than a first-class envelope filled with bad news, perhaps she would be swept into a flock of gulls or cormorants, and it would be the last we saw of her as she headed toward a first-class cabin in the heavens. I was happy therefore when she, too, stirred the limbo bar, as had her brother before her, as had we all *in our day*. There was no winner. Hawaiian Night hurtled toward repose. We of the northeast Atlantic returned to the Pacific Islanders their paradisal heritage, returned to them this imagery of travel advertisements. Had I ever been more surfeited by a simple falling into darkness? We gathered up lost children, we looked for stray garments, a blue ribbon draped across the tennis net on *Court No. 3*, a pair of cross-training sneakers separated one from the other, we restored the beach balls to the closet in the clubhouse, plucked up that doll sprawled haphazardly in the gravel parking lot beyond the pool. Somebody's cocker spaniel fetched a mossy tennis ball, left it at my feet, and would not be placated until I tossed it for him again. Moments later the hound was back.

Drawer

She called it an *armoire*, which was the problem, which was why he had dragged it onto the beach behind the house, and surveyed its progress over the course of a week, the elements driving down their varieties upon her *armoire*, their drama of erosion upon her *armoire*, a winter of steady rain, and had she been willing to call the *armoire* a *chest of drawers* like anybody else maybe they never would have arrived at this moment, or maybe *he* would never have arrived at this moment, he would not have found himself on the deck, in the rain, overlooking the beach, overlooking the *armoire* buried in sand up to the bottommost drawer (the work of tides), strands of kelp like accessories arranged around it, gray driftwood, lobster buoys, a Clorox bottle, a red plastic shovel, the pink detached arm of a chubby doll, plovers piping there, alone on the wet deck with a stiff drink despite the newness of the day, with a Sears deluxe crowbar with lifetime warranty he intended to use on the *armoire*, if you want to know the goddamned truth, specifically the top drawer of the *armoire,* which was locked now as it had always been locked in his presence, though when they bought the imitation *18th century, Sheraton-style armoire* at a flea market in the city, it hadn't bothered him then that the drawer was locked and that she had taken control of the little antique key, with its pair of teeth, *Anyone should have been able to pick that goddamned lock,* open that drawer, and yet, for all his accomplishments in the world of *franchise merchandising,* he couldn't do it, though maybe he had picked it and had forgotten, plenty to forget in these last few days, maybe he'd asked the boys with the cooler and the Frisbee who'd chanced along the shoreline, maybe he'd asked if they'd give a hand opening this *armoire,* using her word when he said it, but they had backed away, politely at first, then vehemently, into a temporarily radiant dusk, even when he called after them, *Show a neighbor a little good cheer! I got a thousand and one jokes!* Hadn't bothered him at first that he had no key to her *armoire,* had no tongue to share the word with her, the tongue which calls an *armoire* an *armoire,* not a *dresser,* not a *chest of drawers,* as his father and his father had said it, hadn't bothered him when the *armoire* was damaged in the *relocation* to the seaside, *just a chip off the side, just a dent,* but she'd gotten *apoplectic,* she'd taken photographs of the *armoire,* poorly lit Polaroids, she'd called the dispatcher at the van lines *demanding compensation,* though they had a hundred other pieces of furniture, deck chairs, poster beds, and a *joint bank account,* and she had her own room to work in (painted a stifling blue), and he'd left her alone, he'd walked upon the beach whistling lullabies, but he'd never learned how to say the word *armoire* with any conviction at all, and he would have included *demitasse* and *taffeta* and *sconce* and *minuet,* actually, he'd gone gray trying to learn all these words, he'd become an *old unteachable dog* trying to learn how to say these things, how to say *I love you* he supposed, an isolated backyard hound in bare feet upon the coastal sand the goodly heft of a crowbar and the way wood gives under such an attack he would burn the damned thing plank by plank and heat the house with the past tense of her, would burn her diaries, leaf by leaf, in the *antique potbelly stove,* weather descriptions, breezy accounts of society functions, he would consume her secrets and her reserve so hidden as to be hidden even from herself, Lord, these people who never gave a goddamned thing.

Pan's Fair Throng

 Fairest *monarch* of our empire, *great king*, conduce in me, lowly tanner of hides, a righteous song as I embark to tell the tale of your origins, spinning for townsfolk the narratives of the province whence you come, that savage northern province of brigands upon highways who accost travelers with blunt, crusted foils called, in those lands, *squeegees*, or in due course how you came from the prolific farms of *Jersey* to rule over all this principality of scribes and divers musicians, how you brought probity to scoundrels of disputatious cast. Lead me as you have led others, eternal administrator, *make your tongue my tongue* as my inscriptions cover this stone and I tell of your reign, to those in the crib, to those upon sickbeds rank and odiferous; let it be me, the tanner, who paints your masterpieces, paints your portraits in tongues of men, as if tales were altarpieces of historical churches, let me be as a butterfly with your paintbrushes, as you *climb down from your folding chair.*

There was a lad, born in the first third of our century, precocious stripling, much given to reverie and to silence. In his bedchamber, he labored over problems mathematical and geometrical, never venturing forth, even should he chance to see a fair maiden dancing on the village green beyond his mullioned windows. He paid no mind to her jolly braids, nor to her furious dancing, nor to the particular brother of this particular girl, a woeful prince (for any comely lad of means was potential regent during the bloodshed and disorder of our *interregnum*), whose acute melancholy was said to have been owing to his terror of ascending to the throne. No, our future king secreted himself in his chamber, covered with animal skins, studying magics and potions through which he might better the station of workers of fields and shopkeepers and salespersons of viands and pickled vegetables. The lad's formula, for the upstanding meritorious valor of aforementioned salespersons, was said to have been called the *Formula of Surplus Value*, completed by him in quill on goat's parchment, under a candle that, according to spell of witchery, never burned down.

One day, our yet-to-be monarch and chief agonist, buoyed by the influence of a thick Turkic potion known as *espresso kaffee*, and because of faintest impropriety of speech that by and by inhibited the correct recitation of spells, turned the comely nervous prince — Maxwell Hennesy Charming, brother of the *flapper maiden* already mentioned — into a performing monkey, or hanuman. As I say, it was inadvertent. The young artist of physick was making as to formulate a concoction of *creamy distillate* for his beverage. Nevertheless, wherefore Prince Maxwell, with fashionable opiated eyes and bulbous cheekbones, had dressed in long flowing garbs that might as well, in a dreamer's tossings, have been the robes of women, now, as hanuman, he became the *dandy*. Breeches of a dusty rose and a blue waistcoat with diamonds and rubies all upon it and stones as these days are called by the name *rhinestones*, such that he shimmered when he crawled on all fours or hung from a bough by his serpentine tail. Wherefore Prince Maxwell had been known to help a blind woman of our village, Miss Hogg, ahead of the carriages thundering by at street trivia, only to be named *infernal scamp* on deliverance of her to the farther side, as hanuman the prince was a rake and a Lothario, and would as soon inflict his manly endowments on a maiden as he would devour a banana in payment for his games of chance. I tell you, *I never liked that particular prince*, when he was under the curse, and would occasionally seize his tail and dip it into inks or poisons.

The family of Charming, a lordly assemblage of counselors and barristers, made suit against our young hero for having turned Prince Maxwell into a *tree monkey*, and this case was duly heard, on a day marked by grand hailstones. *Well it is remembered in my village*, how we had to flee the collapsing of thatched roofs, the merciless raining down of godly disapproval, but the courthouse, never have you seen such astonishing manufacture, with steps made out of *the same pink marble used for imperial towers of clerks*, and a roof that held fast beneath all assault. The carriages in which the barristers arrived to disgorge the principals of this story pulled fast to the curbstone and lords hastened indoors. Two or three footsoldiers were yet crushed by the hailstones so that their brains ran out into the street, *each of them a mother's son, alas.* Yet I was lucky among towns-people to sit in witness of that trial, in a box marked for commoners. A rabid bitch kept us in our place by gnawing ceaselessly if any of us should so much as take modest breath.

The courtier Ebenezer Sloane served as the plaintiff's counsel, and his miserly and shifty eyes were such that all present agreed he'd have bartered away his mother's petti-coats if circumstance permitted. So *wide* was he that his frilly collar scarcely closed about his neck and but a tiny residuary chin protruded from his mounds of bulk. When cogitating earnestly — which was not often — folds of skin on Ebenezer's forehead would move and bulge, as if flowing of the humors to the skull so required.

The king, of course, not yet so crowned, was merely a young knight given to solitary and religious pursuits, and among witnesses and barristers he had none of that splendor we lately associate with his personage. Charges against him were read out by a lady in the employ of the judge — though some say *it is more than employ* and that saucier pursuits in her instance might be more accurate. I'm speaking of Lady Calderon, Duchess of Fidget, who next declaimed, *Hear ye, hear ye, unworthy taxpayers of back alleys and fundaments of this very stinking mound of livestock droppings, we are gath-ered in this space to discuss the fate of this young magician, he of the oily pockmarks and unwashed parts, here to con-temn in strongest terms what has confounded the very order of our local nature, an irrefutable slight against the family of Charmings, consisting of Maxwell Charming now deceased or metamorphosed into a primate from Asia Minor, his sister, the lovely Andalucia Charming, a father, Lancer Charming, Esq., his wife, Lady Charming, all drug into these premises to seek restitution for the fact of their nobility and station infringed upon by this young man of origins foul and mean.*

The duchess, that *sow* — with mane of black curls, eyes jaundiced from gourmandish quaffing of mead *eight days per week;* a bosom that would barely be contained in her evening gown; pearls like a profane rosary circumnavigating her patchy neck, her lips horribly pursed. It was evident from the first syllables of her declamation that any celestial muse of justice *would not necessarily adjudicate in this tragical matter.* And yet at the *woeful charges* an uproarious tumult issued from the cronies of the Charmings. Jailkeepers rustled their irons at the corner of the space. Dogs grimaced and spilled their putrid salivas about us. It was a pretty show. And sure the king turned even bluer than his constitutional imperial shade, for his very term seemed about to come due, and if not capital execution then such tortures as *being branded with fiery iron, eyes excavated with wooden spoons, leg eaten off by ravenous boar.* Yet the king was prepared to meet his woeful fate without complaint: he was humble before persecutors.

Just then the queen — *Heart beat softly! I have given away a portion of the end! May my listeners forgive me!* — or rather the young Andalucia Charming assumed the throne of witnesses before our magistrate so deaf and blind that it is said he lingered for days though the courthouse be emptied, and she was sworn in, *under enchantment,* because the likes of which she spoke had never been uttered in a courtroom before or since, *Your honors, worshipful townsfolk, I have nothing but love for that contemned man, my heart throbs at the apperception of his fine manly features, I would unsheath myself of these fetters of rank and privilege and live with him as a lover, adrift upon breezes of sentiment, I would have no more divisions between folk, I recognize none, there shall be only love!* Consternation upon the courthouse. In later times it was said that this enchantment was not the king's own, yet whichever the origin, its most devastating magic was upon *the very head of our king,* who loved Andalucia at once and from that moment forward, as a rich illumination hovered about her. Her braids, her gladsome lips, her downcast eyes. Who would not love the queen? Who would not kneel to declare for her?

The king thereupon rose to mount his defense, unaided by barristers.

I am a lowly inventor of magics and alchemical poultices, he began, *neither kith nor kin of any here on this* terra firma, *and my poor parents moldering six feet down, and I am called here for no reason but that I have increased the local population of apes by one, a feat which does not deprive the world of a living thing, nor does it infringe, as milady says, on the divine aspect of nature, since whichever way I chance to pivot is nature, and the same with you, for what is man but nature's most frolicsome plaything, and I would not undo my enchantment, but would rather accept my fate, yet that this young woman should perish in a foul grief at the loss of her brother, a prince, and so, out of respect for her loveliness, I vow to remove this curse upon hanuman and restore this savage to Prince Charming, meanwhile to ensure the preservation of some qualities of his former apish state, namely a robust and amusing demeanor, so that he might talk freely with the fairer sex, and with passersby upon the street. If my fate is commuted until nightfall tonight I will total the figures and assemble the tinctures needed for this magic.*

The king, having no clear idea of *how* he had made the prince a monkey in the first instance — when, in like mishaps, he had changed a charwoman into hedgehog, and then, on attempting to return her to a former shape, had made her instead into *a large snaking desk lamp* — was agitated about the prospects for his next formula, but knew that his passionate affinities were enough to liberate him from the courthouse, as indeed a *lady of the court,* in sunshiny curls and clutching a velvet accessory in which were housed her several gold pieces, rose up from the audience, in recognition of his fancy oratories, and cried out, *That man shall be king!* (For it had been said that the most just and enterprising of our many princes would *ascend to rule.*) This being a piece of prophecy that she was in no way equipped to repeat, as I have heard that this selfsame heavily rouged and plucked woman of the court was later pauperized *by making wagers upon sport between poultry.* Next, the town gossip, Mudge, afflicted with a peculiar ocular condition known among chirurgeons as *wall-eye,* as with a smart additional set of bicuspids, this Mudge strode, all inflated as when the peacock in thick of venery attempts to impress his mate, into the street to cry to all who would listen, *New regent, romancer or necromancer? New regent chooses a Charming bride and dazzles all!* Those of us gathered likewise spilled out into a dripping besmirchment of hailstones and forthwith made riot in merry dancing.

The king, as sunset fast approached, was not, of course, able to find any oath that would restore the hanuman —

which beast he had caged in his bedchamber so that while laboring he was subjected to a torrent of abuse in an excessively ornamented verbiage, *Hey, fair and pungent youth, I would not be the damned prince again! I'm happy just the way I am! I'd rather be mummer before thy endless processional of monarchical brats than be again that cur!* Moreover, the animal made the king so excitable by tactics of percussive nattering and drumming upon the bars of his gaol that his lordship kept mixing the parts of lizards and the vomitus of small birds *incorrectly,* with the effect that his housekeeping, his Oriental rugs and French chaises, magically yielded to a sequence of *stuffed antelopes.* With this in mind, the king, short of time, saw no other recourse but to make appointment with *the most feared and reviled citizen of our village,* the pustulating warlock known hereabouts as Levi the Dispatcher.

The Dispatcher, as any here will assent, could not be found by searching, because such gray and black places as he sequestered himself were one day apparent down neglected thoroughfares and next entirely vanished. Only prayers of desperation, in combination with the production of ducats and other gold curios, would produce the dreadful troll of a man. Thus, the king, not yet coronally adorned, walked the streets in rags muttering in low tones, *Oh, good Christian gentleman Levi, I will give you a tenth portion of my treasury, should I ever ascend to the magnificence of rulership, if only you will dig me out of this infernal quackery into which I have plunged myself.* At which, finally, like lightning upon meadow, the foul warlock stepped out of a most ostentatious carriage called a *sport utility vehicle,* and confronted the incipient monarch, while picking encrustments out of his large nose, *Wait, let me be an answerer of riddles. Somewhere a neurasthenic lad is converted into a chimp and the bumbler who brought to pass this enchantment comes hither to have him restored. The further action of this drama? That shall cost you a pretty sum, my lordship, as you well know.*

The king's pockets were unfortunately spacious, indeed quite *ventilated,* and therefore he agreed to a special arrangement called *margin* (I have only passing acquaintance with the transaction), and this arrangement concluded the warlock rose, red curls like a kerosened halo, up above the streets to declaim the following lines of verse, no doubt composed by himself in a joyful interval, *Prince, oh prince, once so charming, your fine sports become alarming, yet since your future needs be farming, your apelike features we are harming,* during which moment, according to manifold witnesses, a jocose Prince Charming did suddenly appear upon the avenues of our fair city, smiling broadly and bestowing blessings on *women of mean reputation,* while here in our tale a ghoulish laugh issued forth from the warlock and he performed a number of somersaults and fell to earth before the king, saying, *It is done, and now I require of you a token of your esteem.* At which point the king ran him through with a dull blade. Manly act of a manly king.

And the king knelt down and prayed to the gods for whom we are justly pawns and made himself grateful. Promptly, upon returning to the court, he ascended to the throne, promptly he was trothed to the queen — until that felicitous day known as Andalucia Charming — and promptly, too, they produced a lovely daughter, the hunting princess named

Diana, who wore frocks of blue and bows of red and who married a court musician. For some years all was right in the kingdom.

Wait just a moment, blessed auditor, bestow on me your forgivenesses, for I seem to have misplaced a portion of the tale, such a large helping, in fact, as to be said to constitute *a second plate.* Fervent apologies. I urge you to return to *the enchantment in the courthouse,* of which I have earlier spake, having to do with the queen's sudden and fervid declaration for the king, though he be the man who changed her own brother into a *performing monkey,* etc. and so forth. This forgotten section of the story, which I append, concentrates on the author of this particular enchantment, namely, the giant of Sandy Spit, known among neighbors and plaintiffs as Maurice.

He wore foul jerkins instead of proper clothes, to begin judiciously enough, blouses that had been sweated through with undignified perspirings for many fortnights or even months; he was fat, he was of such girth that when he ate too much his *own house* burst open along the joists; his breath smelled of goat's milk that has been left out in the hot sun to accumulate gobs of cheesy rankness, he rarely even wetted himself down nor wore a gay cologne. And further to his miserable condition Maurice was alone raising up three progeny, a girl in her middle years, flaxen like himself, name of Kurt, a secondborn girl and boy both with dark mien, like the giant's deceased wife, many years departed. Their names were Elsa and Stibb.

Nearly every inquisitive scamp who hears such tales requires to have satisfied *the exact largeness of the giant,* and so here I essay solution to the enigma, to common good of both young and old, *Just how big was the giant?* Since I only saw his children, I give surmise founded upon reports from travelers to distant precincts, who say of him, *taller than church spires, taller than the biggest oaks, taller than the cliffs at Mahon, tall enough to reach up to the green cheese in the night sky and steal himself a fermenting hunk, massive enough to light his pipe from the morning sun, giant enough to trample the oceans for footbaths.*

As the giant was their father, headmaster of hearth, bringer home of manifold pork products including pork loins and pork lips and sausages, his three children had no choice but to love him, yet for some ages they had noticed that he was *very dismally sad*, given to fits of grave sobbing and beating of breast, which would then cause floods in the streambeds of our land, this melancholia dating to the demise of his goodly wife, of course; these many years, he had stayed singularly awake into the caliginous night muttering *Love is an appellation known to all, and so why must I be so solitary unto the hereafter just my wee children but no woman such as might love me and care for me despite my accursed appearance? Why am I destined to march unaccompanied along my path, all men fleeing my footfall?* Upon encountering him, sleepless and cross, in the morning, the children confabulated many wiles and stratagems to distract the giant from woe, including the imposition of elixirs such as *St. John's Wort* into his tea, which Maurice liked of such strength that it had been known to corrode iron kettles. None of these stratagems succeeded, alas, and the giant of Sandy Spit would therefore, in the midst of his fever, maraud upon the land, abducting children, devouring livestock, visiting horrors upon gentlefolk. In such a fell mood, the giant one day espied before him in the road, like a poisonous ant that needs to be crushed before habitations of the day can continue, a small fleeing figure, namely *the once and future Andalucia Charming,* now queen of our demesne, who had been bathing in a small, clear loch, a reservoir of agreeable drinking waters much traveled by lithesome harvesters of corn and other truck, and having spent an afternoon feeding berries to one of these lads, the queen Andalucia, clad only in a womanly undergarment — as mischievous youths had absconded with her further draperies — she now fled home, hoping to arrive at the castle before her most admirable mother, thereupon to make appropriate tributes to the staff such that they might *neglect to mention* to her progenetrix this dishonored state.

Thunder upon the land. The giant caught glimpse of the small, curvaceous, and perfect queen, and soon fetched her up in his fulsome palms, and here the giant held her to his eyes, being much afflicted in the matter of nearsightedness, at which he immediately became a convert to the argument of Andalucia's beauty. She was like a smoky crystal with its flindering lights, she was like unto the handsome portraits that hung in houses wherein his parents had once begged for alms, she was lily of field, bird of air, she might *make wolves eat only herbs and sing madrigals. Upon my honor,* Maurice cried, and of course the sounds were audible across the land, as if a rogue city-state launched *infernal bullets and arrows* toward our cities, *I believe a goddess has crossed into my wilderness and that I must devote myself to her service henceforth and always.* The queen attempted to reply, of course, but Maurice squeezed her so tightly in his fist she fainted dead away, making no audible reply.

Well aware is your storyteller of his dependence on conjuring and mysticisms in this song, yet elegance and divine symmetry demand that he should now admit that the giant performed next as any gentleman of honor would under like circumstances, viz., he too made an oath *of devilish properties.* Said he, over the sleeping body of the queen, now laid alongside a rutted winding track which snaked into the town, and here I must profess again that the poem is of his own composition as I myself prefer blank verse, *Witches, warlocks of the night, restore this sleeper to her sight, make him next she sees be hers, the giant here who offers prayers.* And with that he reclined beside her to await her waking and subsequent veneration of himself. Yet he had squeezed her so tightly, that she didn't wake, *and didn't wake, and didn't wake, and didn't wake,* days commenced to resemble fortnights which soon resembled seasons, and she did not wake, and no traveler dared disturb the vigil of the giant. New roads were dug to circumnavigate his vigil, until such time as he came to believe he had *killed his fairest love,* his second love, and that, by arrangement of deities and constellations, he was therefore beyond *grace* and doomed to wander the earth, bereft, or perhaps to spend too much time in contemplation of ribald masques and plays. Off he marched in winter to relinquish himself to that paltry luck.

Thereafter, the queen, located by good gentlemen on horseback, was gathered onto a chestnut mare to be driven to town for *a grand adjudication,* namely the trial of that youth, much spoken of above, who would shortly be king.

Sleeping, she was transported by these gentlemen, and sleeping delivered to her splendid parents, and she did not wake until, *struck by a hailstone,* she opened her eyes, to espy the next king of our land making his way up the steps, ascending to his destiny, which is to say *she opened her eyes to the felicity of love.*

Now, *the giant galloped amok upon the lands,* dear friends, as, in his madness, he tore stands of oak and birch and flung them this way and that, and a blindness fell upon him like a fever, and a terrible ringing like of a thousand bells did assail his ears, and he knew himself to have come to a fork in the road in the deserted netherlands beyond all our maps. No longer did wolves, nor bears, nor leopards harbor themselves there, idling in anticipation of smiting some passerby, no, life had fled and only the giant Maurice called it home, that complete oppositeness of light, at the edge of which his lonesome welps, Kurt and Elsa and Stibb, made themselves hoarse with beckoning. He did abandon them. And yet in his lonesome thrall, *nonetheless a ray of melioration,* though no sophistry or legerdemain or clerical bluster would raise him from his spot, for suddenly he conceived what the lonely man must always come to know *that he is but a dream of sleep,* his term mercifully instant and insubstantial; so the giant was a dream, yes, and with him such excellent figures of dreams past as Rapunzel, and Snow White, phantastes all, the fine prince called Valiant, arrayed beside the giant, each of these with recitations of his or her heroic pilgrimages, no differences between one and another, for all stories issue from one origin, one maelstrom, *the demiurge Pan;* all things from his dark, implacable brow are fashioned; and this is the imbroglio, fellow citizens, for I have come to recognize myself as the dream the giant had, the giant dreams of me and I dream of the uneasy king, who knows his reign must one day end, each of us a fervency in another's sleep, *there is no teller of tales,* no protagonist, only the interior of a portrait painter in our village, who in the hours before uncovering the easel of her labors, before she sleeps, tells her own daughter *Once upon a time.*

for Elena Sisto

The Carnival Tradition

one

This was fifteen years ago in Hoboken. The storefront apartment on Madison Street. Her front step served as a landing pad for local strays.

One stray was a shepherd-and-lab mix, one was a lab-and-shepherd mix, and one was a mix of so many breeds that it was impossible to say what it was a mix of. One of the dogs was jumpy, skittish, given to aggression; the other two were sweet, friendly, covered with fleas. Well, they were all covered with fleas, actually. She could never tell which of the three was the skittish individual. When she came home to see one slumbering, she never knew whether to be worried, whether to greet this stray with a loving, if tentative caress upon the top of its sloping canine skull, or whether to steer around it according to that antediluvian proverb about dogs. She kept forgetting the markings on the offending beast.

How much had this anxious, panicky dog suffered at the hands, she guessed, of Hoboken's sinister political action clubhouses, where they kicked at it, or shot at it with their pearl-handled revolvers, in the weeks leading up to *the important school board election?* Which beloved local business owner had waved off this hound with a tire iron as it loitered behind his auto body shop?

And was it really three strays? Maybe it was only two? Maybe the dog that was the shepherd-and-lab mix and the dog that was the lab-and-shepherd mix were actually *one and the same dog* and she just hadn't paid attention to its coloring, hadn't seen him from all the angles, hadn't seen him in all times and all places, frolicking, urinating. The way the dogs reclined on the step, in the afternoon sun, it was hard to know which dog was which — one stretched lengthily, as if prepared to be roasted on a Southeast Asian spit, another coiled like a soft pretzel, gnawing at abraded limbs. Sometimes the lab-and-shepherd mix had a scorched black expanse along its vertebrae mildly overgrown with a henna tone, other times it was more flaxen, the color depicted on panels of American cereal boxes. The mutt, on the other hand, had black spots. M. J. Powell was almost sure that it was one of the two shepherd dogs who served as her occasional adversary — shepherds had that reputation, anyway, or at least they did when she was a kid.

She was on the way home from New York University, where she was in a graduate program at the Tisch School of the Arts. She was a blonde and she was a dancer; she was inches from the surface of a teak floor; she wore leg warmers and unitards for weeks at a time, knew the salesgirls at Capezio, she had worn the bloody toe shoes of the child ballerina; there was Stravinsky in her head, passages from Nijinski's diaries, she had learned to count complicated time signatures, sevens and nines; the church she attended, the church through which she lived and breathed, was the Judson Church, where everything a body could do was an expression of the dance, the beautiful and the homely equally expressive meanderings of bodies in space. *She was a dancer.* She put her finger down her throat in the ladies dressing room on the fourth floor before rehearsal. Just the other day. She'd gouged her own knuckles, on bicuspids and incisors, trying to get her hand out of the way of her own heaves. She was uninsured. She wrestled her hair into a bun. Her toenails were cut to the quick. She had excellent turnout. She was a dancer coming up the block with a black leather satchel from Coach over her left shoulder, with the strap of her white silk blouse unstrapping under the strap of the satchel; she couldn't do anything about the blouse, the strapping and unstrapping, because she was also carrying a box of twelve plastic thirty-two-ounce bottles of soda in a variety of brands and types, and she was close to dropping them, these twelve plastic bottles; she could feel them beginning to yield; she could feel the muscles that attached her arm at her shoulder, *and the particular hypertrophy of these muscles, minute striations of myofilaments, interdigitated rows containing the muscular protein actin,* and she knew all this because she was about to be tested on it for a class in *kinesiology,* and if she had been dancing instead of studying, as she would have preferred, maybe this wouldn't be happening, this painful hypertrophy in *the region of the clavicle,* if she had danced, had slotted certain midwestern hardcore tapes into her battered portable cassette player, stood at the barre, attempted to metaphorize the flight of the curveball of Ron Darling (a pitcher she liked), and mixed this with certain repetitions out of Lucinda Childs, Sufi mysticisms, silences and pauses that didn't mean anything now in a specific way, but would probably mean a lot later, *if so then maybe the whole story would have turned out otherwise.*

The block was empty, the block on Madison between Fifth and Sixth, a block of mostly industrial buildings, loading docks that no longer loaded. The box of sodas she carried, in a variety of types and brands, was overwhelming, and she could see, though her sunglasses were sliding down her nose and neither elbow nor finger was available to restore them to the perfect bridge of her nose, that, up ahead, one of the *dogs* was indeed on the step, as there was always one. But which? And why couldn't security be routine in the matter of where you had your stereo and your jewelry and your paperbacks and your inherited lamps? Closer now, she could almost make out, it was either the lab-and-shepherd mix or it was the shepherd-and-lab mix and was it the one that was going to take a hunk out of her unprotected calf, so that she would never dance again and would have a hideous and disfiguring scar. Like that night when she was a little drunk and was first bringing home her boyfriend, okay more than a little drunk, absolutely dyslexic with surfeit of drinks, and they were coming up the step and she had said to him, *Nevermind about the dogs,* and then the dog had begun to growl, on the crumbling step of the landing, and then when she tried gamely to overleap the dog, as though stepping over the dog were to step across the nuptial threshold, the dog had nipped at her. She'd felt a disturbance of air. She'd jumped. She was known for her ability to jump, to perform the entrechat and the grand jeté, and this was therefore a professional jump. The dog didn't make contact, understand, but nipped at her, and then her boyfriend-to-be yelled at the dog and waved his arms until it skulked down the steps and waited, for a time, in the empty expanse of Madison Street. Growling. Yes, she was certain of it, it was that dog with the *shepherd* in it, as opposed to the dog with *lab* in it, an unbalanced dog, a dog from some deep troubled realm of doghood that didn't recognize that it was a companion species or had a history of protecting and admiring humans; it was part timber wolf, and it intended to bite clean through her Achilles' tendon and to disable her; it had unlearned its domestication. There was a desperation to its movements, when it moved, a desperation of the sort that animal psychologists refer to as *liberty hysteria*. It would run up and down the street, this way and that, unknowing, anxious, deprived of the strategic constraint of home.

Naturally, *as she began to mount the three steps that ascended to the entrance of her building,* carrying a cardboard box full of twelve bottles of soft drinks in a variety of brands, the dog began to growl again. And the street was empty, and she was alone, and she had this party to prepare for tonight. That was it, see, there was a party, in less than an hour and a half, she was a busy woman, and didn't have time for this dog on the step, and she was a little panicked, if also resolute, and somehow the dog sensed this (they can smell the fear), and began to become agitated, at first growling quietly, but then barking continuously, and the two of them, she and the dog, fell into a mutual refusal to yield, a refusal to go forward, she wouldn't go forward up the step, she was afraid, the dog wouldn't budge either, wouldn't attempt its violence, but wouldn't move. They stared at one another in this way, the dog bared its rotting smile; she attempted to refix her grip on the cheap, corrugated cardboard box that housed the sodas (an ineffectual box that the discount-beer-and-soda place had given her). Then after one of those prolonged cinematic intervals that had much to do with the flood of relevant chemicals into the viaducts of the circulatory system, a prolonged cinematic instant that involved recollections of the German shepherd that lived up the street in Wilton, the stray *lunged* and the cardboard box *gave out*, as she instantly recognized it was designed to do, and there were bottles rolling, into the street; this way a pair of Diet Cokes; in another direction, some tonic water; there a lone bottle of orange soda that she shouldn't have bothered to purchase. Who drank orange soda? She tumbled, fell backward, down the two steps, *onto her butt*, gouged a big hole in her black nylons, smudged her miniskirt with soot, and the dog lingered on the edge of the top step, fierce, insistent, in full possession.

The sun declined under the ridge adjacent, upon which sat Union City, abruptly rendering the facades of Madison Street in umbral gloom. Bottles of soda continued to hasten away. A gray Honda Civic ran over one of the Diet Cokes with the pop of a cheap firearm. She began in the most forceful language to admonish the hound, *You stupid dog, I have things to do, okay? Beat it!*, which antagonist continued to bark anyhow. Remember the dog that your neighbor had that one summer when you rented a house on the Jersey Shore or on the Cape or in Southampton, the neighbor who rarely went outside except to remonstrate with his kids and to turn the sprinkler on his desertified lawn? Remember his rottweiler, that miserable rottweiler, in the spattered cage out by the garbage cans, who, when his owner went to the local watering holes, would bark, at painfully unpredictable intervals, four or five hours at a clip, a mournful, desperate barking? If you tried to rectify the barking, with a couple of dog biscuits or a bowl of Kal-Kan, you would find his lonesomeness was nothing compared to his desire to devour all intruders or passersby and therefore yourself? This scene was like that.

She blushed. She summoned her bravest and most firm voice, low in the register, *Get out of here, come on, really, go to the meats department at C-town, or something, I don't have time.* Some resolve of her youth had given out and she felt suddenly helpless. The dog refused to yield. She was getting ready to hit him with her handbag, which had not a single blunt object in it (*Anna Karenina*, a plastic twelve-ounce bottle of water, three lipsticks, a wallet, a holder for tampons, a hairbrush, several varieties of breath mints, two ballpoint pens, an address book, a spiral-bound notebook), but which nonetheless would be useful as a device for a throttling, though maybe she could also use several bottles of soda as missiles, which, under compression of carbonation, would scare the hell out of the dog. But before she could effect the plan, the two additional dogs swung wide around the corner of Madison and Sixth, sprinting according to their *liberty hysteria*, following a navigational sense invisible to *homo sapiens sapiens;* they soon fell into position at her crumbling step. Maybe they had been intent upon another destination. Not now. It was a territorial thing. The three were assembled, the stray dogs of her neighborhood, all in disputation, each wanting ascendance of her step, its view, its majesty. One of the two at the bottom of the step leaped at the shepherd-and-lab mix, *it was the mutt*, and they fell into a real commotion. Somebody's neck was going to be perforated. So aggravated was the altercation that a neighbor was moved to lean out a window across the street, to complain,

— What's the idea? We got a business here. We can't work with that racket going on. Give it a rest.

— Then give me a hand, she called in reply. — Or they'll be at it all day and all night and they'll drive us all crazy.

The window slid shut.

— At least call the police, she said. — Or the fire department. Or whoever it is you call when you're trapped in a stray-dog dispute. I mean, *come on*.

She added dulcetly:

— You asshole.

The window, designed and constructed in an era when manufacturing industries still had windows, when offices had windows, when *window* meant *access to fresh, unrecirculated air*, as opposed to double-thick water-retardant panes that insurance corporations will not allow open lest some employee should have the good sense to plunge to his or her final end, landing on the roof of an El Dorado, bouncing to the left, crushing a gifted young Slovakian flutist making her first visit to the United States, *the window slid up*, and the aforementioned small business owner, of Hoboken Tool and Die Corporation, again leaned out.

— You're on *this* block, honey. This is my block. I been working on this block since before you were a glint in your parents' eyes. Get my drift? I grew up here. I didn't move here because it's cheaper than Greenwich Village but with good access to the city. Understand?

The window slid shut, the dogs continued to tangle. Moments later, though, the large gray steel door with multiple locks at the loading entrance of Hoboken Tool and Die swung ominously open, and out came the C.E.O. and major shareholder of the corporation, Anthony Somebody, slack in the middle section, okay he was *fat*, wearing a knock-off of a Van Heusen shirt purchased at the outlets in Secaucus, short-sleeved, blue flannel slacks that he was having trouble positioning at the waist (either up or down). Arms folded. Similarly, coming upon the scene, a crosstown bus screeched to a halt, between Fifth and Sixth, while Anthony labored toward the curb on his bad knees. These two events at once. Anthony offered no rationale for coming to her aid. Schoolchildren, in the windows on the lee side of the bus, pointed at the dogs, one of which had now drawn blood from another. *Five bucks on the shepherd!* The bus meanwhile, at its designated stop, attempted to disgorge an older woman with a walker who was wearing a plastic Ziploc bag on her grayish hair to protect her coiffure from moisture. A hush on Madison Street. The senior unable to disembark. The bus idling. Voices of children on the bus.

— Got a problem, little lady? called Anthony, from his side of the thoroughfare.

As though it were not plainly obvious. There was this party, for example, and the party was to publicize this *gallery* that she was starting, with her boyfriend, except that she was not certain if her boyfriend was still her boyfriend or not, because there were semantic difficulties, for example, how did you *define* boyfriend, because the only time he seemed as though he were her boyfriend was at parties; it was an association that only made sense in the ignoble atmosphere of parties; when not at parties, there was silence, estrangement, distance; when she tried to rectify silence, as by attempting to figure out what her boyfriend might want from her, certain outfits, certain attitudes (condemnation of popular culture), she found that he didn't want her to make attempts to please, but he didn't want her *not* to want these things either — when she called him a *dick* for flirting with Maria at a dinner party, for example, he didn't like it and wouldn't speak to her for three days, but would have liked her less if she had ignored the whole thing, the flirting, which she was inclined to do; one week he loved her, the next she could tell that her body disgusted him, even though her body was perfect, at least according to standards of a Lincoln Kirstein or a George Balanchine; and she had put her head over the toilet that very morning and felt the compressed-firehose surge of Raisin Bran and fresh peach slices, after which she toweled off, applied lotion to her hand, gargled, all this while waiting for him to go to work, *God, when you were feeling the superabundance of rich creative license, you imagined a dancer's body;* her body would be used up and injured in five years' time, cartilage harvested from both knees, maybe sooner, and anyway this kind of abstract posturing and psychologizing about relationships was really boring, made her weary; when women imagined they were supposed to talk about *relationships,* she could tell that they were uncomfortable, outmaneuvered, they were looking to protect themselves against male *liberty hysteria;* it was another way of being *terrified,* really; but, as long as she was enumerating problems, there were cocaine problems, for example; there was this guy who would deliver to their address, a reasonable Middle Eastern guy, who once even offered to put her in touch with a client of his who worked as a psychotherapist; this dealer would come by to Madison Street and buzz the capricious buzzer, there was a period wherein they had to see this guy every night, and it was uncomfortable, him telling them that their records were shit and their sofa was shit, and it wasn't the expense of the cocaine, since her parents had some money that they were giving her, it was that *her boyfriend never bought any of it;* in fact, he didn't seem very effective at earning his own cash, and so there was the problem of him owing her money for the cocaine and owing her money generally, so that she would occasionally brood over exact figures of indebtedness. Even sweet moments, like when they rented a car and drove up the Hudson and went to a farm stand and bought pumpkins, stood in a pick-your-own orchard, ill-reciting fragments of poems, *That time of year thou may'st in me behold,* even in sweet moments, she was calculating debt, *I don't honestly believe that you have given back a proportionate amount and even if money is irrelevant and I have enough money to a pay a larger portion of the rent it doesn't mean that I can forgive in perpetuity the fact that I have spent more than you even if I say I love you,* or she was thinking of a moment when she had gotten up in the middle of the night to guzzle orange juice and had seen him in the kitchen, at the far end of the odd commercial space that was their apartment, with a rolled-up bill and a mirror and lines and she pretended she saw nothing.

Her boyfriend had scraped the "I" off of the sign in the storefront window where they now lived together and it no longer said *Madison Electric,* as it had once, but now said *Mad Son Electric,* and that was the name of their gallery, and they had written a press release replete with art-critical language that her boyfriend had somehow acquired during his all-but-dissertation career as an analytic philosopher; the press release used *liminality* and *numinosity* and *dialectic,* and it referred to *tactical strategies of subjectivity in post-modernism,* and the *Hoboken Reporter* had picked the whole thing up, on the page opposite the police blotter, where the paper recorded with gusto a recent surge in arrests for public urination attributable to all the new restaurants downtown, and then on the facing page, *New Gallery Brings a Touch of the Village to Midtown,* featuring a photo, *M. J. Powell and Gerry Abramowitz in front of the former Madison St. Electrical Corp.* (He clutched a thrift-store overcoat around himself; his black self-inflicted haircut stood on end.) There would be guests, there would be drinks, there would be the wildness. No time to waste.

— I can't get this guy and his friends off my step, I dropped my case of sodas, M. J. called to Anthony Somebody, on the far side of Madison. — I have a party starting in an hour.

— That's nothing, Anthony said. — Couple of dogs, right? Pretty girl like you. Could be worse. Could be rats.

Anthony stepped off the curb. As though stepping across the Hudson River itself, separating this Jersey side from that NYC side, but at the moment of this historic voyage from the curb there was, unfortunately, *a convergence of bad luck.* A pair of young guys in sweatshirts driving what was probably a stolen Camaro slowed, and the driver of this vehicle waved at Anthony Somebody, and Anthony waved back, and one of the dogs bolted between parked cars on M. J.'s side, and everything was possible in this moment, the movements of the *dramatis personae,* dancers upon a proscenium, all converged, another bottle of soda popped, the Camaro swerved, *struck the crosstown bus,* and Mrs. John J. Vincenzo of Adams Street was thrown clear, from her perch on the steps of the crosstown bus, *over her walker,* and onto the pavement, onto accumulations of automobile glass, and there was a muffled cry from her, and a screech of tires, and the Camaro from the '84 model year rumpled like an expensive suit after an evening of embraces, and Anthony Somebody, attempting to wade into the street, attempting to contribute in a civic way to a dangerous congregation of hounds, fell to the curb, grasping for his leg, so that M. J. could see the comb-over on the summit of his head. At first, she thought Anthony's injury was a bluff, a way to deny aid in the midst of civic upheaval. But Anthony had lurched forward between Hyundai and Ford Escort, *Goddamn it!,* collapsing onto the ground, immediately hiking up blue flannels to reveal navy blue socks of the sort that you might get at one of these haberdashers on Union Square where a guy on a stepladder served as discount law enforcement. Anthony began to rub his ankle, blaspheming softly.

M. J. slipped across the great divide of Madison, behind a police car drawing near. — You okay?

Anthony apparently knew from the block these kids who were driving the Camaro that had smacked the crosstown bus that had disgorged Mrs. Vincenzo, the bus which had formerly housed a dozen private school kids from the Catholic school uptown, *Joey, is that your brother's car, does he know you took his car out like this, you're out joyriding you smack up your own brother's car?* It was a customized car, too, and Joey was the younger brother of the guy at the corner grocery near her, the younger brother of the guy who owned the grocery who no longer much spoke to M. J., because, she suspected, she kept using the store address for parcel deliveries from the catalogues. One day when she strode in for a can of lentil soup, the guy and his wife were calling out to her from behind a wall of corrugated-cardboard shipping containers, from J. Crew and Tweeds, *Miss Powell, could you please take some of these boxes over to your place, because we're having trouble moving around in here, in the store.* Blouses and sweaters and linen jackets and black leotards and jeans and swimsuits and hats. The younger brother, who had been loitering in an aisle near the canned goods, had volunteered to help carry her boxes. Joey. And Joey and his pal Mike were now out of the car (near a prone Mrs. Vincenzo) inspecting the front end, repeating their own decorous obscenities, pacing nervously.

Gerry got the idea for the gallery in a certain bar on Second Avenue. In Manhattan. They used to go there after thesis recitals at Tisch. One girl's performance involved a relation to *dirty laundry;* she had brought out a laundry bag and put on a tape of a song featuring miserably chortling synthesizers, and, amid kinesthetic combinations that resembled the process of giving birth, she scattered laundry across the stage, halter tops, underwear, tights. No dry-clean-only items. It was after this piece that Gerry got the idea. Probably soon after. He had moved in, she had just invited him to move in, and he remarked that the gallery scene in the East Village had been *indispensable,* and with so many musicians living in Hoboken now, so many artists, there was a real scene, there was Maxwell's and there were all these bands, and things were really happening, it was the right time for a gallery, in Hoboken, a gallery, a *samizdat* kind of thing, that would reflect the local artists, like there were definitely some great artists out there, and there was all the loft space, and they could sort of serve as a hub, *a nexus,* for all of these artists, and maybe there would be a Hoboken style, like there was southwestern style. M. J. had taken some art history courses in school; she'd taken this one course where, on the final exam, she'd compared Piet Mondrian's reduction of the vocabulary of classical painting *to the way a student on a final exam attempts to reduce the movement and vocabulary of the semester's work down to a single essay question,* and she had received an A for the paper and therefore for the term. She then elected to reuse this idea, a semester later, for the mid-term on the *Abstract Expressionists and Their Era,* this time receiving a C minus. Where the hell *was* Gerry, while policemen hovered over Mrs. Vincenzo like the mob in deposition paintings; while Joey and Mike argued with the driver of the crosstown bus; while the children who'd been on the bus were spilling out onto the street, *Five dollars on the black lab! That's not a lab!* Gerry didn't know too many artists. He'd dated a woman from Barnard who painted portraits of her wealthy family in the style of court paintings from the fifteenth and sixteenth centuries and he'd approached her for the *Mad Son Electric Opening Gala.* M. J.'s cousin Nicky Jarrett, who'd gone to Cooper Union and who specialized in sculptures featuring *balloons with smiley faces* on them — shunts and fuses and tubes housing balloons which then inflated and uninflated, circularly — had also refused. The artists she'd known years before were not artists anymore. They were graphics designers. *What was art, but something that you could get into a bank lobby, or something that a large law firm or junk-bond brokerage boutique acquired through a committee on decorations to sell later at a profit;* or, as Nijinsky said, *I felt disgust and therefore could not finish the ballet.* The Mad Son Electric Gallery had made more progress with the *Hoboken Reporter,* in terms of *media penetration,* than it had made with the artists who might show upon its walls. Gerry had begun to call frantically around town asking if anyone knew any artists at all who worked in Hoboken, any artists who worked in the loft spaces over in the midtown section of Hoboken near the projects, and sometimes, at dusk, he wandered the streets, gazing in windows.

In the meantime, M. J.'s studies in physiognomy and sports medicine and the Alexander Technique made her ideal for the diagnosis of Anthony Somebody's ankle sprain. His large, homely ankle was up on her thigh, and she was pulling delicately on it, examining. Anthony's eyes: woeful, as though he'd been driven off twenty yards from some game of boys, lifelong, watching myopically from a distance, as boys called out, *No fat kids allowed.*

— A sprain is basically a pulled tendon. Diagnosed by a history. Ever sprain it before? Rest, ice, compression, and elevation. That's your road to recovery. After the swelling goes down after a couple of days, you should do range-of-motion exercises, like balancing on the affected foot. Or you could try tracing letters of the alphabet, easy ones first. *H.* Or *L.* That way you avoid joint instability.

— If you could just help me get up on my feet, Anthony said.

He was worried and distant.

— I'm not sure you should be walking on it. That's what I'm saying, M. J. said. — I mean, you probably don't have a fracture, because that would be obvious. I saw a girl fracture her leg once.

Anthony wrestled his foot out of her control. He began to stand.

— Joey, get your butt over here, Anthony called.

— The Camaro in the eighties will *never* be like the Camaro in the seventies, Joey was mumbling.

— Or what about that '67? With the V-8 and the 350 cubic inches, Mike, his friend, observed. — Sweet on that.

— Parts. That's your whole problem.

— Something goes bad.

— Look, I'm leaking.

— Oil pan. Definitely.

— Joey!

A policeman sauntered over, from where Mrs. Vincenzo lay upon a bier of shattered glass; the sun dipped below the rim of Union City; M. J. plucked off her sunglasses; holiday lights, blinking holiday strings, which Gerry had laboriously hung in the window of the Mad Son Electric Gallery, were by timer engaged, and in these lights *it became clear that the dogs had disappeared, had fled;* and so the way to the gallery was free, and the *interpenetration* of all these people, all these events, caused by dogs, seemed for the moment to be just a mistake of interpretation, nothing more. M. J. felt better. She could just go inside now and get busy with arranging soft drinks (the case of wine was already inside), cheeses, and maybe these pratfalls of the afternoon would be part of the coverage of the *Mad Son Electric Opening Gala:* an old woman on a walker stretched out flat on Madison Street, her voice declaiming irritably on the matter of *sciatica,* a car totaled on the rear of the crosstown bus, kids sitting out on a sidewalk with a portable radio blasting a tune about basketball sneakers, Hispanic men getting out of cars trapped in the snarl up the block, car horns like monarchical cornets, *because of dogs.* Joey and Mike, wearing black tour T-shirts, each with a long, narrow ponytail snaking down his back, hoisted Anthony to his feet. All M. J. had to do was open the door to the building. She was tired. An ambulance came up the block from the wrong direction. Its muffled siren. And before her in the street lay a pristine bottle of orange soda. She scooped it up and went back to make a gift of it to Anthony.

— Sorry for the trouble.

As though he had never met her.

— Thanks. He unscrewed the lid fast. Orange soda was fountained. He brushed a dribble off himself.

— We're having a little art opening later. Come on by.

— Uh, prior engagement.

Back on her side of the street, a guy sat himself on the hood of a station wagon, in front of her building. He too drank her soda. Her Diet Coke. *What kind of operation you running here, huh?* He gestured at the gallery. She let it all go, headed for the door, and the three steps seemed steeper, more demanding, as if this were part of her performance and the audience behind would be watching. She loved her boyfriend, at least right now she loved him, even if he didn't seem to have many friends, even if there were nights when she would come home from school and she would find him alone in the house, with the videocassette recorder fired up, the one that they'd gotten from her parents, beside it a sequence of horror films that he loved since his childhood. *Who are we going to invite to the gallery opening?* she asked. *Don't worry about that. That's the easy part.* They had addressed a few invitations, maybe thirty, but would any of those people actually come? There were a few people he knew from his day job in the city, as bibliographer for the *Encyclopedia of the History of Religions.* He would get a dozen index cards with names like Mercia Eliade or Reinhold Niebuhr on them; he would go down into the maze of stacks at Columbia, see what he could see, a *Festschrift* published in The Hague, some old numbers from the *Religious Anthropology Quarterly.* Akhenaton's or Moses' conception of monotheism. If he did enough of these cards, hourly, he'd have enough money to pay, temporarily, for his long distance calls, in which he invited friends from Austin or Burlington to come to Hoboken for the show. She searched deep into the recesses of her purse. Nope, not in that front pocket, maybe in the zippered pocket in the front, and, okay, if not there, don't panic, they're in the back pocket, she never put them in the back pocket, *okay, shit, where are the keys,* she had no pocket on her skirt, of course, women weren't supposed to have pockets, but she checked nonetheless, absurdly patting down her front and her rear as though there were pockets, then back around again, the entire sequence, front pocket, back pocket, interior pocket, glancing toward the mayhem on Madison Street, *where the hell was Gerry,* and why weren't her keys in here? Her mind rushed back over the last half hour. When she was fighting with *the dogs,* did she have them then? Had the keys fallen out when she had stumbled on the sidewalk? Was there a snapshot in her recollection of a purse overturned, a glint of her silver key chain on the sidewalk? She tried the knob, an old rusty thing on the metal door. It didn't give.

Across the street, Joey and Mike, helping Anthony down the sidewalk.

A homeless guy had shown up from a squat in one of the nearby industrial buildings. *The homeless situation was expanding here in Hoboken,* M. J. believed; once there had been these hotels down by the terminal, the Hotel Victor, for example, a hotel that existed as a satellite business around the Irish bars, watering holes where floozies and drunks who had lost the week's wages on dog races would console and antagonize one another. These were the hotels where these men lived, beside immigrant women and their children; anyhow, when that garish restaurant opened next door, the one with the loud sound system and the waitresses with silicone implants, well then, the hotels had to close, couldn't afford the upwardly adjusted rents, these people couldn't afford to live where they had always lived and so they were going to have to leave. Some penniless adventurer had spray-painted protest language on the door of the Hotel Victor, *Where will these men go?* And there were multi-colored T-shirts appearing in town, with this language upon them, with the dingy Victorian façade of the hotel and its sign, and beneath, *Where will these men go?* But even the adventurer who had spray-painted the hotel was worn down by the futility of political opposition in the medieval town given entirely to political patronage, under federal investigation for the worst public schools in the state, and the men who lived in the Hotel Victor were loosed upon the street, and it was about that time that she started to notice one of the midtown homeless regulars, Aaron was the guy's name, or at least that was what people called him, a delicatessen owner told her, and Aaron, the interesting thing about Aaron, in addition to the fact that he usually wore a hockey helmet which was *to keep in his brains*, the unusual thing was that he was, she believed, *a gay homeless person*, which you didn't encounter every day, although she imagined, after all, that problems like mental illness struck in equal percentages across demographic categories. Underneath the grime and the strawberry-blond beard and the hockey helmet, Aaron seemed delicate, fine, frail, a scarecrow, and his gestures were balletic, as with the male dancers she knew. *I want to write poetry. I want to compose ballets. I am God,* as Nijinsky said. She could imagine making a piece for Aaron to dance, and it would have a lot of Nijinsky's word associations for Aaron to recite while dancing. Aaron was frequently darting around bus stands pointing frantically at things and people who were not immediately apparent, and waving a half-empty bottle of Miller Genuine Draft. There were perfectly sane homeless people, of course, and unlucky homeless families, but Aaron wasn't one of these. He was a deinstitutionalized homeless person. It would have been difficult to get him to perform combinations properly, though maybe he could have been videotaped, phrase by phrase, as in the abstract videos of Cunningham that M. J. liked; and what was he doing here, at the head of Mrs. Vincenzo's prone body, as she regaled paramedics?

— The one young man who started that restaurant on Washington Street. I knew him when he was just a boy. His parents are very proud of him. Very proud. Told me that he got the idea for it from eating sandwiches over to the Jersey shore. This goes back a ways. My own boy was in the armed forces then.

— Mrs. Vincenzo, you shouldn't talk.

— I'll talk if I want to.

— Buddy, just move off a couple feet, here, give the lady some fresh air, the paramedic remarked to Aaron, over whose face then passed a dark cloud of rejection. Meanwhile, adjacent, the operator of the crosstown bus, on the radio, — A fender bender type thing. A flat. Young lady been nice enough to give away some of her soft drinks, and the kids? They all drinking sodas. Some playing cards.

— You want me to get that open for you? Offered the guy on the hood of the station wagon, motioning at M. J.'s front door. — Could open that *easy*. Just need a credit card or something. Let me do it.

Every northeastern town had its eccentric with *the artificial tan*. Many of these characters got their tans from local tanning salons, and Hoboken had a tanning salon, but it was on the uptown end where M. J. rarely traveled and anyhow she believed that *tanning salons involved irradiation*. Fair of skin, as her family were all fair of skin, she was from a long line of ivory that in winter looked delicate and in summer looked unhealthy, *people of the ice*, this ancestry of Anglo- and Irish-Americans who by birthright didn't have to live in towns that were built up on swamps as Hoboken was, *she was white*, and this gentleman on the hood of the station wagon was tanned through some means, through an applied juice, a poultice, an Egyptian henna or some such, which he attempted to mete out over himself evenly, under cover of night, in a harsh bathroom fluorescence.

— I'm supposed to be having a party in less than an hour. The guests are coming really soon. Where's my boyfriend? He's supposed to be here.

— You just need a credit card is all.

So his neighborliness revealed itself as an attempt to get to her credit cards, which, in any event, were her parents' credit cards, namely a Visa card issued by her parents' bank and an American Express Platinum. All of the money, or requests for money, flowed back to that originary trunk, as all her parents' money flowed back to the central bank and its charter for which Washington voted, when president, in 1791. All money referred to the original money of British feudal lords, which, transferred, supplemented, by plastic cards, karats, ducats, nuggets of gold, stock certificates, bonds, computer printouts of mutual fund holdings, was nonetheless merely a recognition of the origin of money, held by people who did not tan well and who did not need to apply juices to their pale veneers. She assumed, moreover, that all original money was stewarded *by men*, because women were held to be forgetful and given to mercurial temper and who were anyway inclined to leave the control of money to others, who had pockets. The men were all in a bar someplace, mired in self-hatred, flattering courtesans who would look hideous in the morning, they were pondering the box-office dominance of a certain Austrian bodybuilder whose accent made him sound startlingly like a fascist; it was almost impossible *not* to imagine that this Austrian, who may possibly have used juices to tan his

(155)

veneer, was a fascist. She used to come home at night and Gerry would be sitting at the kitchen table with the local phone book open and she would ask what he was doing, and he would say, *Reading the phone book.* She would ask why he was reading the phone book. He had no explanation, he was just reading, and when again they were attempting to think of people to invite to the *Mad Son Electric Opening Gala,* he'd turned to reading the white pages, unable to make contact with her in a way that satisfied either of them, uncertain, even, what it was to make contact; Gerry improvised, *Looking for rock stars,* because there were these Hoboken bands and they just lived up the street, they all had day jobs, one guy copyedited for one of the larger publishing houses, and you used to see them on the buses going into Port Authority and Gerry was thinking he was going to invite these celebrities to the *Mad Son Electric Opening Gala,* but then he never did, nothing came of it.

— You don't have your own credit card? M. J. said. — Because I'm not sure I want to sacrifice one of my credit cards for a lock. I mean, they're not really mine, anyway. They're for emergency use, and if I lost one, I'd have to notify the bank.

— Suit yourself, the *tan man* said.

— I don't give a hoot if he was the greatest singer of the century! Mrs. Vincenzo shouted. Aaron rocked beside her in recognition of her oratory. — I'm saying he ought to come back and visit the town where he got raised up. Doesn't make good sense. My boy was in some trouble here in town before he went off to the services and I still lived here with the neighbors and the friends who seen what I've been through. They understood my troubles. This is where I'm from. I'm not going to be from anywhere else.

— Mrs. Vincenzo, said one of the paramedics, — would you be willing to get into the ambulance now?

A dispute broke out between the kids playing cards, a black kid and a white kid and soon several others had gotten into it, and they held the white kid down and they pulled off his sneakers, probably cost $37.50 apiece, tied two laces together, the kid cried out *No! No!* but they held him down. Now M. J. noticed that harvest of sneakers, draped on the power lines. The instigators flung the sneakers up, tried to get them to drape over the lines. *Please, no, those are brand-new sneakers!* They were calling him *faggot*, because what else did you call a kid, you called him a *faggot*, that was the worst thing you could be. She looked at Aaron to see if he registered this, whether a lifetime of being mostly hated by your peers was enough to be a predictor of madness and alcoholism, but Aaron had wandered toward the crosstown bus and was now disputing its route with the driver.

— Must not use the crosstown bus very often, the driver said, — because it's been some years this bus here been going down Madison. *Other* bus goes down Washington, so now people on this side of town, they don't have to walk so far, like the people on the other side, they mostly don't have to walk so far.

— Maybe it's not your house, the guy from the station wagon remarked.

— What did you say? said M. J.

— I mean maybe you're trying to get me to bust you into a house doesn't belong to you.

— Want to see my driver's license?

— Could be this isn't even your street. Maybe somebody else lives here. Driver's license? Hey, you can *buy* one of those.

— That's really rude. What you're saying is just rude.

The face of the *tanned guy* (she supposed now that he was called *Norbert*), indicated a substantial cruelty heretofore concealed. She could tell that he would not be a resource *in her hour of need*. Meanwhile, the cars on the street in a furious klaxoning. The ambulance, the crosstown bus parked side by side. Police beside paramedics. A fireman wandered through asking if his services were needed. At the corner, a traffic cop who had appeared to wave rush-hour flow onto Seventh Street had recognized a friend among the assembled. He stepped out of the intersection to chat with this rotundity of sweatsuit. Traffic languished. Next, there was a street vendor, one of Hoboken's sellers of ices, with a cart and a dozen bottles, chipping away with his pick, loading on raspberry syrup; around him three or four friends heaving crimson dice, talking fast in a froth of Spanish and English: results of first games of the football season, difficulties of wives, *how a couple of Anglos in the wrong neighborhood gonna jack up the rents,* this town where they had gotten halfway through demolishing the ferry terminal so that they could put up *top-dollar developments like amusement arcades, shopping centers, luxury condos,* you could neither take a ferry from the terminal nor use the location for anything else; it was the Committee for a Better Waterfront versus the people who had lived there since they were kids, played stickball on the blacktop over by Observer Highway; the people who lived there were mainly *for* development, even if it brought nothing to them but wrecking balls and Food Courts; and this very theme had now erupted on Madison Street, before the flickering holiday lights of the *Mad Son Electric Gallery* of Hoboken, whereupon a BMW-owner, wearing Ray-Bans and a yellow power tie, climbed out of his convertible, and took it up with the men by the street vendor, and yet they all agreed, everyone agreed, *You think it's a bad idea to have a beautifully designed series of buildings down there, and some shops, with the Empire State Building, right cross the water?* The men, in their basketball jerseys and worn baseball caps, jeans and construction boots, wordless, *That's a good idea,* the young urban professional continued, *which will improve real estate values in the neighborhood. It's better for the tax base. There will be jobs.* Strapped himself back into his car, satisfied with urban planning, and there he sat, immobilized in traffic.

— Over my dead body a bunch of trees down there on that water! Over my dead body! We don't need no more parks! We got plenty of damn parks already! That's just going to cause filth from pigeons and rats! We need tax monies! observed Mrs. Vincenzo.

Autumn, *county fair of tonalities.* People filed out of workplaces, out of tenements, onto stoops. Last time they could do so for months. Leaves clogged the street, the sewer lines. Where had these leaves come from? They were three blocks from the nearest tree. Northeast storms had blown through earlier, as storms did this time of year, and the limbs of the trees, those that remained in the Mile-Square City, were picked clean; each new gust brought a dusting of yellow symbols of decay. Clearly, it wasn't only M. J. who made a poetics, a worldview, out of a drop in the temperature and a diminishment of light. *I tremble like an aspen leaf,* Nijinsky said. Her parents' house had beautiful autumns. When the weather was fine, she practiced out on the lawn, while the man next door clipped graying blooms from his once bright hydrangeas. She bobbed above the clean lines of a box hedge, perfecting leaps, *faint with hunger.* She was always hungry. She was always cold.

The tawny huckster with the scheme to break and enter, Norbert, accepted her offer of a *Major Video, Inc.* lifetime membership card and began working on the lock, which seemed to involve scoring the paint job on the door frame with the edge of the plastic lamination. Gerry Abramowitz had his own Major Video card. This one could be sacrificed. From desperate sprees of video rental Gerry returned, in his usual nervous way, uncertain, taciturn, with a home festival of science fiction films and teen sex comedies. *Talk to me a little bit,* she asked. He'd laughed. He stayed up watching films after she'd gone to sleep and left early with his stack of bibliographical index cards. Her locksmith *pro tem* tried buzzing the tenants on the first floor. He bent the video membership card until it had a veiny fracture in it. M. J. was almost certain, in the light of streetlamps, that guests for the party had now begun to assemble. There was a couple in bowling shoes and Hawaiian shirts, his and hers, hair slicked with the grease of the period, Tenax or Vaseline; there was a guy with heavy tortoiseshell frames and a secondhand madras jacket. All bantering. M. J. would not meet these, her guests, on the front step, locked out, having given away Diet Coke and orange soda. It was humiliating.

— The Carnival Tradition, from Bakhtin, said the madras jacket.

— I thought it was Bakunin, said the woman.

— That's anarchism.

— I know what anarchism is. You've got your B's confused.

— We could go to the Middle Eastern place, you know.

— Uh, no civilization endures without temporary suspension of the rules of civilization.

— Let's wait a few more minutes.

— Got a cigarette?

Whereupon the door to the building next to M. J.'s opened, being 619 Madison, *known drug location,* according to law enforcement circles, known for its *potent smokable form of cocaine.* They had never given her any trouble over there, in the *known drug location.* They were vital and spirited American entrepreneurs. The door, a flimsy old composite affair, into which had been installed cheap stained glass, from Sears, swung back, and out of it came the dream within this dream, a cherub, a teenaged boy from next door, a Hispanic young man, an Edgardo or Jose or Miguel, perhaps, a fraternizer with users of the *potent smokable form of cocaine,* but with a perfect Hispanic celestial quality that he, young Angel, would have until he was older, had put on a few pounds, become a working stiff, traded beauty for dignity; for now as perfect as a boy in Hoboken could possibly be in pressed jeans, black work shoes, James Dean windbreaker, expertly tousled black hair, having strode out of a jailbreak movie, carrying somebody's turntable, *she couldn't help thinking that he was stealing the turntable,* and when he saw the crowd outside the front door, he turned, as if to rethink the plan, to secret himself indoors, away from the authorities. Did anyone still buy

LPs? Even that store down by the PATH terminal where the gruff stoner with sideburns and ponytail wordlessly dispensed obscure rock and roll on vinyl — Syd Barrett, Lothar and the Hand People, the Nazz — even that store was on its way out; so why would Angel, the Hispanic cherub, *steal a turntable?*

She started down the steps toward him.

— I'm locked out here. Next door. And I got all these people coming over to see our new gallery here, and I'm wondering if you might know someone in the building here, or maybe —

A premeditated recognition on the part of Edgardo or Miguel.

— I gotta take this over to my friend's.

— Oh, come on.

The turntable, balanced precariously on wrought-iron railing.

— Can I get over on the roof? M. J. said.

The rashness of the proposal, maybe, persuaded him to change his mind. What white girl from the suburbs would propose *going over the roof*? A conspiratorial grin broke out on his unblemished face.

— Sure, the roof. You could go over on the roof.

She asked if he would show her how, notwithstanding political implications of wanting to be *shown how*, wherein a woman asked a man for instruction, affected an unknowing because of the stylized exchange of information that might follow; she still liked it when a guy would *show her how*, whether it was how to program certain technological appliances, the coffee machine, the stereo, how to operate a handsaw or how to hit a backhand, and perhaps it would have been that way with Gerry, if he had known *how to do anything,* but he didn't know much, a few knots from when he had taken sailing lessons in the suburbs, but he could fix nothing, and once a couple of weeks ago she had found him, inexplicably dangling a hasp in front of the windowsill, as if one could be used on the other, *What are you doing with that hasp?* He knew about Frege, Austin, Kuhn, but his evasions on home repair subjects were appalling. *Can't we get someone in to fix that?* She inflated this evidence, on the front step of her building, into a notational system of romance: you and your lover showed one another *how to,* according to diagrams, and then when you knew *how to,* you moved on to the next person, to have them show you *how.* Once an object in question was fixed, you needed it broken again, or replaced by another, *and fast.* And the question before her now, by way of reminder, was *how does a girl steal onto the roof of her building?*

— Gonna put this back in the basement, Angel said. — Hang on.

Then he returned. Together they occupied the warped stairwell. Cinder block. Exposed ceiling bulbs dangling from frayed electrical lines. Lead-based paints flaking from scuffed walls. She followed him. With each flight of stairs, their pace increased, their gasps and exhalations, their anticipations, and she not only managed to keep up, but to drive Angel on more furiously, though she'd eaten nothing but a rice cake since throwing up breakfast. At last, they each grabbed the banister on the red *emergency ladder;* they hoisted themselves up; at last, they pushed back an old rotting hatch; at last, they heard a scattering of pigeons. They were on the roof.

Night had fallen across the landscape. Dramatically. Beyond the nub of green that was Stevens Institute of Technology at a distance, night upon the World Trade Center, night upon Hoboken high-rises, night upon the spectacle of New York City, night upon the Hudson, night upon the ships of the Hudson, night upon the garbage barges and their peppering of diapers and six-pack holders, night upon the history and politics of the tri-state area, night upon the Newport Mall of Jersey City, night upon Liberty State Park, night upon Edgewater, night upon Fort Lee, night upon the George Washington Bridge, night upon arteries great and small, night upon marshes and blacktops and rail yards and baseball fields and electrical substations. Who could turn from it? Who could neglect it? Night had come, even while the town below undulated with dispute and jubilance.

Did she say the next words before acting, on the roof, in fresh moonlight, words that had to do with kissing a complete stranger *from a different economic class and ethnic heritage* on the roof of a *known drug location*, while the guests for her party were amassing, or did they kiss first, words occurring like spontaneous, retroactive evocations of the riptide of subcutaneous wishes? Where did the thought come from, in this furnace of retrospection? What made her do these incredibly stupid things? Because she'd been hung up for so long, out in front of the building, and was just grateful, at last, to have *gotten her ass indoors*? Or was it some quality in Angel himself? Wasn't there a moment when she'd thought about it and realized that this might not be the smartest decision she ever made? No. Things had been connected together, conjoined. There was no fulcrum with which to pry them apart. This was part of what had come before. How blissful not to have to make a particular decision but to yield to what was already as obvious as if it were mixed up with propositions of physics. She thought, or she said aloud, *Let me kiss your spectacular Caravaggio mug*, and she knew that he knew they were going to kiss too, like candidates for elopement; the kiss was unclear as a romantic gesture, but forceful as an observation on the nature and duration of the month of October and what the end of October meant: onslaught of holiday madness, mixed precipitation, folly in the street, *We're young! We're beautiful! We're supposed to make out!* He held her off. *Let's get over the fence.*

Barbed wire, rusted by age and emissions of sulfurous compounds, separated her building from the *known drug location.* Coiled above the flush edges of the two buildings, bolted into cement. Remorseful visitations of conscience implicit in the difficulties of barbed wire. But these visitations of conscience didn't last very long. Angel (real name Mike) seemed, of course, as if he was made to go over barbed wire, which was a generalization on M. J.'s part about things she didn't understand, to which people who had a lot of stuff were given in the consideration of those who didn't have as much. Nevertheless, Angel simply found a spot that was well traveled, and he pulled some heavy work gloves out of the pockets of his windbreaker, set them down, took off his windbreaker, tossed it like a proverbial cape so that it draped on the fence, gripped the fence in work gloves, vaulted over. Plucked the jacket from the barbs. Now the fence separated the two of them.

— I can't go over *that,* M. J. said.

What about the party? What about the people gathered in the street outside? What about her career as a dancer? Did she want to marry? Did she mean to procreate? Had she been a good friend to her good friends? Had she attempted to remember the kindness of parents, for whom she was an only child? Had she taken in stray pets? Given to charity? Looked for the good in others?

— I'll lift you over, Angel said.

— You weigh about ten pounds more than I do.

— *No problem.*

— You can't.

He stood at the spot where he had climbed over himself. The barbs were speckled with gouts of blood. Maybe it was the light. Blood of the fiscally challenged, blood of laborers, blood of suffering addicts who flocked to the *known drug location.* While their wives or parents slept, when the attention was off, they came up Madison Street, incanting, skulking, sweaty, desperate, to 619 Madison. They banged upon the door. They didn't own enough layers to put off the cold. It was no fashion statement. Angel reached out his arms. She didn't have much faith. She climbed up on the ledge that separated the buildings, and with an expressive *saltation,* a *frisson,* she landed in his hands, arms around his neck; she could smell him now, and he smelled funky, like a human, and up close she could see the planes of his cheeks, hairless and boyish. It was true. He could lift her up. She was air, she had perfected the designs of the universal choreographer and made her body insubstantial like a bird's, *A bird is a messenger of death for people who have no feeling.* There ought to have been even more splashy lifts and embraces, but instead the sequence culminated predictably. That is, her black miniskirt became entangled upon barbs, and there was the shredding of fabric giving way, a sliver of her miniskirt, and her tights too, and then she felt the sting of it, the barb, and she thought about her immodesty, her exhibitionism, about tetanus. *That skirt was expensive.* He put her down, she touched herself on her thigh, with the shyness that had overwhelmed Anthony at the apperception of his sprained ankle, *What was she doing here?* She recognized, on her own roof, a dismal arrangement of browned spider plants and expired geraniums irresolutely tended here by the cat lady up on the third floor. M. J. was bleeding.

And he was all over her, suddenly. His brutish hands upon her caressing. There were endearments, *You are the prettiest girl I ever seen. Never kissed any blond girl before, so pretty like you.* His hands like sandpaper, like a *hasp.* The excesses of a Manhattan skyline, at this remove, like a Big Bang inconceivably past; a blanket had been thrown over something more perfect, of which the stars were an indication, perforations of night. *What was the thing that endeared Gerry to her,* back when he still endeared himself, and why were endearments of people she loved so inaccessible? Objects always stood in for what was missing, a certain slutty color of nail polish that he bought for her one Passover that she had never worn, but which she kept at hand. Objects were like orange traffic cones on the right shoulder of the highway of intimate relations. That's why she was here on the roof, with a Hispanic boy in his late teens kissing her neck in a way that was sort of unpleasant now that she was thinking about it. It was hasty, not like the long, slow tentative daubs that Gerry favored.

— Hey, she said. — Slow down, okay?

He was pushing down the strap of her silk blouse, trying to get at her breasts. Maybe it was romance, and maybe romance was exactly like *the dance,* maybe its gestures were that familiar, that immutable, even if everyone felt that they arrived at these gestures through their own impulsive ramble. Maybe the arabesques, the fouettes, the pliés of dance could be superimposed on love; maybe these gestures of dancing were just love in a deconsecrated space. The way a certain brushing of lips against a cheek then led to a collision of pairs of lips, the way the lips then moved toward a nipple, it was as reliable as the movements of *Ballets Russes.* She tried to distract herself with terms of her childhood education, *maître de ballet, port de bras.* She tried to think of other possible interpretations for brutishness, until *a terror started to swell* in M. J. Powell. It started small, as discomfort, swelled into revulsion, and then assumed the *actual size* of terror, which is always one size larger than its container. Maybe terror is implicit in all anonymous sexual encounters. Maybe that's what's good about these encounters, maybe that's what made degradation, when consensual, effective. But she felt nausea, a faintness. He turned her around a few times as if this were a child's game. Which direction did she face? It was wet, on the roof; there were puddles from the last storm. There was the stench of wet towels.

— Not here, *please,* come on.

His manual circulations upon her became more urgent. Here, on her exposed shoulder, he romanced a certain mole. Her nipple, at the summit of a faintest incline, was now exposed to the air. His hips were fast against hers.

— I want to show you our place. I want to show you our gallery, she said, *reaching for a sequence of words that might put a stop to it.* He showed no indication of understanding the *we* implicit in *our,* that locution with which couples reinforced their reign over single persons.

— *Stop,* she said.

She pushed against him. He resisted. She pushed harder. He pushed back. She pulled away. He held on. She pushed again. He pulled away, holding on. He pushed back. She fell away. He held on. She pushed. He resisted. He pushed. She covered herself. She pulled away. She changed directions. He held on. She pushed against him. He resisted. She pushed. He resisted. She pushed, he resisted. And suddenly, disgustedly, he put a shoulder against her, the whole of his upper body, and she was free, *and her liberty was foul.* She bolted for the door at the far end of the roof. But before she could get there, there was a commotion behind her. A neglected attic closet of memory opened, forth came the image of a blanket, left from a picnic up in the north during a summer visit to the Green Mountains, a blanket, at dusk, aired on a laundry line, at night, disturbed by heavy wind. She was out with a friend, and behind them they saw it, the blanket, and its *animus* was expressed by the gust, a malevolent spirit that sent them, as girls, howling into the pantry, inconsolable. It was behind her, this very *entity,* tackling her now, and she was on her back. How horrible the words in the moment that they appeared in her mind, *You are on your back,* while another part of her noticed the masonry on the edge of the building. It needed attention. And there were car horns, in the distance; her hand dipped in the meniscus of a puddle; her own hyperventilations, sixteenth notes, remarkably constant. This was simply an arrangement of bodies she had once experienced, during an audition, nothing more, and just when her sorrow was beginning to accompany her terror, just when she was beginning to wonder what threat would be used to ensure silence, he whispered, *I ain't gonna hurt you,* and she found, instead, that he was rolling over her, hefting her up, she went over onto her right side, and then *onto him,* and she was on top, and the first thing she did was slap him hard across the face, *You already hurt me, you fuck,* she said, and he did nothing, didn't smile, didn't speak, and then he took her hands, coinciding, she noticed, with an infrastructure of spotlights scintillating in the heavens on the Manhattan side of town, near the Maxwell House factory, where there had formerly been a robust, *good-to-the-last-drop* fog, all days, all times; he took her hands; he *fitted them around his own throat,* tightened his grip on her hands on his throat; there was no swiveling of hips, there was no grinding at her, there was no recognition, no sexual anything; only hands on her hands, and the tightening at his throat. She struggled to pull away, *What are you doing?* He struggled to keep her hands around himself, and his breathing became labored, if only she could see better in the dim light of the roof, she was murdering him, he was slipping away, and yet he was tightening the grip, *Let me go,* she angled her legs off of him, began to pull away again, *Are you out of your mind?* Looking up at her, plaintive. Suffocation of the earth, putrefaction of the land, foulness of marshes, reeds and egrets and muskrats and snappers all replaced by the even fouler *rattus norvegicus* to make this town of Hoboken, so cars could be stolen, substandard buildings constructed, bribes paid, drunks displaced, so bond traders could purchase their condominiums. Then she was *off*, heading for the door, racing for the door, expecting him to finish her off in the stairwell, to impale her through the heart on the diamond stylus of his stolen turntable, to fire the exploding bullet of his class war into the base of her skull. But when she tried to ascertain his whereabouts, *he was gone*, except for his voice, *It's your town now*, calling after her, *Your town now.*

The front door of the Mad Son Electric Gallery swung back almost exactly on time, seven P.M., that evening in October, for its opening gala, and the guests outside, who numbered exactly seven, were unaware that anything much in the way of a delay had taken place. M. J. Powell, temporarily sobbing hostess, could hear, on the other side of the door, Gideon Katz, the boyfriend of Lori Fine, her dancer friend from NYU; Gideon was a mathematician, extremely talkative, and his specialty was *knots*, and Gerry Abramowitz loved him, loved everything about him and his knots, how beautiful they could be in the telling, no symbolism to them at all, just knots with numbers describing them, *An invariant, you know, that's any number you can assign to a knot which doesn't change if you twist the knot or pull on it, like if you wrap a piece of rope around a banister and don't tie it and just pull on one end, it comes off the banister, well except that they're not knotted around anything. They just are. So that example doesn't count. On the other hand, if you have*

*two ends in front of you, you cross one over the other, one way
would be the positive way and you can assign a number of one
to that, the right strand going over the left, a positive crossing,
see, and the other way would be negative. So any kind of knot
has an algebraic length, get it? The minimum is if you pull on
it to get rid of the loops, and so forth.* Had to be Gerry that
Gideon was talking to. Who else could it be? Who else
would tolerate a disquisition on knots? *No knotted knot has
a crossing number less than three, see, but, unfortunately, it's
also true that there's knots that have the same invariant but
aren't the same knot, so it gets complicated.* Maybe Gerry had
lost his key too. He had left his key in the library up at
Columbia, the library for Asian languages, where they had
once gone together to kiss, because he liked it so well, its
dim, neglected stacks. Books and kissing were related somehow. When she appeared in the threshold of the doorway, to
the seven excited guests here for the *opening gala,* she could
see that Gerry was not among them. What a disappointment. And she was a complicated figure to the assembled,
too, and instead of attending to them immediately, she
watched as, going up the block in the distance, a shade, carrying some bulky object, hastened off. *If you have a loop
with two crossings in it, then you can pull it and flip it and
twist it with just an unknotted loop.*

— Are you okay? Lori said. M. J. saw herself as she must
have appeared, torn skirt and stockings, face wet, hair mat-
ted, an open gash on her thigh.

— A long story, she said. — Come on in.

Here was the part that Gerry would have loved, because
it was the part he designed himself. He often made sketches

of things, on scrap paper, not terribly adept sketches, but sketches anyhow. One day she'd found the plans for the gallery, scribbled in this style, on the coffee table. Just sitting there. For her. Then she began the job of realizing this interior for the Mad Son Electric Gallery, according to his vision; no whitewash since Tom Sawyer's was applied with such method. They had taken the whole of the weekend, and while they were laboring, they were laboring *together*. It involved putting the old sofa, with the stuffing unstuffing, out onto the street, where it disappeared at once. Other furnishings, such as they had, were hidden under white sheets, so that the effect, *in toto*, was of perfect eggshell, a blank slate, incomplete potential, like in the great galleries. All these years later, fifteen years later, she remembered the sad parts of the story, but the good parts too, as one thinks of youth after it is gone, a laugh, a goof, a riot, made some bad decisions, made some worse decisions, made awful decisions, *smoked a Quaalude,* slept with a boy on antipsychotic medication, wrecked a car, watched thirteen dawns in thirteen towns, loved people otherwise spoken for, wrote a life story, threw it out, spent recklessly, gave a dog to the ASPCA because it barked, quit speaking to a guy and his friends, *gave up dancing,* above all, *gave up dancing.* Tried out for Arnie Zane and Bill T. Jones, stayed up nights, didn't get the job, and then the knee problems, and then social work school, after which she got married to somebody, some other guy. Oh, it wasn't worth going into. What was attractive became repulsive, this particular habit, this particular inhibition in the beloved, you were married and your heart was *in the freezer in the basement.* But all that weekend they painted the interior of the gallery, she and Gerry, that was a good weekend. The disappointments from later on never interfered with the memory of washing paintbrushes and rollers with Gerry, holding his hands under the faucet. His hands: long and narrow, fingernails incredibly short, the hair on his hands strawberry blond. All this, his hands under the faucets, the big soft part at the base of his thumb. If she had these hands, fifteen years later, in her own hands, if she had back her youth, she knew she would prize these things in a way she hadn't then.

The exhibition? The opening?

It took a few moments to sink in. They were huddled in the doorway, in the glare of interior light, her guests. Two or three of them squeezed into the doorway, like Keystone Kops hastening into a comic interior. The paint job was semigloss. The bright illumination of track lighting and the spots that Gerry had erected around the ducts on the ceiling ricocheted from these blank walls. Across the space, into corners, back into the space, the glare of it. Blank walls. Exactly blank. Completely blank. Blank without interruption. As the first two guests lurched into the space, more were just behind, crowding behind them. It wasn't like every corner had been swept clean. M. J. could see that colony of dust bunnies, making its way, as always, from the heating register under the bay window into the center of the floor. But it was the walls that arrested everyone. Whiteness of the white walls, absolute blankness of the display, absolute poverty of ideas contained in it, M. J. could feel it even where she stood, the moment where each of the guests tried to evaluate whether or not they should consider themselves *suckered* by the gallery interior. By the implicit privation of the space. There was no exhibition. Or, at least: *no art.* The art at the Mad Son Electric Gallery *was the gallery,* was the fact of its presentation, was its concept, was its appearance, was its history, was its ambition. There was a discouraging silence, while each of them made his or her way past each of the dividers that separated the exhibition space, looking, making sure there wasn't some tiny, postage-stamp-sized *statement* somewhere that might account for what they were *not* seeing.

Gideon was the first to get the drift. By exercising the powers vested in him as a doctor of philosophy in mathematics, he found that the piece of art that most fascinated him was the table on which the case of wine sat, still in its box. A pair of sawhorses with a door across the top of them, a sheet thrown over the whole thing, bottled wine on top. *Meaning is usage, after all. Right? An interpretation of a gallery, not a gallery itself. You rope it off, but the ropes themselves are the artwork. Something like that. I can get behind it. Let's drink.* A good preliminary theory, anyway, unless it was the people contained in the gallery who were the show, a bunch of youngsters from the Mile Square City of Hoboken, NJ, who had come through intersecting routes, to be here, at this moment of disappointment. M. J. stood at the mirror by the front door, attempted to fix her makeup. There was Gideon and Lori, and the three locals — musicians, one of whom had once played bass for Yo La Tengo. There was her cousin Nicky Jarrett, who never said *boo,* his girlfriend of the week, called Annabelle. They all made themselves comfortable. *The ancient crushed grape* flowed from a decanter.

Gideon acted as steward for the event, carrying the first and second and third bottles around, pouring out their contents, mopping up the overturned glasses.

Later, with the sprawl of them sitting on the floor laughing, drinking out of plastic cups, she roamed out onto the step. There were two strays now. One of them was Gerry.

two

Late in every possible way. Late to engagements major and minor; late when it was crucial to be on time; late when it made no difference; late when lateness was clearly his fault; late when he was at the mercy of others; late in the mornings (for having slept late); late in the evenings (for having stayed up late); late to the birth of his godchildren; late to the World Series game, *that October classic;* late to movies, notwithstanding trailers; late to plays; late to job interviews; late to the doctor and dentist; late to dates and romantic escapades; late when remorseful about lateness; late when careless; late when happy, late when sad or impervious to feelings, increasingly late, and it had always been that way. He was always leaving someone, arms folded, irate, in a lobby or on a street corner. He'd even been late to his *accident*, that frivolity of kids in their twenties. He'd waited until later, a decade later, after giving up on New Jersey, before finding himself on a stretch of interstate between Brattleboro and Northampton, on a rainy autumn afternoon, at dusk. *He'd been drinking sure.* His was a flying car. He swerved onto the shoulder, gravel percussive in his treads, and then the car lifted off, and there was a blissful moment of flight, too brief. The front tires struck earth and his car began to negotiate the fields of New England, rolling lengthways, like a steed getting friendly with the mud, three or four of these gymnastic tumbles. Inside, alone, upside-down, right way around, *a game*. It didn't leave him time to think of his death, although death was a possibility. How were the cars behind him accounting for this sequence, in which a rental car plunged off the road into a meadow? What did they think as this rental car rapidly approached a majestic American linden over near some cows; wasn't it clear that he would frontally strike the American linden, now, scattering the cows, and what did those cars back on the interstate think. There was nothing to do but strike the tree. His aloneness was poignant to him later: if none of the cars on the interstate skidded onto the shoulder, to offer help, well, there would be no one to acknowledge his *last end;* there was barely time for conjecture as the car was tele-scoped by the tree, and his arm, his left arm, the arm with which he wrote diary entries and scribbled doodles that a quack therapist had once called *evidence of a fine, questing mind,* his left arm was pinioned by the engine when the engine came up into the front seat of the rental car, pin-ioned between steering wheel and engine, when the air bag failed to inflate. He fractured his arm so multiply that even a half-dozen invasions by eager surgeons couldn't alleviate his suffering. *We can give you ninety percent movement, defi-nitely.* He had fifty percent movement. And there were pieces of aeronautically perfected metal in there now. He had an elbow made of plastics, a titanium humerus, bone grafts in the radius and the ulna, and *pain all day.* Pain in the morning, pain in the evening, pain when he slept. He hadn't known anything about pain until a state policeman with an infernal apparatus pulled him from the wreckage. The arm hung from him sideways as if it were the *right* arm and he had wrongly assembled himself with right attached to left side. Pain commenced. Medication commenced (Percocet, Percodan, Dilaudid). Now there were two things that were chronic in his life, namely, lateness and pain.

It wasn't a story he *told*. In fact, the accident enraged him, especially the retelling of it. The necessity of medication enraged him. The lackluster sympathies of acquaintances enraged him, their troubling cases of tennis elbow, their arthriscopic interludes.

On the other hand, there were tales of the past worth remembering. There were consolations in memory. There were narratives of things lost. That party at the Fosters' house, for example. In Darien. The Fosters' *house?* It wasn't a house. It was a *mansion*, and the Fosters — though you wouldn't know it from Nick Foster, whose only distinguishing characteristic was an inclination to set things on fire — went as far back in American history as America went back; there was a Foster who was the law partner of Button Gwinnett or Roger Williams; there was a Foster on the bridge in the battle for Concord and Lexington. And Nick Foster's grandfather had made a lot of money in millinery, hydroelectrics, espionage, some grand American business. He'd made a lot of money, and they had this mansion, and outbuildings next to it, for the butler, the cook, the maids, the groundskeeper. They had a river that meandered through their yard. *Stream* was the more appropriate term, maybe even *creek*. The creek had a waterfall on it. He couldn't believe it, back when he was a teenager, that anyone had so much money that they were allowed to *own a waterfall,* and horses, too, and miles of trails. So many miles of trails that there were always kids wandering around there. He had taken Lynn Skeele to the Fosters' property to woo her, though no wooing was done; instead they exchanged stories of the past, that raw material of all present association, lies about the past, false memories, hyperboles, concentrations of remorse. He miserably frequented trails with Lynn Skeele, boasting that he had shot things with a twenty-two-caliber rile. As if a twenty-two could impress Lynn. On the contrary, Lynn knew what all residents of Gerry's neighborhood knew: his surname was Abramowitz. In a town full of Burnses, Sutherlands, Talmadges, Griswolds. He was Abramowitz. He was Jewish on his dad's side and he didn't wear a *yarmulke,* but he sure didn't wear Lacoste shirts or L. L. Bean either. Lynn Skeele didn't want to hear about it, the kind of stuff that won you friends in Young Adult novels. He grew up skeptical. His skepticism was a seedling in the old forest behind the Fosters' mansion, and Lynn Skeele and the others might have wiped out this seedling of skepticism with a little kindness, but instead they fed and watered it. He was Abramowitz.

It was no particular honor that he'd gotten invited to Foster's Halloween party. It was not evidence of diversity in the matter of invitations. Foster invited every student in their class. All the sophomores and juniors at the day school. And he invited the kids on his street, Brookside. Most of the kids from the school didn't want to come to Darien to go to a Halloween party. A lot of them were from the next town over. They had mischief in their own neighborhoods. They soaped windows on the hospital in their own town.

Gerry Abramowitz's mother had theories about Halloween. Her maiden name was Callahan. She was a psychologist.
She argued that, according to recent monographs on the
subject, Halloween was a counterproductive American holiday tradition, inherited from Druids and other pre-civilized
groups, one which encouraged *liberty hysteria* among children of the upper-middle class (the term, of course, derived
from the *Diagnostic and Statistical Manual,* third edition),
itself a dangerous condition of lawlessness upsetting to children even as they coveted it. *Liberty and security are at opposing ends of an essential continuum, and security is important
enough in the ego formation of children that liberty should
be tightly controlled in order to create and nourish feelings
of safety.* The real ghouls depicted in Halloween outfits, in
masks, his mother argued, were the ghouls of lawlessness
residing in young people. When faced with drugs, explosives,
incendiary devices, pint flasks, premarital sex, well, children
of the suburbs began to panic, to beg for regulations, *for
maximum-time allotments for television-watching, for cur-
fews, and so forth.* His mother went further. The most popular costume of the Connecticut region was the *vagrant.* The
bum, as the young called this sinister figure. And who was
this archetype? He was the children despairing of themselves, of course, of their place in affluent civilization. He
was their feelings of homelessness and dispossession writ
large. The windows that got soaped, the shaving cream in
the mailboxes, toilet paper in all the trees, *liberty hysteria,*
an upsurge of the stratum of destructive fantasy that must
be suppressed in a democratic society if it wished to func-
tion securely, equitably, peaceably. Gerry's mother therefore
concluded that the Fosters' party was an affront to commu-

nity standards. Gerry had no business being there at all, but his father had the final say.

Party, blessed word, blessed state, thank God for parties, for ounces of dope, harder drugs. That hippie shit, that vestigial *tune in, turn on, drop out* business that mainly expressed itself in sleeping overnight in front of record stores until concert tickets went on sale — this was horse shit. And yet *partying* was a holiness. It survived even a squabbling over music. A little squabbling at a party was a good thing. A fistfight over a *billiards table, drinks flung at a girl, someone's car stolen, beds of parents befouled with teenage bodily fluids.* Get the intoxicants together! Night had descended! So his parents loaned Gerry their Jeep, because other parents were doing it too, and he was driving it over to Foster's place, though he could have walked; this was his mother's negotiated compromise: *I don't want you walking miles in the dark and the cold on a night like this.* His father intervened, at last, *Let the kid do what he wants. I could swear you were a kid once, too.* Looking up from the day's most active trading. Gerry exploited this gap in consensus, procured the car keys, drove.

There was one kid he would know well at the party, Julian Peltz. Peltz was of the persecuted faith, too, Gerry was sure. He was of the wanderers on the globe. But Peltz would never answer any questions about it. A cloud passed over Peltz's face when Gerry asked, *Is your family German or Polish, or what?* Peltz was not noteworthy in any way. He wasn't good in school, wasn't good at sports, wasn't extracurricular, didn't play chess, had only one record: a scratchy copy of *Classical Music for Young People,* conducted by Leonard Bernstein. He was a guy in school whom people liked all right but with whom they would stop to talk only if unobserved. However, a subject on which Peltz was really well informed was *human sexuality,* and that was why Gerry liked him. Since his own mother was a mental health professional and every discussion on any subject was laden with doctoral revelation, Gerry couldn't stand talking to her about sex, *Honey, I know that you're expressing your need to individuate, but it's important that you understand my authority and allow me access to your bed and your underthings when I am in the process of cleaning your room. And furthermore, Gerry, I need to know about how much information you've gathered in your social network on the issues of the erotic drives. Can we have an honest dialogue about this?*

His social network consisted mainly of Julian Peltz. At lunch, at school, Peltz constructed quizzes. *You know what frottage is, right? It's really cool. Like you're on a bus, okay. You're on a bus and it's really crowded, crowded with girls, let's say. And there's no room left to sit. You're going to the big game and you're on this bus, with all these girls, and you know you could just sort of brush up against one of those girls, while she's standing there, you brush up against her using the lower part of your torso as the targeting mechanism, right? And then everybody clears out of that end of the bus and bingo, you get a seat. It's really easy!* Gerry antiphonally replied: *You are totally fucked up.* Nevertheless, he had an alibi when his mother entrapped him and demanded if he knew what *protection* was, or how a girl's menstrual cycle fluctuated, or the precise location of the clitoris. Peltz had explained all this to him, over the years, had given him a package of rubbers. There'd also been the instruction of

Mr. Smith, school psychologist, of whom everyone said *he touched students inappropriately.* (Peltz: *I'd just about pay someone to touch me inappropriately. How come I always get overlooked when the inappropriate touching is going around?*) Mr. Smith recently slipped a rubber on a banana for the tenth grade kids. Gerry knew about protection. Gerry had ideas about love. Gerry was therefore able to rebuff his mother's theoretical overtures. Meanwhile, Peltz: *Today I'm going to tell you about a particular taste of some guys, which is how they like to go down between their wives' legs during the time of the month, when . . .* Or one day it was necrophilia, and how Peltz said that necrophilia was a perfectly reasonable *lifestyle choice,* especially since it only required the consensual input of one adult, so what difference did it make? *Victimless crime!*

Often Gerry would show up at school, late, and kids would be loitering out front, getting ready to go to their first classes, and he'd see Peltz a hundred yards off, talking to a tree or to a dog or to a chipmunk, probably on subjects such as double-digit inflation or Jimmy Carter's *adultery of the mind.* No one noticed Peltz's loneliness. If Peltz neglected to show up for school, it would have been weeks before anyone would have inquired. He was a library assistant, it was true, and probably, eventually, people would have had trouble checking out their library books, but, at the same time, he was of such diminutive stature that he was almost invisible behind the counter in the library, and Gerry wasn't sure anyone really knew Peltz was there. They probably believed the checking-out procedure was automated. The line would back up, if he vanished, and people would demand copies of *I Never Promised You a Rose Garden* and

A Separate Peace, and there would be library complaints, because Peltz was dead.

Loud popular music emanated from the Foster house. The Californian idiom, *soft rock*, like a perfumed glob of used toilet tissue or a sample of imitation American cheese food product or meatless chili. He liked the crass stuff coming out of England and New York City, where people couldn't play their instruments very well. But *soft rock* was no surprise here. Peltz was standing at the edge of the driveway poking dead leaves with a stick. His absurd ringlets, about which he constantly complained, could not be combed down. He was dressed the same way he always dressed, in the regulation *nondescript corduroy trousers and blue pullover sweater.* So much for the costumes of a Halloween party. Gerry was careful to lock the doors of the Jeep. Somebody's car would get rolled before night was over. Its canopy would be crushed. And allowing his own parents' car to be crushed would be a sign of *adolescent pathology,* and he would be grounded until receipt of his first social security check.

— You're late, Peltz said.

— Nice costume.

— I'm a White Anglo-Saxon Protestant, Peltz replied.

— Lots of thinking went into that.

— What are you?

Gerry, too, wore *nondescript corduroy trousers,* matched with a navy blue turtleneck.

— I'm a lupus sufferer.

Peltz mulled it over.

— They look just like everybody else, Gerry said.

— What about the skin problems?

— The turtleneck is covering my rash. I'm telling you, we have hopes and fears just like you do.

Another car pulled up. Parked on the lawn. Out of it came a procession of attractive girls, more girls than should have been able to fit in a Honda Civic. Amazingly, these classmates were also wearing *nondescript corduroy trousers. But with frilly blouses.* They paid no attention to this pair of boys, these interlopers of Eastern European extraction secreted in the shady grove of the Fosters' yard. The girls themselves disappeared in and out of shadows of oaks and maples on their way across the enormous lawn. As if these sylphs were the muses of his fantasies and daydreams, Peltz announced that he had a plan for the evening. *In order to make the party more happening. Multiple conquests,* he elaborated. *Like see that carload of girls just got out here, well, there's Nancy Van Ingen, heir to the Weyerhauser paper fortune, at least I think her dad is somehow involved with those paper products, paper towels, and next to her, that's Bernie Cooper, a Rockefeller through an aunt, her family goes back to the dawn of time, which was when her family rented out the space on cave walls for the guys who did the cave paintings. They were already going to France for vacations, see, and they cornered the market in cave walls. Next to her is Annie Winningham. Annie's great-great-grand aunt owned the boat where the Boston Tea Party took place, actually sold tea to protesters at a huge markup, and that's not all. Lots of them are inside, heiresses, women who'll rule the world, Gerry, they'll rule the world. They're related to the kings of all different countries, they're related to the kings of Monaco and Estonia and Macedonia and Bhutan, and one of them is actually the God Queen of Krakatoa, no shit, these girls, they're coming to this party expecting that something memorable is going to happen, that there's going to be a surprise, because it's Halloween, and even though these women will probably figure out later on that really they'd rather be with* other heiresses, *not with the guys they're supposed to marry, well, eventually they'll get married anyway so that their fortunes can be given away to kids instead of to charitable foundations. We still have to be ready to offer them the stuff that they need, Gerry, we have to be able to tell them, look, we have pot, we have booze, and we're ready to teach you what premature ejaculators on the football team won't be able to teach you how to, you know, experience it, feel the whole thing, feel the feeling called love. But that's what we have to be able to do. We know all there is to know about love. We know everything. That's what I'm saying, Gerry. Heiresses of Fairfield County, they're here for us.*

Gerry didn't believe a word of this speech, but it was made more impressive by the sight of the Fosters' mansion, which loomed in the distance. Up over the rolling hill just ahead was the sand trap where the foster patriarch once practiced his chips and putts, back before liver disease. Gerry sprinted to the edge of it, out of the sheer enthusiasm for sprinting on a night in October, but at the lid of the trap he almost tripped over a *body.* Sand billowed. He tumbled to the side of the trap. It was Lyle Hubbell. Wearing the obligatory *nondescript corduroys,* of course, affixed with a few patches, a T-shirt, a denim jacket. Lyle Hubbard, completely unconscious. Expressions of shock issued from Gerry, instinctively, at the insult of this corpse. And yet it was consistent with Hubbell's character that he was here. Hubbell failed all the tests of human company. And he was always *sneaking beers.* It was said that the diet sodas that Hubbell frequently carried around school were actually filled with intoxicants. He was even rumored to have his own distillery out in the woods, by the retirement facility next to the school. Since, in this tableau, there was a six-pack of pull-tab Millers in Hubbell's left hand, and a couple of loose cans nearby, prejudice on the matter of his condition was justified.

— Bodes well, Peltz remarked.

— I almost kicked him in the head. You know, head injury leads to a lifetime of impulse-control problems.

— We could put a sign up. *Teenager trying to escape from feelings of isolation, use caution.* People would steer clear.

Next, on the landscaped walkway, the goldfish pond, brightly illumined with subaqueous lamps. The pond was in season, too, because the color of the fish, their unearthly orange, was a near match with the pumpkins, actual and plastic, that were strewn widely across the premises. The fish were demonic, possessed. Casting off their usual lethargic demeanor, they streaked from end to end in the little pond, as if unfed or disturbed by pressure from without. Perhaps it was the fact that two teens, Steven Dodge and Eloise Falk, were sitting in one end of the water, the pond rippling well above their waists, ruining their outfits. They talked calmly, as though it were the most natural thing in the world. Julian Peltz wished them a good evening with exaggerated felicity. They looked up briefly.

— Definitely talking about sex. He's claiming that he really loves her deeply and that it will be really meaningful for him to express the depth of his profound love for her in this special way. And she's stuck. If anything, she's more into it. Abramowitz, let's be clear. Guy and a girl, getting wild, it's the girls that are driven to a frenzy. That's why all those other girls, like Nancy Van Ingen and Polly Firestone, they need men like us, who can offer them the real experiences of love.

— So we head off in different directions, each with our really bad social skills and we try to get these girls interested in us, and then later we compare notes?

— Brilliant.

— If you say so.

Foster's greyhounds came bounding out of the orchard on the west side of the main house. Freed from lethal injection, they had reservoirs of energy, in accordance with which they were cantering from the gazebo where Nick Foster had once pretended to hang himself. One of them paused, by the parked cars, to lift a leg on a Mercedes. Then off toward the house again. Gerry and Julian didn't have time to reflect on the immediate need for shelter from these marauders, because the dogs were immediately surrounding them, snouts low to the ground as if bent upon retrieval of their primeval mechanical rabbit. In lead position, a whippet, ribs multiply protruding, kicked up divots on the magnificent lawn, moist from the rain that month; in second position, but gaining, since the whippet seemed to be tiring, was an Irish wolfhound, a tall example of the species, too, close to four feet, a mighty hound with a blood-curdling grin, which just then veered around Peltz, before vanishing into darkness at a full gallop; in show position, the Fosters' exotic pharaoh hound, a breed brought to Spain during the Saracen invasions and later exported abroad, thus a dog as old as civilization, *in third place, yes, but exerting enormous pressure on the leaders!* Look at him nosing on the wolfhound! He could almost sniff the underside of the larger dog's tail! *Rest of the pack several lengths back, an afghan, a borzoi, three of your traditional Anglo-Saxon greyhounds. Banking around the house, they poured it on, heading for the home stretch, frolicking in draperies of mist!*

They were heading for the next property over, probably, which was not a private residence, but, rather, the grounds belonging to the Cherry Lawn School. An *alternative school,* noteworthy for its accumulation of boys with long unwashed hair and acne who dotted the front steps of the administrative building smoking cigarettes. Gerry's mother thought the school was *fabulous,* because it was so much like a minimum-security penitentiary, but apparently it didn't make any money, and was therefore doomed. Moreover, the Cherry Lawn School was a *zoning nightmare,* and it provided *known drug addicts* with an address at which to receive shipments of *controlled substances* which they then passed on to *impressionable young persons of Darien.* There was a tennis court in front of the Cherry Lawn School upon which no one had ever, to Gerry's knowledge, played a single set of tennis. There was a tetherball court with grass growing through its tarmac. The young men of Cherry Lawn, meanwhile, were like the greyhound starvelings of the Foster Mansion and Plantation, and they fed these animals with whatever institutional food was offered at the Cherry Lawn School, Swedish meatballs, salisbury steak, chicken teriyaki, pizza squares, tuna casserole, minute rice. One of the greyhounds was called *Warren G. Harding;* one was called *Zachary Taylor,* one was called *Franklin Pierce.* Gerry was pretty sure there was also a *William Henry Harrison* and a *Millard Filmore.* In this way, the young men of Cherry Lawn learned about the less-well-known presidents, as it was these presidents who most interested the Fosters, a family bent on assembling a complete set of presidential dogs. What breed would you choose for James Earl Carter? Miniature schnauzer?

Gerry and Julian arrived at the house itself. As you know, George Sheldon, historian and popularizer, described the house in his *Artistic Country Seats,* dwelling at some length on its *effect of length and lowness; the finishing of the great hall in immemorial pine. Next to Dutch doors of the south side are transomed English basement windows. Above the mantel in the parlor sits a large hood supported by four brackets whose intervening spaces each show a lion triumphant in relief,* and so forth. Designed in the Shingle Style by Lamb and Rich in 1885, not long after their completion of the Hinckley commission on Long Island. The Foster home betrayed its influence. The main entrance at the end of the walkway required passage onto a luxurious porch that sleeved the residence on three sides: the den, the dining room, the hall, the parlor, and the pantry, where the most magnificent face of the porch, fitted out in unavoidable rattan porch furniture, overlooked the Fosters' Illyrian waterfall. But here, where Gerry stood, in the front, was the intended entrance. However, no one answered when the two of them called at the front door. There was the warbling of a convex piece of vinyl, Linda Ronstadt, distantly. They pushed their way inside. The screen door swung shut behind them as if controlled from the spirit world. The hall was lit only in candles, but not the sort that you got in a dozen box at your department store. These were altar candles from northeastern Protestant churches, where Gerry had occasionally been as a young boy, during the interval in which his mother attempted to give him *a range of denominational experiences,* so that he would better understand *the social ideology* of his peers, so that he could better make up his mind later in life about *the contested space of American spiritual experience.* What he figured out during this period was that the dispossession of American Judaism was native to his spirits. He was a Jewish boy. He ascribed to the religion of a people who didn't belong anywhere, unless you counted the promises on some mystic scroll. Gerry's United States of America was a Jewish country, because it was a nation of people cast wide, like seed cases, in some awesome planting, broadcast upon gales.

He grew accustomed to the trembling candlelight, to the stillness of the main hall, to the conflagration likewise dancing in a walk-in fireplace there, and then he noticed that there was a *headless man in the foyer.* A man holding his own head. A man wearing clerical garb of Puritan faith, holding a bloody head with stump under one arm. A specter who now broke the silence in an eerie and familiar voice to speak to the two of them.

— You aren't wearing costumes either? How come nobody's wearing any costumes? It's Halloween. Don't you kids have any fun? The whole *point* of Halloween is to wear a costume.

The groundskeeper. Gerry knew his son. The kid was an athlete, the Platonic ideal thereof, a halfback with a strong need to assault others. This kid only had one eye. Nate, that was this kid's name, would show you his eye socket, too, pin you down in some corridor, if he really wanted to intimidate you. He'd wanted to intimidate Gerry a number of times, so now Gerry knew exactly what an eye socket looked like: the surface of Mars, pinky-yellow with red irrigations, much adorned with encrustments and green slime. The same information was confirmed by a friend of a friend of a friend who had also seen it. Everybody talked about Nate's eye socket. And maybe the dismembered head that his dad carried under his arm, tonight, with the *fake blood* all over it, was an evocation of the part of Nate's dad of the day when he had to come back home one afternoon to find that the boy *had lanced a baby blue,* playing with a plastic sword ordered from a cereal manufacturer. Or maybe it was just that Old Man Foster preferred his groundskeeper to wear a ridiculous costume on Halloween, indicating class difference, even though Nick Foster had no interest in costumes at all and didn't want any kind of costume party. Mr. McGloon, the groundskeeper, had the cassock up over his *actual* head and was therefore peeking through the space between buttonholes:

— Your friends are already leaving, I think.

— We didn't see anyone leaving. We saw some girls *coming in,* Peltz said. Julian often contradicted persons of authority, even when it was inadvisable to do so. It made Gerry want to get the hell away from him sometimes.

The headless clergyman, weary from labors, sank onto the divan beside the fireplace. He pointed, wordlessly, to the three porcelain bowls that were laid out, with cheesecloth draped across their mouths, on a Shaker sideboard. Though the main hall was noteworthy for its absence of activity, Gerry nonetheless glimpsed the retreat of a pair of toe shoes near the top of the great staircase. Candles trembled anew. A pedal steel guitar shivered in the backdrop of the distant Linda Ronstadt album.

— This is the part where we touch the cold pasta and it's supposed to feel like brains, Julian said. — Or is it pasta that's supposed to feel like intestines? Or Jell-O that's supposed to feel like a liver, right? I can't remember. Anyway, it's foods you'd find anywhere. You're meant to believe they're guts.

— Just go on in, McGloon said wearily to Peltz. The groundskeeper's flushed visage now protruded from the neck-hole of his vestment. He gazed away from the boys, through the window by the divan. Across a colonnaded porch.

Peltz nodded dismissively. And then he uttered the words that would become pivotal in any midlife recollection of the Fosters' Halloween party. — I'll be right back. *Nature calls.*

He gestured in the direction of a theoretical half-bath under the staircase, as if he already knew the layout. In the sinister light of candelabras, space and design were in the eye of the beholder. Sure there was a bathroom, next to that *secret passageway* there. And maybe this door, to the right, led to the dining room, maybe not. He would wait for Peltz there. Was this the true location of the party then? Was this to be its epicenter? It was a question asked across the recent decades of polite society with increasing vehemence. Parties, according to most celebrants, had to have a centermost emanation, a spot of perfect celebration, over and through and above the *hang-ups and put-downs* that always threatened a party. A popular theory indicated that the center of the party was always identical with a particular person — Danny Henderson, for example, the guy from up the street who never took anything seriously. Not even one thing. Henderson had never been known to make any utterance but that it was at the expense of some poor classmate. When you were with him, you had best not take anything seriously either. By this hour, Henderson would have cast off his regulation outfit; he would be wearing only the bearskin rug from the parlor next door, like Marianne Faithful during the Stones bust. He would be *mooning* kids from the debating team. Therefore, according to this first theory, *the center of the party was a particular person,* and all good times were his or hers to execute, as puppeteer works the strings of marionette. Yet a competing theory held that *the center of the party was always a room.* The room, for example, where two guys were reciting entire recordings by a certain British improvisational comedy troupe. Passing a joint between them. Everyone was laughing. *This isn't Argument! This is Abuse!* Or maybe the room where a snaking line of white girls attempted to do a version of a dance entitled the Bus Stop to the Linda Ronstadt recording or to its successors. Any of the rooms in Grasslands, which was the name of the Foster residence (there were some good jokes about that!), was liable to be the center of the party, because they were all impressive spaces. However, according to yet another theory (this elaborated by a minor writer of the Prague School), the center of the party was neither inherent in person, nor in place; it was located, rather, in *mood.* As it happened, the mood was frequently *intoxication,* the obliteration of day's cares in the here and now of drink. Genuine Miller Drafts were stashed in an additional refrigerator, in the basement, by the billiards table. Children loitered there. Think of the feeling of a thirteen-year-old, forbidden by his uptight folks to consume any such fermented beverage as he reached into the refrigerator for the first can. His algebra homework far from his mind. The difference between *compliment* and *complement* far from his mind. The Emancipation Proclamation far from his mind. He was at the center of the party, because he was *intoxicated.* And it was good.

Meanwhile, the fourth and final theory of *party topo-graphics* held that the center of the event was *unstable,* was always *elsewhere from where you found yourself,* no matter the room, the mood, the company. A seeker of the center of the party was according to this theory never at the center of the party himself or herself, by definition, and all party-goers, by definition, were seekers of the party. The essence of the party was *migratory, impermanent, provisional.* You felt you were *there,* at the party, your glass was newly filled, and right across the undulating sea of witnesses you saw a teenager with whom you knew you were destined to have exquisite romance — her eyeliner like the lines in Picasso drawings, just as certain, just as enduring — but as you began to cross the room, knowing that this was the place and this was the time, you began to feel the center of the party spiraling away. The party tacked upwind, came about. Suddenly, you were lost. Suddenly, you were having a con-versation with Glen Dunbar about standardized tests. *What's the best model for taking standardized tests? Do you think it's best to rule out one of the questions definitively, and at what point? Or should you really try to work out each answer before you give up on a particular question?*

But Gerry was alone and therefore certain that he was missing whatever it was he was supposed to be experienc-ing. He was in the Fosters' dining room. The table, draped in a white silk tablecloth, was laden with confections. Not with the individually wrapped Tootsie Rolls or two-packs of Devil Dogs or Twinkies, boxes of Dots, holiday servings of Jujyfruits, M&M's, Mars bars, Snickers, Three Musketeers, Charleston Chews, Bazooka Joe gum. No, the table was piled high with *baked goods,* with eclairs and cupcakes and

Tollhouse cookies. Repulsive. Who wanted to eat *homemade* crap? Nick Foster had probably hacked up rhinoviral gobs into the batter, laughing, before stirring vigorously. On a silver serving tray, however, Gerry found a single bottle of German imported beer. *How had it come to be here, this German beer, illegally proffered to minors, and why did it seem to be the solution to the difficulties inherent in the Fosters' party?* The chairs had been removed from the table, to permit party-goers to circulate, but there were no party-goers. At least until Dinah Polanski crawled from under the table, drunk.

Dinah Polanski. She already wore bifocals. Behind her spectacles, the lenses of which resembled bulletproof Plexiglas, her eyes wandered in contrary directions. And yet even wall-eyed Dinah was wearing the obligatory *nondescript corduroy trousers,* along with a gray cardigan sweater from the Land's End catalogue. In her case, the look was *fashion abomination.* Dinah had apparently donned it in imitation of Nancy Van Ingen and her crowd. She had not arrived at her outfit through the adventure of personal expression. Maybe it was the fact that Dinah was hefting an extra eight or ten pounds and had dun brown locks that ruined the effect of her reliable and understated garb. And beyond the fashion problem there was the further deep historical indignity that Dinah had been following Gerry around Fairfield County, turning up as regularly as a Connecticut raccoon, since they were six years old. She'd been trying to get his attention for some reason, even when, because of his unremitting neglect, it was self-destructive to do so. Her motives were unclear. In the last year, however, these efforts had been focused almost exclusively on recounting for Gerry the intricacies of a certain science-fiction novel entitled *Dune*. In the present instance, Dinah launched in immediately with only the briefest introduction —

— I was over next door, and I noticed that they had all the books of H. P. Lovecraft. And Edgar Allan Poe. Stories of Poe, and also the works of H. G. Wells. I like all of those books. Just really wonderful, you know? Then I noticed that they had a copy of *Dune*.

Dinah's face was aglow, and close to his now, as he attempted to work a church key on his imported German beer. Gerry backpedaled to achieve a requisite conversational twenty-four inches of distance from Dinah's rheumy face, and so that he might prevent salivary driblets from showering upon him, but as he retreated she followed, always closing in to a range of twelve to fourteen inches, a distance more frequently associated with conversational styles of the Mediterranean nations. He could see a patch of dermatitis on her brow. She was in need of a cream of some kind.

— *Beyond a critical point within a finite space, freedom diminishes as numbers increase.* That's Pardot Kynes, first planetologist of the planet called Arrakis. . . . He dies in a landslide. Well, the House of Atreides, you know, comes to this desert planet, and there's only these worms, gigantic worms, miles long, and these smugglers and their spice. The spice is called *melange*. And there's this tyrant. Baron Harkonnen.

Gerry found himself against the east wall of the dining room, against the *throne* that Lamb and Rich had helpfully built for Nicky Foster's great-grandfather when he sat at table, and Gerry actually climbed up onto this *high seat*, as described in the plans for the house. He repeated words he had used before, *Sure, yeah, great, I'll definitely read it,* while plotting to flank Dinah, the clamorous science fiction commentator, and make for the door, but then a really awful thought hit him. Since Dinah was the first girl he had spoken to here at the party, and since he had already agreed to a competition with Peltz having to do with conquest of as many girls as possible, *did this not imply that he needed to attempt some kind of seduction* of Dinah Polanski?

An enumeration of the girlfriends of Gerald Callahan Abramowitz up to this moment is now essential. Happily, this history is brief, because in spite of Gerry's reputation for amiability, he had little experience with the fairer sex. Ginny Williams, for example, who lived up the block, was really good at weaving. This is what his mother said, *Ginny Williams, she's a sweet kid. Her mom says she's crazy about weaving.* Ginny also drew pictures of insects. The two of them had nothing to talk about, though they had often shared rides to school. She had never watched a baseball game even once. She had a permanent excuse from physical education because of scoliosis. She had a pet rabbit. Gerry had never seen Ginny's neck. It had never been displayed. Perhaps she was a lupus sufferer. Her wrists were lovely, though. Like carvings of ivory. Anyway, he had asked her to *go out* with him, when he was thirteen, because he had heard from older adolescent males that this was what you were supposed to do. You were supposed to ask this particular question of girls, though he had no idea *where he would go with Ginny* if she said yes. He was very nervous when he posed the question. She was too. They were in front of her mailbox. Ginny Williams, with her beautiful coppery hair, yanked the mouth of the mailbox open and looked in. Closed it. Yanked it open. She would have to take time to think about his question, she told him. He was surprised at the warmth this exchange heated up in him. Then she started to cry. *Why are you crying?* He said. *I never expected anybody to ask,* she said. She retreated into her house. And never did reply.

Later, there was Lisa Talmadge. He had liked watching Lisa Talmadge play soccer, but he never really got to know her. Lynn Skeele rebuffed him, as described above. Susie Harris was sweet on him in band. She offered him cigarettes during breaks. He played the acoustic bass, quite badly. She played trombone. In spring, band adjourned. She had urged that they swap instruments. But he had no embouchure. Later, on a trip to Jamaica with his family, Gerry had met a girl at the pool. When you're an only child, you meet kids at the pool. Every day, at the pool, she was there, in a green French bikini. Anne, surname unknown. She was incredibly smart in addition to being beautiful. She lived in Scarsdale, which, by ten-speed bicycle, was far away. There was a common theme to his encounters with these girl schoolmates. He suspected it had to do with his Ashkenazi gene pool. Late at night, he suspected this, though his father lectured him contrarily, *My kid is not going to let this stuff get him down, correct? My kid is going to persevere.*

— *The Fremen were supreme in a quality the ancients called "spannungsbogen,"* that's what Muad'Dib says. He's this guy . . . His name is Paul. He's just a boy at the start of the story, but then he gets chosen, you know. First he's the

(199)

duke of the house of Atreides, after his dad dies, and then, well, he sort of goes after the post of emperor of, you know, the universe.

— Did you memorize the whole book?

— I've read it a bunch of times.

Upstairs, Linda Ronstadt came to an end and was replaced by the Eagles. *Desperado, when will you come to your senses?* An appallingly blond girl whom Gerry had never seen before peeked into the dining room so fleetingly that in recollection, it was more like a head floating into the space than anything else. Was she wearing a tutu? Or was it a lie of remembering?

— Dinah, can you just step back like one foot?

Dinah Polanski blushed horribly, as though he had stumbled upon a *core failure* in her short life and probed it callously, without respect. Yet at last she stepped back into the North American conversational range. What a relief.

— Frank Herbert was living up in the Oregon area, she said, — working as a newspaper reporter, and he had this vision of what humans would be like when Old Earth, that's us here, you know, with our energy crisis, took off into, you know, into space. Must have been really something. One night he was writing advertising copy for ladies' hats, and the next night he knew about Arrakis, the wasteland. It's kind of romantic, I think. You have your home on this planet Earth, this little polluted dump, and you imagine your future home, a desert planet, out in space. It's romantic.

Gerry was uncertain whether this observation of Dinah's, in the backwater of the dining room, was coincidence — *two teenagers in a room will inevitably begin talking about love and its idioms, no matter the manifest content of their conversation.* Was she secretly trying to tell him something, at last, trying to incite to the surface any recumbent possibilities? Maybe that spot under the table where she'd been hiding led somewhere, to a mattress. Since Julian Peltz never showed up after going off to *drain the snake,* Gerry had no choice but to presume that *the romantic* was the goal of the Halloween party. After all, love was the scariest thing. Love was the uncanny force that people recoiled from on Halloween. They made these costumes to stave off things and people who proposed the responsibilities of love. So Gerry seized the initiative. *Who cared if Dinah had really thick glasses, because when she smiled she actually conveyed, you know, enthusiasm, which was pretty rare, and in contact lenses she might look kind of good, actually, like when she talked about things that actually interested her.*

— Dinah, want to kiss me?

An eternal and unbearable instant lingered between them.

— Are you trying to fool with me, Gerry Abramowitz? Because I'm not like all those kids at your keg parties and at your football games.

— I wasn't —

— Because even if I followed you around when we were in grade school doesn't mean anything now, because we're older, and maybe we have other things to think about, like getting into good colleges. I'm not going to squander valuable time having meaningless encounters with boys. I'm going to think about early applications to the Big Three.

Gerry began to apologize, but in the midst of this apology the sliding doors to the library, on the north face of the dining room, swung back, as if according to plan, and with this coincidental opening, feelings of relief pulsed vitally in him. And Dinah said, *I want to show you what the book looks like,* and Gerry understood now that *the book* was in this instance an ideal category. Not the particular novel by Frank Herbert, but *the book* itself, the notion of the preservation of impressions of the past, the book as Ark of the Covenant. He couldn't return in the direction he had come. That was timid. He had to continue pursuing the essence of the party through the house, and it was okay to take his imported German beer with him. Therefore, it was the library to which he came next, and the amazing thing, considering that Fosters' old man edited some magazine featuring think pieces about the corrupt labor movement and the moral bankruptcy of the Left, was that the entire library was composed of rack-sized spy novels. Mysteries. Maybe an odd title on the theory of backgammon. Must have been hundreds of these paperbacks. Thousands, maybe. Dinah was his companion as he strode across this threshold, and immediately he could hear Foster's dad discoursing on subjects relating to *Our disgraceful abandonment of the Shah in his hour of need, and likewise the inability of the American people to understand the aims of our involvement in Asia, the urgent need to oppose the dark purpose of the Eastern bloc wherever it arises.* He was holding a drink, Foster's old man, and wearing a tweed jacket, khaki trousers, white dress shirt, paisley bow tie. He was gesticulating with one of those *extra-long cigarettes* that was about to deposit its payload of ash on the floor. Gerry expected that Old Man Foster, in laying out his Cold War policy doctrine, would have adults as his audience, but there were no adults in the room. Instead, Nick Foster's dad was talking to two guys playing *Pong,* that Pleistocene video game. There was an enormous television set in one corner of the den and these two teens were so deep into the couch there that they seemed to have been upholstered into it. The only free movement left to them was in their arms, by which they might control remotes.

For those not lucky enough to have experienced this old world home entertainment concept, it amounted to a *reductio ad absurdum* of all that is suggested by today's video age. Each of two players controlled a small white oblong parallelogram on a vertical axis of the black television screen. Each attempted to hit a small white square with his vertically scrolling parallelogram so that it would carom back at the other guy. If one player missed and the square traveled to the edge of the screen, he lost. Very simple. This particular match, taking place between the two silent guys on the couch, had been going on at great length, perhaps since puberty. The square, the metaphoric tennis ball, went back and forth between the guys on the couch, neither of them acknowledging one another, neither of them acknowledging Foster's old man, as he hypothesized: *The decision to pardon the former president was a dramatic misstep, because the former president needed to stay and fight the charges against him, in order to vanquish the resistance of our American youth:* the circular imperatives of Mr. Foster's soliloquy were ordered and ratified by the movement of the square back and forth and back and forth and back and forth and back and forth and back and forth and back and forth.

— Mister Foster, did you happen to see Julian Peltz come through here?

Gerry had seen cars out front. He knew there were people in here *somewhere*. He knew there were young people *having fun,* and he knew there was a lightness of conversation, *the riposte, the rejoinder, the one-liner, the shaggy dog story,* the tangle of flirtation that came with talk. Happening all around him, happening wherever he, the Jewish kid, was not.

— The young women are upstairs. And the young men are not far away. Please don't interrupt me now.

— Sorry, Mr. Foster.

He stepped around Foster's dad, as though the old man were decorative. A number of paperbacks were stacked there, and these toppled. Early le Carré novels fanned out around the older man's feet. Mr. Foster picked up one of them, and with expert aim flung it into the fireplace, which even now, as Gerry watched, seemed to be robustly fueled with Trevanian and Robert Ludlum. At the far end of the den was another recessed divan, carved out of pink marble, and while the present action took place, a pair of girls from school motionlessly slept. It was essential for Gerry to investigate this phenomenon. Who were those girls exactly, and would it count, in the enumeration of conquests, if he kissed one of them on the lips?

— Gerry. Wait. Don't you want to see it?

Dinah Polanski. The book. He'd almost forgotten. *How quickly attachments came and went.* Dinah had been scouring the east wall of the den, a small section of hardcovers, looking for her title. Now she had it. She was waving it like it was an illuminated spiritual text. She would bring *the message to the people,* though the people had shown that they were much more interested in yeast, fermentation, hunks of mutton, swords.

— Just a second, Dinah!

He leaned over the sleeping form of Sally Burns, for her identity was now apparent, Sally, who wore *nondescript corduroys and a pink turtleneck sweater.* She was blond. Didn't the Anglo-Saxons turn out any girl children who were not blond? A tiny strand of drool, like a synthetic fiber, fresh from its vat of plastics, stretched from her lips. With an index finger, Gerry interrupted this circuit of drool connecting lip and chintz throw pillow so that the moisture instead coiled around his index finger. He put this finger to his own lips, and the liqueur of Sally Burns's mouth was now upon his own. Her drool tasted like bubblegum. And celery. He composed the following love lyric, *I always thought you were really good in that mock debate that we had in history on the subject of abortion and I was proud that you supported a woman's right to whatever it was you were supporting, but I didn't say anything to you about it, because I'm just some guy. It's not my right to choose. I support a guy's right to get the hell out of the way when a girl has a decision she's going to make. It was kind of you to let me do the cross-questioning of that one ninth grade kid and it was great when he was so frustrated that he turned red. If you ever wake up, be sure to remember that I had all these compassionate thoughts about you.* Sally Burns's friend, Dee Maguire, was laid out parallel, in the opposite direction, head to Sally's feet, one hand draped over Sally's hips. Gerry had never seen anything so beautiful in his life, and yet gazing upon it he suddenly felt like a shoplifter, and so he made his way around the end of the divan, and from there toward the door to the pantry.

— Gerry!

— All this nonsense about our having come to the end of a consumer society! Mr. Foster thundered. — It's industry that has made this great nation what it is. Take the Panama Canal, a good example, and why we should have to —

Meanwhile, on the television screen in the den, the white square went back and forth and back and forth and back and forth.

Nick Foster probably had imagined a party in which lots of mischief was accomplished to the detriment of neighbors near and far, such that adult males of Darien would, in a collective rage, climb stepladders fetching down the toilet tissue from the willows and forsythia and dogwoods, all the next day, while their wives worked over the outsides of the french windows with a bucket of water and a scrub brush. Yet this vision would never come to pass. The *matériel* for Halloween's fiendish assault on norms and standards was still stacked on top of the countertops in the pantry. There were three or four cartons of toilet paper on the floor, two dozen cans of Noxema mentholated shaving cream, a box of Ivory soap bars. Gerry also noted that the Fosters possessed a number of sets of china, not just one set, but two or three, including stuff that looked old and hand-painted, perhaps in an Asian country where the folk arts flourished until recently.

He then stuck his head inside the kitchen, which was porcelain, magnificent, and spotless. A young black woman sat, reading a hardcover at a breakfast table. She paid no attention to Gerry, as if it were rude to pay attention to him, as if any interaction would be rude, and he knew, from experience, that he likewise was intended to be neglectful of this black woman, this *staff person*. This was just the kind of thing that they did here. This was the way *the system worked.* It's what she expected, it's what her employers demanded.

— What's it like working for the Fosters?

— Beg pardon?

— Working here. For the Fosters.

— What are you talking about?

— Just asking.

— You should mind your own business. Her voice diminished to a whisper. — Don't you worry about what goes on in somebody's house. You wouldn't understand anyhow.

— No, I would understand.

The black woman waved him off.

— I don't have time for nonsense.

He would have pursued his convictions, but beyond Gina the cook's fiefdom of particulars, he could see *someone* in the laundry room. A girl. A beguiling and comely *someone.* Girls, from a distance, and the heartbreaking recognition of their superiority to boys, their fleeting perfection, the curve of them in jeans, the strap of a bra peeking out of a V-neck sweater, smudged eyeliner; there was nothing more perfect than that smudge of eyeliner; a sobbing girl (perhaps disconsolate over some brutality of the world, the starvation of distant children, the local athlete with his neck broken); weeping girls; disheveled girls; girls at dusk; girls in autumn; girls running; girls laughing; girls growing up. Here was a girl, mostly concealed in a luffing of white sheets, bleached and dried, sheets in the process of being folded. What a relief from the tense atmosphere of the kitchen, from the Victorian stiffness of the parlor. This girl was trying to fold king-sized sheets, twice again as wide as she was, longer than she was. She was dressed in white corduroys, and a white velour turtleneck sweater, and so she was a vision of simulated virginity and piety. Polly Firestone. The mere syllables of her name summoned nobility. She could purchase multiple sets of new sheets if she wanted. And yet where on another day he might have resented it, the way in which the name Firestone summoned nobility, the way in which the name Abramowitz sounded like a name for a manufacturer of carpets. Nevertheless, there was a pathos to Polly's travails in the laundry room. Despite her inability to manage the king-sized sheets, she didn't seem at all resentful. In fact, she was radiant, and lit in profile, across planes of cheekbones, by candlelight, by a pair of hatless jack-o'-lanterns on a shelf with the powdered detergents. Polly Firestone, in a flattery of candlelight, resembled the heavenly servant girls of Flemish painting, and her every movement summoned the music of zithers from a heavenly bank of cumulonimbus clouds. There was a stack of a dozen sheets already piled on the dryer, folded in a number of oblong and imperfect ways. Now, as Gerry watched, Polly turned her attention to that most vexatious of folding responsibilities, the fitted sheet. Would the young heiress, of the Philadelphia Firestones, know the proper way to fold *a fitted sheet*? Would she at least be able to argue for the proper strategy in folding this sheet, having been informed through some matrilineal ritual that Gerry's mother would eventually write about for the *Cultural Anthropology Quarterly*, in a monograph that would include a note saying, *Jane is not the subject's real name. It has been changed at the insistence of her family.* Would Polly jam the fitted sheet up into a ball, as the vast majority of Americans had been doing for almost fifty years now, proving that class difference was not as rigid as it had once been? No, Gerry Abramowitz divined: Polly had known the theory of folding since birth.

— Hi there. Polly Firestone said, without looking up. — Aren't you a little late?

He manufactured the appropriate ennui. Boys of Darien avoided caring perceptibly about anything, the trajectory of that revolving plastic disk that was about to float into their hands, chased by a golden retriever. *It was routine.* Everything was routine. Boys could walk across a festooned gymnasium into the arms of a girl at a dance as though it were like getting the mail. Without evident feeling. He would attempt these skills, though they were foreign to him.

— Everyone keeps saying that.

He felt a powerful urge to reach for a laundry marker on the shelf above her, so that he might *connect her freckles.*

— Where is everyone?

— If you got here earlier, you wouldn't be asking.

The exchange might have been considered flirtatious, at least according to his mother's theory, *Disregard as Complex Coital Strategy,* but he decided that the tone was actually *intended* to be callous. *No festivity without cruelty.* Gatherings of kids always had their body counts. He thought of Peltz, and of the dwindling of his own opportunities at the party. Time was passing. He didn't even have any candy to show for himself.

— Will you kiss me? he asked.

— No. Why would I want to kiss you? What's your name, anyway?

— Gerry.

— Oh, yeah. Are you going to help me carry all this bedding?

— Must be a lot of beds.

— Have any gum?

He did have gum, of course. Sugarless, according to recommendations of four out of five doctors. She handed him the stack of flat sheets as she worked to finish up the fitted counterparts. And it was true, she had a perfect intention, a complete knowledge of tactics, if not the total command of muscular adjustments required for fitted sheets. Later in life she would be as good at folding sheets as the German army was at lockstep, but she would *pay* someone else to do it. The transfer of sheets into his arms, an important symbolic exchange, and the exchange of gum, these required the abandonment of his beer, unfinished, on a rattling Maytag dryer. Polly demurely snapped the gum as she led him down the corridor at the rear of the house. Through the pantry. There was an empty gallon crate of ice cream sweating off its remains that he hadn't noticed earlier. And in a door jamb, at the rear of the pantry, was the Fosters' *genealogical measuring station.* Nick Foster had once been *little Nicky,* who smiled recklessly and admired the action of waves on lifeless Long Island Sound. A wobbly line, made with Old Man Foster's golf pencil, indicated *Nicky, Age 6yrs, 6mos,* another, *Nicky, 8th birthday,* and so on, likewise for his little sisters, whom Nicky had terrorized into submission, and who were nowhere to be seen this night, Annabelle and Grace. With his mother, they had relocated, probably to the Fosters' *pied à terre* in the East Fifties. Next right was the servants' staircase to the second floor, half in shadow. He bolted up these back stairs, and Polly, who waited behind, likely understood the implications of these researches. Every kid who came to the Fosters' house had to know its complete architectural layout, as if this were to understand all American power, its implied antagonism of classes, its scant beachhead against wilderness, its scantly concealed totalitarianism. Polly was impatient, though. She sighed. Nevertheless, he embarked on his frolic, without leaving aside the fitted sheets, no, carrying them upon his person. There weren't enough lights at the top of the servants' staircase. There were low doorways, irregular construction, pneumatic tubes, messages from below. Spiders everywhere, their astounding constructions brushing against his brow, *spiders of finality, existing beyond the great net of causality.* The servants' rooms were closed, storage vaults, now, in which boxes of neglected dolls' dresses and cadets' uniforms moldered. An aunt had climbed these stairs in search of Christmas ornaments, several years past, never to return. But Gerry survived these adventures. But soon he passed into the larger corridor of bedchambers on the second floor. These were constructed on a plan of increasing size and ornament. The bed in each was more floral than the last. Simple double beds gave way to fabulous poster beds with too many pillows. (A subject on which subject his father had recently expatiated, *Interior designers make their margin on the pillows. It's a percentage of whatever fabric you use, so they buy these pillows, different kinds of fabric, put the pillows all over the goddamned place. Any time you want to sit down, you dislodge pillows.*) There were sheer window dressings, draperies as convoluted as the waterfall outdoors, there was wallpaper with velvet upon it. And a television in every room, a stunning luxury from Gerry's point of view, since his mother's regulations allowed him to watch two hours of television per week. No more. He was permitted to bank time from one week and use it toward the following week, but more frequently he squandered it spinning the dial.

All the screens in the various rooms of the second floor of the Fosters' house were tuned to horror films. From the sacred to the profane: *Bride of Frankenstein* juxtaposed with *The Fly*, *Plan Nine from Outer Space* with *Night of the Living Dead*. In every room, a huddle of teens, as if born there, each in his or her Platonic cave, taking in the broadcast fuzz of UHF stations. Gerry and his sheets swept past one of the guest rooms, where the mirror over the vanity captured in reverse the image on the screen, Raymond Burr, from the original *Godzilla*, rumbling in monotone about destruction and waste, *This is Tokyo. Once a city of six million people. What has happened here was caused by a force which, up until a few days ago, was entirely beyond the scope of man's imagination. Tokyo, a smoldering memorial to the unknown, an unknown which at this moment still prevails.* In the deep space of the mirror image, featureless backs of teenaged heads. For a second it seemed that these were the *faces* of his acquaintances, each a blank mask. In each of the six bedrooms, this stultified tableau. In each, Gerry stopped and inquired after the story:

— *I was a Teenage Werewolf*, said Margaret Nagle, stirring from anesthesia.

— The part where he's in front of the bathroom mirror? Gerry said. — You know, sprouting fresh growth on his —

— Didn't get there yet.

— Want to kiss me, Margaret?

And so on. From one tomb of lethargy to the next. The sheets, in his arms, grew heavy. Wherever he paused he leaned against a wall with this burden. As with any kid of his age, he avoided the *master bedroom*. Everyone knew that the beds of parents had been protected with hexes of witchcraft and if you glimpsed them, especially unmade beds of parents, you'd be turned into a *pedophile* or a *foot fetishist* or one of those guys who could tell you the weather on the day of Lincoln's inaugural but couldn't hold a job. According to blueprints of the second floor, the master bedroom was immediately to his left, here, at the top of the main staircase, where Danny Henderson and Pete Mars, the harlequins of his school, were engaged in a sinister prank. They were attempting to roll an enormous fire extinguisher down the main staircase of the Fosters' house. A chemical fire extinguisher. As Gerry came upon them at the summit of the staircase, Henderson, practical joker, tried anew to lift the extinguisher. This should have been feasible, since Mars was captain of the wrestling team. But no. There was a danger of herniated disks. They dropped the extinguisher again, narrowly avoiding crushing metatarsals. The thud of the cylinder on ancient beams rippled along the main staircase.

— Can I get by? Gerry said.

— Don't help us or anything, Abramowitz. What if we had an emergency? Sheets might come in handy in an emergency like this. You never know.

— I promised to get these sheets to Polly Firestone.

They twisted the extinguisher around, another revolution, and its penile hose swiveled and whacked Gerry on the back of his thighs as he passed. Henderson giggled, and then, in a heroic attempt to keep the rusted bottom of the extinguisher from fouling the maroon carpeting that ran the length of the main staircase, he put another tremendous effort into lifting it up. But, having failed to warn Pete Mars, he dropped it altogether and only Pete's body block kept them, Danny and Pete and the fire extinguisher, from plunging down the staircase.

— Make sure the pin is still in the handle, Gerry volunteered from higher ground. — Or you'll discharge chemical foam all over the house.

— Shut up, Abramowitz, Mars said. — What are you, fire safety commissioner or something?

— Yeah, Henderson said, — buzz off. This fire extinguisher's been in this house longer than you've been in this town. You jerk. If we wanted your opinions, we'd torture you.

Their remarks emboldened him to push by, to descend. His relatives had been oppressed in every country in Europe. His suffering was immemorial. And there was no time to dwell on slights, because Polly Firestone was waiting by the screen door that led to the porch, and, beyond the porch, into the woods. She'd disposed of her sheets.

— You're still late.

The forest beyond her, beyond the porch. Remember it? There used to be forest in Fairfield County. A little forest anyhow. Woodpeckers, foxes, turkeys, muskrats, skunk cabbage, trees thickly competing, trees for climbing. The idea of tree-climbing outlasted the moment when it was age-appropriate to climb trees, well into your teens, you were alone in the woods, in the density of woods, you had one eye out for the right arrangement of boughs that would reward your nimbleness. Conifers were better than deciduous trees. They dropped their mattress of needles below. Here was one, on this very spot, and before you could get too panicky about the heights involved, you were halfway up the tree, never mind stories you heard, that kid in the wheelchair, that one who fell to his death, you were halfway up the tree, with a view. Just like all those real estate people were always saying. You had a view. *I'm what I see, lord of what I see, I'll give it back sometime, I'll be a kid again, later, a kid who can't do anything right, can't say the right thing, can't put a sentence together or sing in tune, a kid cutting through the woods, on the way home, but for now I'm surveying the expanse of my empire.* That forest you remembered with a catch in your throat was itself a falling off from a prior forest, a primeval forest that was more grand, more impenetrable, more wild than the forest you remembered. The moment you sentimentalized, therefore, was a watered down conception of something more genuine that preceded your nostalgia by centuries. Thus, any true account of a suburban forest should feature a neglectful hunter grinding down a home-rolled cigarette in a bed of pine needles, underneath the very tree you once climbed, this after he has drunkenly fired thirteen times into a white-tailed deer fawn, to make sure it won't move anymore, after which he vomits during disembowelment of the animal. *It's for the best that we're out here pruning the weaker individuals of this herd today because otherwise these animals will get into your gardens and eat your landscaping.* The hunter grinds out the stub of the cigarette in the bed of pine needles, and the woods burn.

In the case of the Fosters' Halloween party, the ignition was different.

Polly led him out, down the steps, and then they were at the bank of the creek. All the time Gerry had spent in the house, in the consideration of its interiors, turned out to be time squandered. If the elusive center of the party could be said to be anywhere, according to the barometers like *median chatter decibels, recycling potential, egg fertilization percentages,* and so forth, it had to be here at the bank of the Fosters' creek. The waterfall — a dozen feet of glacial moraine with a froth overspilling it — emptied here, into the creek, which in turn went meandering into town, under the Boston Post Road, over by the Good Wives' Shopping Center (where they filmed *The Stepford Wives*), down into the Five Mile River, which emptied into the Sound, which emptied into the Atlantic. A host of the invitees from Nick Foster's Halloween extravaganza were gathered in this vicinity. On the banks. In a window upstairs, an LP skipped in its last groove. No one made an effort to correct it. *Carnival dynamism* was the eminent force: *The center of the party was wherever the greatest amount of intoxicants was located,* and therefore here was the missing keg, in the shallows of the river, where it was cool, and one of the girls who had come with Polly Firestone, Nancy Van Ingen, was knee-deep in the creek, handing effervescences of beer back to the celebrants on dry land. Nancy's beige corduroys were wet up above her knees. Her carelessness seemed oddly seductive. There was an expectation in the air, Gerry recognized, and it had to do with more than beer. Polly Firestone accepted his pile of sheets.

— Someone's going over the waterfall in a barrel.

— No, stupid. Her face obscured by a mound of bedding.

— What's your costume anyhow?

— Florence Nightingale, Polly said. — Or maybe I'm a fresh tampon. Just put on one of these.

— A sheet?

Was it a *toga event*? A stylized reenactment of ancient Greek civilization? Or a Mayan sacrifice? An impromptu surgery on the first volunteer? Or were these the chasubles of priests, these sheets? The hooded garments of southern prejudice? It wasn't that anyone was taking *off* their *nondescript corduroys,* but they were all beginning to wrap the Fosters' sheets around them, the doubles, the full-size sheets, the queens from the guest rooms. It was surprising that the kids would look this stupid. You almost never found that among teens. Their objection to being Young Republicans was that Young Republicans dressed badly. Gerry wasn't sure he could do it, wear a sheet, but his hesitation was interrupted, when Julian Peltz called to him, suddenly, from behind a nearby spruce. He could see one of Peltz's hands, plump, diminutive, beckoning.

— Be right back, Gerry said to Polly Firestone, who no longer listened. She was complaining to Lynn Skeele about having to read Henry James for English class.

If it was the last good conversation that Gerry Abramowitz had with Julian Peltz, it was still more troubling than good, as conversations were when friendships sheered apart. Julian led them out toward the winter tee of Old Man Foster's practice course. Peltz was quiet where he had been prolix; pale where he had been rosy; uncertain where he had been witty and sure-footed. Moonlight had brought some crisis down upon him. Though the front yard had been like a crowd scene from some movie, it was empty now. There were just the two of them, the boys of Darien with the unusual surnames. The groundskeeper had doused the flaming pumpkins, or switched them off. There were just a few exterior spotlights. If, in the backyard, facing the creek, adolescence was arriving at its crescendo, elsewhere in Darien it was *business as usual.* Two boys sat at the edge of a tee. They hadn't soaped a window, they hadn't rung a doorbell and fled, they hadn't beaten a smaller kid, they hadn't stolen anyone's candy, they hadn't smoked pot, they hadn't seen vampires.

— Time to tally up? Gerry said. He was trying to be good-natured, though the circumstances no longer seemed to merit it.

— Okay. Peltz hesitated.

— Let's see, I had a longish chat with Dinah Polanski. About some book she was reading.

— Dinah Polanski?

— I know, I know. Maybe it was going to be the best I could do for the evening. How did I know? Anyway, I didn't go through with it. She wanted to talk about college. I saw Sally Burns asleep on a *chaise longue.* She looked beautiful. She probably wouldn't care, since she was asleep, right, but I got all cowardly and couldn't do anything. Dee Maguire was with her too. I saw the Fosters' cook in the pantry. She didn't want to have anything to do with me. Who else? Polly Firestone. I used all my debating skill. Not a chance. She's sort of nice, though. So it was just a lot of conversations, really.

Julian didn't say anything. Because there was history between them, Gerry knew intuitively that Julian hadn't talked to anyone that night, hadn't said a word to any of the other kids, hadn't spoken to any girl, hadn't even attended the party, if attendance meant exchange of human pleas-antries. Peltz, when born, had been rubber-stamped *Lonely No Matter What,* so it seemed, didn't matter what crowd he was in, what birthday he was celebrating. He was sixteen years old, but he might as well be forty, or sixty-three, or eighty-five. The valleys of his character were carved out and he would dwell in them from now on. Gerry understood what it was like to have a friend with bad prospects, a homely friend. It didn't mean that you didn't care for some-one, just because they were awkward or had horrible acne or rarely went outside. On the other hand, it was also important to know when a friendship was *stale.*

You know the reputation that Percocet has, among major pain relievers, for nightmares, for taking the component material of dreams and distorting them? Part of chronic pain, when you are a sufferer thereof, as Gerry Abramowitz was, at the time of this remembering, had to do with *terror,* simple implacable terror, the atavistic memories like *I'm going to be left out on the steppe and fed upon by wolves, because of my disability.* If you closed your eyes, on this your present medication, to embark on the family of human experiences known as memories, you'd find that you were automatically inclined toward the most painful of these reveries, as if Percocet, especially when taken in excess of the recommended dosage, could relieve physical discomfort only by creating a mental analogue. So when Gerry embarked on this outline of the Foster's Halloween party, in recollection, a bleak outcome was assured.

— Want some of this beer? Julian had evidently found a can somewhere on his travels. It foamed liberally. He handed it over to Gerry for a sip. — I've been thinking, about the plan, and you know, about whether or not it was a good plan. And I decided that for me, it really wasn't that good. I had some reservations, about the rules and regulations of it, you know, even at the beginning. And not just because I don't think I ever, you know, just had a *conversation* with a girl. Not even once. Well, maybe once or twice, but not very many times. I should have known, but I realized pretty fast, you know, that I couldn't get anywhere near where you were going to get with all those heiresses, because you're a natural. You're a *guy*, and everybody likes you, and when you walk into a room, everybody's happy that you're there, even if they don't show it, and I thought about how the plan, well, it had a thing about it that wasn't on the level. You know, there was a part of it that wasn't entirely honest, and the more I was out here thinking about it, the more I was thinking that maybe I just couldn't live up to it exactly. Not in the way I thought it. Because I just can't talk to people the way you can talk to people, I get panicky, then I do something stupid. And so that's why I went out the window of the bathroom. It was a small window. There were a couple of kids outside who saw me come out, you know, out of the window, but I didn't want to explain. So I just ran off into the woods. I sat out there in the woods, and my ass got really moist, from sitting on stumps and logs. And that's how it went.

They passed the can of beer back and forth.

— So you're saying I went through a conversation where I asked Dinah Polanski to kiss me —

— You asked her to kiss you?

— While you were going out the window of the bathroom?

— Well . . . yeah.

— And why did you do that?

Some people had cruelties inflicted on them because cruelties had been inflicted on them in the past. These initial cruelties acted as magnets for further cruelties. You saw the wound, you saw the way victim loved the wound, you saw the way he tended it, how lovingly, how pridefully, and you couldn't do anything but reopen this wound. In fact, it was almost *pleasurable* to be the source of renewed trauma for this unfortunate, because it was something the victim knew well. Therefore, you were reassuring him even while you were inflicting discomfort. That's how it was. Friendships turned on a dime. When Gerry ran off and left Julian on the golf tee, on the winter tee, when Gerry went to join the throng beside the creek, he knew he was doing something awful, but the worst part was that he had no remorse. There was a total absence of sympathy for Julian. He couldn't even imagine there was an inside to Julian Peltz; he couldn't imagine that Julian wasn't just some ugly kid with braces on his teeth who worked at the library and who was constantly *hanging around.* It was only later that Julian's face, receding in sheets of night, floated through the heavy conscience of Gerry Abramowitz.

Wearers of sheets prepared for a migration across the river. Down into the river they went, allotheistic teens, shawls wrapped snugly around them, to ford the river called Tokeneke, rock by rock. Toward what goal did they proceed? Toward Nicky Foster, on the far bank, where, lubricated by the consumption of beers, Nicky was preparing to set fire to his familial acreage. In its entirety. He had a gallon of high-octane fuel, he had *a tiger in his tank.* His pyrotechnics would begin with a bonfire, and then it would engulf the entire far side of the river. The fire would have to travel almost a half-mile before it would hit the Goodells' house, over on Hamilton, and the local volunteer fire department would arrive *way before that*. There were spots where there were no trees anyhow, just underbrush. Nicky would call the fire department himself, since he had learned the number for all local emergency personnel in the pursuit of a certain merit badge in his troop of boy scouts. There would be no accident or injury. And his audience, *the faithful*, would be transfixed by his spectacle. The first drenched handful of them, one or two sliding down the muddy bank and back into the river, now labored to reach Nicky's side. They clutched at roots and branches, pulled themselves from the creek. Where was Julian Peltz now? In that forest somewhere, so that he, the other Jewish kid, could serve as the appropriate sacrifice for Nicky Foster's destruction of property? Tied to a sugar maple and left to broil?

It was like Gerry had offered him up.

Polly Firestone, her name afterward an emblem for the excesses of the Fosters' party, stretched out a hand to Nick Foster. Nick helped her up onto the bank. She fished in the pocket of her *nondescript corduroy trousers*, which she wore underneath a twin-sized sheet, for a disposable lighter, one made by a large multinational plastics corporation. Nick took the proffered lighter, struck it in the conventional way, and before the rest of the kids were even up on the bank, the bonfire *lit up that Halloween*. A pair of cedars was engulfed. Some eyebrows were singed. It was all more than they had ever expected in their short, careless lives.

His mother's paper on the circumstances of the party and the reaction to it in the local press, which later appeared in the *Deviant Behavior* biannual (volume nineteen, number two), turned on a line from Nietzsche, as Gerry interpreted it in his middle life, *Rejoicing monsters, they are capable of high spirits as they walk away without qualms from a horrific succession of murder, arson, violence, and torture, as if it were nothing more than a student prank.* His mother's prose was subdued, with a faint trace of wistfulness: *The songs of contemporary youth worship imaginary possibilities immanent in abstraction: liberty, heroism, revolution. But more practically the freedom connoted in these lyrics, to take the first example, is the abandonment of pregnant women, the abuse of controlled substances, the victimless defrauding of banks and financial institutions, narcissism, selfishness, untimely death. A lineage might be supposed in which libertarian and anti-governmental rhetoric leads directly to destruction of property and violence against parents and leadership entities. See below, e.g., deposition statements of defendants in what I'm calling the Foster Case. I have appended the testimony of one boy, sixteen, who I'll call Jim, accidentally injured when abandoned in the woods by other party-attendants. The reliable conclusion is that restriction is the proper environment for youth, that time of life that I can only refer to as ethical apprenticeship, during which privileges such as decision making and liberty ought to be controlled, abridged, even eliminated for a period of about seven years from onset of puberty, while ethical and normative values are instilled. Arrest, according to this formulation, is benevolent, arrest is compassionate, arrest is creative, arrest is planning for a serene future.*

Gerry Abramowitz, the legal aid lawyer of Providence, RI, insisted on the language of identity politics, Percocet or no Percocet. He was a *disabled person*, not a handicapped person. And yet, in his privacies he thought of the injured arm not as some poignant but surmountable problem, but as *the Claw*. Finally, all places and times of youth had been reconsidered until they did nothing but refer to or predict or reflect back upon the Claw. The useless and homely Claw. Everything was *Before Claw* and *After Claw*, and these places he was remembering that were *Before Claw*, they receded at an alarming rate, like distant galaxies, hurtling toward a margin of space where, in a dazzling and romantic nothing-ness, they were refracted distortedly: Connecticut, the years when he was in college, the year when he lived in Hoboken, in brief faux–connubial bliss, the following year in Jersey City, all *Before Claw*, before the weekend when he decided to go look at *autumn foliage*, alone, because he couldn't find any-one to go along. What a stupid way to spend a weekend. If he had just stayed home, if he had gone to see movies in the city, then he wouldn't be doubling up on Percocet, remem-bering. Everything *Before Claw* was better than the mono-chromes *After Claw*, everything was sweet and acute in the time *before*. Now daily life was pale and thin, a low-sodium canned broth; *After Claw* was all survival, how admirable it seemed to survive another year, to have a few friends whom you had known for a while. *After Claw*, shampooing was a victory; *After Claw*, knowing the birthday of two or three people was the height of solicitousness; *After Claw*, being polite to the guy in the dry cleaner up the block was very good; *After Claw*, thanking a bus driver was remarkable; *After Claw*, trying a new cuisine was adventurous; *After*

Claw, remembering to vote was heroic; *After Claw,* feeling like taking your clothes off in the presence of a lover was an astonishment (easier to watch television); *After Claw,* the Weather Channel was the most serene and beneficent institution on earth; *After Claw,* it was the little things: not having a malignant tumor, not having your hair fall out from chemotherapy, not having a colostomy shunt; *After Claw,* a child that didn't scream was beautiful, as was a geranium that blossomed once, a cardinal that landed on the feeder, a mailbox without a letter from the tax authorities, a cereal that tasted okay, a government that did something about poverty, a neighbor who told you to close your windows before a storm, a friend who wanted to talk, a sky that cleared. *After Claw,* everything that was *before* was better than it had actually been; *After Claw,* all was poignant and diminished and sad, and all that was *Before Claw,* was shiny, new, and lost.

When the sirens began, there was a rush toward the cars parked in the driveway. Sheets were abandoned on the lawn. The girl parked in the car next to him was from Wilton, it turned out. They barked out a short conversation. She was the one he'd seen before *wearing a costume,* a tutu of crinoline, in gold, with white tights. And he met her again six years later, in the city. Same girl. Three times he had idealized her, therefore, once when he was a kid and she was pleasant to him, once when he was in his twenties and she was leaving him, and once in this remembering. But when the carnival of youth left town, leaving behind its crushed Styrofoam cups, dismembered Kewpie dolls, and beer vomit, *idealism hitched a ride,* in its wake only symptoms of withdrawal. Remembering was a flu then, remembering was a sickness, and his skin crawled, and his nose ran, and his eyes were red, and he couldn't get comfortable with the temperature in this cramped apartment, and blowing his nose was impossible, because of his bad arm. The girl in the tutu drove a Volvo now, and picked up her own girl in a tutu from the ballet school in Larchmont; and if she called, he deferred to the answering machine, and failed to call back. It was a delirium of stories in which the principals never quite met, never quite spoke, never quite loved, never quite left. The pieces didn't match and never would, but the pieces were almost identical. The girl in the tutu pirouetted by him on his bad side, and he knew now, indisputably, he was older.

Wilkie Fahnstock,
The Boxed Set

The ground-breaking, innovative collection you have before you represents a new milestone in the history of Bankruptcy Records, a profound effort to bring to the public one of the representative lives of the last century. Bankruptcy here endeavors to depict Wilkie Ridgeway Fahnstock in a format he personally favored during his lifetime, that of the old-time magnetic tape cassette — in this instance a ten-volume anthology of such cassettes, one for each of the important periods of

Cassette One

(A)

"There was a lot of space in the living room to dance. My sister had a hula hoop and she used to put on Neil Diamond's early work, like 'Mother Love's Traveling Salvation Show.' Now she's a social worker in Sandusky, Ohio, with two kids named Jenny and Mike."

1. Peter Ilyich Tchaikovsky (1840–93), 1812 Overture, Op. 49, *edit.*
2. The Beatles, "I Saw Her Standing There" (1965).
3. The Beach Boys, "I Get Around" (1965).
4. Byrds, "Turn, Turn, Turn" (1967).
5. Bob Dylan, "Tambourine Man" (1966).
6. Otis Redding, "(Sitting on) The Dock of the Bay" (1968).

Fahnstock's life, including the Greenwich Years, the years in Kingston, Rhode Island, etc. (See our Website for more information about other exciting Bankruptcy releases, including collections like the home videos of the McGill family of Poughkeepsie, NY ("Shannon's fifth birthday party" "Summer Theater Production of OUR TOWN, 6/21/76!"), and the laser-disk-only release of STAR TREK EPISODES I REALLY LIKE by Rochester, NY, software designer Greg Tanizaki.)

The earthquake-like cannon blasts of Tchaikovsky's *1812 Overture* serve here as an éclat for Wilkie Fahnstock's 1964 birth, without complications, at the Mercy Hospital of Greenwich, CT. His mother, Elise Fahnstock (née Roosevelt) was and is a classical music *fanatic,* and Tchaikovsky and other classical greats such as Beethoven and Mozart were often spinning on the playroom hi-fi near Wilkie's crib, especially in renditions by Arthur Fiedler's Boston

7. Tommy James & the Shondells, "Mony, Mony" (1969).
8. Jimi Hendrix, "The Star-Spangled Banner" (1969).
9. Simon and Garfunkel, "Bridge Over Troubled Water" (1970).

(B)
"The most important place to learn about music was on the AM-only radio dial of my mom's station wagon. Cousin Brucie, Wolfman Jack, Imus in the morning, and Harry Harrison."
10. Bobby Sherman, "Julie, Do You Love Me?" (1971).
11. Three Dog Night, "Mama Told Me Not to Come" (1971).
12. Smokey Robinson and the Miracles, "Tears of a Clown" (1970).
13. Jackson Five, "I Want You Back" (1971).
14. Edwin Starr, "War" (1972).
15. Dobie Gray, "Fade Away" (1972).
16. Ohio Players, "Fire" (1972).
17. The Allman Brothers Band, "Ramblin' Man" (1972).
18. James Taylor, "Fire and Rain" (1971).
19. Looking Glass, "Brandy (You're a Fine Girl)" (1972).
20. The Brady Bunch Kids, "Candy" (1972).

Cassette Two
(A)
"Danny Berry's dad accidentally killed someone mountain climbing — roped snapped and the guy sailed into a gorge. Danny liked really dark stuff. He turned me on to

Pops. Later, when Wilkie briefly tried to learn the violin, he surreptitiously played records of the Bach Cello suites (the Pablo Casals recording) in an effort to fool his mom into believing he was practicing.

Tragedy struck in 1970, when Elise Fahnstock's marriage to Stannard Buchanan Fahnstock ended in acrimonious divorce — to the sounds of Simon and Garfunkel's *Bridge Over Troubled Water*. Wilkie's dad took to an apartment in New York City in order to date a succession of chainsmoking, high-fashion models. Poor Wilkie! Poor little sister Samantha! Suddenly the tender pop classics of the middle and late sixties — the sunny harmonies of the Beach Boys, the raucous fun of Tommy James and the Shondells, the prepubescent funk of the Jackson Five — gave way to the darker moods of early seventies "progressive rock" stylings. Wilkie, alone in his room (in a succession of split-level Tudor homes throughout the County of Westchester), was

Pink Floyd. I remember reading the lyrics to 'Brain Damage' and thinking it was really scary."
1. Gary Glitter, "Rock 'n Roll" (1972).
2. Deep Purple, "Smoke on the Water" (1971).
3. Led Zeppelin, "Black Dog" (1971).
4. Focus, "Hocus Pocus" (1972).
5. Traffic, "John Barleycorn Must Die" (1973).
6. Yes, "Roundabout" (1972).
7. Edgar Winter Group, "Frankenstein" (1973).
8. Elton John, "Philadelphia Freedom" (1973).
9. Alice Cooper, "School's Out" (1972).

(B)
10. Jethro Tull, "Skating Away on the Thin Ice of a New Day" (1974).
11. Emerson, Lake and Palmer, "Hoedown" (1973).
12. Pink Floyd, "Money" (1972).
13. Hot Butter, "Popcorn" (1973).
14. Genesis, "I Know What I Like (In Your Wardrobe)" (1973).
15. Mike Oldfield, "Tubular Bells" (1973).
16. The Who, "Baba O'Riley" (1971).
17. Electric Light Orchestra, "Roll Over Beethoven" (1972).
18. Moody Blues, "Legend of a Mind" (1968).

Cassette Three
(A)
"Had to hide my Kiss albums from my roommate in freshman year. But now I'm proud of them. These

contemplating the multiples of Rusty Staub baseball cards while the ominous chords of Mike Oldfield and Pink Floyd floated through his depressive consciousness on a monophonic Zenith brand "record player." Of course, the surge of *national drug experimentation* was also a part of Wilkie Fahnstock's adolescence, as with so many of his peers, and on cassette two (actually dubbed from a moldering Memorex ninety-minute tape found in an old summer camp foot locker), we see for the first time the "heavy" music of such acknowledged "drug" bands as Led Zeppelin, Alice Cooper, and the Moody Blues, especially as these portentous sounds vied for Wilkie's attentions with the simple easy confections of Elton John.

Now, as Fahnstock's parents shipped him off to the Phillips Academy at Andover, as Elise Fahnstock — newly betrothed to Fred Bolger, the reinforced-carton magnate — undertook a demanding career as Metro-

days, Kiss records sound really cool."
1. The Tubes, "White Punks on Dope" (1975).
2. Kiss, "Rock 'n Roll All Nite" (1974).
3. Lou Reed, "Sweet Jane" (1973).
4. Roxy Music, "Re-Make, Re-Model" (1972).
5. David Bowie, "Rebel, Rebel" (1973).
6. Queen, "We Will Rock You" and "We Are the Champions" (1976).
7. Ian Hunter, "Once Bitten, Twice Shy" (1976).
8. Sweet, "Fox on the Run" (1976).
9. The Who, "Squeeze Box" (1976).

(B)
"When I got older I started to learn to play Frisbee and hackey sack."
10. Bruce Springsteen, "Rosalita" (1973).
11. Grateful Dead, "Truckin'" (1972).
12. Bob Dylan, "Tangled Up in Blue" (1975).
13. Neil Young, "Cortez the Killer" (1975).
14. Joni Mitchell, "For Free" (1972).
15. Fleetwood Mac, "Go Your Own Way" (1975).
16. KC and the Sunshine Band, "Get Down Tonight" (1975).
17. Daryl Hall and John Oates, "She's Gone" (1977).
18. The Eagles, "Hotel California" (1976).

politan Museum docent, as Stannard Fahnstock relocated his consulting business to Marblehead, Mass., the collection succumbs to a brief infatuation with the dazzling surfaces of "glam" rock, characterized by the abundant makeup of bands like Kiss and David Bowie. (Fahnstock tried, at this point, to get a few other prep school chums interested in forming a band featuring fire-breathing and spitting up blood, but given his own character — bad hair combined with high grades, unflattering eyeglasses and a poor sense of rhythm — this plan was doomed from the start.) On the B side of cassette three, however, there's a precipitous turning toward the introspective, Californian singer-songwriter stylings of the seventies. Probably it was peer pressure. Probably it was the influence of his boarding school contemporaries. In any case, it's as if Fahnstock comes home across the big Atlantic puddle. Take it easy, dude! Skip trigonometry! Smoke a reefer!

Cassette Four

(A)

"*I knew this guy, Mike Frew — he went on to become a big lawyer for Greenpeace — used to wear dog collars and listen to the Stranglers. He broke in punk rock big for my school. Single-handedly. He had these dances featuring the Bee Gees and the Pistols albums.*"

1. Peter Gabriel, "Solsbury Hill" (1976).
2. Iggy Pop, "Passenger" (1977).
3. Elvis Costello, "Radio, Radio" (1978).
4. Sex Pistols, "Anarchy in the U.K." (1977).
5. Devo, "Satisfaction" (1978).
6. Stranglers, "Hanging Around" (1977).
7. Blondie, "Hanging on the Telephone" (1977).
8. The Police, "Walking on the Moon" (1979).
9. The Clash, "Safe European Home" (1978).
10. Sid Vicious, "My Way" (1979).
11. The Dickies, "Tra La La (The Banana Splits Theme Song)" (1979).
12. The Vapors, "Turning Japanese" (1980).
13. Plastique Bertrand, "Ca Plane Pour Moi" (1979).

(B)

14. Patti Smith, "Horses" (1976).
15. The Dead Boys, "Sonic Reducer" (1977).
16. Bee Gees, "Stayin' Alive" (1976).

Just as this easy-listening nationalism took root, however, there was *the shot heard round the world.* The punk rock explosion! The revolution! Wow! Safety pins! In the space of a few short months, Wilkie Fahnstock turned away from the soft-rock conventions of the mid-seventies entirely and embraced instead the anarchic celebrations flowing out of London's King's Row.

Meanwhile, after years of loneliness and romantic starvation in high school, and with only the simple addition of a diet of beer, speed, and filched prescription medication, Wilkie Fahnstock suddenly achieved campus celebrity as an oddball, *the guy with the Devo albums* — just as he was being expelled from Andover for curfew violations. So it was back to Mamaroneck High to complete the twelfth grade without a letter *in any sport.* (I can report here that Fahnstock did, however, finally manage to "cop a feel," as he put it, from Pauline Vanderbilt of

17. Television, "Marquee Moon" (1977).
18. Richard Hell and the Voidoids, "Blank Generation" (1978).
19. Talking Heads, "Warning Sign" (1978).
20. B-52's "52 Girls" (1980).
21. Ramones, "Rock and Roll Radio" (1979).
22. Sex Pistols, "God Save the Queen" (1978).

Cassette Five

(A)

1. Orchestral Manoeuvres in the Dark, "Enola Gay" (1979).
2. Peter Gabriel, "Games Without Frontiers" (1979).
3. The Cure, "Boys Don't Cry" (1980).
4. Patti Smith, "Rock and Roll Nigger" (1979).
5. Modern Lovers, "Road Runner" (1972).
6. M, "Pop Music" (1979).
7. Human Sexual Response, "What Does Sex Mean to Me?" (1980).
8. Klark Kent, "On My Own" (1980).
9. Pretenders, "2000 Miles" (1983).
10. dB'S "I Thought You Wanted to Know" (1979).
11. Rockpile, "Teacher, Teacher" (1982).

(B)

"I spent most of college drinking beer at the campus bar and buying clothes from that nice girl at the used clothing store in Newport."

Park Ave., NYC, a fellow Andover casualty, while in the next room her close-and-play mangled a copy of Blondie's "Heart of Glass." Oaths of eternal fealty followed.)

At home in Westchester, Fahnstock managed to parlay acceptable board scores and indifferent recommendations into an acceptance at the University of Rhode Island, a school which (according to atlases available to the compiler of these notes) was a mere road trip from the recherché and enigmatic Moonstone Beach of the Rhode Island coast. A known nudist bathing location! Fahnstock, with his beer-related paunch and excessive chest hair, was often a sight at Moonstone playing, with various nursing students, volleyball *en deshabillé!* The best music for nudism, at least in those days, was *funk*, and thus it blasted from the sound system of Fahnstock's car. We located, in the glove box of his 1982 Volkswagen Rabbit, a battered compendium of funk and "new wave" classics to

12. Funkadelic, "Hardcore Jollies" (1978).
13. Talking Heads, "Once in a Lifetime" (1980).
14. Brian Eno, "Kurt's Rejoinder" (1976).
15. Gang of Four, "Outside the Trains Don't Run on Time" (1981).
16. Public Image Limited, "Poptones" (1981).
17. Pere Ubu, "Dub Housing" (1979).
18. Blondie, "Rapture" (1982).
19. The English Beat, "Ranking Full Stop" (1979).
20. ABC, "The Look of Love" (1982).
21. R.E.M., "Sitting Still" (1983).

Cassette Six
(A)
1. The Replacements, "Unsatisfied" (1984).
2. Hüsker Dü, "Celebrated Summer" (1984).
3. Minutemen, "History of the World, Part II" and "This Ain't No Picnic" (1985).
4. Cocteau Twins, "Lorelei" (1985).
5. Dead Kennedys, "California Über Alles" (1980).
6. Violent Femmes, "Good Feeling" (1984).
7. Black Flag, "Slip It In" (1984).
8. James "Blood" Ulmer, "Are You Happy in America?" (1982).
9. Laurie Anderson, "O Superman" (1982).
10. The Smiths, "What Difference Does It Make?" (1984).

support the selections from this period.

In 1984, Fahnstock, turning aside the advice of his more liberal friends, and notwithstanding his countercultural personal habits, nonetheless voted in his first presidential election *for former California governor Ronald Reagan.* Proving that the G.O.P. can indeed be a big tent, he did not however endorse the conservative "hair" bands of the period — Poison, Ratt, Whitesnake, Loverboy. He concentrated instead on the nascent pop form known as "hardcore": the sound of the empty landscapes of the American plains, without Dolby noise reduction or compression. Dairy farms in foreclosure. Permafrost. Songs a minute long, played at four hundred beats per.

A period of retrenchment followed, featuring a flirtation with the local, NYC-related phenomenon called Rap or Hip Hop. Fahnstock learned of it at after-hours clubs, where he spent far too many nights during these summers in col-

(B)
11. The Beastie Boys, "Cookie Puss" (1982).
12. Run-DMC, "Rock Box" (1983).
13. New Order, "Bizarre Love Triangle" (1984).
14. Echo and the Bunnymen, "Never Stop" (1984).
15. Van Halen, "Panama" (1984).
16. Velvet Underground, "Jesus" (1970).
17. Bruce Springsteen, "Born in the U.S.A." (1983).
18. Michael Jackson, "Beat It" (1983).
19. The Feelies, "The Boy with the Perpetual Nervousness" (1979) and "On the Roof" (1986).

Cassette Seven

(A)
"Don't ask me about the mid-eighties."
1. Van Morrison, "Sweet Thing" (1969).
2. Bob Dylan, "Most of the Time" (1986).
3. Big Star, "September Gurls" (1972).
4. Yo La Tengo, "Five Years" (1984).
5. Chris Stamey, "Cara Lee" (1985).
6. They Might Be Giants, "Dead" (1984).
7. Victoria Williams, "The Holy Spirit" (1987).
8. Robin Holcomb, "Going, Going, Gone" (1988).
9. The Proclaimers, "I'm Going to Be (500 Miles)" (1988).
10. A.C./D.C., "Back in Black" (1978).

lege. Rap gave way almost immediately to various *artists from the past*, the Velvet Underground, Bruce Springsteen, Bob Dylan. And this organic past sustained him overland to rehab in Minnesota, where, *admitting complete defeat* (in Hazelden parlance) less than a month after graduation, he dogged female cocaine addicts and disdained a belief in God until transferred summarily to a halfway house in Queens. He then turned up briefly at confirmation classes at Greenwich Village's Grace Church.

A succession of bad day jobs gave way to a bad streak of *sobriety jobs*, as they are called in the *demimonde* of recovering types, at a succession of New York fashion magazines — in copyediting, and then fact-checking departments. At *Self*, for example, Fahnstock worked closely with beauty columnist Denise D'Onofrio, whose office beat box listed toward Janet Jackson and Paula Abdul, and whose gin and tonic he accidentally sipped at an Xmas party, scaring himself witless,

11. Hall & Oates, "You Make My Dreams Come True" (1984).

(B)
12. R.E.M., "It's the End of World As We Know It (And I Feel Fine)" (1987).
13. Elvis Costello, "I Want You" (1987).
14. Prince, "Sign O' the Times" (1986).
15. Captain Beefheart, "Low Yo Yo" (1973).
16. Metallica, "Enter Sandman" (1990).
17. The Cucumbers, "My Town" (1987).
18. Pogues, "Fairytale in New York" (1988).
19. Tom Waits, selections from RAIN DOGS (1986).
20. The Silos, "Let's Go Get Some Drugs and Drive Around" (1990).
21. The Feelies, "Sooner or Later" (1991).

Cassette Eight
(A)
1. Sonic Youth, "Teenage Riot" (1988).
2. Ciccone Youth, untitled instrumental from *The Whitey Album* (1988).
3. The Pixies, "Here Comes Your Man" (1990).
4. Jane's Addiction, "Stop" (1991).
5. Sugar, "That's a Good Idea" (1992).
6. Pavement, "Summer Babe (Winter Version)" (1992).
7. Syd Barrett, "Golden Hair" (1972).

such that he fled home on the PATH train to his sixth-floor walkup in downtown Jersey City, and didn't come out again for a week. When he did, it was to relapse.

Have we spoken already of the Garden State and its influence on Wilkie Fahnstock? Of its flat, Netherlandish aspect? Of the local bands of Hoboken? How in the cauldron of that old waterfront town he went through a sort of flowering of compassion for fellow man, however short-lived, as evidenced by his sudden, precipitous decision to take in rehab acquaintance Kristina Ruiz, fleeing at the time a pugilistic husband, so that the two of them might share that tiny space, Wilkie's apartment, *chastely, platonically,* until a furious row, after which Wilkie slunk home again to Westchester.

It was *back under the roof* of his stepfamily, two years sober, ashamed, unemployable, that Wilkie Fahnstock first saw the MTV video (measuring worthlessness by the amount of daily

8. Sebadoh, "Brand New Love" (1992).
9. Television, "Rhyme" (1992).
10. Slint, "Nosferatu Man" (1988).

(B)
"In 1991, I was living in the basement at home. I'd take out the trash for my mom. I had an idea for a screenplay. I was going to get a broker's license."
11. Nirvana, "Smells Like Teen Spirit" (1991).
12. My Bloody Valentine, "Glider" (1991).
13. Pearl Jam, "Jeremy" (1991).
14. The Pixies, "U.Mass" (1992).
15. P. J. Harvey "Rub Till It Bleeds" (1992).
16. Liz Phair, "Fuck and Run" (1993).
17. Sebadoh, "Spoiled" (1993).
18. Morphine, "In Spite of Me" (1993).
19. Vic Chestnutt, "West of Rome" (1994).
20. Dog Bowl, "Love Bomb" (1992).
21. Nine Inch Nails, "Head Like a Hole" (1992).

Cassette Nine
(A)
1. Nirvana, "Heart-Shaped Box" (1993).
2. Hole, "Doll Parts" (1994).
3. The Breeders, "Cannonball" (1993).
4. Offspring, "Genocide" (1994).
5. Half Japanese, "Roman Candle" (1989).
6. G. Love and Special Sauce, "Blues Music" (1995).

consumption of that channel) for a song entitled "Smells Like Teen Spirit." Another relapse ensued. However, his sheer delight in the movement of rock and roll fashion — in the direction of the so-called *grunge* music — revivified Wilkie Fahnstock enough to apply to law school, financed mainly by his reinforced-carton magnate stepfather. This plan lasted about one year (1994), as did Wilkie's marriage, contemporaneously, to law classmate Arlene Levy, of Scarsdale. On the occasion of their first anniversary, Arlene informed her own parents that Wilkie's refusal to study, his concentration on such disagreeable racket as The Shaggs, and his crack binges were unacceptable. Thus, Wilkie took an apartment by himself in Park Slope, Brooklyn, and began to write his roman à clef (untitled), of which, after six months, he completed thirteen pages. Applications to the writing and film programs of city institutions were to no avail.

7. Beck, "Loser" (1995).
8. Guided by Voices, "Goldheart Mountaintop Queen Directory" and "Hot Freaks" (1994).
9. The Shaggs, "Philosophy of the World" (1972).
10. Fly Ashtray, "Barry's Time Machine" (1995).
11. Smashing Pumpkins, "Today" (1995).
12. Stereolab, "Lock Groove Lullaby" (1994).

(B)
13. Soul Coughing, "Screenwriter's Blues" (1994).
14. Bad Religion, "Television" (1995).
15. Rancid, "Roots, Rockers, Radicals" (1995).
16. The Sixths, "San Diego Zoo" (1995).
17. Boss Hog, "Nothing to Lose" (1995).
18. The Innocence Mission, "Happy. The End" (1995).
19. Neil Young, "The Ocean" (1995).
20. Guided By Voices, "Atom Eyes" (1996).
21. Steve Earle, "Ellis Unit One" (1996).
22. Rage Against the Machine, "Bulls on Parade" (1996).
23. White Zombie, "More Human Than Human" (1994).

Cassette Ten
(A)
1. John Cage, "In a Landscape" (1948).
2. Frédéric Chopin, "Nocturne #1" (1839).

Bringing us to the present. The tale, then, of a confused, contemporary young person, a young man overlooked by the public, a person of meager accomplishment, a person of bad temperament, *but a guy who nonetheless has a very large collection of compact discs!* For this reason, Bankruptcy Records presents to you the music of Wilkie Ridgeway Fahnstock in his thirty-third year. The last WASP (one of them anyway), the last of this nation's culturally homogeneous offspring deluded enough to believe in the uniqueness of this cultural designation, a young man whose *beloved rock and roll* has finally apparently become a thing of the past, a quaint, charming racket from another eon. We present to you, ladies and gentlemen, the life and music of an undistinguished American!

3. U. Srinivas, "Saranambhava Karuna" (1994).

4. Frank Zappa, "Get Whitey" (1995).

5. David Lang, "Face So Pale" (1993).

6. Thurston Moore, from the soundtrack to HEAVY (1996).

(B)

7. Brian Eno, "Ikebura" (1993).

8. J. S. Bach, "Contrapunctus XIV," from DIE KUNST DER FUGUE (1750).

9. John Coltrane, "Stellar Regions" (1965).

10. Carl Stone, "Banteay Srey" (1992).

11. Aphex Twin, "1" (1994).

Production, Remastering, and Sequencing at Bankruptcy studios by Mike Hubbard.
A&R by Jules Hathaway.
Liner Notes by Rick Moody.
Special thanks to Wilkie Fahnstock, and the Fahnstocks of Mamaroneck, NY, and Marblehead, MA.
http://www.chapter11.com

Boys

Boys enter the house, boys enter the house. Boys, and with them the ideas of boys (ideas leaden, reductive, inflexible), enter the house. Boys, two of them, wound into hospital packaging, boys with infant pattern baldness, slung in the arms of parents, boys dreaming of breasts, enter the house. Twin boys, kettles on the boil, boys in hideous vinyl knapsacks that young couples from Edison, NJ, wear on their shirt fronts, knapsacks coated with baby saliva and staphylococcus and milk vomit, enter the house. Two boys, one striking the other with a rubberized hot dog, enter the house. Two boys, one of them striking the other with a willow switch about the head and shoulders, the other crying, enter the house. Boys enter the house, speaking nonsense. Boys enter the house, calling for Mother. On a Sunday, in May, a day one might nearly describe as *perfect*, an ice cream truck comes slowly down the lane, chimes inducing salivation, and children run after it, not long after which boys dig a hole in the backyard and bury their younger sister's dolls *two feet down*, so that she will never find these dolls and these dolls will *rot in hell*, after which boys enter the house. Boys, trailing after their father like he is the Second Goddamned Coming of Christ Goddamned Almighty, enter the house, repair to the basement to watch baseball. Boys enter the house, site of devastation, and repair immediately to the kitchen, where they mix lighter fluid, vanilla pudding, drain-opening lye, balsamic vinegar, blue food coloring, calamine lotion, cottage cheese, ants, a plastic lizard that one of them received in his Xmas stocking, tacks, leftover mashed potatoes, Span, frozen lima beans, and chocolate syrup in a medium-sized saucepan and heat over a low flame until thick, afterwards transferring the contents of this saucepan into a Pyrex lasagna dish, baking the Pyrex lasagna dish in the oven for nineteen minutes before attempting to persuade their sister that she should *eat the mixture;* later they smash three family heirlooms (the last, a glass egg, *intentionally*) in a two-and-a-half hour stretch, whereupon they are sent to their bedroom, until freed, in each case thirteen minutes after. Boys enter the house, starchy in pressed shirts and flannel pants that *itch so bad,* fresh from Sunday School instruction, blond and brown locks (respectively) plastered down, but even so with a number of cowlicks protruding at odd angles, disconsolate and humbled, uncertain if boyish things — such as shooting at the neighbor's dog with a pump action bb gun and gagging the fat boy up the street with a bandanna and showing their shriveled boy-penises to their younger sister — are exempted from the commandment to *Love the Lord thy God with all thy heart and with all thy soul, and with all thy might, and thy neighbor as thyself.* Boys enter the house in baseball gear (only one of the boys can hit): in their spikes, in mismatched tube socks that smell like Stilton cheese. Boys enter the house in soccer gear. Boys enter the house carrying skates. Boys enter the house with lacrosse sticks, and, soon after, tossing a lacrosse ball lightly in the living room they destroy a lamp. One boy enters the house sporting basketball clothes, the other wearing jeans and a sweatshirt. One boy enters the house bleeding profusely and is taken out to get stitches, the other watches. Boys enter the house at the end of term carrying report cards, sneak around the house like spies of foreign nationality, looking for a place to hide the report cards for the time being (under the toaster? in a medicine cabinet?). One boy with a black eye enters the house, one boy without. Boys with acne enter the house and squeeze and prod large skin blemishes in front of their sister. Boys with acne treatment products hidden about their persons enter the house. Boys, standing just up the street, sneak cigarettes behind a willow in the Elys' yard, wave smoke away from their natural fibers, hack terribly, experience nausea, then enter the house. Boys call each other *retard, homo, geek,* and, later, *Neckless Thug, Theater Fag,* and enter the house exchanging further epithets. Boys enter the house with nose hair clippers, chase sister around the house threatening to depilate her eyebrows. She cries. Boys attempt to induce girls to whom they would not have spoken only six or eight months prior to enter the house with them. Boys enter the house with girls efflorescent and homely, and attempt to induce girls to sneak into their bedroom, as they still share a single bedroom; girls refuse. Boys enter the house, go to separate bedrooms. Boys, with their father (an arm around each of them), enter the house, but of the monologue preceding and succeeding this entrance, not a syllable is preserved. Boys enter the house having masturbated in a variety of locales. Boys enter the house having masturbated in train station bathrooms, in forests, in beach houses, in football bleachers at night under the stars, in cars (under a blanket), in the shower, backstage, on a plane, the boys masturbate constantly, identically, three times a day in some cases, desire like a madness upon them, at the mere sound of certain words, words that sound like other words, *interrogative* reminding them of *intercourse, beast* reminding them of *breast, sects* reminding them of *sex*, and so forth, the boys are not very smart yet, and, as they enter the house, they feel, as always, immense shame at the scale of this *self-abusive cogitation*, seeing a classmate, seeing a billboard, seeing a fire hydrant, seeing things that should not induce thoughts of masturbation (their sister, e.g.) and then thinking of masturbation anyway. Boys enter the house, go to their rooms, remove sexually explicit magazines from hidden stashes, put on loud music, feel despair. Boys enter the house worried; they argue. The boys are ugly, they are failures, they will never be loved, they enter the house. Boys enter the house and kiss their mother, who feels differently, now they have outgrown her. Boys enter the house, kiss their mother, she explains the seriousness of their sister's difficulty, *her diagnosis*. Boys enter the house, having attempted to locate the spot in their yard where the dolls were buried, eight or nine years prior, without success; they go to their sister's room, sit by her bed. Boys enter the house and tell their completely bald sister jokes about baldness. Boys hold either hand of their sister, laying aside differences, having trudged grimly into the house. Boys skip school, enter house, hold vigil. Boys enter the house after their parents have both gone off to work, sit with their sister and with their sister's nurse. Boys enter the house carrying cases of beer. Boys enter the house, very worried now, didn't know more worry was possible. Boys enter the house carrying controlled substances, neither having told the other that he is carrying a controlled substance, though an intoxicated posture seems appropriate under the circumstances. Boys enter the house *weeping* and hear weeping around them. Boys enter the house, embarrassed, silent, anguished, keening, afflicted, angry, woeful, *griefstricken.* Boys enter the house on vacation, each clasps the hand of the other with genuine warmth, the one wearing dark colors and having shaved a portion of his head, the other having grown his hair out longish and wearing, uncharacteristically, a tie-dyed shirt. Boys enter the house on vacation and argue bitterly about politics (other subjects are no longer discussed), one boy supporting the Maoist insurgency in a certain Southeast Asian country, one believing that *to change the system you need to work inside it;* one boy threatens to *beat the living shit out of the other,* refuses crème brûlée, though it is created by his mother in order to keep the peace. One boy writes home and thereby enters the house only through a mail slot: he argues that the other boy is *crypto-fascist,* believing that *the market can seek its own level on questions of ethics and morals;* boys enter the house on vacation and announce future professions; boys enter the house on vacation and change their minds about professions; boys enter the house on vacation and one boy brings home a *sweetheart,* but throws a tantrum when it is suggested that the *sweetheart* will have to retire on the folding bed in the basement; the other boy, having no *sweetheart*, is distant and withdrawn, preferring to talk late into the night about family members gone from this world. Boys enter the house several weeks apart. Boys enter the house on days of heavy rain. Boys enter the house, in different calendar years, and upon entering, the boys seem to do nothing but compose manifestos, for the benefit of parents; they follow their mother around the place, having fashioned their manifestos in celebration of brand-new independence: *Mom, I like to lie in bed late into the morning watching game shows,* or, *I'm never going to date anyone but artists from now on, mad girls, dreamers, practicers of black magic,* or *A man should eat bologna, sliced meats are important,* or, *An American should bowl at least once a year,* but these manifestos apply only for brief spells, after which they are reversed or discarded. Boys don't enter the house, at all, except as ghostly afterimages of younger selves, fleeting images of sneakers dashing up a staircase; soggy towels on the floor of the bathroom; blue jeans coiled like asps in the basin of the washing machine; boys as an absence of boys, blissful at first, you put a thing down on a spot, put this book down, come back later, *it's still there;* you buy a box of cookies, eat three, later three are missing. Nevertheless, when boys next enter the house, which they ultimately must do, it's a relief, even if it's only in preparation for weddings of acquaintances from boyhood, one boy has a beard, neatly trimmed, the other has rakish sideburns, one boy wears a hat, the other boy thinks hats are ridiculous, one boy wears khakis pleated at the waist, the other wears denim, but each changes into his suit (one suit fits well, one is a little tight), as though suits are *the* liminary marker of adulthood. Boys enter the house after the wedding and they are slapping each other on the back and yelling at anyone who will listen, *It's a party!* One boy enters the house, carried by friends, having been arrested (after the wedding) for driving while intoxicated, complexion ashen; the other boy tries to keep his mouth shut: the car is on its side in a ditch, the car has the top half of a tree broken over its bonnet, the car has struck another car which has in turn struck a third, *Everyone will have seen.* One boy misses his brother horribly, misses the past, misses a time worth being nostalgic over, *a time that never existed,* back when they set their sister's playhouse on fire; the other boy avoids all mention of that time; each of them is once the boy who enters the house alone, missing the other, each is devoted and each callous, and each plays his part on the telephone, over the course of months. Boys enter the house with fishing gear, according to prearranged date and time, arguing about whether to use *lures* or *live bait,* in order to meet their father for the *fishing adventure,* after which boys enter the house again, almost immediately, with live bait, having settled the question; boys boast of having caught fish in the past, though no fish has ever been caught: *Remember when the blues were biting?* Boys enter the house carrying their father, slumped. Happens so fast. Boys rush into the house leading EMTs to the couch in the living room where the body lies, boys enter the house, boys enter the house, boys enter the house. Boys hold open the threshold, awesome threshold that has welcomed them when they haven't even been able to welcome themselves, that threshold which welcomed them when they *had* to be taken in, here is its tarnished knocker, here is its euphonious bell, here's where the boys had to sand the door down because it never would hang right in the frame, here are the scuff-marks from when boys were on the wrong side of the door *demanding*, here's where there were once milk bottles for the milkman, here's where the newspaper always landed, here's the mail slot, here's the light on the front step, illuminated, here's where the boys are standing, as that beloved man is carried out. Boys, no longer boys, exit.

Ineluctable Modality of the Vaginal

Arguing about Lacan's late seminars, about the *petit objet a*, or about the theory of the *two lips*, about the expulsion of Irigary, I think that's what it was, though I'm willing to bet most couples don't argue about such things, at least not after two or three margaritas, probably not under any circumstances at all, but then again we weren't really arguing about that, not about French psychoanalysis, not about the *petit objet a*, not about Irigary and that *sex which is not one*, but about some other subject altogether, it's always something else, that's what was making me so sad, how it was always some other subject, a subject that was bumped aside, some isolate, hermeneutical matter that I couldn't pin down in an Upper West Side bar while he was assuming his particularly vehement boy expression, a kind of a *phallocratic* face, or a *carnophallogocentric* face, a *politics of face simulation*, a phallic politics of facial deformation, it should have been about *finances*, this argument, or about the economic politics of sexuality, or about his inability to allow into debate the discussion of matrimony, which he always said was *a social construction of commitment, rather than a commitment itself,* and if I could agree with the liberating theory of contingency, *the contingency of committed relationships,* then I would see that this social construction of commitment was irrelevant, just something that magazines and television programming tried to hard-sell me, and it's not that I disagreed, at all, I understood that marriage had feudal origins and *was thus about bourgeois power and patrimony,* but I took issue with the fact that we could never even discuss the nuptial commitment, because if we did he said that I was assuming a *fascist totalizing language, a feminine language in the becoming of male totalitarian language,* and then he would start to drink to excess and his face would flush and we couldn't touch each other for a week or more, well, maybe it was on this occasion that I did say it out loud as I too had drunk or was just plain fed up, maybe I *raised my voice a little,* admitted that he was a *phallocrat,* that despite his seminars in Marxist aesthetics, or whatever, Walter Benjamin, women disgusted him, that the way he required the first and last word, the alpha and omega, was an oppressive thing, always the last word, always a dead stop, which was when he got going on some nonsense, on algorithms of the unconscious, on *Borromean knots, those psychosexual and linguistic constructs that are essential to the conjunction of language and consciousness, the gossamer moment of ontology, the knot that binds, the erotic, the feminine,* couldn't be untangled, couldn't be separated and formulated outside of feminine consciousness, these knots, a *girl thing, Borromean knots,* I don't know, up until then we might have found the spot where we agreed that we didn't disagree, and we might have listed the things we agreed on, a history that swept backward behind us, we agreed on being in that certain bar on the Upper West Side and, prior to that, we agreed on certain jukebox selections, Tom Waits or Leonard Cohen or Joni Mitchell if available, and, prior to that, we agreed on a sequence of semesters and vacations, ebbing and flowing, and prior to that, we agreed on moving in together, cohabiting, and, prior to that, we agreed on a certain narrative of our meeting, a narrative which spun out its thread in this way: both of us trapped on the subway one night when it rumbled to a stop between 96th St. and 72nd St., both of us reading, coincidentally, *The Lover* by Marguerite Duras, straphanging, talking and giggling during the quarter hour that the Number Two was hobbled in the express tunnel, the injustice of collapsed trains, it was sweet, and I asked for his number, because he was too shy to do the asking, or so we agreed later, and, in my black tights with the *provocative stylized tear,* he said, which was actually an accidental tear on the thigh, and in my gray miniskirt, which was only slightly racier than office garb, I was the one who was *ready to move,* ready to yield to some *subliminal discourse of romantic love,* we agreed on this narrative and recounted it periodically, refining and improving, *concretizing or reifying its artifice,* and he occasionally included actual passages from the Duras, blunt short sentences, claimed to have read these to me, to have read them aloud in the subway tunnel, as we hung on those straps, though there were no actual straps (it was a train that had only poles and transverses), and though I was actually reading Djuna Barnes, and later anyhow he always said that *the romantic was a destructive force,* responsible for all the worst poetry of the nineteenth century, responsible even *for the theory of Total War, because by extrapolation, there would be no war without the romance of the Empire, the romance of nationalism, the romance of purity doctrines,* he even said that he no longer liked Duras, whose idea of upheaval was *decadent, alcoholic,* still we wrote this story together, shared the quill, about a time when we had been irresistible, when we used to burst into one another's apartments eager to fling off *layers of fashion,* when we used to cry out, making use of that philosopher's stone of romantic mythology, *jouissance,* I admit it, that time was lost, and when in the singular precincts of our separate offices we tried to locate that time, that fabulous unity, it was as part of our intimate folklore of abundance, rather than a part of *actual experience,* and that was maybe the real argument, the one we didn't have in the Upper West Side bar, that was the *stiff breeze,* and our relationship was a Mylar balloon slipping out of a toddler's fist, helixing around and around up into the elsewhere of the musky New York City skies, landing distantly back in time, during the Sandinistas, during El Salvador, during Iran-Contra, fogbound in the dim past, we had loosed our balloon, even if all this simply made him furious because he always said that *I would not stay on a particular subject,* that was the problem, the culture of femininity asserted as its moral right a fuzziness with respect to meaning, *You're a sloppy thinker!,* I arrived at a point, he said, through a kind of labial circulation, *a vicus recirculation,* as Joyce said, meaning probably both *vicious* and having to do with Vico, but maybe viscous, too, as in labial, viscous, heavy with a heavy menstrual fluidity, *You won't stay on the point, you exceed and overflow,* he said, in the bar on the Upper West Side, in the seventh year of our entanglement, our Borromean knot, but I insisted that staying on the point was his way of dictating the terms of the discussion like arguing about whether *oval table* or *rectangular table* as preliminary to *détente,* and if he was willing to let the point vacillate, then maybe he would know *what it was like to be on my side of the negotiating table,* to be me as I was perceiving him, *overcoming in a flutter of jubilant activity obstructions of support in order to hold him in my gaze,* perceiving that he didn't care for me any longer, perceiving that we had come to the time in which it was probably right for me to engage the services of a good realtor, *No,* he said we were existing in *segmentarity,* but I said if he would let go of the point, and *wear my skirt,* feel the constriction of tights for the purposes of being professional without being provocative, being an adjunct without being a *castrating cunt,* as one guy in the department said of a colleague who didn't try to be a little bit sexy, if he could wear my skirt, he would understand how sad this was all making me, and this is why I was *on the verge of tears,* in the wood-paneled bar on the Upper West Side, though I refused to allow him to touch me as I cried, as I also refused to use tears strategically, they were just how I felt and I would not conceal it, they were *a condensation and displacement,* sure, but they required no action, and I was, it's true, a woman with a doctoral degree who *believed against all reasonable evidence that there must have been some justifiability to the Western tradition of marriage,* and who happened now to be crying, and who happened to be sad more often than not, who happened to have a striping of mascara on her cheeks, okay, but this only made him madder still, and there was a whole elegant spray of his logic about how *feminine language undoes the proper meaning of words, of nouns,* and that's when I said that *he had no idea what it was like, would never know what it was like, that all of his bright, politically engaged, advanced-degreed tenure-track friends would never know what it was like to be a woman, the fact of hips, cervical dilation, labia major and minor, childbirth, breastfeeding, hot flashes, premenstrual rage, an outside that is an inside, circularity, collapse of opposites, it was something that he would never know about,* and basically, I went on in my tirade, he secretly really liked it when I cooked, the percussive clanging of pots and pans, the poring over ancient texts like *The Joy of Cooking* or Julia Child, he liked to see me doing these things, and after I cooked there was always this stunning moment when the meal was done and the dirty plates and cups and saucers were teetering in a stack around us, in our tiny roach-infested kitchenette, there was this moment of arrest when he would feign a distracted expression, a scholarly absence, as if the life of the scholar were so profound that practicalities didn't enter into it, and it was then that I understood that I was supposed to do the dishes myself, the dishes were my responsibility, even though I had done the cooking, the same was true on the days when he climbed down from his *Olympian, woman-hating aerie* and deigned to broil a tasteless piece of fish, some bland fillet that he always overcooked, and I was still the one who had to do everything else and had to sponge down the table afterward, and I was the one who ended up making the bed, and doing the laundry most of the time, washing his fecund jogging clothes which I had to carry, reeking, to the Laundromat, and his streaked BVDs, and I was the one who ended

up buying the toilet paper, and I was the one who remembered to call his mom on her birthday, and I was the one
who wrote the checks that paid the bills that placated the
utilities who ensured that the electricity flowed into his
word processor and printer and modem, and, I told him, I
had done this in the past because I loved him, but that I was
thinking maybe that I didn't love him that much anymore,
because I didn't know how anyone could be so cruel as he
was, cruel enough to cause me to feel that I didn't know what
my point was, or that it was inappropriate of me to even
attempt to have a point, and yet as Irigary said, *The "elsewhere" of the feminine can only be found by crossing back
through the threshold of the mirror,* so, I observed again,
*the Dark Continent of the social order, you'll never know it,
you'll never know the possible world of the possible universe
of womanhood, this Oriental city-state that exists parallel to
your own stupid, unreachable, masculine world, you want to
tame it somehow and never will and you'll die never having
tamed it, femininity,* and the barmaid came around, and she
was wearing very tight jeans and a T-shirt that was too short,
purchased, I observed, at Baby Gap, so that her pierced
belly button saluted us provocatively, she was like some
teenaged toy girl, Hasbro waitress, she was the past of female sexual slavery, and in a moment of calculated witless-
ness he *gave her the once-over,* paused dramatically to look
at her breasts and her middle and the curve of her hips,
Another round, please, and, of course, this was the thrust of
his argument, as his argument always had a thrust to it, a
veiled entelechy, namely, that he was above domestication,
couldn't be bothered, still I had my teeth into him, and there
could be no distraction, as I would complete the argument,

and would be through with him or else have some other kind of resolve even if fluctuating, *Okay, then prove to me in any substantial way that you know what it's like to be a woman and what our experience is like here where the legislature insists on control over how we use our bodies, prove for one second that you have an idea about what I'm talking about because we are at an impasse here where you either have to be intimate with me or lose me, the way I'm feeling about it, prove that I haven't wasted years trying to have a conversation with a total stranger,* at which point in a stunning delivery of high affect, *a prepersonal intensity corresponding to the passage from one experiential state of the body to another,* on short notice, his own eyes began to brim with tears, as the next round of drinks came, even as he began to weep he checked out the barmaid's rear as she retreated from our booth, beginning with a theatrical sigh his story, *There's something I haven't told you about myself,* and I said, *You're kidding, right, because we have lived together for a long time and I have read your IRS returns and I have typed portions of your dissertation because you were too lazy to type them yourself and I have listened to you puking and cleaned the bathroom after you puked and if there's something more intimate than all that, some preserve of intimacy that I have not managed to permeate yet I'm going to be a little upset about it,* with an expression of dreadful but stylized seriousness, his crewcut scalp furrowing slightly, from the brow upward, and he admitted that it was true, that there *was* something he hadn't told me, a certain charcoal secret, a lost cat in the fringed outback of his psychology, and he said, *Think of human sexuality as a continuum with inertia at one end of it and satiety at the other, two ends that meet somewhere we can't see*, please not the language of the department office right now, could we try to keep this in the Vulgate, he ignored me: he was just a kid, scrawny, homely, no good at ballgames of any kind, last to be chosen when choosing up sides, happened to be friends with this one girl, the beauty of the middle school, theirs was the profane friendship destined to be crushed in the imposition of social order, something like that, when the mists of childhood receded once and for all she would have nothing to do with him, but in the meantime the two of them ate Twinkies in the lunchroom, traded secrets, as all these athletes and student councilors came by to talk to her, ignoring him, unless to inquire about aspects of algebra or geometry likely to turn up on an examination or pop quiz, *would it be all right if they copied from him,* they were ambling by in order to impress Sapphira with the fruits of their boyish masculinity, they would perhaps say hello to him then, and then later in the halls it was if he were masked or cloaked or otherwise concealed, outside of the radiating force of Sapphira, no longer her satellite, moon to her great Jovian significance, her efflorescent girlhood, she would telephone him for forty-five minutes after the bus ride home and speak of how Kevin or Tom or Lenny had tried to get her to agree to this or that *home breast exam,* or the like, and then one afternoon when her parents were vacationing or on business, in autumn, leaves the colors of unrestored frescoes, Sapphira invited him over, arranged in hushed tones to meet, and once inside the door, *I have an idea for you, you are so wonderful, you are my best girlfriend, you are my one and only, and I want you to be just like me, come on in, girlfriend, sister of mine,* and next he knew they were in her room, and she was helping him off with his jeans, helping him off with his T-shirt, and helping him *on* with her white underpants, and then her trainer bra, and then her plaid, pleated field hockey skirt, her eyelet camisole, and then they were in her parents' bathroom, with the vanity mirror, turning him, as on a Lazy Susan, to appreciate all angles, scattering widely upon the glass table the pencils and brushes of her trade, and, *God, here is the difficult part, I was so aroused, I have never felt so passive and so aroused, as she ringed my eyes with her lavender eyeliner, as she brushed on the mascara, as she rouged me, covered my actual physical blushing with her Kabuki cultural blushing, as her hands danced all around me with delicate embraces, it was as though she had a hundred arms, like she was Hindu statuary, I had never been so loved as I was loved now that I was a girl, I had never been so esteemed,* and she even had a wig, which was sort of a bow-headed thing that a cheerleader might want to wear, with short bangs, and Sapphira herself had been a cheerleader so she ought to have known, even if she was only wearing chinos and sandals and a sweatshirt that afternoon, *And she even painted my toenails in a red-umber, the color of menstrual efflux, and it was true, as I lay upon her bed with the fringe skirt, and she hugged me and called me her rag doll, that I had never felt so scorched as I felt then, and I knew, I knew, I knew, I knew what I was, so outrageous in my elevated state that I had to run into the bathroom to gaze on myself all over again, feeling a racing in myself that I had never felt before, the teleology of desire, the bound and cauterized site of the feminine, that's how it was, and I was so ashamed, and so ashamed that she knew, and she knew that I knew, and she visited upon me a knowing smile, and it was that smile that did it, that toppled the care-*

fully erected façade, and I began demanding, Get this stuff off of me, Get this stuff off me, even as I knew now what she was to those guys, to Kevin or Tom or Lenny, she was no different from what I was then, I could have provided for their needs as well as she, could have provided the trophy, the object, the ravishment they desired, I had become America's delightful exotic doll; this was a heartfelt display to be sure, and obviously it would not have been polite for me to turn away this difficult and generous admission, but I was still *upset,* you know, I was still *deterritorialized,* and if he tried to explain that this assumption of the clothes of *the slut from up the street* gave him access to femininity, I was going to have to get shrill, I was going to swallow a hunk of him, with my vagina, if necessary, some hunk of bicep or quadricep, *Who, then, is this other to whom I am more attached than to myself, since at the heart of my assent to my own identity it is still he who agitates me?,* I told him we needed to *leave now,* we needed to pay the check, goddammit, for once in our lives we would pay the check without arguing about whose turn it was to pay, because we needed to leave now, and there was a flurry of settling up and tip-leaving, his hands trembled at the astronomical sum, his *essential tremor,* and the bottled blonde with the decorated navel didn't even give him a second look as she swept the six ones and change into her apron and carried the two twenties back to the register, and we eased between the empty conversations in the Upper West Side bar, the discussions of cars and shares in the Hamptons and good mutual funds, and I, in my *tempest,* insisted on a cab, though we had in the past argued about whether taxis were an expense that fitted into the extremely narrow budget that we were trying to observe, and, if truth were a thing that could be revealed by argument, if truth were some system of layers that you could husk when your relationship had assumed its permanent shape, then it was true that our pennilessness, our academic poverty, surrounded by this Rube Goldberg contraption of cosmopolitan New York, by the limousines, by the price-gouging restaurants, by the dwindling number of our classmates who practiced the *life of the mind*, by our undergraduate classmates who were now psychiatrists, or lawyers, or boutique money managers — this academic penury was wearing us away, sanding us down, burnishing us until like the professors of our own youth, we were hollow mouths, reciting things we no longer felt or cared at all about, we were the culmination of a genealogy of ghosts, Marx, Freud, Derrida, Lacan, Nietzsche, Reich, syphilitics and cocaine addicts and income tax evaders, and I asked where in this arrangement was room for what I had once loved with an enthusiasm dialectical, rhizomatic, interstitial, defiant, the possibility that *thinking* could save lives, as at the moment when I first heard him lecture, back when he was the assistant for *Intro to Film Analysis*, when he paced the proscenium by the blackboard in that room off of 116th, back when he smoked, chain-smoked, barely made eye contact with those restive kids, how I loved him, back when he said, *Anorexia, the scurvy on the raft in which I embark with the thin virgins*, misquoting it turned out, in order to make a point about Audrey Hepburn in *Breakfast at Tiffany's*, he wanted to make a difference and I wanted to make a difference, or a *differance*, a deferral, a deferment, a defacement, I recognized my own image in the eyes of that boy who was recognizing his own image in me, a flickering in candlelight, candles about to be blown out in the hushed, sudden interior of a bedroom, *flickering in the pink night of youthful graces,* all that was gone now and we had opened the windows of the taxi because the air was thick as bread, and we said nothing, and the taxi idled in traffic on Broadway, my stubbly legs crossed one over the other, I needed a shower, and I felt cross and shameful, unemployable, old, I felt he would leave me for a younger woman, like the barmaid, a trickle of blood at the corner of her perfect lips, as I pronounced these assessments, these solemn truths about us, *facteur de la verité,* as the taxi with its geometrically increasing fare expelled us on 120th and we paid the cabby a month's salary and we walked past Grant's Tomb, cromlech, dolmen, barrow, in our necropolis, what it was to be a woman in this afterlife, giving an extra bit of effort in the going hence of what you once loved, he said nothing, the key turned in the lock, it tumbled the bolts, as if the idea of the key were the perfection of an ancient ethics, I couldn't believe that I would have to lose what it seemed like I was about to lose, what it once seemed like I might *always have,* all the lights in our apartment had burnt out in our absence, he always left the lights on and the bulbs were always blown, *Let's compromise,* he said, running his hands nervously across his Velcro crewcut, adjusting his eyeglasses, *I'm so tired of fighting,* and I didn't know what I was going to do until I did it, though there was a certain inevitability to these next moments, and I slammed the door, and I pulled the metal folding chair from under the kitchen table, situated it at the end of the table, situated it for spectatorship, *I have a vagina,* I said, *I have a uterus, I have a cervix,* he nodded wearily, and I said, *Man's feminine is not woman's feminine,* and he nodded wearily, and I told him to quit nodding, and I asked him if he happened to know where his *shoehorn* was, and he shook his head, no, and I said, *Of course, it's a trick question, but I know where your shoehorn is, because I keep it with mine, as with so many other things you couldn't be bothered to think about,* so I walked into the interior of the apartment, which was not so far that he couldn't hear the emanations of my breath, *Look,* he said, *I don't know what I've done to cause so much difficulty, but I apologize, I honestly do, let's let it drop, I love you,* and I could feel my steep decline coming on, as when the low-pressure system moves in and drives off summer filth, yet having made the decision, I couldn't let go of it, or maybe it's more credible to say that it was obvious that I could feel like subjecting him to this painful scrutiny and at the same time not feel like doing it at all: *I demand that you deny me that which I offer you,* that sort of thing, a Saturday, a post-structuralist Saturday, the night on which I urged my lover to give me a pelvic examination on the kitchen table, which he refused, of course, *Oh, the old biology is destiny argument, it doesn't suit you at all, and don't you think you're acting childishly?,* was and wasn't, in my view, and the torrents of my argument were and were not forceful, and this *was and was not* erotic, this argument, like the arguments that produced that old sweet thing so much gone from us now, and the resolution, it seemed to me, would be ephemeral, would never be what I suspected it would be, and so I went on with the display nonetheless, climbing up on the kitchen table now, holding, among other props, the two shoehorns, the one from a Florsheim on 8th street, plastic shoehorn of imitation cordovan, and the other a shiny metallic stainless steel shoehorn of my own given to me *gratis* when I had bought, on

Madison Avenue, this pair of sandals I was wearing, peeling off the ivory sandals, yanking down my beige nylons and then also my lingerie, satin and from Victoria's Secret, and then I hiked up my skirt, a thin, rayon, slightly clingy wrap in a floral print, cream with navy blossoms thereupon, and I shoved a throw pillow from the sofa under my lumbar region, and I leaned back such that I was facing him, it facing him is the right term, since, now, he was facing away, having assumed what was happening, at last, and I readied my shoehorns, greased slightly, *They're cold, they're always cold, when they come for you with the speculum it is always cold,* with a splenetic passivity, he mumbled, *Don't I need a light of some kind,* but I had one of these, a penlight that he himself used when grading papers late at night in our tiny apartment, when he did not want to wake me, and I embarked on my tour, *Look, look, look, spread wide the external petals at either side,* and I helped him along, as he seemed a little unwilling to commit, *never mind that first trompe l'oeil for now, that little nub, move indoors, where the walls are pink and ridged like when the sand upon the beach is blown by successive waves, which means that estrogen is present, because when menopause strikes the rugae will vanish, straight ahead, if you please, the cervix has a different texture, sort of a pearly pink like gums, dense fibrous, thick, rigid, averages four centimeters across, and the hole is a tiny dark spot, the os, like the hole in a bagel that swells to threaten its cavity, in a nulliparous woman it's a hole, if you've had children it's more like the creases in an old balled feather pillow, then up through there is the uterus, of course, you can't see, up there, endometrium, now lined with blood and sludge, the color of ugly seventies wall-to-wall carpeting, my sludge,*

after which we head north up into the pear, because it's
shaped like a pear with a sleeve around it, and at ten and two
o'clock in the pear, little holes, oviducts, and these go around
each ovary, like treble clefs, they wrap cursively around each
ovary, each end fimbriated, and in mid-cycle during ovula-
tion, one egg gets primed to be released on one side, sucked into
the tube from the corpus luteum, and then there's the hydatid
of Morgagni, and the Mesosalpinx, and the Epoöphoron, and
the Fundus of the Uterus, and the external abdominal opening,
basically open all the way up there, all the way up, unpro-
tected, vulnerable to the approach of the fleet of chromo-
somes, the little Navy SEALs coming up the canal here,
although you have to wonder at the fact of it from an evolu-
tionary point of view how a perfect vulnerability makes for the
reproduction of a species unless that ends up being the locu-
tion of our biology, of our position in things, or, to put it
another way, the victim, in your construct, *the penitent,*
always has the upper hand, always has control, hidden from
you, present and absent, both; yes, an uncomfortable position, holding the shoehorns in this way, arched over myself,
while he took command of the penlight, while he tried to
neglect his responsibility, and I mean uncomfortable in a lot
of ways, I mean that I didn't want to watch his expressions
of remorse, I didn't want to think about what I was doing, I
was better off looking at the stuccoed ceiling, an interior
style that always made me feel really claustrophobic, the
simulated remodeling ease of stucco, and if at this point the
penlight didn't do the job, didn't illuminate, what did I care,
now, alone or married, fertile or infertile, pregnant or bar-
ren, what did I care that he had gone now and left me on the
kitchen table, had gone to the bedroom, I could hear him

now padding away, the door only partly ajar, I could see the dim clamp light on his bedside table illumined, I could see him brushing his teeth in that furious inconsolable way he had, he sawed at his gums, and now he was reading, of course, reading in volumes that no longer comforted, reading to repair the differences, what was all this talk, all these pages, all this prose, all these sentences, what was it all for, I thought, on the kitchen table, holding two shoehorns in this way so that I was open to the world, its first citizen, its first woman, its original woman, naked on the kitchen table, like a repast, I left off talking, my outrage lapsed, what had we been arguing about, what was the source of the argument and where did it take us, *don't leave me here like this,* all your broken bindings, your printing presses, your history of histories, I climbed down off the table and began straightening things up.

Surplus Value Books: Catalogue Number 13

Note: Dawn in Springfield, where I am writing these words, dawn, hue of oatmeal, Springfield, city of former industrial glory. Something, some animal, has overturned the large aluminum trash barrel I recently purchased from a national discounter, scattering two insufficiently sealed bags across the backyard, one containing a number of the *sexually explicit magazines* that have served as my companions in the last several years. How I wish I were making coffee. Maybe I will make coffee; in fact, maybe I will embark herewith upon description of my expensive *home brewing station* of a Germanic or ersatz-Germanic design; my coffeemaker has a timer and a grinder; I will confess, *bibliophile*, that frequently I allow the coffeemaker to serve as my alarm, my *carpe diem*, first a high-pitched screech, no more than a second or two, then the beans that I have scooped into the grinding portion of the technology during the prior night's rash of scotches, these beans, in a clockwise motion not unlike the movement of planets around the sun, not unlike the sun's motion around the galaxy, not unlike the galaxies as they helix around the circular nothingness of *creation,* these beans fall upon knives, roasted and seasoned beans slipping down through the grinding stage of the Germanic *home brewing station,* and then into the filtering area, where a reusable Mylar filter with *thousands of tiny filaments* will begin trapping and collecting this elixir of Araby to allow it to achieve maximum viscosity; about this time, where I am lying on a full-size box spring that induces unbearable lumbar pain, I begin to hear the blubbering of the local fluorinated tap water in the *stem section* of my German *home brewing station.* The water is beginning to achieve its electrically induced convection current, in the stem section, the water is beginning to reach its boiling, I can hear it, as the grinding noise has penetrated the scrim of my disappointment and I have reluctantly opened my eyes and concluded, again, that I need to launder the sheets, which duty, by nightfall, I will have abjured; never mind all that, I can hear the buoyant chemistries of the German *home brewing station,* and now I can *smell* the beverage, my addiction, my blessing, my nightingale, my helpmeet; it is drifting from the kitchen, across the dining room, across the thick wall-to-wall in the dining room with the Beaujolais stains and the woolen gobs hacked up by my incontinent Abyssinian, down the little corridor, the smell of my coffee, the certain basis for any claim of the Divine, coffee, all the beans, all the varieties, I have lingered in the boutiques of shopping malls devoted to its worship, Eritrean beans flavored with betel juice, perhaps a bit of almond or absinthe, perhaps some Percocet or Vicodin to further amplify my caffeinated comforts, a frame or two of my lost childhood snuck into this taste, ice cream cones past, double scoops, my lost parents and the liqueured desserts, I admit it, even *house blends* can seduce me, even *house blends* suggest the high art of roasting and flavoring, even house blends suggest a sunrise when the non-union farm laborer is hunched in the mottled shade of the glorious shrub picking green fruits, a dream fit for a victorious conqueror, even the production of these notes (on books I'm featuring this quarter) were composed in a Javanese ecstasy. I have searched among the possessions of dead people, pinchpennies, those with obsessive-compulsive disorder, those who never read, I have searched in second-hand stores in towns like Rockville and Cincinnati, and I did it all for coffee, oh coffee, of thee I sing, profits, lives, loves, passions, all this for thou, oh muse, oh goddess, oh bean, oh coffee.

All books fine in original dust jackets, unless otherwise noted.

1. (Anthology). *Kiss My Ass, Motherfucker, Gonna Blow Up Your Damn House.* Seattle: Squatter's Collective, 1979. Essays on direct action, including one by Tony Puryear, later author of an Arnold Schwarzenegger vehicle, *Eraser,* also including the first ever appearance of National Book Award Winner Eileen Brennan *(Several Generations of Forlorn Women)* under her pseudonym, Elsie Tree. We had the book in our co-op back in Ann Arbor back in the late seventies. At the time, my roommate, who eventually directed

aspirin commercials, insisted that influenza was organized and disseminated by the Central Intelligence Agency in an effort to neutralize the American counterculture. $15

2.   (Anthology). *Prose by Don.* New York: Unfounded Allegations, 1978. Hardcover edition of this sampling of literature by authors named Don, including Don DeLillo, Donald Antrim, Donald Barthelme, Donald Westlake, Dawn Powell, Donny Osmond, Don Knotts, Donald Sutherland, Don Giovanni, Don Vito Corleone, and others, also including excerpts from the autobiography of a Nutley, New Jersey, electrician, Don Vyclitl, of Ukrainian origin. Slight foxing to jacket, otherwise fine. Later titles in the series included the two-in-one volume *Works by Zephediah* backed with *A Couple of Unpublished Scraps by Hamilton.* $35

3.   (Anthology). *Words, Blossoms, Cars.* Austin, TX: Cooked Books, 1968. All contributions are unsigned, although, according to scholars like Tommy McCandless at Western Kentucky Technical Institute, they include Frederick Barthelme, a seventeen-year-old Mary Robison, Rikki Ducornet, Ann Lauterbach, and others, as well as excerpts from manuals on how to disassemble and reassemble the first Ford Mustang, several arguments against popular modifications of the *Monopoly* board, and some poems in the style of

Mallarmé. This copy signed by Barthelme with appended disclaimer, *I don't know what the hell you're talking about, I had nothing to do with this book, I like your suede shoes though. F.B.* $45

4.   Blake, Kenneth M. *Elocution*. New York: Ticknor and Fields, 1986. First American edition of this novel concerning a group of Oxbridge scholars who cook and eat their landlady, and who later assume command of British forces during the Falklands War. Not long after, the author himself was convicted of cooking and eating his landlady. This copy also signed, rare as such: *Bon Apetit! K.M.B., 7.7.87.* $50

5.   Carrington, Leonora. *Chilblains*. Paris: Editions Aveugle, 1921. Little known *roman à clef* by the great surrealist. A library copy, actually stolen from the Widener, at Harvard, by yours truly. The story goes thus. I was desperately in love with an art history student, Anna Feldman, she of the blond bob, she of the palindromic name, she of the ballerina's frame, she of the turnout, of the veils and scarves, of the BMW 2002; having espied her at a fast food joint in town (I was working at a used bookstore), I had taken the opportunity to follow her on a couple of occasions, always at a discreet distance, never in a way that would have intruded. I'd been reading Carrington's books in the confines of the Rare Book Room at the Widener: *For as the reader will*

recognize, my famishment is immense. I was fascinated with the way the heroine in Carrington's
novel could change herself at will into the South
American mammal called the *nutria.* I'd felt that
Anna Feldman would especially appreciate the
image and the book. Getting it past the sequence
of alarms in the Widener was a chore, I can tell
you, even though security was comparatively lax
in those years. When I finally attempted to present Carrington's volume to Anna, after months
of conspiring, the future art historian was aloof,
refusing the token of my affections outright. This
copy, therefore, though it is in the original edition,
has some lonely, dispirited marginal commentary
in my own hand, of a mildly misogynistic cast
(from which illness I later recovered, I assure
you). I offer it at bargain price. $75

6. Dactyl, Veronica (Davis, Lydia). *How to Compose
a Detective Novel.* Washington, DC: Sun and
Moon, 1987. Pseudonymous how-to primer, by
the fiction writer and translator widely considered one of the most elegant and arresting of
twentieth-century American voices. Davis, as has
often been noted, *writes and produces slowly,* and
now it's clear why. Acting on information provided me by a Katonah, NY, accountant, I have
learned that the identity of this shadowy, elusive
crime writer, Veronica Dactyl, is none other than
the exquisitely *luxe* prose stylist herself. This
primer reflects Dactyl's fifteen years of writing

mysteries mainly for the French market (*L'Ami, L'Amour, Le Mort,* for example, was a bestseller after the release of the Mickey Rourke vehicle) and as such was not a hit on this side of the pond. Now that the association is clear, Dactyl will no doubt have a higher profile among collectors. Price-clipped, with some writing on title page, though not in the author's hand: *Happy bday B., you should always have a career to fall back on, love, Mom.* $100

7.   Firth, Desmond. *The Benzene Ring.* New York: Linden Press, 1986. Outrageously funny first novel about the publishing business. Released posthumously. Which reminds me. After my years at the bookstore in Cambridge, where I was getting minimum wage and amassing enormous credit card debt, I decided there was little choice but to retreat to the groves of academe, where, although I'd never had much success, *I had learned to respect and admire books.* My list of likely institutions included several top-flight northeastern universities, to which I intended to apply in both the English literature and philosophy departments. I was also interested in at least one *art history program,* so that I might be closer to a certain beloved expert in forgeries of pre-Columbian native American artifacts, namely, of course, Anna Feldman. Desmond Firth, friend of a friend, had gone to SUNY Binghamton before getting his job in New York in the computer

books division of New American Library. Our mutual acquaintance, a ticket scalper, memorabilia collector, and paraplegic called Benny Fontaine, therefore suggested I call Firth to discuss the academic business with him. Since I'm a little disinclined to make or return any kind of phone call, it took longer than I anticipated to make contact with Firth, even if from reports Firth was eager to talk to me. However, by the time I dialed the unlisted number of his Jersey City apartment, he had already thrown himself in front of a Manhattan-bound PATH train. At rush hour. The Newport Mall station. For reasons unexplained. Persevering without Firth's help I made application to some regional universities on my wish list, including UMass, only to be rejected from all these departments. $15

8. Ford, David. *Demanding That You Deny Me That Which I Offer You: Lacan as Advanced Capitalist in the Age of Post-Post-Structuralism.* Santa Monica: Danger! Books, 1994. Including instruction in viaticals, topologies, rhizomes, and the *petit objet a.* $25

A Fascinating Letter

9. Gelb, Mortimer. *TLS* from Gelb to Chip Mandible, dated 14 July 1973. Clearly typed on an early IBM electric without correcting key. The author was a minor playwright (*Death on the*

Back Nine, e.g.), known mainly in the Providence area (including a disastrous tenure with the Trinity Repertory Company), but here he writes in his capacity as director of Woonsocket Camp for Boys (note letterhead), to the stepfather of a camper given to vexing kleptomaniacal tendencies. Gelb's preoccupation, from a disciplinary standpoint, is with a vanishing collection of 1969 New York Mets baseball cards. The card featuring Nolan Ryan was later recovered. A fine example of how an early covetousness can pave the way for effective business tactics in later life. $900

10.   Holberg, Susan Emmerich. *Blue and Gray Notebooks: A Novel.* New York: Alfred A. Knopf, 1985. *New York Times* notable book of 1985. Haven't read it personally, and I don't have to, but with a minuscule print run (1,500 copies), a meager advertising budget, negligible promotion, it has all the signs of an income-generating bonanza in my sector of the business. Especially now that the author, having appeared nude on the jacket, is a sensation! Dealers have been shadowing Holberg coast to coast on the promotional junket for her more recent *White Male Oppressors.* Listen, *deplorable* is the only appropriate term for the conduct of my professional brethren. If we can't treat the authors of these works with dignity and kindness, our business is going to wither before our eyes. On the other hand, I personally brought

a shopping cart full of seventy-three copies of this first novel to Holberg's in-store appearance in Boston. I actually had to get a homeless fellow from the Common to help me carry the shipping containers. I guess, *in a spirit of business conciliation,* I should offer my strategy: I would carry five copies forward in the reception line, run back to the shopping cart — where my pal Spike would hand me five more — wait through the queue a second time. When, on each occasion, I reached the dais, where the author was rubbing her arthritic wrist, I would *alter my expression slightly,* from careworn sadness to earnest befuddlement, completely deceiving the poor, exhausted Holberg. When the rest of the crowd, with their dog-eared paperbacks that will never be worth *a wooden nickel,* were through extracting signatures from her *(This is for my friend Kitty! She wants to be a writer too!),* I asked Holberg if she wouldn't mind signing *just a couple more.* There were in fact forty-nine additional copies left, and Spike gamely brought them forward. When I hinted that I might be associated with one of the larger *chain merchandisers,* Holberg obligingly complied. After twenty-five copies, however, she handed the Sharpie back to me. "Why don't you sign them all yourself? Nobody'll know the difference." This copy near mint, rare as such, with an interesting inscription, *The author's hand as complex promotional swindle, S.E.H. 6/16/85.* $150

An Unusual Association

11.   Holberg, Susan Emmerich. *White Male Oppressors*. New York: Alfred A. Knopf, 1996. It wasn't long after my initial conversation with Holberg, that, at a yard sale, I stumbled upon this copy of her second novel, inscribed to none other than *Anna Feldman!* The inscription reads in part, *One broad to another, enduring fealty, don't let the bastards grind you down.* I was drinking an Irish coffee, about ten in the morning. This was in Glastonbury, Connecticut, I believe, and the people having the yard sale — their belongings flapping from hastily strung laundry lines — were the Weavers. When I cornered the woman of the house, a pudgy, outdated example of the nineteen-fifties bombshell wearing the *obligatory pelican blue eye shadow,* I demanded to know where she'd gotten this first edition of the Holberg. She remarked that there was no reason to use threatening language. I'd used no such thing. She'd gotten the volume at the library sale in town, simply because she liked the dust jacket, with its leering platoon of American militarists. Supposedly, Mrs. Weaver claimed, she didn't know Holberg personally, had no idea of the value of the book (which in fact had one of the Weavers' orange stickers on it: *50¢*), and was in the process of declaring bankruptcy. I felt I needed to keep the Glastonbury residence of the Weavers under surveillance for a

few days, from the far side of Oakdale Blvd., yet I noticed nothing out of the ordinary, except for Mr. Weaver's tendency to sob while cutting the lawn. Around the back of his ranch house he would go, on his riding mower, his face a mask of anguish. $275

Very, Very Unstable In the First Place

12. (Institutionalized Writers) Klingman, Finley. *Sun, Shine Down Upon Besieged Humors*. Amenia, NY: M.A.O. Press, 1987. A rare peek at the drawings and poems of one of the foremost of American *outsider artists*, Klingman committed himself in the late seventies upon becoming convinced that computers were beginning to *speak to one another*, a perception that certainly wouldn't seem unusual these days. I met him thereafter and found him passionate, articulate, resigned to his fate. He was also an outstanding Scrabble player, specializing in sequences of two- and three-letter words that all fell, mercilessly, on triple-word scores. These feats were accomplished while Finley delivered lengthy tirades about particle physics and German phenomenological thinkers. This chapbook is number thirteen of a limited edition of twenty, signed by Klingman, and thus especially rare, as he believed that signing anything would alert authorities to his political resistance and thereby bring torture down upon his head. $1,000

13. (Institutionalized Writers) Meyers, Mirabelle.
     County Dreambook. Amenia, NY: M.A.O. Press,
     1987. Another in the M.A.O. series. With Meyers's
     poetical attention to dismemberment, ecstatic
     sexual union, forced homosexuality, religious
     themes, she'd have been a natural for any contro-
     versy relating to government funding of the arts,
     but, astonishingly, her work never came to the
     attention of Helms, et al., even though she was
     being housed in a state facility and even though
     M.A.O. received grants from N.Y.S.C.A. in 1987
     and 1988. Meyers's free-verse poems are all the
     more astonishing (with their heavy plagiaristic
     reliance on conservative publications like the
     National Review, the *New York Post,* the *Washing-
     ton Times*), when you consider that she was a col-
     lege dropout and former *domestic engineer* from
     Corinth, NY, whose husband was the local grocer,
     and whose children were dyslexic. The author
     died while incarcerated, penniless and neglected,
     and this is therefore her only work, one of a num-
     bered twelve copies. I am forced to price it at a
     threshold it deserves. You would be lucky to have
     known Mirabelle. Those who did miss her.

                                              $2,500

14. (Institutionalized Writers) Poole, Samuel. *In Sup-
     port of a Reliance Upon Power Tools.* Amenia, NY:
     M.A.O. Press, 1988. Yes, I knew him, too, during
     that dark interval of my own. I loved them all, my
     friends inside, they were good people, and it's no

reflection on their own dignity that they didn't have the kind of insurance that would allow them to stay in private psychiatric hospitals, or that their illnesses were of such sturdy architecture that they could not lead productive lives, as I have been able to do, by finding a line of work that made harmony with who they were, with their gears and engines. One night, I saw Sam Poole, *actually floating in the corridor of the hospital;* I awoke, in the ward, tiptoed quietly out into the hall, knowing that there was no loneliness like the loneliness of the mentally ill, knowing that my solitude would never be corrected, no matter how many days I waited in front of the brownstone in Back Bay where Anna Feldman settled with her husband, the tax lawyer. Every thread of my short life had come to a frayed end. Out into the hall I went, across the hall, to whisper at the mesh of the window, out at the county road, empty at that hour but for a tractor, laden with bales, that labored away from me with hazard lamps flashing. I was as astonished as you would be, to find then, Sam, in his dressing gown, unshaven, *drifting,* as if in a heated, kidney-shaped swimming pool, several feet above the cracked, heaving linoleum. In his sleep, but nonetheless chattering like a suburban housewife. The night orderly was slumped in a chair by the nurse's station. And thus there was no observer but myself, none but myself to ask of Sam the questions that had afflicted me and others in that institution, but Sam would answer no questions. That was *not* the sort of oracle he was. Instead, amid his jeremiads were the words *Son, you get on out of here now. This is no place for a kid like yourself.* Since Sam was asleep his remarks were somewhat disordered, but this is how I reconstructed this particular morsel of advice. I founded the M.A.O. Press to preserve Sam's literary legacy, and, yes, it's true, Sam Poole argued, while drifting lazily in the corridor of my psychiatric hospital, that no matter the darkness of any life, we should always be grateful for the *band saw.* $2,500

A Run of Defaced Mailers

15.   Mailer, Norman (Duffy, Tyrone). *Advertisements for Myself.* New York: Random House, 1959. Tyrone Duffy, a graduate of Cooper Union in New York City, began mangling and defacing copies of Norman Mailer's work in the early eighties, and displaying them in galleries mostly associated with the East Village scene. In interviews, Duffy has refused to acknowledge any particular feeling for Mailer (*but how could you have a feeling for Mailer,* beyond being appalled that the writer once stabbed his own wife). Duffy claims to have selected Mailer for his art — which incorporates doodles, notations for saxophone solos, grocery lists, bank statements, diary entries, and quarrels with the texts themselves — because the lesser

Mailer titles are readily available at used book-
stores. This subsequent collection of Duffy's work
(as opposed to Mailer's), amazingly owned by a
product manager from the Glock Firearms Corporation (Frank Gilman), is an example of the
aleatory quality of all the best literature, *how it
conjoins reader and writer blessedly,* how it is
never complete until there is a reader who can
make of the work what she or he wishes, using it
to line their birdcage, using it for ecstasy or articulation of dreams, using it to imagine their own
log cabin in the empty forested regions of Western Canada or Cincinnati skyscraper in the shape
of a flamingo; all this collecting of the perfect
copy of everyone's book, you and I know that collection is merely autobiography. Mailer now
becomes Tyrone Duffy, and while Mailer might
still haunt the Promenade on Brooklyn Heights,
walking a pug and smoking a cigar, Duffy's Mailer
crowds him out. Late at night the author senses it
and trembles. $750

16. Mailer, Norman (Duffy, Tyrone). *Tough Guys
Don't Dance.* New York: Random House, 1983.
$500

17. Mailer, Norman (Duffy, Tyrone). *Ancient
Evenings.* Boston: Little, Brown, 1983. I should
admit that I am a great appreciator of spines of
the book, their simple elegant signs of authority.
I like the multifary of jackets, I like the simple

three-color jackets of an earlier time in the century, I like the type jackets of Salinger, I like the jackets of Gallimard and all French publishers. But as for books themselves, I care minimally; I didn't even open most of the books you see on this list, it's true. Opening them would damage the spine. But I did, however, at a certain time in my life, read the opening pages of *Ancient Evenings*. I have no idea how the rest of the book turned out, but the opening was among the most beautiful things I've ever read, and I can tell you exactly where I was when I read this opening; it was during my *Cambridge experience,* before the arrest, and I was working in the secondhand bookstore and going home at night to an apartment I shared with a guy called Reginald, at which point I would *hit the lush hard* and then climb up on the roof of the apartment building (a three-story townhouse sort of a thing), as if it were the roof of the world. It was there one night I was reading the opening of *Ancient Evenings* by flashlight when who should go past, down below, on the verdant Cambridge street where I lived, but Anna Feldman, like a specter from a future I would never have. I called to her, *Anna! Hey, Anna! It's me, up here on the roof! I'm up here!* Was it a harbinger of my decline that there was an unmistakable hastening away of her footstep at the sound of my voice? Did I imagine it? Or was I my own adversary, and she just my catalytic muse? I threw the book after her, from the roof,

its leaves, its boards, like wings flapping, flight-
less, tumbling, foliating, to earth, in the little area
beside my neighbor's recycling cans, *If I can't
have you,* I believe I shouted, *I'll have nobody, I'll
be noteworthy for my absence, for recoiling! I will
make a temple to your unattainability! I will worship there! I will charge exorbitant fees to the members of my congregation! I will found a mystery
cult! I will become a preacher!* $900

18. Moody, Rick. *Garden State: A Novel.* Wainscott,
     NY: Pushcart Press, 1992. Hard-to-find hardcover
     edition. Signed. $325

19. Olafson, Olaf. *Um Yœghrönte då Kzœpøqubniòõs-
     ghemen der Vhä¥çhnachtÿshesse!* Ostuni, Italia:
     Editore Zanare, 1921. Arguably Olafson's tower-
     ing achievement, certainly one of the most com-
     pelling of early twentieth-century philosophical
     works, this argument dates from the years after
     the author was shipped from Oxford directly to
     Broadmoor, where he was compelled, in his mad-
     ness, to address the indeterminacy of, indeed, the
     total *inability* to prove the existence of any other,
     of any love, of any parent, of any pet, of any
     friendly acquaintance met in passing at a coffee
     shop, anyone. The work is based of course on a
     brain-in-a-vat hypothesis that came to Olafson as
     delusional inmate, at which time he suffered with
     a hysterical cessation of *all sensory data;* not eyes,
     nor ears, nor taste buds, nor olfactory receptors,

nor even the surface of Olafson's skin would receive data. He was left entirely alone without intellection. This work, then, is a repudiation of all that comes to us from Descartes's *cogito ergo sum* and from the positivists who still cast a long shadow on Olafson while he was pursuing his studies in England. So profound, so uncompromising is Olafson's nihilism that he might have prevented this work ever *coming to light* (of what value is publication if you don't believe that any reader exists?), were it not for his brother Hans, who in 1920 took the author to southern Italy, to a region of olive trees, the luscious teal of the Adriatic, *La Città Bianca*, the narrow streets and medieval basilicas, the whitewashed alleys, dating all the way back to the occupation of the Masapians from distant Croatia (they ritually consumed their young). In these austere yet strangely celebratory streets, young Hans, desperately morose, sat with his brother Olaf (drooling, incoherent) at a table outside a local café and ordered for him *uno cona di gelato pistacchio.* Whereupon a great light, like that which brightened Theresa in her ecstasy, enlightened him and he could *see* and he could hear the music coming from the basilica, there were women in their shawls, there were dogs in the piazza scratching their fleas and sidling up to the *turisti* for food, there were carts and horses and fresh cherries and this fabulous *gelato,* and thus were born for

Olafson the twin discourses of all his philosophy,
negation and recreation. $2,500

Translated by a Goddess

20. Pizzicato, Sergio. (Anna Feldman, trans.) *Illusionism in Mannerist Painting and Since.* Chicago:
University of Chicago Press, 1991. By *mannerist,*
Pizzicato referred, of course, to the period *after*
the great paintings of the Renaissance, when
what was so routine, the masterpiece, gave way
instead to frescoes and canvases that while
delightful seem suddenly to reflect not the perfection of human imagination, but rather its imper-
fections, its artifices, its dodges and feints.
Pizzicato suggested this illusionism in his own
sleights of hand, by addressing forgeries as
though these were genuine paintings of the
period, by footnoting texts that didn't exist, by
creating fraudulent citations for his bibliography.
He was discredited at the *università* in Rome. He
was then arrested, as the story is recreated, by the
polizie at the Pantheon itself, while listening to a
group of American teenagers singing madrigals,
while afternoon sun streamed in through the
opening in the ceiling, while he ate from a bag of
french fries purchased just up the block at a
McDonald's franchise. The charge, of which he
was entirely guilty, involved incorporating into his
work uncited quotations from the early poetical

works of Pope John Paul II. After serving out his
incarceration, he left Italy altogether for Ireland,
of all places, where his monumental interpretation began contextually to appear as what it was,
the most creative of all Italian postwar works of
fiction. But this is all beside the point. If Pizzicato's contention is that the illusionism of man-
nerism is *more* realistic than the realism of the
Renaissance, if artifice — magnificent, playful,
salacious, decadent, sullen — is more real than
the studies from cadavers of Leonardo and
Michelangelo, then what of Pizzicato himself?
Can we really be sure there is a Pizzicato? And if
Pizzicato is himself, say, a bank teller from
Phoenix, or an incredibly bored naval cadet (on
six months of submarine duty), or a dealer in rare
books and manuscripts, what of his translator?
Her early work, as I have already pointed out,
was in Pre-Columbian forgeries, and so why the
sudden interest in Italian painting, in the period
after Italian painting was any good? Was it a crisis in her personal life? Was she heartbroken
because of the defection of a lover? Had a beautiful young bibliographer of the greatest of expec-
tations been suddenly sundered from her by the
constabulary forces of Back Bay, who mistook
his constant serenading at her window, his ritual-
istic garbage-can rifling, his worship of her utility
bills and postcards for a derangement? Was it
possible that she realized that all of her life's
ambitions were just elaborate put-ons, that no

author, no hack, no unpublished scrivener, was anything but an articulation of God's devotion to his own rich creative energies, just a mutable symbol, therefore, a little placeholder? Was this the truth of Sergio Pizzicato, and thus of Anna Feldman herself (and me, too, if we're being consistent)? Thus Pizzicato's inscription on an English translation must be spurious. Nevertheless, I price it as though it were real: *Pizzicato, hit et nunc, 4.1.1992.* $1,500

21. Straw, Syd (Harris, Susan). *The John Cage Story.* New York: De Capo, 1999. First novel by the singer/songwriter and former lead vocalist for NYC's Golden Palominos. Not a story of John Cage, the composer, in the conventional sense at all, but rather the story of Straw's thirteen months caring for her ailing father (song-and-dance man Jack Straw) as he relinquished himself to lung cancer. What's reliable in the fluxus of grief? Nothing, and the twittering of birds, the wind chimes on the snowed-in porch, the sound of a leak in the basement, the notations for her own wordless canticles at her father's bedside nonetheless *suggest* the inadvertent beauty that was so essential to Cage's work. Those of us who have now outlasted our own parents will find this a worthy investment at an attractive price. This reading copy signed, in a fascinating association, for short story writer Amy Hempel, author of the influential *Reasons to Live* and *Tumble Home:*

Thanks for the week at the beach, you are my idol,
love Syd. $350

By Jerome David Salinger

22. Salinger, J. D. *The Diamond Sutra: A Cookbook.*
Unpublished manuscript, typed on a Royal, from
the late sixties or early seventies. Mimeographed,
not photocopied. Contains no mention of the
Glass family, but does meditate at length on vege-
tarianism, Taoism, baseball, and the electric
period of Miles Davis. Includes some mournful
anti-war poems that are quite moving. Signed by
the writer to a friend, *Tom,* rare as such. $30,000

23. Vidal, Gore. *The Diagnosis of Collectors.* Providence: Burning Deck, 1983. The title here alludes
to the pathology of collection, and not only that
pathology of book collectors, clearly the most disturbed of the breed, but also to hoarders of
antiques, of miniatures, ceramic bears, *Star Wars*
paraphernalia, Kiss action figures, early video
games, *Gidget* novels, Jell-O molds, LPs of progressive rock acts of the seventies, garments worn
by Elvis Presley, and so forth. Vidal, the author
among other things of a masterpiece entitled
Myra Breckinridge, correctly posits collecting as a
pathology of the amorous in a Capitalist economy;
it is things that make us happy when conversation begins to reveal itself as a paltry substitute.
I loved words when people were nowhere on the

horizon and having begun to have a taste for
them, for all that was summoned by words in my
skull — a wealth of imaginary comforts — the
world with its people seemed but a discount substitute, Anna Feldman with blond bob has
goslings now, trailing after her on the beach at
Nantucket, no doubt, where the sun this week is
bright and plovers scatter at her feet. Little Dee
Dee and Marie and Liza, each carries a stick with
a length of kelp spiraling around it; each makes
hearts in the sand, writes names; am I the bad
guy from some videotape that Anna puts on in
the living room so that she might kiss her husband, the tax lawyer, before repairing to the
garage to call her lover on a cellular phone, her
lover never to be possessed but in motels and
hotels, and in her imagination; who has conceived of whom, Anna or her collector, and from
which book did they get the idea? $350

24.   Wittgenstein, Ludwig. *Coded Remarks: 1919–1920.*
      Not a manuscript so much as a series of remarks
      written in a simple code that the author used
      occasionally in all his many diaries (a=z, b=y,
      et cetera). Sometimes this cryptographically
      rendered manuscript took up matters of philos-
      ophy, sometimes not. The significance of the
      period described here, however, is that it con-
      cerns Wittgenstein's *lost decade,* during which he
      mainly taught elementary school in Austria.
      (Later, he was driven from this his homeland by

the *Anschluss.*) The coded remarks contained in
these pages, however, most often concern themselves with Wittgenstein's fantasies about working class men, the *angelic and brutal boys,* who
inhabited a park nearby, creeping from copse to
meadow on the prowl; or, at least, remarks on
these boys, some quite lengthy, are interlarded
with exacting and unyielding truths of Wittgenstein's daily life after the First World War, *Ate
Dover sole. Stupefied by the continuing manifesta-
tions of sensuality in myself. That the lion should
speak is by no means guaranteed, though possessed
of a tongue.* Commentators are at loggerheads, as
commentators always are, as to whether the boys
in the park actually existed for Wittgenstein in
the carnal sense, whether he possessed them,
knew them, saw them frequently, or whether, having occasionally observed them, he merely imagined a sinful compulsion, in his view, thus
engaging in what was hardest to admit to himself, the need for a physical articulation of a love
he felt strongly, *If my body should sing the perfect
round tones of an oratorio across a forbidden
boundary of shrubs, is it not inevitable that its cry
should be unmistakable?* Of course, there are par-
allels here, and not only in that Anna Feldman
was also of Jewish ancestry, somewhat assimi-
lated, married *goyim,* thus diluting whether
intentionally or by happenstance her bloodline.
I've already intimated, moreover, the possibility

that your bibliographer has exaggerated the tone and frequency of contacts with Anna, because, as with Wittgenstein, his experiences with the sweet mayhem of *intrapsychic libidinous exchange* are limited to a few meaningless couplings, after which he found himself suddenly alone. In conclusion, there is a mystical level to this collection of excerpts torn from the famous *lost decade* of Ludwig Wittgenstein, as in the inscription on the title page, in his elegant but somewhat florid cursive. Am I correct in how I decipher the words? Perhaps it says *To any friend who would labor here for my full and complete confession I bequeath herewith the force of my affliction.* When I showed it to my friend Don, the U.P.S. delivery man who comes to visit occasionally, his interpretation was as follows: *To any fiend who lives here in complete decomposition of beneath hereafter the fast forward of my afterlife.* We argued strenuously about it. I told Don that his high school education wasn't up to the task of handwriting analysis. Then I signed for the packages he'd brought. The final word on interpretation I leave for myself, unless some institution is willing to pay the absurd price I suggest below. Wittgenstein's inscription does not say *To any friend,* nor does it say *To any fiend.* Actually, as you should have guessed, it says, *To Anna Feldman — who should labor here for my full and complete confession — I bequeath the price of my affection.* Of course, it's anachronistic, this signature, unless Anna is a *condition of the universe,* a condition of all language, a condition of nighttime in Springfield, MA, unless Anna is merely an aspect of longing, the longing I have always felt, and therefore an inscription in all the books ever produced. How I miss her. $100,000

Demonology

They came in twos and threes, dressed in the fashionable Disney costumes of the year, Lion King, Pocahontas, Beauty and the Beast, or in the costumes of televised superheroes, protean, shape-shifting, thus arrayed, in twos and threes, complaining it was too hot with the mask on, *Hey, I'm really hot!*, lugging those orange plastic buckets, bartering, haggling with one another, *Gimme your Smarties, please?* as their parents tarried behind, grownups following after, grownups bantering about the schools, or about movies, about local sports, about their marriages, about the difficulties of long marriages, kids sprinting up the next driveway, kids decked out as demons or superheroes or dinosaurs or as advertisements for our multinational entertainment-providers, beating back the restless souls of the dead, in search of sweets.

■   ■   ■

They came in bursts of fertility, my sister's kids, when the bar drinking, or home-grown dope-smoking, or bed-hopping had lost its luster; they came with shrill cries and demands — little gavels, she said, instead of fists — *Feed me! Change me! Pay attention to me!* Now it was Halloween and the mothers in town, my sister among them, trailed after their kids, warned them away from items not fully wrapped, *Just give me that, you don't even like apples,* laughing at the kids hobbling in their bulky costumes — my nephew dressed as a shark, dragging a mildewed gray tail behind him. But what kind of shark? A great white? A blue? A tiger shark? A hammerhead? A nurse shark?

She took pictures of costumed urchins, my sister, as she always took pictures, e.g., my nephew on his first birthday (six years prior), blackfaced with cake and ice cream, a dozen relatives attempting in turn to read to him — about a tugboat — from a brand-new rubberized book. *Toot toot!* His desperate, needy expression, in the photo, all out of phase with our excitement. The first nephew! The first grandchild! He was trying to get the cake in his mouth. Or: a later photo of my niece (his younger sister) attempting to push my nephew out of the shot — against a backdrop of autumn foliage; or a photo of my brother wearing my dad's yellow double-knit paisley trousers (with a bit of flare in the cuffs), twenty-five years after the heyday of such stylings; or my father and stepmother on their powerboat, peaceful and happy, the riotous wake behind them; or my sister's virtuosic photos of *dogs* — Mom's irrepressible golden retriever chasing a tennis ball across an overgrown lawn, or my dad's setter on the beach with a perspiring Löwenbräu leaning against his snout. Fifteen or twenty photo albums on the shelves in my sister's living room, a whole range of leathers and faux-leathers, no particular order, and just as many more photos loose, floating around the basement, castoffs, and files of negatives in their plastic wrappers.

She drank the *demon rum,* and she taught me how to do it, too, when we were kids; she taught me how to drink. We stole drinks, or we got people to steal them for us; we got reprobates of age to venture into the pristine suburban liquor stores. Later, I drank bourbon. My brother drank beer. My father drank single malt scotches. My grandmother drank half-gallons and then fell ill. My grandfather drank the finest collectibles. My sister's ex-husband drank more reasonably priced facsimiles. My brother drank until a woman lured him out of my mother's house. I drank until I was afraid to go outside. My uncle drank until the last year of his life. And I carried my sister in a blackout from a bar once — she was mumbling to herself, humming melodies, mostly unconscious. I took her arms; Peter Hunter took her legs. She slept the whole next day. On Halloween, my sister had a single gin and tonic before going out with the kids, before ambling around the condos of Kensington Court, circling from multifamily unit to multifamily unit, until my nephew's shark tail was grass-stained from the freshly mown lawns of the common areas. Then she drove her children across town to her ex-husband's house, released them into his supervision, and there they walked along empty lots, beside a brook, under the stars.

■   ■   ■

When they arrived home, these monsters, disgorged from their dad's Jeep, there was a fracas between girl and boy about which was superior (in the Aristotelian hierarchies), Milky Way, Whoppers, Slim Jim, Mike 'n Ikes, Sweet Tarts, or Pez — this bounty counted, weighed, and inventoried (on my niece's bed). Which was the Pez dispenser of greatest value? A Hanna-Barbera Pez dispenser? Or, say, a demonic *totem pole Pez dispenser*? And after this fracas, which my sister refereed wearily *(Look, if he wants to save the Smarties, you can't make him trade!)*, they all slept, and this part is routine, my sister was tired as hell; she slept the sleep of the besieged, of the overworked, she fell precipitously into whorls of unconsciousness, of which no snapshot can be taken.

In one photograph, my sister is wearing a Superman outfit. This, from a prior Halloween. I think it was a *Supermom* outfit, actually, because she always liked these bad jokes, degraded jokes, things other people would find ridiculous. (She'd take a joke and repeat it until it was leaden, until it was funny only in its awfulness.) Jokes with the fillip of sentimentality. Anyway, in this picture her blond hair — brightened a couple of shades with the current technologies — cascades around her shoulders, disordered and impulsive. *Supermom.* And her expression is skeptical, as if she assumes the mantle of Supermom — raising the kids, accepting wage-slavery, growing old and contented — and thinks it's dopey at the same time.

Never any good without coffee. Never any good in the morning. Never any good until the second cup. Never any good without freshly ground Joe, because of my dad's insistence, despite advantages of class and style, on *instant coffee*. No way. Not for my sister. At my dad's house, where she stayed in summer, she used to grumble derisively, while staring out the kitchen windows, out the expanse of windows that gave onto the meadow there, *Instant coffee!* There would be horses in the meadow and the ocean just over the trees, the sound of the surf and *instant coffee!* Thus the morning after Halloween, with my nephew the shark (who took this opportunity to remind her, in fact, that last year he saved his Halloween candy *all the way till Easter, Mommy*) and my niece, the Little Mermaid, orbiting around her like a fine dream. My sister was making this coffee with the automatic grinder and the automatic drip device, and the dishes were piled in the sink behind her, and the wall calendar was staring her in the face, with its hundred urgent appointments, e.g., *jury duty* (the following Monday) and *R & A to pediatrician;* the kids whirled around the kitchen, demanding to know who got the last of the Lucky Charms, who had to settle for the Kix. My sister's eyes barely open.

Now this portrait of her cat, Pointdexter, twelve years old — he slept on my face when I stayed at her place in 1984 — Pointdexter with the brain tumor, Pointdexter with the phenobarbital habit. That morning — All Saints' Day — he stood entirely motionless before his empty dish. His need was clear. His dignity was immense. Well, except for the seizures. Pointdexter had these seizures. He was possessed. He was a demon. He would bounce off the walls, he would get up *a head of steam*, mouth frothing, and run straight at the wall, smack into it, shake off the ghosts, and start again. His screeches were unearthly. Phenobarbital was prescribed. My sister medicated him preemptively, before any other chore, before diplomatic initiatives on matters of cereal allocation. *Hold on you guys, I'll be with you in a second.* Drugging the cat, slipping him the Mickey Finn in the Science Diet, feeding the kids, then getting out the door, pecking her boyfriend on the cheek (he was stumbling sleepily down the stairs).

She printed snapshots. At this photo lab. She'd sold cameras (mnemonic devices) for years, and then she'd been kicked upstairs to the lab. Once she sold a camera to Pete Townshend, the musician. She told him — in her way both casual and rebellious — that she didn't really like The Who. Later, from her job at the lab, she used to bring home *other people's pictures*, e.g., an envelope of photographs of the Pope. Had she been out to Giants Stadium to use her telephoto lens to photograph John Paul II? No, she'd just printed up an extra batch of, say, Agnes Venditi's or Joey Mueller's photos. *Caveat emptor.* Who knew what else she'd swiped? Those Jerry Garcia pix from the show right before he died? Garcia's eyes squeezed tightly shut, as he sang in that heartbroken, exhausted voice of his? Or: somebody's trip to the Caribbean or to the Liberty Bell in Philly? Or: her neighbor's private documentations of love? Who knew? She'd get on the phone at work and gab, call up her friends, call up my family, printing pictures while gabbing, sheet after sheet of negatives, of memories. Oh, and circa Halloween, she was working in the lab with some new, exotic chemicals. She had a wicked headache.

▪ ▪ ▪

My sister didn't pay much attention to the church calendar. Too busy. Too busy to concentrate on theologies, too busy to go to the doctor, too busy to deal with her finances, her credit-card debt, etc. Too busy. (And maybe afraid, too.) She was unclear on this day set aside for God's awesome tabernacle, unclear on the feast for the departed faithful, didn't know about the church of the Middle Ages, didn't know about the particulars of the Druidic ritual of Halloween — it was a Hallmark thing, a marketing event — or how All Saints' Day emerged as an alternative to Halloween. She was not much preoccupied with nor attendant to articulations of loss, nor interested in how this feast in the church calendar was hewn into two separate holy days, one for the saints, *that great cloud of witnesses,* one for the dearly departed, the regular old believers. She didn't know of any attachments that bound together these constituencies, didn't know, e.g., that God would *wipe away all tears from our eyes and there would be no more death,* according to the evening's reading from the book of Revelation. All this academic stuff was lost on her, though she sang in the church choir, and though on All Saints' Day, a guy from the church choir happened to come into the camera store, just to say hi, a sort of an angel (let's say), and she said, *Hey Bob, you know, I never asked you what you do.*

To which Bob replied, *I'm a designer.*

My sister: *What do you design?*

Bob: *Steel wool.*

She believed him.

She was really small. She barely held down her clothes. Five feet tall. Tiny hands and feet. Here's a photo from my brother's wedding (two weeks before Halloween); we were dancing on the dance floor, she and I. She liked to *pogo* sometimes. It was the dance we preferred when dancing together. We created mayhem on the dance floor. Scared people off. We were demons for dance, for noise and excitement. So at my brother's wedding reception I hoisted her up onto my shoulder, and she was so light, just as I remembered from years before, twenty years of dances, still tiny, and I wanted to crowd-surf her across the reception, pass her across upraised hands, I wanted to impose her on older couples, gentlemen in their cummerbunds, old guys with tennis elbow or arthritis, with red faces and gin blossoms; they would smile, passing my sister hither, to the microphone, where the wedding band was playing, where she would suddenly burst into song, into some sort of reconciliatory song, backed by the wedding band, and there would be stills of this moment, flashbulbs popping, a spotlight on her face, a tiny bit of reverb on her microphone, she would smile and concentrate and sing. Unfortunately, the situation around us, on the dance floor, was more complicated than this. Her boyfriend was about to have back surgery. He wasn't going to do any heavy lifting. And my nephew was too little to hold her up. And my brother was preoccupied with his duties as groom. So instead I twirled her once and put her down. We were laughing, out of breath.

On All Saints' Day she had lunch with Bob the angelic designer of steel wool (maybe he had a crush on her) or with the younger guys from the lab (because she was a middle-aged free spirit), and then she printed more photos of Columbus Day parades across Jersey, or photos of other people's kids dressed as Pocahontas or as the Lion King, and then at 5:30 she started home, a commute of forty-five minutes, Morristown to Hackettstown, on two-laners. She knew every turn. Here's the local news photo that never was: my sister slumped over the wheel of her Plymouth Saturn after having run smack into a local deer. All along those roads the deer were upended, disemboweled, set upon by crows and hawks, and my sister on the way back from work, or on the way home from a bar, must have grazed an entire herd of them at one time or another, missed them narrowly, frozen in the headlights of her car, on the shoulders of the meandering back roads, pulverized.

Her boy lives on air. Disdains food. My niece, meanwhile, will eat only candy. By dinnertime, they had probably made a dent in the orange plastic bucket with the Three Muske-teers, the Cadbury's, Hot Tamales, Kit Kats, Jujyfruits, Baby Ruths, Bubble Yum — at least my niece had. They had insisted on bringing a sampling of this booty to school and from there to their afterschool play group. Neither of them wanted to eat anything; they complained about the whole idea of supper, and thus my sister offered, instead, to take them to the *McDonaldLand play area* on the main drag in Hackettstown, where she would buy them a Happy Meal, or equivalent, a hamburger topped with *American processed cheese food*, and, as an afterthought, she would insist on their each trying a little bit of a salad from the brand-new McDonald's salad bar. She had to make a deal to get the kids to accept the salad. She suggested six mouthfuls of lettuce each and drew a hard line there, but then she allowed her-self to be talked down to two mouthfuls each. They ate indoors at first, the three of them, and then went out to the playground, where there were slides and jungle gyms in the reds and yellows of Ray Kroc's empire. My sister made the usual conversation, *How did the other kids make out on Halloween? What happened at school?* and she thought of her boyfriend, fresh from spinal surgery, who had limped downstairs in the morning to give her a kiss, and then she thought about *bills, bills, bills,* as she caught my niece at the foot of a slide. It was time to go sing. Home by nine.

My sister as she played the guitar in the late sixties with her hair in braids; she played it before anyone else in my family, wandering around the chords, "House of the Rising Sun" or "Blackbird," on classical guitar, sticking to the open chords of guitar tablature. It never occurred to me to wonder about which instruments were used on those AM songs of the period (the Beatles with their sitars and cornets, Brian Wilson with his theremin), not until my sister started to play the guitar. (All of us sang — we used to sing and dance in the living room when my parents were married, especially to *Abbey Road* and *Bridge Over Troubled Water.*) And when she got divorced she started hanging around this bar where they had live music, this Jersey bar, and then she started hanging around at a local record label, an indy operation, and then she started *managing a band* (on top of everything else), and then she started to sing again. She joined the choir at St. James Church of Hackettstown and she started to sing, and after singing she started to pray — prayer and song being, I guess, styles of the same beseechment.

I don't know what songs they rehearsed at choir rehearsal, but Bob was there, as were others, Donna, Frank, Eileen, and Tim (I'm making the names up), and I know that the choir was warm and friendly, though perhaps a little bit out of tune. It was one of those Charles Ives small-town choruses that slip in and out of pitch, that misses exits and entrances. But they had a good time rehearsing, with the kids monkeying around in the pews, the kids climbing sacrilegiously over that furniture, dashing up the aisle to the altar and back, as somebody kept half an eye on them (five of the whelps in all) and after the last notes ricocheted around the choir loft, my sister offered her summation of the proceedings, *Totally cool! Totally cool!*, and now the intolerable part of this story begins — with joy and excitement and a church interior. My sister and her kids drove from St. James to her house, her condo, this picturesque drive home, Hackettstown as if lifted from picture postcards of autumn, the park with its streams and ponds and lighted walkways, leaves in the streetlamps, in the headlights, leaves three or four days past their peak, the sound of leaves in the breeze, the construction crane by her place (they were digging up the road), the crane swaying above a fork in the road, a left turn after the fast-food depots, and then into her parking spot in front of the condo. The porch by the front door with the Halloween pumpkins: a cat's face complete with whiskers, a clown, a jack-o'-lantern. My sister closed the front door of her house behind her. Bolted it. Her daughter reminded her to light the pumpkins. Just inside the front door, Pointdexter, on the top step, waiting.

Her keys on the kitchen table. Her coat in the closet. She sent the kids upstairs to get into their pajamas. She called up to her boyfriend, who was in bed reading a textbook, *What are you doing in bed, you total slug!* and then, after checking the messages on the answering machine, looking at the mail, she trudged up to my niece's room to kiss her good night. Endearments passed between them. My sister loved her kids, above all, and in spite of all the work and the hardships, in spite of my niece's reputation as a firecracker, in spite of my nephew's sometimes diabolical smarts. She loved them. There were endearments, therefore, lengthy and repetitive, as there would have been with my nephew, too. And my sister kissed her daughter multiply, because my niece is a little impish redhead, and it's hard *not* to kiss her. *Look, it's late, so I can't read to you tonight, okay?* My niece protested temporarily, and then my sister arranged the stuffed animals around her daughter (for the sake of arranging), and plumped a feather pillow, and switched off the bedside lamp on the bedside table, and she made sure the night-light underneath the table (a plug-in shaped like a ghost) was illumined, and then on the way out the door she stopped for a second. And looked back. The tableau of domesticity was what she last contemplated. Or maybe she was composing endearments for my nephew. Or maybe she wasn't looking back at my niece at all. Maybe she was lost in this next tempest.

Out of nowhere. All of a sudden. All at once. In an instant. Without warning. In no time. Helter-skelter. *In the twinkling of an eye.* Figurative language isn't up to the task. My sister's legs gave out, and she fell over toward my niece's desk, by the door, dislodging a pile of toys and dolls (a Barbie in evening wear, a posable Tinkerbell doll), colliding with the desk, sweeping its contents off with her, toppling onto the floor, falling heavily, her head by the door. My niece, startled, rose up from under covers.

More photos: my sister, my brother and I, *back in our single digits,* dressed in matching, or nearly matching outfits (there was a naval flavor to our look), playing with my aunt's basset hound — my sister grinning mischievously; or: my sister, my father, my brother and I, in my dad's Karmann-Ghia, just before she totaled it on the straight-away on Fishers Island (she skidded, she said, *on antifreeze or something slippery*); or: my sister, with her newborn daughter in her lap, sitting on the floor of her living room — mother and daughter with the same bemused impatience.

My sister started to seize.
The report of her fall was, of course, loud enough to stir her boyfriend from the next room. He was out of bed fast. (Despite physical pain associated with his recent surgery.) I imagine there was a second in which other possibilities occurred to him — hoax, argument, accident, anything — but quickly the worst of these seemed most likely. You know these things somewhere. You know immediately the content of all middle-of-the-night telephone calls. He was out of bed. And my niece called out to her brother, to my nephew, next door. She called my nephew's name, plaintively, like it was a question.

■ ■ ■

My sister's hands balled up. Her heels drumming on the carpeting. Her muscles all like nautical lines, pulling tight against cleats. Her jaw clenched. Her heart rattling desperately. Fibrillating. If it was a conventional seizure, she was unconscious for this part — maybe even unconscious throughout — because of reduced blood flow to the brain, because of the fibrillation, because of her heart condition; which is to say that my sister's *mitral valve prolapse* — technical feature of her *broken heart* — was here engendering an arrhythmia, and now, if not already, she began to hemorrhage internally. Her son stood in the doorway, in his pajamas, shifting from one foot to the other (there was a draft in the hall). Her daughter knelt at the foot of the bed, staring, and my sister's boyfriend watched, as my poor sister shook, and he held her head, and then changed his mind and bolted for the phone.

After the seizure, she went slack. (Meredith's heart stopped. And her breathing. She was still.) For a second, she was alone in the room, with her children, silent. After he dialed 911, Jimmy appeared again, to try to restart her breathing. Here's how: he pressed his lips against hers. He didn't think to say, *Come on, breathe, dammit,* or to make similar imprecations, although he did manage to shout at the kids, *Get the hell out of here, please! Go downstairs!* (It was advice they followed only for a minute.) At last, my sister took a breath. Took a deep breath, a sigh, and there were two more of these. Deep resigned sighs. Five or ten seconds between each. For a few moments more, instants, she looked at Jimmy, as he pounded on her chest with his fists, thoughtless about anything but results, stopping occasionally to press his ear between her breasts. Her eyes were sad and frightened, even in the company of the people she most loved. So it seemed. More likely she was unconscious. The kids sat cross-legged on the floor in the hall, by the top of the stairs, watching. Lots of stuff was left to be accomplished in these last seconds, even if it wasn't anything unusual, people and relationships and small kindnesses, the best way to fry pumpkin seeds, what to pack for Thanksgiving, whether to make turnips or not, snapshots to be culled and arranged, photos to be taken — these possibilities spun out of my sister's grasp, torrential futures, my beloved sister, solitary with pictures taken and untaken, gone.

EMS technicians arrived and carried her body down to the living room, where they tried to start her pulse with expensive engines and devices. Her body jumped while they shocked her — she was a revenant in some corridor of simultaneities — but her heart wouldn't start. Then they put her body on the stretcher. To carry her away. Now the moment arrives when they bear her out the front door of her house and she leaves it to us, leaves to us the house and her things and her friends and her memories and the involuntary assemblage of these into language. Grief. The sound of the ambulance. The road is mostly clear on the way to the hospital; my sister's route is clear.

I should fictionalize it more, I should conceal myself. I should consider the responsibilities of characterization, I should conflate her two children into one, or reverse their genders, or otherwise alter them, I should make her boyfriend a husband, I should explicate all the tributaries of my extended family (its remarriages, its internecine politics), I should novelize the whole thing, I should make it multi-generational, I should work in my forefathers (stonemasons and newspapermen), I should let artifice create an elegant surface, I should make the events orderly, I should wait and write about it later, I should wait until I'm not angry, I shouldn't clutter a narrative with fragments, with mere recollections of good times, or with regrets, I should make Meredith's death shapely and persuasive, not blunt and disjunctive, I shouldn't have to think the unthinkable, I shouldn't have to suffer, I should address her here directly (these are the ways I miss you), I should write only of affection, I should make our travels in this earthly landscape safe and secure, I should have a better ending, I shouldn't say her life was short and often sad, I shouldn't say she had her demons, as I do too.

These stories first appeared in the following places: "The Mansion on the Hill" in the *Paris Review*, and in *Pushcart Prize #24;* "On the Carousel" in *Fence;* "The Double Zero" (based on Sherwood Anderson's "The Egg") in *McSweeney's;* "Forecast from the Retail Desk" in the *New Yorker;* "Hawaiian Night" in the *New Yorker;* "Drawer" in *Esquire;* "Pan's Fair Throng" in *Conjunctions,* and in a gallery pamphlet at a show of Elena Sisto's paintings; "The Carnival Tradition" in the *Paris Review;* "Wilkie Fahnstock: The Boxed Set" in *Primal Primers,* and on Word.com; "Boys" in *Elle;* "Ineluctable Modality of the Vaginal" in *Lit,* and in Fiona Giles's anthology *Chick for a Day;* and "Demonology" in *Conjunctions,* in *Pushcart Prize #21,* in *O. Henry Prize Awards,* in *The KGB Bar Reader,* and in *Survival Stories.*

Quotations from Nijinsky are from the excellent Joan Acocella translation; quotations from Nietzsche are from the translation by Douglas Smith.

For encouragement and support: my family, Julia Slavin, Amy Hempel, Mary Robison, Susan Minot, Mary-Beth Hughes, Heather McGowan, Elizabeth Gaffney, George Plimpton, Bradford Morrow, Alice Quinn, Bill Buford, Gregory Crewdson, Fiona Giles, David Ford, Adrienne Miller, Margaret Nagle, Dave Eggers, Laura Iglehart, Courtney Eldridge, Bill Henderson, Michael Pietsch, Walter Donohue, Michael and Nina Sundell, all at Yaddo, all at Cranberry's, and the most extraordinary Melanie Jackson.